HUNTER

By

Sherrill Nilson

HUNTER

Adalta: Vol. II

By

Sherrill Nilson

Illustrations and cover by
Kurt Nilson

Copyrighted Material

This is a work of fiction. All characters and events portrayed in this novel are fictitious and are the product of the author's imagination. Any resemblance to actual places or persons, living or dead, is entirely coincidental.

HUNTER
Adalta Volume II

Print version ISBN 13: 978-1-7322729-1-0
    Ebook version ISBN. 13: 978-1-7322729-3-4

Cover art and illustrations copyright (©) Kurt Nilson
    Published by

Green Canoe, LLC
    3702 S Harvard Ave #172
    Tulsa, OK 74135

For my Family

Yarak, in (adj): Hawk in prime fitness and condition
orig. Persian: yarakhi= strength, keen to hunt
—*Breckfalconry.com*

Kern—German for kernel, seed

Chapter One

Tessa Me'Cowyn paced from her window to her bed to the door. She pressed her ear to the varnished oak. She could hear clashes of metal on metal, shouts, screams, running feet echoing up to the corridor, growing closer, louder, ever more threatening.

Or was this finally rescue?

After weeks as a hostage in Readen's keep, the elegance of the furnishings, the thick rug, the private bathing room didn't make Tessa feel any less trapped.

She dropped into a chair at the table and pushed away her cold, half-finished breakfast. If she didn't get out of here soon, she'd smother. She sucked a breath through her tight throat and looked toward the door. Who's winning?

The door smashed open and splintered against the wall. One of Readen's mercenaries stepped through. His unkempt hair waved wildly in his aroused Air talent.

Tessa jumped to her feet, knife in one hand, fork in the other. Her heart slammed into her throat. Her mind a startled *can't think, can't think*. She stared at his bloodied sword. She stared at the slow you're-all-mine-little-girl smile spreading across his hard face.

She backed away. Her breath refused to come.

He followed, sheathed the sword, unbuckled the belt, let it fall to the floor.

She forced her feet to move, to get past him to the door. He stepped closer.

Her breath stuttered. She choked on his rank smell of sweat, blood, and battle.

"Watched you for days. You're the prettiest of all the hostages." His voice was low, harsh, gravelly with lust.

"I'm a protected hostage. If you touch me, the regent will kill you." Her too high voice squeaked in her ears. Tessa recognized him now— Dix Ward. He'd stared at her every time she went to the main hall at dinner. Stopped her in the halls with a too-friendly hand on her arm until she refused to go anywhere without one of the other hostages and started keeping her room locked. She swallowed the tiny bit of moisture left in her mouth and edged closer to the door.

"The regent"—the sneer was audible in his voice— "is too busy right now. Or off in his cellars again. He won't be Regent long. We're losin' the battle. I'm takin' what I can. Then I'm out of here. Maybe you'll wanna come with me. Time to get a little closer so I can show you why." He unbuttoned his tight breeches, moved to block her from the door, and grabbed for her.

Tessa slashed at him with the knife and jumped back. A line of blood beaded across the back of his hand.

He laughed, bringing his hand to his mouth. His tongue licked the blood. He thrust with his hips. "Such a little knife against this big sword."

She ducked to the right. He moved faster. He seized her arm and slung her toward the bed. Tessa stumbled over his belt and fell on top of the sword.

She rolled away and grabbed the hilt with both hands, scrambling to get a knee under her, trying to jerk it from the scabbard.

He grabbed the scabbard. Tessa held on, and the sword pulled free. He laughed harder and tossed the sheath to the side. "Such a big sword for a sweet little bit like you. I've got a better one you can grab."

Tessa braced herself on one knee, both hands tight on the hilt, and shoved the blade straight up in front of her just as he lunged. It cut up into his chest, buried almost to the cross guard. He looked down. His eyes widened in disbelief and filmed over with the opaque veil of death.

He let out a long breath. His knees collapsed. His body fell on her, flattening Tessa on her back. The sword pommel jabbed into her diaphragm. Her breath whooshed out.

Her face mashed into the hollow of his shoulder, and she couldn't breathe. Her lips clamped tight against the welling blood from his dying heart.

She shoved. Hard. Her hands wouldn't let go of the sword. They were trapped.

Tessa shoved harder, fighting for air. He was heavy. Too heavy.

Twisting to the side, she shoved again. Freeing one leg from her tangled skirt, she hooked it around his big thigh, pushed and pulled herself out from under his torso. The scratchy wool of his jacket dug into her cheek. His body rolled to its back. One arm flopped over and slapped loud on the stone floor.

The sword frozen in her hands, she stood, put her foot on his chest and pulled. It slid out of his chest with a horrible sucking sound.

She shook so hard she could barely stand. The clash of swords and yelling men outside her room receded. The room shrank till all she saw was the blood on the sword, on her hands.

Tessa stumbled to the spindly chair beside the table and rested her head on her knees. Her hands gripped the sword hilt like they were glued.

Gradually her breathing slowed, and her head cleared. She forced her fingers away from the sword and dropped it on the table. Blood stained the white cloth, blending with a spill of bright red preserves. Tessa stared at the sword, refusing to look at the body sprawled near the bed. She staggered toward the bathing room and scrubbed at the blood on her hands, her face, her throat. Tessa leaned over the water bowl for a long time trying not to shake, trying not to feel the blood that soaked her blouse, trying not to think.

She'd watched people die. Her mother—

But this time she'd killed.

Urgent need sent her whirling to the commode. She retched until her stomach muscles could force nothing more out and sank to the floor. The cold flagstones pulled the heat out of her face, out of the image of the body lying twisted and still by the bed. Soothed the nausea that welled from the clammy, wet feeling of the dark purple splotches of blood on her fine blue linen shirt.

She tore at her clothes. *Get them off. Get them off.* She stripped, throwing everything in a corner. Holding a towel under the faucet, she soaked it and scrubbed her body everywhere she could reach, trying not to see the blood and the pink-tinged water dripping on the floor.

But he might not be the only mercenary roaming this wing of the keep. She forced herself back into the other room, breath coming in hard gasps. She froze. His body sprawled on the floor, blood seeping between the flagstones.

Biting hard on her lip, Tessa un-froze, grabbed the coverlet from her bed and threw it over the body. It missed his head, and his open eyes stared at her. The man would have raped her. He'd laughed at the sword in her hands, seeing only the beautiful face, the long silver hair.

Shaking, muscles quivering, adrenaline washing out of her, she pulled open her wardrobe, grabbed a tunic and split skirt and pulled them on. She fell into a chair. How did one ever get over killing someone, even in self-defense? *How could I do that? How did I know what to do when my mind couldn't work?*

Minutes passed. The yelling, the sound of battle faded to silence. The long sword lay on her breakfast tray still leaking blood into the splotch of bright red preserves. *I'll never be able to eat cherryapples again.* Tessa forced her legs to support her and moved past the broken door into the hall. She had to get away from the body lying on her floor, get away from the blood, get away from the room that hadn't even been a *safe* prison.

She ran. And smashed into a broad chest. Hands gripped her arms hard. Tessa screamed and fought, kicking, biting, struggling to get loose. Her chest was bursting, her throat tearing with frantic screams.

"Hush, lass. Hush. Do you na know me? Hush, now. It's Cael, Tessa. It's Cael. Hush, now. Tell me what's wrong."

She stilled and looked up at the broad, deeply lined face almost hidden by his leather helmet. "Cael. Cael." She knew him. Cael, who had been her father's armsmaster for years until he disappeared when she was twelve. Her body began to shake so hard she could only stand because he held her arms. "I killed him, Cael. I killed him."

Cael pulled her to his chest, and she felt him jerk when he saw the body on the floor inside the room. "So I see, lass. So I see. I know him. He's a bad one. You did good, Tess. You remembered what I taught you before I— You did good."

He pushed her away from him, rubbing his hands up and down her arms. "Now remember what else I taught you. You do what you have to do, and then you move on to what you have to do next." He held her gaze, matching her breath for breath until she began to calm, then let go.

Tessa staggered then caught her balance. She looked at his leather jerkin and helmet. "You're one of Readen's men. Cael, how could you be one of Readen's men?" She stepped back.

He looked behind her down the hall. "I can't explain now, Tessa. I have to get away before I'm found. Just don't tell anyone you saw me. Except Krager. Tell him. But only him." He touched her shoulder. "I was right, Tessa. And your father was wrong. You are extraordinary." And he left her standing, staring after him, but calmer, oddly calmer.

He left so long ago she'd almost forgotten him. She talked him into giving her sword lessons when she was ten. They kept at it for two years until her father discovered them, and Cael disappeared. She took a deep, stuttering breath and turned away from the carnage in her room. She had to think about something else, move on to the next thing like Cael said.

Wounded. There would be wounded. *My blocked talents may make me useless as a healer, but I can still do triage and basic nursing.* Tessa skipped over the thought that there would be more blood.

Tessa ran as fast as she could, stopped before she turned each corner and watched for Readen's mercenaries, but she saw only a few dead bodies. Her stomach lurched each time. Four guards stood in the corridor at the bottom of the third stairway. They wore purple and yellow armbands—the colors of the guardian heir—Daryl Me'Vere's colors. Her steps faltered, knees weak with relief. The usurper Readen was defeated.

The lieutenant caught her before she fell. "You're Tessa Me'Cowyn, aren't you?" His voice was so steady, so strong and sure, relief threatened to take her legs from under her. Daryl had won. The rightful heir was back and in control. "Your father is looking all over for you."

"I'll need to get to wherever the wounded are. And someone will need to send for healers."

"They've probably already been sent for, but to be sure—" He nodded at two of the guards who left at a run. "The wounded are brought to the receiving hall. We'll take you there. Not good to be roaming these corridors by yourself. No telling who you might run into."

Tessa swallowed. One of those no-telling-whos had already run into her. "There's a body in my room. I...I..." Her tongue was thick, her words distant in her ear.

He nodded. A flicker of respect crossed the concern in his face. "I'll take care of it."

The doors to the huge receiving hall stood open. All she could see were wounded and dying. She saw no healers. None of the other girls who'd been held hostage with her were there. A few scattered servants helped the injured, doing their best. But they were overwhelmed and under-trained. She was all there was. And she wasn't enough.

The keep's steward, Lerys, stood, red-faced, arms flying, arguing with another lieutenant. "Guardian Roland won't stand for these people bloodying up the hall. Send them to Healer's Hospice. They'll be taken care of there."

Tessa couldn't believe her ears.

The lieutenant was having the same problem. "You need to bring more linens, sir. And fresh. This pile of cleaning rags won't do." He gestured to the mound of cloth in the arms of the servant behind Lerys. Tessa recognized Elda.

Lerys stepped back half a step, palms out in front of him. "The guardian—"

Tessa stepped in front of him. "Guardian Roland isn't here. No one's seen him for two tendays, and these guards need help now."

"Miss Tessa. You shouldn't be here." He turned to the lieutenant, his tone officious. "Have someone escort the holder's daughter to her room. It's not appropriate for her to be—"

She interrupted him. Fury scoured away any fear, any feeling of inadequacy. "Lerys. Bring everything you have. I'll need pallets, sheets, even tablecloths. Whatever we can tear into bandages. I'll need alcohol and all the herbs, tonics, and antibiotic salves you can find. These people are bleeding and dying."

"All I have left are the good linens. I can't have them all bloody and—"

Tessa turned to the tiny housekeeper standing just out of Lerys's line of sight. "Melayne, you know what we need."

The woman nodded and left in a hurry.

"You can't just override my orders." Lerys sputtered and spittle sprayed. He turned to the two guardsmen behind Tessa. "Take her to her room."

They both shrugged. She was a holder's daughter. She outranked the steward.

Tessa ignored him and turned to the room filling with wounded, cursing her blocked talent. She should be able to heal them. Instead, too many would die before the healers arrived. All she could do was sort out the most severely injured, stabilize them and be grateful that she never stopped studying despite her blocked talent. There was still much she could do, and right now it was triage that was most important. *The healers won't be long. Please, Adalta, let the healers not be long.*

She turned to the servant holding the cloths. "Elda, are these clean?" Elda nodded. "Then start tearing them into strips. Fold some pads." The woman laid her bundle down and started ripping.

A young guard with a slashed abdomen lay on the floor just inside the door of the receiving hall. Tessa grabbed a strip from the servant, folded it into a pad and pressed it firm against his belly. She scanned the man beside him. Blood dripped down his chin from a deep slash across his cheek. "Here," she told him. "Hold this here and press firmly. You're better off than he is."

"What do I do if—?"

"It's not a deep cut. Just keep pressure on it till the healers come."

Tessa smiled her best you'll-be-alright smile to take the sting out of her words. She pressed a pad to his bleeding cheek and wrapped a bandage around his head to hold it. Then she moved to the next guard where Elda was already holding a large pad to a young woman's chest. A bloody froth of bubbles seeped from the sides of her mouth and pooled into her hair.

Tessa swallowed a gasp and dropped to her knees next to the pale woman. She lifted the guardswoman's icy hand, noting the blue fingernails. An awful rasping sounded from the wound in her chest despite the pad Elda pressed against it. The too-young woman wasn't going to make it until the healers came.

Tessa tried desperately to connect with Adalta. She tried forcing her consciousness down through the stones of the floor into the bedrock beneath the keep, into the tiny rivulets and streams that ran through the earth. She searched her mind and body for the faintest hint of connection to Water or Earth.

But she couldn't pull the power up, couldn't see the core of the wound, couldn't feel what was needed to heal it. She should be able to manipulate the vessels, bones, and tissues—to realign, to mend. But the images skittered away as they always did.

Tessa opened her eyes. The woman's eyes were fixed on her face, eyes full of fear and pain and questions. She tried to speak, and the words caught, choked off by the frothy blood that bubbled with every feeble breath. Then the fear and the pain and the questions were gone. Tessa watched bright red blood spill from the woman's mouth, and after a long, long moment, pulled the edge of the sheet over the face no older than her own and fought the familiar upwelling of helpless shame. Shame was an indulgence she couldn't afford right now.

She stood, staring down, clasping her hands together till they cramped. *No use crying over my lost talents. She's gone. And I can't bring her back. Even with talent, I couldn't bring her back now.*

"Renewal," she whispered.

"Renewal," said Elda.

Tessa swiped her forearm across her damp eyes and looked for the next person who needed the little she could give. She went back to doing what she could, thankful she never stopped learning about the ordinary healing of herbs, salves, and wound care from whomever she could talk into teaching her on the Me'Cowyn Hold. Thankful they had dared to do so behind her father's back.

The minutes it took the healers to get from the guild house to the hall seemed hours. Hours-long minutes of tearing sheets, pressing thick pads to bloody wounds. Hours-long minutes of washing and bandaging the less critical cuts and slashes she could treat without talent, of covering too many stilled faces. But the healers finally arrived. She directed them to the critically wounded. And she followed —bandaging and splinting, brewing aspirtea, applying antibiotic salves—until the healers finished the urgent cases and could begin to take care of the simple broken bones and lighter wounds.

There was only endless time bending over wounds, wrapping meters of bandages, emptying buckets of bloody water, and carrying pails of clean water from the kitchens. Endless time until Tessa stood up from the young man whose broken arm she helped healer Evya, the guild house mother, set. She staggered. Evya grabbed her before she fell.

"You need to stop. Get some water and some food. Melayne set some out in the little anteroom. She put several cots and pallets in there for us." She looked at Tessa's face. "Don't object again. You nearly fell before I caught you. If I have to, I'll give you an order."

Tessa wanted to grin, but she was so tired she could only raise one side of her mouth. "I don't know if you can order me. I'm not one of your healers."

"Oh, I can give the order. I just can't make you follow it. So consider it a strong suggestion from your healer to eat and rest. You're exhausted, and your talent is so depleted I can't even sense it."

Tessa turned away. She was too tired to pretend. It wasn't depleted —she had no talent.

Tessa rolled to the edge of the cot, choking back a scream. She dragged a deep breath through her tight throat. She wasn't smother-ing. There was no heavy, bloody man pinning her down. She was safe in the small anteroom adjacent to the receiving hall. Was she going to re-live the attack of that vile mercenary every time she closed her eyes? She untangled her legs from the blanket and sat, cross-legged, grounding herself as best she could without a connection to Adalta, ignoring, like always, the rejection she felt when she tried to connect to the planet.

Resting her head in her hands, elbows propped on her knees, Tessa let out her breath. How had she managed to kill her attacker? She should have been too terrified to move. Nothing in her sheltered life prepared her for such an experience. Yet she'd killed him.

She was so tired. She wished for her stepmother, to be held, to be safe in her arms. She felt less like the almost eighteen-year-old she was and more like the seven-year-old she'd been when her talents first failed her.

A light touch on her shoulder startled her. Healer Evya looked down at her. "Ground yourself, Tessa. And replenish your talent. You're depleted. I still can't feel any talent in your channels. Do that, and get some food." Evya gestured to a table with bread, fruit, cheese. Beads of moisture dripped from several pitchers. "When you feel up to it we can use your help again."

Tessa ran her tongue, thick with thirst, across her lips. "How long have I been asleep?"

"Several hours. Your father's looking for you. He was surprised you helped with the wounded and concerned about you. I told him you were resting. He wanted you to know he moved your things to another room. He said there's a dead man in your room. He's trying to find out who rescued you and wanted to be sure you were alright."

Her face creased into a gentle smile. "I didn't know about what you faced, the man you faced. I wouldn't have blamed you if you had collapsed and needed healing yourself. Nor would I have let you work so hard. That's probably why your father didn't think you'd be much help. But how can he not know how powerful your talent is?"

Tessa just shook her head, trying not to react. There was no talent there for Evya to feel. Just a void. An impenetrable wall of nothing-at-all. She stood, forcing a smile. "You're right. I need to eat something. If you'll excuse me?"

Evya stepped aside as Tessa headed for the table of food, ignoring the guild mother's concern. She picked up a plate and reached for a piece of bread.

The image of a tiny bird overwhelmed her tired mind. Blue, with an orange breast and a short, sharp yellow beak. Its wing twisted wrongly, it lay in Tessa's small seven-year-old hands. She watched her younger self feel her way into the tiny body, seeing the snapped bone, the torn muscle, felt the tightness in her forehead as she concentrated, moving the ends of the bone together, fusing them.

And again, she felt the horror as the blood vessel burst, spouting crimson with every rapid beat of the tiny heart. She didn't know how to stop the blood loss, the final convulsion that ended the bird's life.

Her fault, just like her mother's death. Tessa's fault. She'd pushed too hard, demanded too much, known too little.

That was when her hair turned to silver.

Eleven years and the images were as powerful now as then.

She shook her head against the vision of her mother's pale face as the younger Tessa, the bird's blood still wet on her small fingers, raged at her for dying. Raged at her unavailable abilities, her small helpless self.

That was when she lost her talent.

She made herself put food on her plate. There'd been no time to eat since her interrupted breakfast this morning when Daryl's forces had attacked. Next to her Evya poured herself a cup of red juice. Tessa clapped her hands over her mouth, seeing again the image of the bloody sword lying in the bright red smear of cherryapple preserves.

Several mornings later Tessa closed the door to her room and started down the hallway to the smaller dining room for breakfast. She hoped she'd dawdled long enough. Hoped her father had finished and gone about his business elsewhere. She wasn't up to seeing him. To let herself in for another rant on how to attract Guardian Heir Daryl Me'Vere just wasn't what she wanted right now. Head down, taking small steps, she scuffed her feet along, delaying her progress even more. And bumped into someone.

"Omph. Sorry. I wasn't looking where I was going." The speaker was a slender, auburn-haired woman, jacket over her arm, dressed in the split-skirt uniform of the Mi'hiru, riders and caretakers of the magnificent hawk-headed, flying horse, Karda. She was too slender, her face too pale, eyes too hollow.

"My fault. I wasn't either." Tessa reached to steady the other woman. "Are you all right?"

"Yes. I don't look it, I know, but I'm fine. Just really hungry. I'm Marta, Sidhari's rider."

"Yes, of course you are. I'm sorry. I didn't recognize you at first. I'm headed for breakfast myself. May I join you?"

Tessa tried not to stare at Marta as they headed for the stairs. Whatever ordeal she had undergone at the hands of the defeated Readen Me'Vere in the hidden cavern under the keep had taken a terrible toll. Her skin was nearly translucent, her cheekbones too sharp. Tessa could see too clearly the blue veins and the outlines of slender bones in the hand that rested on her sword hilt.

Marta stopped suddenly, her head cocked as if listening to something Tessa couldn't hear.

"Are you sure you're alright?"

Marta laughed. "Yes, and I'm not crazy either. Sidhari, my Karda, was telling me I need to talk to you. You're Tessa Me'Cowyn, aren't you? No one else has your lovely silver hair. So striking against your tea-with-a-little-milk complexion."

"Oh, you're one of the Mi'hiru who speak telepathically to her Karda. Why is your Karda concerned with me?" She ignored the comment about her looks. Beauty wasn't an accomplishment—it just was. Comments on her looks had long since failed to affect her. Her beauty was her father's tool. She hated it.

The two young women settled in one corner of the small dining area with their full plates. Tessa played with her food and watched Marta attack hers and signal their young server for more before she emptied the first plate piled with potatoes, ham, egg toast.

She finally finished and wrapped slender hands around her mug of tea. She tilted her head and looked hard at Tessa. "Sometimes I think I will never get enough to eat. I'm told until the new talent settles in, it

will burn a lot of energy. I just need to keep eating. And grounding."
She took a sip of tea.

Tessa shook her head. "What do you mean, new talent? We're born with all the talent we'll ever have. Except for Readen, of course."

"I'm getting ahead of myself. I don't know how much you know about what happened to me." She raised a questioning eyebrow at Tessa.

Tessa knew Guardian Roland's son, Readen, had taken Marta captive and held her in the hidden cavern below Restal Keep. That's where he'd been when Daryl, the rightful heir, and his forces attacked and retook the keep that Readen usurped from his father and his brother.

She shuddered, unsure she wanted to hear about whatever made Marta look so ill. "It must be painful for you to talk about. You don't need to tell me."

"You have your own history with Readen, don't you? Being one of his hostages couldn't have been pleasant," Marta said.

Tessa looked down and clamped her eyelids tight against the memory. It was several minutes before she could bring herself to speak, her voice soft with remembered pity. "I found one of the serving girls who didn't get away from him in time."

She couldn't stop the shiver that ran through her or the sudden turn-over in her stomach. "I couldn't do anything about it. I had no proof, and he was regent. No matter that he called us guests, I was a hostage with no power to call him to account. All I could do was find someone to take her to the healer's house. They could heal her body, but her mind— "

Tessa looked across the table at Marta. "You know there are people who won't believe you about him, don't you? I've heard the denials already, and you haven't even been asked to tell your story."

"It doesn't matter. Hopefully enough will. But Sidhari is insisting it's important for you to know about the Itza Larrak, and about the way Readen has found to get power. She says you have a choice to make, and you need to know what I have to tell you."

"A choice to make?" Tessa laid her fork on her plate and turned her head away. "Marta, I'm the only child of a powerful holder. The only choice I ever get to make is what to put on to wear in the mornings. And not always then. Just about any other *choice*--" The disgust and despair she invested in the word *choice* were heavy enough to crack the flagstone floor. "Any choice I make not dictated by him has to be carried out with a lot of secrecy."

Tessa looked back and forced herself to smile, willed her manner back into the perfect equilibrium expected of her. "I'm sorry. You didn't need to hear that. But the Itza Larrak? That's an old story. It hasn't been a problem since shortly after the Ark Ship landed the original colonists here. The Larrak were defeated then. What do you mean by power? Readen has no talent. I'm sure you know that."

"Let's go out to the gardens. Roland may not be the best guardian, but I must admit, he created the loveliest gardens I've ever seen. I like to sit out there when I'm feeling overwhelmed by all that's happened. And we won't be overheard or interrupted."

Tessa looked around Marta. "Oh, dear. Speaking of interruption." Her father headed for their corner wearing an irritated scowl. As usual. She forced a pleasant look onto her face and sat straighter. Since the day of the revolt, she felt less and less anxiety every time she saw him. Killing the mercenary had its benefits.

With only the briefest nod to Marta demanded by civility he said, "Tessa, I know you won't bother to do it yourself, so I made an appointment with the seamstress for you. You're to be there in an hour. You need the final fitting for your dress for the reception." His voice was a sharp swipe of impatience.

"What reception, Father?" Tessa's shoulders slumped as if already dressed in her father's expectations.

"Your uncle and his retinue arrive mid-tenday."

"Oh? You've given up on Daryl, then?" Tessa forced herself to keep the anger out of her face. It was too much to hope that he'd abandon his plans to marry her to Daryl.

A flicker of emotion crossed his face. Frustration? He pulled her to her feet and out of Marta's hearing. His grip pinched her upper arm. "Just be ready. I don't know who Hugh will bring with him, but you need to show at your best. Daryl has called in all of Restal's holders and heirs, too. I'm keeping my options open."

His options?

He turned abruptly, made a slight bow in Marta's direction, and walked away.

Tessa rubbed her arm where his grip bruised her. *His options? He's not scheming to marry himself off to the highest bidder. How can I ever get away from him and his breeding plans?* She stared after his straight, tall, uncompromising back until Marta cleared her throat.

"I'm sorry, Marta. He can be very rude. Prime Guardian Hugh Me'Rahl is my uncle. I'm sure Father's mind is busy cataloging all the talents of whoever might be in his retinue, searching for the best breeding prospect to marry me off to." She blinked, hard. *I can't cry. I won't cry in front of her.* "I'm sorry. I shouldn't have said that. Please forget it. Let's walk in the garden. It can't be much colder than this." And she wasn't talking about the temperature of the room.

She wrapped her wool shawl more closely around her as they stepped outside. It was still too early for the pale red sun to have warmed the garden. "I'm not sure what you need to tell me, Marta. I can see you've gone through a great deal. If it's painful for you—"

Marta looked closely at her face. "I know it's not my business, but he can't make you marry someone you don't want to, can he? Surely Restal Quadrant is not that—"

"I'm afraid he can. Restal is not like the other quadrants. Women are...restricted in their choices here. At least women of holder status. And my father is one of the worst." She looked away, her voice soft. "He wasn't always that way."

The two women walked in silence for several minutes. The peace and beauty of the garden's tentative approach to spring, the tiny new leaves glistening, buds swelling on branches, the clean damp earth smells, finally worked their wonder on Tessa's composure. "What is it that you need to tell me, Marta?"

"Sidhari says you need to know this so you can make an informed choice. And I'm sorry but she either can't or won't be more clear. I'm not sure which." She bent down and touched the hint of yellow showing at the tip of a tight jonquil bud. "It's good to see the signs of renewal. Winter is all too long here on Adalta." She straightened and started to walk on. Tessa took a long step to keep abreast of her on the path.

"Only a few people know some of what I'm going to tell you, and I trust you'll not share it with anyone else without great need. I am not native to Adalta. I come from an independent trade ship orbiting the planet—it has been for the last year. My assignment is, or was, to assess the resources and the markets of this planet, and to find a covert way to influence the laws and restrictions against advanced technology here on Adalta."

Tessa stumbled as if her feet stuck to the path. She stared at Marta, trying to wrap her mind around the words Marta spoke in such a matter of fact tone. Adalta was one of the diaspora planets, but it had been hidden from the rest of the colonized planets for five hundred years. When it left Earth, five people had stayed behind and sacrificed themselves to erase all trace of the ship and the planet they'd found. How had Adalta been discovered?

"I wouldn't have told you that part except it's important for you to understand everything that's happened and is likely to happen. One of the other agents from the ship attempted to smuggle highly advanced weapons to Readen."

Tessa stumbled again.

Marta reached out a hand and steadied her. "Probably in exchange for the rare heavy metals from Restal's northern mountains. Readen was not only planning to wrest control of Restal Quadrant from Daryl but to move on Toldar, and perhaps even beyond that. With his father incapacitated, if his attempts to assassinate Daryl had not been thwarted, Readen might well have succeeded."

The slaughter any advanced weapons could wreak against the simple bows and swords allowed on the planet—the thought was terrifying. Tessa wrapped her wool shawl tight around her, but it didn't help the icy cold that froze her. Everyone learned the history of the end day disasters that led to the diaspora from Earth on the Ark Ships. It was why such things were outlawed here. Warfare, fanaticism, xenophobia, and uncontrolled environmental disasters had devastated the home planet. Technology had become a curse Earth could not avert.

"Those weapons would have assured his success. Altan destroyed the one shipment we know of, and the agent responsible was badly hurt." Marta stopped in front of a bush with graceful arching branches swollen with tight buds.

"But Readen's been stopped. Daryl had him taken to the prison near the village of Ardencroft," Tessa said. "What will they do now?" She thought for a moment. "And what does that have to do with me? That's the concern of the guardians like my uncle and Daryl and holders like Father."

The two of them walked on for a few minutes to a bench in a bend of the path. Then Marta stopped and faced Tessa. "I am still not used to talking about this next part. I've only told Altan and Daryl so far. But this is the reason they've asked Hugh Me'Rahl to come here—Readen has found a way to raise power that is not talent."

"But—"

Marta raised a hand, and Tessa stopped.

"You've seen at least one of the results of what he's doing—the young serving girl you helped."

Tessa frowned, puzzled. What Readen had done to the girl was beyond wrong. But what did it have to do with raising power? Cold seeped inside until she wasn't sure she'd ever be warm again.

"Somehow he discovered how to use the energy of blood, sex, and death—even negative emotions—to gain power."

Tessa reached behind her for the bench. She sat. Her memory of that girl, barely beyond childhood, overwhelmed her, and she fought not to empty her stomach on the mulched flowerbed beside her.

"I'm sorry," she murmured. Her throat burned. She swallowed and rested her head in her hands, elbows propped on her knees. "The girl —she'd been tortured. She had cuts all over her. Shallow cuts in places where the nerves are the most sensitive—intimate places. She wouldn't speak. She was broken, her talent shredded."

Tessa sat up and looked at Marta. "I've never seen anyone so terrified, so empty of anything but fear. He didn't do that to you, did he?" Her throat tightened on her next words. "I'm sorry. I shouldn't ask. Oh, shit, I shouldn't ask that kind of question."

Marta sat calmly, waiting for Tessa to compose herself. After a moment, she answered, her voice so low Tessa strained to hear. "He tried. But it was his minion who wielded the knives. The bond with Altan protected me, and Readen wasn't able to touch me." She looked straight into Tessa's eyes. "Can you listen to the rest?"

"Why are you telling me this? It must be so painful for you."

"As I said, Sidhari is insisting you need to know. The Itza Larrak—Readen released it from its cavern prison. And I don't know if that is all he released."

Chapter Two

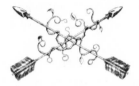

Galen Morel finished currying his horse and walked out of the stall, latching it behind him. He automatically clenched and spread his burn-scarred hands, stretching the fingers wide, curling his right hand around the hilt of the sword hanging low at his waist. His grip tightened, and the scars pulled painfully. He almost didn't have to think about doing the exercise anymore—almost.

He hefted his pack and the sack loaded with seeds, plant. and soil samples he'd collected to his shoulder, winced, and readjusted them, so they didn't rub on his newly healed skin. He forced himself not to hunch over his pain, to hold his body straight, and crossed the rough cobbled courtyard, wet with drizzle, to the small ivy-covered inn.

The healers told him the pain would get better. Burns were an injury even the best healers couldn't heal without at least some scarring. He might never regain full use of his left hand. Thank the far-flung galaxies it was his left. Whether the medics on the ship would be able to help at this stage, he didn't know and almost didn't care.

The few customers in the common room clustered around the glowing magma stones in the river rock fireplace on the far wall. He hung his damp cloak on the drying rack, seated himself at a small table nearby, and ordered ale from the woman who appeared at his elbow.

He watched her eyes skitter across his scarred cheek, down to his hands, back to his face. He should consider himself lucky that they only disfigured one side of his face. She turned away, and he felt an odd disconnect. When had he ever felt anything like this before? This faint hunger for a friendly touch?

Galen looked at his left hand curled around a soft leather ball and squeezed it, willing the muscles and tendons to strengthen. He should still be thanking the two mercenaries who'd worked on him day and night after the fire. When the steamwagon train finally arrived in Restal Prime, they delivered him to the healers, but they were the ones who saved his life.

It was hard not to be bitter. There'd been a time when the woman wouldn't have turned away. When he could have enticed more than pity from her with a glance and a few words. Oh, how he hated Readen Me'Vere. And this backward planet.

When the weapons he was smuggling to Readen caught fire, something went horribly wrong inside him. He ignored the flames on the crates. Ignored his burning flesh and clothes. He fought the men trying to drag him away and put out the blaze that nearly killed him. He struggled to pull the fiery cases out of the wagon.

Galen still didn't understand the strange mental fog, the compelling need that ruled him on that trip to smuggle the weapons into Restal. Readen had done something to him that over-rode all sense of self-preservation. It took the searing pain from the blaze to burn off the compulsion that drove him from the time he last left Readen to the moment he threw himself into the fire. He hated the man with a consummate implacability.

But he wouldn't forget himself like that again. Not ever. He squeezed and stretched his fingers, forced through the pain. No one would ever be able to do that to him again. He knew about talent, and he knew about Readen's magic—not the same as talent, not at all. He resisted thinking the word evil, but there was no other word to describe what Readen did to him.

Galen looked up at the innkeeper's approach. His hood fell back off his head.

"We've some roast kurga left, a bit o' vegetables, and Mina just took a loaf out of the oven, if'n you're hungry." The rotund man tried not to wince at Galen's scarred face and moved to the other side of the table. To Galen's good side. "We'll be gettin' a room ready any minute now, and she'll leave a packet of food on th' kitchen table for mornin'. You said you'd be leavin' early? Gone near a tenday?"

"Roast kurga will be fine." *Whatever kurga is—oh, yeah, like antelope. If this man doesn't stop staring at my face, I'm going to rearrange his.*

The man lingered. Then he gestured toward the seed sack at Galen's feet. "Tis good on you to do yer plantin' duty. Too many from Restal Prime don't bother anymore, an' the land shows it."

The innkeeper fidgeted with the utensils he'd just laid on the table. He took a breath and spoke fast as if to get the words out before he thought better. "Mayhap when you get back to the prime, you'll tell them how bad the circles be gettin'. How bad we need trees'n such planted to stop them as are gettin' bigger."

"Bad, are they?" Galen had no idea what the man was talking about. He'd seen the circles. Not up close--he knew they were danger-ous. But why was it alarming that they were growing? The planet was far from being reclaimed. Barren areas of sterile ground still spread everywhere beyond the forests and the fields of the holds, particularly in Restal Quadrant. Masquerading as a member of the Planter Corps provided the perfect cover, allowing him to travel where and as often as his covert activities for the secretly orbiting trade ship demanded.

He shifted in the chair, and his hand brushed the sack lying on top of his pack. He'd carried that same seed sack around with him most of the time he'd been on Adalta. Maybe if he had to come back to the planet, he would apply for more training. It would make his cover that much more legitimate. It disturbed him that the thought pushed at him.

The innkeeper's mouth curved down. "One of the village boys went missing chasin' a goat too close to the circle to the north. We found his body days later. Mutilated." He turned his face away as if speaking the words pained him. Then he looked back at Galen, anger threading his voice. "We need more trees planted to stop the circles again. Not that we don' need grass and shrub, like the seeds you're spreadin' in the barrens, mind you. We need that, too." He looked around in relief when Mina approached with Galen's dinner and left Galen to it. Like he'd said too much.

I guess that explains why the forests scattered across the continent look like green bowls with black at their hearts from the ship. The trees are planted that way purposely. What in the world are those circles, anyway?

The planters he worked with assumed he knew, and Galen hadn't bothered to find out more than the bare minimum he needed to know for his cover. But then he'd never bothered with much of anything that wasn't directly involved with his assignments for the ship or his entertainment. Not necessarily in that order.

He thought the forests were part of the terra-forming and reclamation the colonists had been doing for centuries. It was the duty of every adult person on Adalta to spend (or pay someone to spend) one tenday a season spreading seed and microorganisms or planting in the barren areas. It offered a reasonable explanation for his current need to be far away from any civilization. The fact that most people did their tenday duty, and often more, amazed him. Though it appeared that wasn't true in Restal. He applied his knife and fork to the kurga in front of him. It was delicious—whatever it was.

His shirt and undergarments were of the finest soft linen, and his trousers of the finest wool, but the unending drizzle made them damp, and they rasped against his pink scars. Galen eased himself down on a large rock, settling his pack and the half-full seed bag at his feet.

Despite himself, he enjoyed spreading the microbe-inoculated seeds as he walked through the barren, unreclaimed landscape, getting further and further from what little civilization there was on this planet, searching for pockets and low spots where wind and water deposited enough soil to allow the seeds to take root.

That was unexpected—his efforts were half-hearted before. No more than what he needed for cover as advance agent for the trade consortium hidden in orbit. But today he wanted to do it, enjoyed the sensuous slide of the seeds through his fingers. That was not a comforting thought. He wanted off this planet. He didn't want to feel any attachment to it.

Where was that shuttle? He fished his data-com unit, his Cue, out of his pack, rechecked the coordinates, pulled the hood of his cloak forward against the soft rain, and resigned himself to a wait. He'd walked the better part of a day and a half to get to this spot.

Riding his horse would have been faster but leaving a hobbled horse here would have been cruel. A rider-less mount showing up back at the inn might cause a bit of trouble, and he'd purposely gone far into the still-unseeded territory west of the village fields. He didn't need anyone looking for him and witnessing the method of his departure. And he wasn't at all sure he was going to come back.

Finally, his ears caught the high staccato whine of rotors. He looked up, searching the bottom of the ubiquitous cloud cover, then sighed in relief. The heli-shuttle dropped out of the clouds into view. It oriented on the com-signal and landed fifteen meters away in a cloud of red dust and flying gravel. Without noticing, Galen grabbed the bag of seed with his pack, ran for the opening door at its base, and leaped up the ramp before it fully extended. He was still buckling in when the shuttle took off. It approached the edge of the atmosphere, the rotor arms retracted, the thrusters took over, and he fell asleep.

A chime alerted him in time to watch the shuttle's approach to the trade ship on the passenger screen. As always, its fractal net shape fascinated him, stretching thousands of meters across the sky. Pods and extensions curled out in every direction, obscuring the original central hub of the ship. The net opened, and the outer view disappeared off screen just before he felt the familiar grav-grab shudder, and the shuttle became another node of the net.

Kayne Morel waited at the entrance of the small personal shuttle deck. Galen knew better than to expect much reaction from his father. Still, the cold, impersonal examination of his face and hands, and the short, "Let's get you to Med Pod. We'll debrief there," was sour milk to Galen's stomach.

"What? No shiny streamers? No Welcome Home canister? No fatherly embrace?" He walked past and headed down the hallway. Kayne didn't respond, nor did Galen expect a response.

SHERRILL NILSON

He hurt. The scars on his chest made it an effort to walk upright, but Galen refused to let his father see it. He concentrated on the hallway, noticed the worn flooring, the chipped finishes at the corners, the slight musty smell that the ubiquitous plants and the ozone scrubbers didn't erase. He frowned.

"I wouldn't have thought things would be so busy up here you couldn't take care of a little basic maintenance," he said.

Kayne looked around as if noticing the neglect for the first time. A brusque movement with his hand brushed away any importance in Galen's remark. "Retooling."

"Surely re-programming for the simple tech they might want on this backward planet doesn't take that much."

"Umm."

So much for conversation. Welcome home, beloved son. If I put my ear to his chest to hear his heartbeat, will it fall off with frostbite? The need for approval and validation didn't grab him as it usually did. If he decided not to return to the planet, he'd be dealing with his father every day. As much as he hated backward Adalta, life without his father everpresent was a strong temptation.

They stepped on the trans-walk that led to Medic Pod. The slight jerk tugged at his scars, and he schooled his face to hide a wince. But his father noticed, and Galen's stomach soured further at the cold look of impatience that morphed into a look of concern. Like the father just remembered the care he was supposed to feel for his son. It was a long, silent twenty minutes. Galen wanted to shout his deliverance when they finally stepped off at the medic hatch.

Two hours later, the director of medic carefully took off the cumbersome ocular diagnostic goggles and handed them to the younger medic behind him. "My assistant's right, Kayne. This degree of healing just isn't possible within the time frame you gave us. Not according to what we know and can do with this degree of burn. I can tell the trauma extended beneath the dermal layers, almost to the bone in a number of places, but most of the nerves and tissues are whole. Newly regenerated and somewhat scarred, but whole. There is little damage to muscle and tendon that renewed training won't set aright."

"So what can you do about his scars, Arlan?"

"Sorry to disappoint you, but nothing. In fact, if this happened here, his scars would be far worse."

I'm standing right here. You're talking about my scars. Galen shrugged his shirt back on and started to say something, but the medic went on talking to his father, ignoring Galen.

"I don't know what methodology or equipment they use down there, but this is amazing. I thought Adalta was a primitive planet. Judging by this, they're far more advanced medically than we are. Our regenerative efforts are crude in comparison. I'm even more eager to get down there when we can finally announce ourselves."

Galen buttoned his shirt and buckled on his sword. He weighed his next words, stifling a sigh. "It was hands-on healing, herbs, and salves. No technology involved."

His father and the director of Medic both laughed. No surprise there.

"You were unconscious for two weeks, or rather two tendays. You don't know what kind of equipment they used," said Kayne.

They left the Medic Pod.

"I know you are hurting, Galen, but that was embarrassing. Herbs and salves." He laughed and put his hand on Galen's shoulder.

Galen shrugged it off, bit his lip, and didn't answer.

He was angry and exhausted by the time they got to the Morel quarters. He still kept rooms there. He'd never seen the need for his own separate space. Most of his time was spent on planet whenever they were in orbit. If he decided to stay on the ship, that would have to change. His father poured a pale blue liquid into two cut-crystal tumblers and handed him one. Galen swirled it around several times then knocked back the whole thing.

"That's meant to savor, Galen, not gulped like medicine. If that's what you need, try this one. It's not so expensive." He reached into the carved antique cabinet behind him and pulled out another bottle, setting it on the polished surface of his antique desk.

Galen poured the thick amber liquid into his glass. This he did savor, enjoying the twist of annoyance that interrupted the concern his father's face was still trying to wear. He looked around. Being in this office was like being in a sitting room a couple of thousand years before on Old Earth. Heavy ruby-colored draperies framed faux windows that "looked out" on formal gardens along one wall—Galen knew his father watched old vids on the screen as if they were his windows to the past. The jewel-toned carpet on the floor was of a style so ancient that Galen couldn't even begin to place it in Earth's history —but then his father was fanatic about Earth's history. And willing to pay what it took to surround himself with it.

Galen wandered past dark wood glass-fronted bookcases lining another wall. An ancient oil painting, carefully protected in a stasis field like the antique books, hung on a third. He stood in front of it for a minute, admiring.

"How could you have been so careless, Galen? Letting the aken-guns get destroyed is inexcusable. I don't have so many that we can afford the loss." Kayne sat back, pressed his steepled forefingers to his lips, and closed his eyes for several minutes. "Who is there in Restal to take Readen's place? Who were his supporters? Or if there is no one who can take his place, how do you plan to rescue him from prison?" He swiveled back and forth in his chair.

"I can probably find someone, but I'll have to be more than careful. Marta is in Restal, and I presume you don't want me to take her into our confidence." He didn't even try to hide the sarcasm. *Thanks for the concern about my health, Father.* Galen knew better than to mention not returning to the planet. Anyway, he hadn't decided.

"Ah, yes. Marta. Tell me about Marta. Is she making progress with the Me'Gerron heir? Will I be able to count on that connection when the Adalta Assembly meets, and we finally announce our presence?"

Galen, studying his father's face, didn't answer right away. "How is it Marta doesn't know her father left her a substantial number of shares in the Consortium?"

Kayne looked at him for several minutes—his eyes narrowed. "And how is it you do know this?"

"You were pushing us into life partnering. Did you think I wouldn't want to know where she stood financially?" His gut twisted a little. Was that shame? Shame was not a feeling he was familiar with.

"I admit there are times when I wonder if you are my son. This isn't one of them. You were evidently not so enamored of her you lost your better senses." He paused. "Those shares are what is financing this effort." He spoke idly as if it were a matter of no importance.

Galen marveled at his father's complete self-interest and lack of conscience at this betrayal of someone he carried responsibility for. The child of a supposed old friend who'd died thinking his daughter was well taken care of. It was an effort for Galen to keep his expression from betraying his thoughts.

He stretched his fingers and winced at the pain. It occurred to him that he felt no sense of failure, of inadequacy. Where was the insecurity his father never before failed to incite? Maybe the fire burned more out of him than just flesh and Readen's strange hypnosis, or whatever it was. He pulled one of the heavy oak antique chairs a little away from the desk and sat, his legs stretched out in front of him. Oddly, the pull on his scars gave him strength. He was almost grateful.

Chapter Three

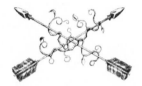

Tessa peered around the doorway of the small anteroom off the main reception hall. The heavy basket of medicines pulled at her arm. Her father was still there, talking to Mother Evya, who laughed at something he said. Tessa leaned back against the wall.

The wounded were gone, moved to the healer's hospices. She'd cleaned up the bloody bandages. She'd bundled the pallets and blankets for the laundresses. She'd almost finished clearing out this small room, and then her father appeared. Would he never leave? The two stood in the middle of the hall. No way to get past them.

Evya laughed again. Why was it he so seldom showed this gracious side of himself to Tessa? She hated feeling like a ten-year-old hiding from her always-angry parent. Anger was the curse of an Air talent, and Connor Me'Cowyn was a strong, strong Air talent. And it seemed his angry wind forever blew in her direction.

Uncle Hugh and his entourage of mating prospects had flown in today. Her father thought she had nothing better to do than to flaunt herself as a prospective broodmare.

All of Restal Quadrant didn't have the same attitude of women as chattel like the Me'Cowyn Hold. She blamed her great-grandfather, who had been Restal's guardian until Errand Me'Vere came along with his stronger talent and usurped him a hundred and twenty years ago.

Connor Me'Cowyn, like his father and his father's father before him, was obsessed with breeding talent to regain the guardianship and the power that came with it. Hence her current situation, hidden behind a cabinet in a tiny anteroom off the hall. Hiding from her father.

A foot scuffed near the doorway. She tensed. He walked around the corner wearing his irritated what-am-I-going-to-do-with-you face.

"Tessa. There you are. You shouldn't be here." He pulled her out of the room. "Evya said you were helping with the wounded. Your beauty won't make up for your lack of talent if anyone finds out. You risk disaster. Have you no sense of what's important?"

He looked at her blood-stained clothes, at her falling down hair and tired face. Tight, pinched lips and tight, pinched eyes marred his expression. He pushed her ahead of him toward the Me'Cowyn apartments. "You're late for your appointment with the seamstress. Most of Restal's holders and heirs will be there. Not to mention the strongly talented men who came with Hugh." He shoved her along so hard she would need long sleeves to cover the bruises. "You're trying my temper, Tessa."

I might as well be his oversized doll and let him show me off today. I'll hide tomorrow. And I'll find a way to get away from him. Somehow. I'll find a way. And it won't be marriage to some arrogant, strong talent whose only care is how true I'll breed and how good he looks with me.

I killed a mercenary twice my size. Getting away from Father should be nothing after that. I'll find a way. I'll find a way.

She pulled her arm from her father's grasp.

Tessa stopped just inside the door to the Great Hall. Her appetite fled. The voices of the few people, mostly men gathered around a cluster of tables at one end of the cavernous hall, bounced off the stone walls. Light from the bronze sconces and torcheres lit the tables, gleamed on the silver and crystal.

She could only see three other women, and she was by far the youngest there. The only single one. The lace trim across the bodice of her long, silver—to match her hair—velvet dress didn't cover nearly enough. At least the seamstress hadn't agreed with her father to have the gown slit up to her hip to show her translucent slip. The dress hung heavy on her shoulders with her father's ambitions. She felt, and probably looked, like a walking icicle.

Marta Rowan and Altan Me'Gerron sat at Guardian Heir Daryl's table. The Mi'hiru still looked pale. Alton's large body hovered over her like a hawk with its chick.

Tessa crossed the room to the table near where her father stood. Connor pulled her around to face Holder Me'Kammin. His foul breath backed her against the table, and she was almost sitting in her dinner plate. His assessing gaze flicked up and down her body.

She twisted away, and Connor drew the elder Me'Kammin aside. The two men stood talking, and Tessa turned to try to talk to Timmon, the holder's son and heir. Timmon—who named their son Timmon Me'Kammin?

He must be at least four years younger than she was. And just the right height—from his perspective, not hers. He was practically dripping drool down her décolletage. His eyes never lifted from the skimpy silver lace, which he was disarranging with his Air talent.

Without her talent she couldn't counter his, so she lifted her nose as if she smelled something putrid, pictured a sword in her hand, pointed in a downward direction, and stared straight at the part of him that was stiffening in his trousers. He stepped back, his smirk faded, his face turned pink. Ugh. Surely her father wouldn't—she couldn't even finish the thought.

A server stepped up to put a bottle of wine on the table, and Tessa moved away, almost running to sit beside Merenya Me'Kahrl, guardian of Anuma Quadrant. Merenya filled a wine glass for Tessa. "You look like you might need this. What do you suppose your father and Me'Kammin are talking about to have him looking so smug?"

Tessa's stomach rebelled. She'd never be able to eat any dinner. "Offering me up like a chicken on a cart hawker's spit. Like he'll probably do to every eligible male here before this is over." She picked up the wine glass and gulped half of it down.

Merenya didn't laugh.

Neither did Tessa.

The Me'Kammins walked back to their table, and Connor took his seat on Tessa's other side. Connor talked about her through most of the meal, smug at the attention the other men at the table paid her, acting the gracious and often funny host, drawing attention to her with pride, making Tessa cringe more than once. What had her father been telling the men about her?

She'd never been more uncomfortable, thankful that her dark complexion hid the red heat that flushed her body over and over. She stopped looking at any of the others and concentrated on her plate. She stuttered a few remarks to Guardian Merenya, who was not hiding the disgust she felt for Tessa's father's behavior on her broad, square face.

Connor stood as the sweet course was served, pulled her up, and headed for the table where Daryl talked to Marta. Daryl looked up then back at Marta with a save-me-from-another-father look. The buzzing in Tessa's head was so loud she didn't hear what her father said, or what Daryl replied. She only saw the red rising on the back of her father's neck. She pulled away and escaped back to their table and the safety of Guardian Merenya.

With the everlasting dinner finally over, Connor, equanimity restored, took her half-full wine glass out of her hand and stood to dismiss her. "You can leave now, Tessa. The rest of the evening will be business you won't need to bother with. I'll meet you in the morning at the mews. Be packed. A couple of my guard will be by early for your pack and trunks." He kissed her forehead and spoke in a low voice: "You looked beautiful tonight, my dear. You did well. I've identified several prospects for you. And not the Me'Kammin boy. I do want you to be happy." He dropped his voice to a whisper. "No matter how many times he's kissed by a pretty girl, he'll always be a toad."

His compliments and joking didn't help. Anger locked her muscles and stopped her breath. She forced herself to push her chair back and started to stand, dismissed like a child so the grownups could talk.

Merenya pulled Tessa back into her chair, snatched her glass and poured wine to the brim. "She needs to stay, Connor." Tessa could hear mocking in her voice. "I realize Restal is rather backward in their attitudes toward women, your hold more than most, but she is your heir. She needs to know what's going on. By the look on your face, you could have heart failure anytime."

He started to grab Tessa's arm. Merenya leaned around her. She rested her eyes on his hand, then lifted them slowly to his face like an angry broodmare berating a cocky young stallion.

Tessa rested her elbow on the table and covered her mouth with her hand, her anger twisting with glee. It wouldn't help for him to see her laughing at his reaction to Merenya. Tessa kept her eyes down, fixed in front of her, concentrating on breathing evenly and keeping her face polite. Connor's face, normally the same tea-with-milk color of hers, was dark red, his silver-touched hair bristled with angry Air talent from his hair-trigger temper. He sat, glaring across Tessa at Merenya. Tessa's stepmother Aldra sat on his other side, eyes wide, her hand over her mouth.

The tall, big-boned Merenya held Connor's angry gaze, her eyes hard. "She needs to know what's going on just as you do. From the rumors I've heard since I got here, there are some very wrong things here in Restal."

Tessa heard Aldra's breath suck in. Connor's hands gripped the edge of the table hard, jerking the heavy linen cloth. Glasses and silver rattled.

Adalta's blessings on Merenya. I wonder if I could convince her to come live with us. Or, even better, let me live with her.

"Yes, Connor. She does." Aldra's voice was soft, and she patted his arm with a be-ringed hand. She held his eyes for several seconds.

He calmed—his temper back under control. "Her husband will be holder after me." Connor's dismissive tone was at odds with the glare directed at the female guardian. Tessa could almost taste his frustration at having to acknowledge her. A woman in what he considered a man's role.

Merenya raised her eyes to the ceiling then back down to Connor's. "How open-minded of you. She's not married yet, is she?" Her slow drawl poked at Connor. The guardian looked at Tessa. "Are you? The way your father drags you around to every half-talented single male in the room trying to make Daryl jealous would seem to say no." She looked around the tables of holders, Hugh, the First Guardian, and his coterie. "Some of them are so old I'm sure you hope they don't notice you. Which would be hard to do, as lovely as you are."

Tessa could only shake her head. *I mustn't laugh. Don't laugh, Tessa. Don't laugh. He's already angry enough. He backed down from Merenya, but no one needs to see an example of his temper here.* She remembered with dread the smug look on his face and that of both Me'Kammins. *And he can still hurt me in too many ways.*

"Is there some reason she can't be holder herself, Connor? She looks to be healthy and intelligent. You're not saying she can't be holder because she's female, are you?" There was a dangerous glint in Merenya's eye as she reached for her wine glass. "Here's to female guardians and holders, Tessa."

Tessa lifted her glass and sipped. "Maybe I'll never marry, Father, and be holder myself." She was careful not to look at him, grateful to hear a ringing chime sound as Daryl tapped his glass with a knife, forestalling Connor's angry response and subduing the nervous chuckles around the table.

I'll pay for that later. But the paralyzing fear of him was gone. Hopefully-but-probably-not-forever gone. *I killed a man trying to rape me. I defied father to help the healers with the wounded. And he just backed down from Merenya. A female. I'll get away from him somehow. I know I can. I must.*

She was almost dizzy with the thought and forced herself to pay attention to what was happening. She watched the faces of the people in the room as Daryl introduced Marta, and the Mi'hiru began to speak. These were some of the most influential people in Restal. And the presence of her uncle Hugh, Adalta's prime guardian, and Anuma's Guardian Merenya, testified to the seriousness with which they, at least, took Marta's story.

Tessa glanced sideways at her father. Oh, dear. He wasn't taking it seriously. He didn't believe Marta. He sprawled in his chair, toyed with his wine glass, whispered asides to Aldra. His face showed nothing of the alarm it should have. She didn't understand it. He had no love for

Readen, the man who had held his daughter hostage. And he'd fought alongside Daryl to take back the keep from Readen.

She saw too many others with expressions of disbelief mixed with pity. What would they think if Marta told them she was not from this planet? It had been centuries since the Ark Ship arrived at Adalta with their ancestors. Space travel was ancient history, almost legend. Their smug complacency would certainly be tried if she revealed the presence of the secretly orbiting trade ship and the smuggled guns. Why wasn't she? Tessa glanced at her uncle Hugh. He knew. She was positive he knew. Probably Daryl and Merenya both knew, too.

The Mi'hiru finished her story of alien monsters and torture. The dead silence that fell as Marta spoke erupted into loud shouting confusion.

Connor stood. His voice boomed above the others, "Mi'hiru!" He shouted again, "Mi'hiru!" finally getting the attention of the room. "Mi'hiru. We all understand what a terrible ordeal you have been through. No one feels worse about that than I do. You have all our sympathies. I'm certain."

Tessa slumped forward, elbows on the table, and dropped her face into her hands. Merenya jabbed her in the ribs, and she sat up straight.

"Don't let them see you flinch." Merenya's whisper was barely audible.

Connor looked around. "I'm sure, like all of us, you've heard the stories and legends of the Itza Larrak and its creatures since you were a little girl. Even though you don't show the scars—Altan is a powerful healer—the torture you experienced in the hands of that jailor must have been unbearable. I'm certain you believe what you are telling us. But isn't it possible you were hallucinating?"

Marta started to speak, but Connor held his hands out, palms forward. "I mean no denigration of the pain and anguish you must have suffered. I notice you said Readen himself never touched you. I am obviously not a supporter of Readen, never have been, but what you are alleging is difficult for me to believe. I can believe it of your jailor—there've always been stories about what happens in the cells here. But Readen? As to this creature—whatever you think it might have been—severe pain and fear can cause us to see things that aren't there. The mind—"

A ferocious Altan Me'Gerron stopped Connor with one upraised hand. But Marta put her hand on Altan's arm and stood. "Holder Me'Cowyn, I don't know what to say to you, other than,"—she enunciated the words clearly and individually—" I. Was. Not. Hallucinating. The Itza Larrak was there. Readen has freed it from its prison in the cavern. I don't know what happened to it. Altan said it was gone when he got there, and no one has seen a sign of it since. But it was there. And it controlled Readen."

Tessa heard an uneasy muttering. Merenya snorted and said, in a low voice, "Sit down, Connor. You're making a fool of yourself."

But Connor went on, heedless, "I'm not the only one who is unconvinced, Mi'hiru. Readen was always ambitious. Would he try to usurp the guardianship, yes. But torture? Wild rumor has always spread about Readen because of his lack of talent. As though that lack proves he is cursed and evil. The Itza Larrak? An old enemy long defeated has suddenly come to life? And I've never heard of blood magic. Talent can't be raised by blood and torture."

Judging by the wild discussion that followed for the next hour and a half, Tessa thought half the people in the keep's hall doubted Marta. She was almost too calm, too strong, despite her pale face and frail body, to have undergone the torture she alleged happened. And Marta didn't mention the powerful surge of new talent that was another reason for her weakness. She couldn't without acknowledging she hadn't been born on Adalta.

Connor's explanation of pain and trauma-induced hallucinations of childhood night terrors convinced too many too easily. They remembered the scoldings used by mothers and servants. "The Itza Larrak will get you if you don't behave."

Few wanted to believe—or admit—that the son of a guardian, known to most of those present for years, was capable of what Marta alleged. They were too willing to blame the jailor who disappeared. They were too willing to share whispered doubts about whether Readen had even been present for the torture. Some had been Readen's supporters, openly or secretly, in his grab for power—recipients of

Guardian Roland's erratic favors who didn't want to lose what they had gained. Though they were doing their best to help people forget their "mistakes in judgment."

Altan looked like he was about to explode. Marta had a death grip on his arm, holding him back. For a few moments, Tessa wondered again why Marta did not just explain that she had never heard of the Itza Larrak. Then she realized that announcing the presence of an agent from a spaceship in hidden orbit who might be smuggling powerful forbidden weapons on planet would not be helpful. Readen was not the only person on Adalta with dreams of conquest. The unity that brought the colonists together in their escape from the socially and environmentally devastated Earth had fractured not long after they landed. Borders were still fluid in many places, and peace all too often splintered. Outlawed weapons that could be secretly acquired would be a tasty temptation.

Tessa reminded herself that many of these people had followed along with, ignored, or participated in Guardian Roland's vanity and excesses. For years they refused to admit the circles were growing out of their hard-won containment, preferring to enjoy the lavish entertainments Roland held too often. They were too accustomed to denying reality, she decided. A return of the Larrak and what that might portend would be more than many of them could handle. Better to leave it for Daryl.

Confusion reigned in the mews the next morning with everyone trying to leave at once. The dry, spicy scent of Karda filled the air. Several huge Karda, hawk heads high, taloned feet fisted in take-off and landing mode, wing feathers and horse bodies gleaming, stood patiently or not so patiently while Mi'hiru strapped saddle rigging and packs on them and boosted riders up. One by one they loped down the landing field to take off. Their great wings thundered, thrusting them upward. In between, other Karda landed and trotted to the mews for their riders. Some for their partnered, others un-partnered and willing to accept riders Mi'hiru assigned to them.

Tessa stood by her uncle Hugh, as always feeling tiny and delicate next to his burly bulk even as tall as she was. She watched as her father clasped forearms with Holder Me'Kammin, who turned to glare at her and walked away. Connor caught her eye, smiled, and shook his head.

She took a deep breath of relief. The thought of Timmon Me'Kammin sent creepy centipedes crawling up her back. She'd escaped that trap.

She swallowed and looked up at Hugh, wondering if she could ask him to take her back to Rashiba with him. "I'm sorry we didn't have much time to talk, Uncle Hugh."

He laughed. "As usual your father kept you occupied searching for a mate. When will he realize that you have your own mind about such things, and he can't force you into anything? You have your own resources. You have your own strengths, Tessa. You need to find them." He looked toward the front of the mews and the retreating back of Me'Kammin, his nose wrinkling as if he smelled something putrid. "Sometimes I wish our laws didn't leave quite so much latitude to the quadrants and holds. Me'Cowyn Hold's laws are too restrictive on its people, especially the women." He looked down the aisle of the mews at Connor, tacking up his Karda Arib and laughing at something Aldra said. "He's terrified for you, Tessa."

"He's terrified for his own ambitions. He's worried that if people come to know about my...talent, no one of breeding will have me, and his political star will fade."

"Aren't you being a little harsh on him? Your talents will come back, Tessa." Hugh looked down at her and gave her a quick hug, almost lifting her off her feet. "When you quit blaming yourself for your mother's death, your talents will come back."

Tessa's face closed. She stepped away to regain her balance. "I know. It wasn't my fault. I was only seven."

"Yes," He put his finger under her chin, tilting her head up. "But you have to know it in your heart, Tessa. In your heart." He tapped her forehead. "Not just your head. And you don't. Not yet." He laughed. "Your father is a good man in spite of his inability to see you for the strong woman you're becoming. He's obsessed with breeding. He always has been, and his father and grandfather before him. He's never accepted the Me'Cowyn's loss of Restal's guardianship. I know he loved my sister. And he genuinely cares for Aldra even though she's not given him other children. You're his hope. He does love you, you know. That makes him a little less an idiot with a hot temper."

Tessa knew her laugh was too shrill. "You always make me feel better, Uncle. He is an idiot. Thanks." *I wonder what you would do if you knew what he has planned for me, Uncle. I wonder what you would do if you knew he broke my arm when I was ten trying to force me to use my talent to heal myself. I wonder what you would do if you knew how many times he made me go days without water, certain I could just call it to me if I were desperate enough. Always telling me it was for my own good. Holding me and crying afterward, saying it was the only way to get my talents back. He was doing it for me.* She opened her mouth to ask her uncle to take her to Rashiba.

"Oh now, lovely fledgling. I can say that, but you still need to have respect for your parent." He put his arm around her and pulled her close. "Take care of yourself. And come visit. Very soon." He looked toward the front of the mews. "I'm coming. I'm coming, Nereya. Don't get your feathers in a ruff." He strode off to his enormous Karda, waiting impatiently in her beautifully tooled saddle rigging. Tessa's mouth still open, she watched him walk away. Too late. Too late. She wanted to curl around the hard bubble ballooning in her chest.

Suddenly the mews stilled. Tessa looked around. Every Karda stood like a statue, heads raised and turned toward the opening to the mews. Sharp staccato cries sounded from high above. A small, black Karda arrowed down in a stoop faster than she had ever seen and hovered at the entrance with a flurry of back-winging. He landed gracefully, directly in the arched entrance to the mews, one foot touching down, then the others, taking only three steps to stop. He hadn't needed to lope down the runway and slow to a stop like other Karda. *What kind of Karda is he?*

The mews was silent. Not a Karda nor a human made a sound.

~I come in search of the Austringer. We will find yarak together~ The voice was loud and piercing and echoed in her head—in her head. She could hear him in her mind. Others had, too. All around her, people grabbed their heads, shaking them in pain. All around her, people stared at this new Karda.

She'd never seen a Karda like this before, never heard of one. Small, sleek, blue-black hawk head and horse body, long, silver-barred tail feathers, silver-and-grey-striped underbody and legs—feet black from pasterns to the tips of the long, curved talons.

The Karda danced in the arched opening of the mews. Its head, with its sharp, hooked beak even more vicious looking than the other Karda's, turned back and forth, enormous black eyes searching. It curvetted, then strode, imperious head high, onto the stone-flagged alleyway, looking hard at each person he passed. Every Karda fell back, giving way to the smaller stranger, bending knees and bowing heads as the gorgeous creature made his way through the center aisle of the mews. Mi'hiru and riders were looking from their Karda to him, confused by the awed reactions. Still, no one spoke.

He stopped, stood statue-still for a moment, then stalked toward Tessa, head cocked to one side, his eye firmly fixed on her. Tessa froze. She heard in her head, softly, in clear bell-like tones, ~Hello, Tessa. I am Kishar. Are you the Austringer I seek? Are you the one who will hunt with me?~

Her knees buckled, and a flash flood of knowing, of strange facts, random visions, grotesque monsters overwhelmed her. Muscles fired with tiny electric shocks through her body. Her back arched, and she fell to the stone floor. Her bones burning to hard coal.

Pain raced through her until, finally, after an eon, she curled into a ball and into blessed oblivion.

Then,

Gradually,

She came back to herself. Her head rang as if hundreds of people were yelling. The cool stone floor she lay on pulled the fire from her body.

She pushed up on one elbow, dizzy, disoriented, surrounded by boots and taloned feet. Had she fainted?

"Do something." Her father's voice. "Tell that Karda to get away from her. Where's Aldra? She needs a healer."

"There's nothing wrong with your daughter, Holder Me'Cowyn.

She'll be fine in just a moment. I think she's been chosen by this Karda." The forced, calm voice was one of the Mi'hiru.

"Nereya says his name is Kishar." That was her uncle's voice. Its authority reassured her. "Wait a minute, Connor, this is not an ordinary Karda. Look at how the other Karda are reacting. Nereya tells me he is someone more than special. She's stunned that he is here. Have you ever seen a Karda like him? I never have."

Tessa pushed up on one arm and opened her eyes. The ringing stopped, and she heard the voice in her head again. That voice—imperious and amused. ~Yes, I am Kishar. Does your father always yell like this?~

Every other voice faded away. Incandescent joy lit her very bones, fright forgotten, the strange knowings and visions folded into the back of her mind as if they had never been.

She twisted to look behind her. The great predator head with its vicious, hooked beak bent down, close to her own.

"Yes. Much of the time. Am I imagining you?" She could hear the laughter in her own voice. But she didn't imagine him. He was very much there—and speaking in her head. In her head—like she knew only a few Karda spoke to their favored riders.

There was a low musical chuckle. ~No, you do not imagine me. I have come for you. You are the Austringer. We will "fight together in yarak. In yarak, we will hunt the urbat.~

"The what? What's an urbat? What's yarak? Is it the Itza Larrak? I don't understand. Are you choosing me? Am I a Mi'hiru now?" But it didn't matter. She reached one trembling hand up to touch the soft feathers of his head beside the fierce beak.

"Who is she talking to? She's not making sense. Aldra, help her. She needs your healing." Her father's voice sounded close to panic, but somehow that wasn't significant to her in that moment, only irritating. She heard faint sounds of stones grating—her father's Earth talent reacting to his fury. Dust motes and bits of straw whirled in a miniature tornado around him.

"Come away, Connor." Tessa's uncle put a hand on her father's shoulder, shielding his eyes with the other, and pulled him away.

"She's fine. She's been partnered. She's talking to her Karda." The tornado subsided.

Tessa sat up straighter, tucking her legs beneath her, and looked at the black head so close to hers. "Is that right? Have you chosen me to be Mi'hiru?"

The Karda closed his eyes, and the hard bubble started to form in her chest again. He was going to reject her.

~No, Tessa. I cannot choose you to be Mi'hiru. I have found you, but not to be Mi'hiru. You are the Austringer. In yarak together—like a hunting hawk on the wrist, fit, ready, eager to hunt—we will kill the monsters the Itza Larrak is calling.~

An undercurrent of sadness in his pathing voice rolled through her, touching her grief for her mother. The bubble in her chest tried to move up into her tight throat, up and down, up and down. It was a mistake. He wasn't choosing her.

He spoke again. ~We will not bond as Karda and Mi'hiru. I will be your friend for as long as I...~

There was hesitation in his voice that Tessa almost missed.

Then he went on. ~As long as we need. It is you who must choose to come with me, you who must choose yarak to fight the evil that comes. I believe you are the one for whom I search. But yours is the choice.~

"What's an austringer?"

~One who hunts with hawks. You will hunt the enemy with me.~

"But I'm not a hunter. I've only ever hunted small game with small hawks." Her whispered voice felt tiny and uncertain. Her chest felt empty—the bubble trying to climb to her throat had dropped into her stomach and was growing spikes. "I can't be the one you search for. It's a mistake. You've mistaken me for someone I'm not." She knew what to be *in yarak* meant—it meant to become a weapon, strong, fierce, and keen to hunt. It was a term from falconry. She was far from being a weapon. And the Austringer was just a legend.

~I do not mistake. If you choose to come with me, you will have the knowing that you need to be the hunter.~

Tessa looked hard into his coal black eyes and listened to his words in her mind. Listened to the strident voice of her father in the background and thought of what her life had been since her mother died, of the choices her father would make for her, the cage he built for her. She looked around. Hugh had his hand on her father's arm, and Aldra was at his other side, holding him at bay.

"I'm fine, Father." She rose to her feet, still a little unsteady, as if her muscles didn't quite belong to her, and put her hand on the side of the strange Karda's sleek neck. "I'm better than fine." Pushed by hope, fierceness pounded through her. Her muscles tensed, her scalp prickled, and her hands fisted as though already feeling the handle of a sword, the grip of a bow. She shook her head to clear it. Her choice was made even before she asked,

"What do we hunt?"

Chapter Four

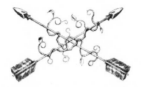

Galen was naked. His feet hovered a few inches above bare ground—dark, roiling dirt that made his whole body clench. Then he was moving. Backward. Fast. He touched the earth on the grass at the edges of the ugliness, between young hybrid poplar-abelee trees. A discordant, tinny thrum sounded, and three creatures rose out of the ugly ground some distance in front of him, their moves sluggish. Stubby, metallic wings unfurled, throwing dust and debris from hairless bodies.

The creatures struggled to stand on four wobbly legs, blinking and pawing at strings of red viscous cauls covering heads and eyes. Large forequarters, huge heads, mouths ringed with back-slanted, shark-like teeth. Long front legs with powerful shoulders. Joints of toothed, dark metal gears. Smooth grey-black skin covered bodies the size of small ponies. Glinting metal scales armored necks and shoulders. Galen was thankful he was dreaming. These were the creatures of nightmares. Noses to the ground, they snuffed at the place where he had been.

~It is an evil place, spawning evil beings.~

He whirled around, almost losing his balance, to face an enormous Karda close behind him. She glowed green and bronze, wings furled tight against her sides, head raised, neck arched.

"What are those things? Where am I?"

The creature's fierce eye and massive size terrified him. He'd never been this close to a Karda. The hooked predator beak was big enough to snap off his head with one quick twist.

~Urbat. Beasts of the Itza Larrak. They are waking.~

The voice was inside his mind. He rubbed his temples.

"What is this place?"

~A Circle of Disorder. It is growing. You must stop this.~

"Me? How can I stop this? Do you mean these creatures?" He staggered away from the edge of the circle, sick and frightened. *This is a dream. This is a dream.*

The creature stepped close and knocked her wing against his shoulder. Excruciating pain fired his scars, radiating down his fingers, up his arms, across his chest, and flamed in the scar on his face. He fell to his knees. His hands on the ground in front of him sank into dark soil.

Spilled seeds burst into green shoots that twined up his arms, branching ever more finely until they reached his shoulders and across his chest. His scars twisted into raised green and brown tattoos that burned like the blaze that maimed him. Fire seared in the scars on his face. A scream waked him. His own.

He swung his legs off the bed. "Lights." He blinked as the room illuminated to the low level allowed during the hours set as "night." He stood, breathing hard, and stared down at his hands and arms. His fists clenched. Tendons popped in his hard, muscular arms. There were no green shoots, no swirling vines. But the scars on his arms were red —afire with searing pain that eased with excruciating slowness.

Thin brown and black lines curled in a complicated design around his wrists like a bracelet tattoo. He rubbed at one, then harder, scrubbing at the marks until his skin was red. But they didn't go away.

He pulled on a robe—the softest thing he could find in his on-ship wardrobe and headed for the nearest observation lounge. He needed to be able to see the planet. Adalta. *Why? Do I think it disappeared in the few hours I've been asleep?* The remnants of the nightmare tunneled like ants through the scars spreading from his fingertips up his arms. His sudden, urgent need to look at Adalta had him almost running. He pulled his sleeves down to cover the delicate lines that circled his wrists, willing them not to be there, willing them back into his nightmare.

He stood staring at the vid screen that covered one wall of the lounge with the image of the planet below. The need to see Adalta was still there, unsatisfied. But then he wasn't looking at the planet itself, just billions of pixels arranged by the ship into a life-like replica.

Except it wasn't life-like. The ubiquitous clouds shifted above the planet's one continent, drifting to reveal glimpses of blue-green water, darker green bowl-shaped forests with dark circles at their centers, patches of gold plains, and the bare brown expanses of barren un-reclaimed ground that covered most of the continent. Beautiful, lifeless pixels. It left him bereft. A gnawing emptiness cramped his stomach.

Seeing any planet from the ship had never been possible. There were no windows, only cameras and digital images. It hadn't bothered him before, so why now? He had to fight the urge to grab his pack and his bag of seeds, commandeer a heli-shuttle, and fly back right that minute. What was happening to his desire not to go back?

He looked at the plants that lined the walls as they lined the jungle-like walls of every space on the ship. The plant-filled room with its battered and familiar furniture eased the tension in his shoulders and neck. Resisting the weird urge to dig his fingers into their soil, Galen rummaged in the canteen kitchen until he found a few cherryapples, a crusty loaf of bread, and pungent cheese someone brought aboard ship. Not ship-side fare. Of course, there wasn't any ale. He was glad one of the other agents had remembered to bring food. Eating ship food changed your body odor, a danger to the clandestine life he lived.

He started to sit at one of the scattered tables in the empty lounge and realized he had the seed bag slung over his shoulder. He looked down at it, irritated. He didn't remember picking it up. In fact, he didn't remember bringing it from planet-side.

For a second Galen wondered if whatever Readen had done to his mind had caused permanent damage. But he shrugged the thought off. It had been several tendays since the fire, and he'd never experienced anything to suggest that. It was the accursed planet. It had somehow gotten under his skin. He stripped the bag off his shoulder and threw it to the floor, kicking it under the table.

The fear, the sense of disconnection, lessened while he ate. His wrists itched. He started to pull back the sleeve of his robe to look at his arm and shook it back down, angry at himself. It was only a nightmare. There were only scars. There were no tattoos. There couldn't be.

A tired looking maintenance tech pushed through the door. Galen thought he recognized him, racking his brain for a name. Geof. That was it.

"Geof. Come sit down. Talk to me. How've you been? Catch me up on ship gossip."

Geof looked a little surprised, then pleased at the invitation. *Am I such a jerk no one thinks I'll talk to them like a real human?*

"Yeah, OK. If you'll tell me what it's like down there. I hear it's pretty primitive." Geof popped the opening in his drink container. "There was a grav disruption in one of the inner nodes. I've been up for thirty-seven hours trying to stabilize it. Not sure I'm done yet."

Galen leaned his chair back on its hind legs. "None of the tech things I've tried to use will work on-planet except the Cues, and they're sporadic—no visuals at all."

"Yeah. Seems like all I've done since we arrived here is chase after disruptions, blown boards, lost com satellites—even overgrown plants sending roots and tendrils into the circuits. Cedar and her biotechs have fits when we have to cut them out. The satellites are all gone. But I guess you know that. All of you on-planet have had a hard time communicating."

Galen took a bite of his cherryapple, ignoring Geof's curious look at it. "Seems like the ship is looking a little seedy, Geof. Is that why? Your crews are all busy chasing lost satellites?" He knew well the guy didn't have much of a crew under him, much less crews. He watched him preen a little.

"Yeah. Not a day goes by without some glitch. I'd wonder if the ship is showing its age or something if we hadn't gone through a major overhaul and systems check before we left the last planet."

He looked around the empty room as if expecting to find a listener under every other table. "But I've heard the Consortium lost a bunch of credits there. We didn't stock enough material for upkeep. Most everything went for trade goods materials. And, according to what I hear, not the kind that they accept on this planet. But you didn't hear that from me." He crossed his arms and tilted his chair back on its hind legs, unconsciously mimicking Galen.

If he sticks his chest out any further, he'll fall over on his back. Everyone wants to think they can be a covert agent like me, or rather like they think I am. But Galen wasn't averse to using the hero worship. Anything to take his mind off why he was so discontented and restless. He rubbed his wrist.

"So, Geof. What else has been happening up here? I've been on-planet for a year. Need to catch up." He refused to look down at his wrists.

Geof leaned forward and stared at them. "Did you get those on the planet?" He reached out a finger to touch them.

Galen jerked back and pulled down his sleeves again.

It was late when Galen left his quarters the next day, grateful the rest of the night had been dreamless. Geof had been a fountain of information. Easy prey for someone like Galen with years of experience—despite his youth—who could drag what he needed out of the unwary. He scrubbed at his face, wondering why he stood in the darkness far to the back of a huge cargo hold, staring at crates of weapons—akenguns. He was headed to breakfast. This was the last place he should be. It could draw attention to the contraband weapons.

He'd come without thinking, not even aware of where he was going. His fingers traced the scars on his left hand. He gripped and released the resilient, leather-covered ball the healers had given him to strengthen his hand.

He shifted the seed sack on his shoulder. Why did he bring it? He never remembered picking it up, but every time he looked down, there it was, hanging from his shoulder. He tried to cover his unease with anger. But his hand trembled, and he almost dropped the leather ball before he collected himself. He couldn't allow whatever Readen had done to him to rule his life.

He concentrated on the crates in front of him. They were ordinary enough. Nothing on the outside hinted at the incipient destruction they contained. But he could feel it. Like an itch under the scars. Part of him wondered how he'd never felt this before, why he felt it now. They were only weapons. He'd spent almost as much time training with such weapons as with the sword he wore on-planet.

Why was he even here, risking discovery? If one of the Consortium directors besides his father found these weapons, it wouldn't bode well. They had no idea of Kayne Morel's plans for the planet. They'd stop him if they knew in advance, but presented as a fait accompli? Galen wondered if they'd accept the riches it could bring. That's what his father was counting on.

He was late for the agents' debriefing with his father. Cedar Evans ran by as Galen left the pod, nearly knocking him down when she stumbled. She stopped and leaned down, hands on her knees, breathing hard. "Galen," she managed to gasp out. "What are you doing here?"

She straightened, pushing sweat-damp black hair out of her eyes, and smiled with her whole face. Gesturing at the bag over Galen's shoulder, she said, "I hope you have some samples in there for me. You haven't been very dutiful about collecting." Even when Cedar tried to frown, the expression on her lively face couldn't be serious.

"Still running the walkways, I see, Elf. What's wrong with your foot? You're not usually so clumsy." Cedar had a bionic prosthesis. She'd lost her foot to infection when she was a child from an alien microorganism on the primitive planet where her parents were assigned. It had been a difficult time. Her father didn't survive.

"It glitches every once in a while. Like just about everything else on this ship since we arrived here."

"How do you ever get your work done, Cedar? Every time I see you, you're tearing through somewhere on your way to somewhere else."

"This is my work, Galen." She gestured to the planters that lined the walkway, spilling greenery. "How else am I going to keep track of how my plants are if I don't check on them every day." Cedar was the botanist in charge of maintaining the plants that lined the kilometers of corridors and grew in every possible space on the ship, filtering the air and providing oxygen support as well as food. She also oversaw research on the flora of the planets they visited

She grinned and looked around. "Or that's what I tell myself. Where am I, anyway? What are you doing in the warehouse pods?" She tilted her head to look closely at him. "You're different somehow."

He flinched.

"No. Don't be ridiculous. Not your scars. You were too handsome for words before. They add character." She grinned. "And you need character. You've depended on your looks for too long, you vain, vain man." She cocked her head to the other side. "It isn't that. There's something—"

"I have seeds for you," Galen said, diverting her attention. Cedar was too perceptive and was one of the few people besides Marta who knew him well. He knew the seeds and soil samples he brought would distract her.

He left her sitting cross-legged on the floor outside the warehouse, filling small plastic envelopes with his seed mixes. She promised to return the bag and the rest of the seeds to him before he went planet-side again. Absorbed in her task, she'd never remember where she ran into him—he hoped.

It was a fifteen-minute trip via four walkways to the node of Planetary Findings where Galen's father was director. Or it would have been if the fourth walkway hadn't jerked to a stop. Probably giving some tech a headache.

It was several minutes before the walkway started moving again. The sudden jerk pulled at his scars. He stepped off at the Planetary Findings node and found the debriefing room.

His father looked up from the head of the long table, "Nice of you to join us, Galen."

Four other agents sat grouped near Kayne. Galen slid a chair out halfway down the table and sat, nodding to the others. He didn't respond to his father's gibe. At one time or another, he'd worked with three of these people. Paulla was assigned to Akhara Quadrant, Thom to Rashiba Quint, Merrik newly posted to Restal. Tiny-but-fierce Dalys, assigned to the Coastal Hold, was the only one he hadn't worked with. He was assigned to Anuma and Rashiba—that was his father's fiction.

His actual assignment had been to foster revolt and smuggle weapons to Readen.

"Where's Marta?" he asked. Her area included Restal and Toldar Quadrants.

"She's mixed up in whatever's happening in Restal and sent her report in," said Thom. "There was a revolt. The First Guardian, Hugh Me'Rahl, flew out there for a few days. I've heard nothing about what he discovered."

Galen bit his lip. He'd started to tell them what he'd heard of Marta's story, but for some reason, shadowed to himself, he didn't.

"We'll get to all that." Kayne's voice could cut titanium. Any banter or friendly conversation that might have started stopped cold at his tone. "You've all been on-planet for most of the year. What can you tell me that you haven't reported via your Cues? I want resources, political updates, personal contacts. Let's hear what you have. The spectra-sonic engineers reported some strange changes in the subsurface dynamics of the planet—whenever they could work around the blasted EM fluctuations. What does anyone know about that? Dalys, you first, since you fly over the planet on one of those Karda creatures."

"I'm stuck in the Coastal Hold on the back side of the mountains. I don't know anything except rumor."

"Give us rumor, then."

"The Mi'hiru messengers that pass through my guild house have only said that the Circles of Disorder in Restal are growing. There's a great deal of concern about that. It could be related to what the engineers are sensing."

"What are those circles? The electromagnetic fluctuations are most severe over them. Whatever is happening sub-surface radiates out in lines from the ones in Restal."

"They are the remnants of some ancient cataclysmic war or disaster —the alien invasion that left Adalta so barren of life before the colonists arrived. I flew around a number of them on my way from Rashiba to the coast. The Karda refuse to fly over them no matter how far out of the way they have to detour. They—" She stopped, looking around. "I know this sounds strange, but the circles give off a rancid feel of…evil." Her uncertain voice twisted up on the last word.

Kayne rolled his eyes. "I suppose you're going to say something about magic now. Like Marta."

Dalys's head gave a tiny shake, but she held his irritated gaze.

"I've heard the same," said Paulla. "It is my understanding that these circles, whatever they are, are contained by planting certain hybrid trees and phyto-remediating plants around them. Over the centuries, they've shrunk to what they are now, spots varying from many to a few kilometers in the midst of huge planted forests—almost all the trees are Earth species, of course, with a few hybrids. The locals fear these areas. I have to agree with Dalys. They do feel toxic, and I've been warned away from them several times. I don't want to explore them any closer than I have."

Older by a good bit than Dalys and Galen, Paulla had no qualms about telling Kayne what she thought. She went on, "You can scoff all you want, Kayne, but there is something here that is impossible for me to explain. Hands-on healing, the strange magma stones that burn hot but can't be lit by fire. I swear one of the people in Akhara Prime can do something with the weather beyond just predicting it. And her predictions are eerily accurate. Infallible." Kayne's face started to redden, and she stopped.

Thom spoke up, changing the subject. "As near as I can tell, there is nothing in our current inventory, or in what we're currently programmed to produce, that we can find a market for. Or will even work. All the trade samples I took to garner interest failed. Every one of them except, oddly enough, our data-com units and, thanks be to the endless stars, the heli-shuttles. Products work for a short time and then, poof. Nothing. This low-tech place wants to stay low-tech. We've wasted nearly a year trying to garner interest in products that not only don't work but are illegal with their current restrictions on technology. We'd do better to research nineteenth century Earth's mechanistic technology for something they don't have here yet."

He paused. "They do use steam power for a few things. Some mills." His voice trailed off as Kayne glared at him.

"You said there was something happening subsurface, Father," said Galen. "What is it?" He could tell Kayne was struggling to control himself. This news was not what he wanted to hear. It was as if, in spite of the agents' regular reports from the planet, scattered as they'd been when the com satellites disappeared, this information was new to him. Though Galen knew he'd been told. And often.

"It's happening in Restal Quadrant where you say these circle things are growing. The spectra-sonic engineers say there are lines of what they think are deposits of some unknown mineral extending threadlike from what must be these circles, always orienting toward another. Mineral deposits that should take hundreds of thousands of years to form are spreading. Slowly but detectable to the scientists and close to the surface, sometimes breaking the surface. Data from the spectrometric analyses says they're unique and unknown. Maybe a new allotrope of carbon. Galen, you need to gather some samples for them to test."

He rapped the table with his fist. "The probes we sent to bring them up failed. If it's an unknown mineral, and we can discover a use for it, it could be priceless. And if it's generated by these circles, we need to discover what they are, too. This planet is the first hint any trade ship has ever had that there is another sentient species capable of space travel. We need to discover everything we can about these Larrak, even though it appears they were destroyed. Their artifacts remain, apparently in these circles." His intensity was palpable.

The meeting went on for the rest of the day, the discussion alternated between the politics of this tech-resistant society and lists of trade resources. Galen was exhausted when the briefing ended. But his father wasn't finished and held him back when the others left to shuttle back to the planet. He wasn't sure how to tell his father he might not want to return to the planet—though his determination to never go back was fading. He shifted the seed bag on his shoulder. The seed bag that he couldn't seem to leave behind. It would not be a pleasant conversation.

"Damn Luddites." Kayne threw his stack of paper across the table.

Galen had a sudden memory of an old man telling stories of the first colonists by the fire in an inn on Adalta. He remembered the old man's pride in those Luddites Kayne cursed. He described the Adaltans' dedication to the complexity of life and their determination that they save what they could of life on Earth. Their frantic search on Earth in those last days to find a suitable habitable planet mostly barren of life where they would be able to recreate what they loved of Earth. Their joy when they discovered Adalta.

Their struggle to gather the seeds, the rootstock, the eggs, the embryos—everything they could load on the immense Ark Ship. Everything they would need to rebuild vibrant life on what they thought was a completely barren world. The unexpected discovery of sentient life—the Karda—who welcomed them as allies. Their courage and struggles to survive in the fight against their common enemy. The Larrak, the vicious aliens who were destroying the planet—the cause of its barrenness.

"Sometimes I wonder if the damn planet itself is conniving against us." Kayne's voice brought him back. "These colonists are so smugly satisfied with what they have they won't even consider anything more technological. When it comes right down to it, with all this talk today, there is not much we have to offer them they can't do for themselves. Damn Readen for moving too fast. Why couldn't he have waited for the weapons? And damn you for letting them get destroyed. We'll be ruined. I sunk everything I have into this venture."

His raving went on for another good five minutes. Galen tuned him out again and worked the leather ball with his fist. He clenched and unclenched his hands and watched the subtle moves of the strange lines on his wrists—refusing to think about how they appeared.

Kayne like the approaches to a planet choreographed, every move planned, and Adalta wasn't following his lead.

The crux of the matter was that Kayne had stolen—borrowed, he insisted—Marta's stock in the consortium beginning right after her father died. Now he couldn't pay it back.

The akenguns were all Kayne had to trade. But they were forbidden by law on Adalta and therefore prohibited by the Trade Federation that oversaw the various trade ships. Nothing more advanced than bows or swords was allowed on the planet by law and custom. Smuggling the weapons to Readen Me'Vere in exchange for the valuable minerals so plentiful in the mines of northern Restal was only the beginning of Kayne's plans to strip the planet. And Galen had been embroiled up to his neck on horseback in the disastrous project.

I didn't find myself embroiled by accident. I was an active participant. He looked down at his scarred and deformed hand. *I did this to myself. And it can't be undone.* A brief flash of the gold and green Karda came and went in his mind. Pain flared—shot from his fingertips to his shoulders and across the scars on his chest and face. Then it was gone.

"Readen is our best and possibly only hope," said Kayne, jerking Galen's attention back again. "You must figure out how to contact him and get him free. His ambitions to rule Adalta are the perfect foil for our purposes. Forget trade. Forget friendly relations. No other trade ship, not even the Federation, knows about Adalta yet. We can strip it and move on, and no one will ever know as long as we erase the records from the ship's data banks."

"How are you going to convince the other directors? Especially Glenn Voigt. They won't stand for such blatant piracy. They never have in all our history since the Diaspora." Galen had to force himself to swallow the hatred that threatened to spill out at his father's mention of Readen. It overshadowed what his father was saying until he heard his next words.

"Because it's that or complete financial collapse. We spent too many resources finding this planet and gathering the goods to trade—the goods they won't accept. Our directors won't sacrifice the future of the families that live and work on this ship for the sake of an outmoded principle. Families who have been on this ship for hundreds of years. They won't want the Trade Federation to take control."

He leaned across his desk. His voice rasped against Galen's skin. "But that's my problem. Yours is to get Readen back in power. I'll switch your territory from Anuma to Restal. Use the excuse of needing more training in the Planters Corp. That's been a useful cover."

Galen forced calm into the muscles of his face and body. He knew he had no choice. He was returning to Adalta. *I can't stay here—forced to face my father day after day.* Life on the backward planet was suddenly the better alternative.

His father's eyes bored into him. "You will not fail again. I will leave you on this accursed planet if you do. I will sail away and leave you here to rot."

Chapter Five

Tessa leaned into Kishar's shoulder, brushing his coat, cleaning it of sweat until it shone, then combed out his mane.

"That's good, Tessa. Now let's take care of his wings and tail feathers." Cerla, the stocky, brown-haired Mi'hiru assigned to oversee her training and to instruct her in the care of the Karda, pulled out a small bottle of thin oil and a fine paintbrush, its hairs spread fanlike.

"It takes very little oil, so little you wouldn't think it necessary unless you'd seen a neglected Karda. And it helps with rainy days. It's difficult enough to fly in the rain—they don't need to be without the oil that helps shed the water and dampness. They produce some naturally, but we ask them to fly in the wet more than they are ordinarily inclined to."

Cerla was one of the cadres of women chosen for a lifelong bond by a Karda. They were dedicated to the big creatures and trained to care for them. Proficient in weapons and hand-to-hand fighting, they were among the few who could communicate with the Karda—empathically and sometimes telepathically.

They served as messengers and flew with Karda Patrol wings in every quadrant. Scattered over Adalta in the primes and on the larger holds, wherever there were Karda, there were Mi'hiru. They lived in the guild houses attached to the mews with other single women—healers, weavers, teachers—who preferred the convenience and protection of communal living.

"Your schedule indicates you have a session with the cartographer in about thirty minutes, so I'll help you this time."

Tessa didn't look up from the flight feather she was brushing with oil. "Um, Cerla? I don't need lessons with the cartographer."

"Yes, Tessa, you do. Being able to recognize landmarks wherever you fly is important. It's a lot to learn, I know, but you will only need to learn about Restal for now. I'm sure you'll be back periodically. You can continue your studies of the rest of Adalta then."

Tessa undid her waist-length, silver hair from its knot and twisted it up, gathering back the strands that strayed. "Oh, drat. I've gotten oil in my hair again."

She wiped her hands on her dirty work shirt for too long, then forced them to be still, fisting them tightly. *How do I explain this strange new ability?* "No, Cerla. I don't need the cartographer's lessons. I always know where I am and how to get where I need to go."

Cerla laughed. "I'm sure you think you don't need it, but—"

~She does not need lessons about maps. She is the Austringer. She knows.~

The Mi'hiru whirled to look at Kishar. "Oh, I don't understand how you can make your words heard in anyone's mind. I can only communicate empathically with other Karda no matter how hard I try." She started to chew on a fingernail then spit and rubbed her mouth with her sleeve. "Ugh. That oil tastes awful. I never learn." She paced the back of the large stall, back and forth several times, frowning.

"All right. Tell me the distance and directions to the Me'Neve mines."

Tessa's answer was immediate: "A hard, three-day flight four degrees west of magnetic north." She bit her lip at the suspicion on Cerla's face.

"You've been there."

"No. I've never been there."

"They have to haul their ores across your father's land. You must have learned from that. What is the distance and direction to the Isomil sawmill in Akhara Quadrant?"

Tessa huffed out an exasperated breath, swiping a strand of oily hair off her face. *She doesn't believe me.* She closed her eyes for a moment and focused. A clear line formed in her mind, crossing through Toldar and into Akhara Quadrant. "Most of a tenday flight south and east of Toldar Prime. And if you want to know how long it takes by wagon or horseback, you will have to extrapolate from the flight time. And how can you even know if I'm right?"

Cerla didn't respond for a few moments. Then, her voice rising with both apology and confusion, she replied, "I'm from there. Go explain to the cartographer why he won't need to interrupt his work to teach you what you already know. If you can. Then go on to the arms salon to meet Armsmaster Krager for your workout. I won't say your weapons lessons because you've no need for those either from what I've heard."

Tessa laughed. "I don't understand it either, Cerla. It makes no sense that I do always know how to move, how to attack, how to defend. Even with the bow, I never miss. But my muscles protest loud and often. I may know *how* to move, but it doesn't help when my body fails because I haven't developed the strength to do what I shouldn't know how to do. I hurt all over all the time." She rubbed her aching shoulder, shaking out her arms. *And how I can do all that with my talents still blocked is even more mystery than you think.*

"Tessa." The imperious voice jarred through the mews.

Oh, please, gracious galaxy. Not father. Not now. She looked at Cerla. "Is there any place I can hide? I was hoping he wouldn't be back before I left. His trip home was too short."

Cerla's tone was apologetic. "I'm afraid not. He'd yell at me instead of you like he did when you ran away yesterday." She grabbed up soiled cloths, brushes, nearly empty oil bottles and slid around the opening of the stall. "Sorry to abandon you but—busy, you know." She ran for the tack room before Connor Me'Cowyn reached them.

Tessa moved to Kishar's side, leaned against a solid front leg, and waited for her father to find her, wishing Kishar could help her.

~I'm afraid you will have to face this on your own, Tessa. You will be facing things that are much more dangerous than your father soon.~

Tessa jumped at the feeling of Kishar's voice in her head. How could she ever get used to this? It made the inside of her head itch. And she groaned at the amusement in his voice. She concentrated on thinking the words to him. It wasn't easy, but she felt blessed. Very few riders could speak telepathically to their Karda partners. One more confusing ability to get used to.

~It's not funny, you know. I've been placating him all my life. I've never flat denied him before.~ She reached up and twisted a strand of Kishar's long black mane across her face. ~I just want to hide.~

"Tessa, Great Adalta, you're filthy. And what is that you're wearing. Work clothes? You've let yourself go while I was away. Why are you wearing something that looks like what a Mi'hiru or a female patroller would wear? And your hair. It's a mess. Is that oil? Take it down and brush whatever that is out. No. Get yourself to our apartments in the keep and wash. Change into the dress I chose for you. Leave your hair down—your clean hair—tonight. We're sitting at Daryl's table, and you need to look your best."

How many times have I heard those words? You need to look your best for This Man of Great Talent. You need to look your best for That Man of Great Talent. They rang louder and louder in her head. They burned into her skull until she was sure there was a sign branded on her forehead—Brood Mare for Sale.

She turned and reached into the shelves that held Kishar's grooming tools, grabbed the long shears, shook down her hair, and started cutting. Hunk after long hunk of silver hair floated to the floor of the stall before her father could move. His face froze halfway between fury and disbelief.

"What are you doing?" His voice boomed in alarm, and feathered heads popped up over the sides of the stalls all through the mews. Connor started for her, furious, and reached to grab the scissors. Kishar mantled his wings and stepped between them, knocking Connor back.

Tessa kept cutting. Glistening strands of silver hair dropped in a ring on the floor of the stall around her like a fallen halo. Short clumps stuck up every which way on her head.

Finally finished, she turned to the speechless, red-faced Connor and said, "Kishar and I are leaving tomorrow. We'll be scouting for the Planting Expedition that leaves in a tenday for the circle north of here. So Cerla and Kishar say I need more experience being—"

"No, you are not." He was shouting now. He dodged around Kishar's wing and grabbed her arm, shaking her until she could barely keep her feet on the ground.

~Yes. We are~ Kishar reached out with a taloned foot, grabbed the back of his jacket, plucked him neatly off his feet, and set him outside the stall.

Kishar's pathed voice rang, and every head in the mews turned to look. ~We leave in the morning. The Austringer and I.~

Connor's hands flew to his head, covering his ears, and he dropped to his knees.

A few days later Tessa scrubbed her hands through the newly cut hair flying in a scraggly silver halo around her head. How freeing it was. No longer would she spend hours on the elaborate hairdos her father insisted she wear. Her waist long weight of silver hair was gone. Gone. She laughed out loud and grabbed the handle on the saddle pommel in front of her.

They'd been on their own and away from Restal Prime for several days. She'd learned to build a fire circle, to make a crude camp, to cook her meals, to make a rough bed from cut evergreen branches, to organize her packs, and to keep the many long straps of Kishar's rigging from getting hopelessly tangled when she stowed them at night.

~Dive, Kishar. Let's dive again. You said I need the practice, so let's do it.~ She adjusted the goggles over her eyes, leaned forward, and the Karda dove for the forest beneath them faster than any Karda she'd ever ridden. She could feel the muscles of her cheeks pushed back by the force of their headlong stoop. Her stomach tried to stay behind as he pulled up, just skimming the ground, and darted through the ancient forest of immense, wide-spaced trees, twisting and turning through them.

Tessa clamped her thighs and leaned close over his neck, one hand on the pommel handle and one hand wrapped in his mane, holding on for dear life. His upraised wings almost closed over her head as they darted through a narrow space in the tangle of trees. She braced against the sudden jerk of his hind legs shoving off the trunk of a tree, one then the other. He twisted through crossed branches, wings folding tight then snapping open. They broke into a clearing, and the Karda swooped back up, wings beating hard, and her insides did another roll.

~That's the fastest we've done yet,~ she shouted, telepathically.

~Modulate your voice, please,~ Kishar pathed, ~I can hear you fine if you speak softly. And I will have less of a headache if you do.~

~Sorry. Sorry. It's--all so--exciting.~ Even her inner voice was having a problem speaking clearly as the wingbeats of the Karda tossed her back and forward in the saddle, from high cantle to pommel, legs clamped, knees securely wedged under its horns. She struggled to gain her rhythm, to sync her movements with Kishar's wingbeats, grateful her muscles were getting accustomed to the forceful back and forth, up and down.

~And so much fun. I know you've told me how dangerous our job will be. But flying is…is…Oh, I can't find the words for what flying with you is. It's incredible. You're not like any other Karda I've ever had the privilege to fly with. Of course, I couldn't talk to them like I can to you.~

She laughed and threw her hands up over her head as the Karda found a thermal and rode it up. She was learning to sense the thermals herself. With his tutoring, the warm upward-moving air currents were almost visible to her.

~That's true enough. And possibly a mixed blessing for them.~

Tessa drew her hands back down, chastened at the hint of sorrow behind his teasing. It wasn't the first time—she'd sensed it before in her beloved Karda. He wasn't like any other Karda. His small, sleek body, long tail, and short, wide wings lent him agility no other had. He had the characteristics of a sparrow-hawk rather than the larger raptors the other Karda resembled. His ability to maneuver in the forest and his ability to land in a small space without loping to a stop were unique. The soft feathers at the edges of his wings made him as soundless as an owl in flight, unlike the thunderous beats of the others' wings.

They circled wide up the thermal until the air got too cold then began a slow glide down toward the trees, moving north. ~Bow practice now. It is late, and I am hungry. We will need to camp soon. Find us a deer.~

Tessa bit her lip. This wasn't her favorite thing. She didn't understand why Kishar had chosen her as the Austringer. She loved the target shooting he insisted on. And she was good at it. Despite never having held a bow before, from the beginning, she seldom if ever missed where she aimed, and as her muscles strengthened, she got even better.

Except for hunting, when she seldom hit her target. She hated the killing. She was supposed to be a healer, not a killer. Healer, not hunter. Would she ever find yarak? Would she ever be the keen hunter Kishar expected her to be?

But she obediently flipped the second set of lenses down on her goggles, and the forest leaped up at her. She scanned the forest below for some time, finally spotting a small herd of deer searching for a resting place at the edge of a pocket meadow. ~There. Do you see them?~ She pulled her short recurve bow out of the straps at her legs, strung it, and fished an arrow out of the quiver. ~I don't like doing this. It feels so wrong.~

~We are going to eat this deer, not kill it for sport. And you must practice. The urbat will rise soon.~

~All my life I have wanted to become a healer. Now I'm a killer.~ Her fingers fumbled the arrow, nearly dropping it, and her throat tightened. *It feels so much like another failure. I can't heal because I lost my talent. So I kill instead. But Kishar says I must, and there is no one in my life I trust like I trust him.* She swallowed the lump in her throat and pathed, ~I hope I do better this time. I don't want to go back to boiled, dried meat and vegetables.~

~Indeed,~ said Kishar, and he folded his wings for a stoop, diving directly at the herd.

Tessa flipped the extra lenses back up and nocked her arrow as they streaked toward the ground and the unsuspecting deer. Just before

Kishar had to pull up, she loosed the arrow. ~Did I get it? Did I get it?~ She stopped—she was yelling again. ~Sorry.~

The Karda swooped up out of the tiny clearing and, tail twisting wheeled to vertical on one wing. The force of the sharp turn pressed Tessa hard against the cantle at her back. ~I believe you did, though I might have to finish it off.~ He headed down again, snatched the struggling buck from the ground and broke its neck—the rest of the herd disappeared through the trees. Kishar dropped the deer, turned so quickly Tessa's head whirled, and landed with precision in the middle of the pocket meadow surrounded by towering trees.

She pulled off his rigging and fished a brush out of her packs. They were both tired and hungry, but this was the first thing she always did when they stopped for the day. ~You're more important than my empty stomach,~ she said, forestalling his usual objection. ~And we've hardly stopped all day. Dinner can wait.~ She had to wait till her stomach settled anyway. Killing the young buck went against everything she yearned for. And Kishar forced her to do it every day.

But she'd had almost a whole tenday of freedom—ten days without pressure from her father to be the perfect young woman, the perfect breeder, the perfect avenue for his ambitions. She shook her head, reveling in the freedom of her short hair. Such a simple thing—a haircut. Taking the scissors to her waist-length, silver hair had cut her free of her father's expectations and ambitions. She ignored the sliver of guilt trying to slide in sideways. A tenday of freedom from him. A whole tenday of feeling so light she could almost fly herself.

Tessa finished brushing the Karda and oiling the feathers that needed it. She minutely inspected them at the end of each day, painstakingly following every instruction for the care of Kishar Mi'hiru Cerla had given her before she left Restal Prime. She checked his feet—each talon and the hard, horny pads that formed when he fisted his long claws into landing mode. They couldn't afford a crack or an embedded stone, however tiny.

~I know it doesn't do any good to ask, but I do wonder who takes care of Karda where you come from. Wherever that is in the middle of the mountains.~

Kishar laughed. ~Many ask. No one answers.~ Then the timbre of his voice changed, deepened with something too close to sorrow. ~Tomorrow, we go to the circle. You need to see what is happening there before we fly back to Restal Prime to join the planters and the wagon train.~

Tessa let his foot drop.. ~So soon? Are you sure I'm ready?~ She swallowed hard.

He didn't answer, butted her with his head, and walked off toward the small deer she'd killed. She went to build a fire for her dinner and prepare her camp for the night. One more thing she'd learned to do. *At least I can build a fire now. No more cold food and cold nights and wasted matches.* She ignored the old pain not being able to light the wood with talent always gave her. She'd lit her first candle with talent when she was three. No more. The talent was gone.

Before she banked her fire and curled herself into her blankets for the night, she spent an hour practicing the sword forms that were so strangely natural to her, blanking her mind, sealing off the pain in her muscles, enjoying the movement of her body.

Tessa shifted in the saddle. A long night on hard ground made her stiff. It was the middle of the fifth tenday since Kishar had come for her. Every day since then, she'd spent training with the Mi'hiru, practicing sword and bow in the arms salon, learning to ride the agile Karda, dodging and turning through the wide spaced trees, gliding up thermals, learning to live alone with no one but Kishar for company and guidance.

She gloried in the long glides, exulted in the swift stoops that took mere seconds to bring them from thousands of meters high in the air to skim across the ground, causing her stomach to lurch. Learning to shoot her short recurve bow from Kishar's back and timing his wing beats, so she didn't accidentally put an arrow through a wing had brought pride she'd never felt before.

Kishar could always tell when she loosed her arrow, which helped keep his wings out of the line of fire. She learned even faster when his dodging threatened to snap her saddle rig straps and fling her off his back. And her unexpected natural ability helped. She could hit anything from his back now no matter how fast they flew, no matter how small the target. Even a fast-moving target.

She pulled the goggles off and rubbed where they rested against her forehead. Today was different. Today they searched for circles.

~Which direction should we fly?~ Kishar asked.

~What? I don't know. How could I know that? Why would anyone want to know that? The circles are too dangerous.~ She might know the distance and direction of any place she had ever heard of, but Circles of Disorder were a blankness in her mind.

~You do know. Search for the nearest circle.~

Tessa moved to put her goggles back on.

~Not with your eyes, with your mind. You are the Austringer. It's not just about your ability with sword and bow. It is also knowledge of the Hunter you hold inside you that must begin to open. You know where the circles are.~

~But...~

~I do not ask for what you cannot do.~ His voice was stern and formal as it always was when she said she couldn't do something.

She sighed and tucked her goggles into her saddlebag. She could find her way to any place on Adalta that she had the slightest knowledge of. Usually, a clear line appeared in her head, and she knew where and how far the place was. Except the circles. Where that clear line should be was nothing. ~I can't tell where it is. What do I do?~

~Close your eyes and search.~

Well, that sounds simple. Like learning to shoot between his wings or stay in the saddle while he twists through the woods is simple. Right.

She resigned herself to days of closing her eyes and "searching" fruitlessly while he told her repeatedly, ~I do not ask for what you cannot do.~ She stared at the top of his regal head, un-focused her eyes, and tried to clear her mind. How many times had she done this, reaching down into Adalta, searching futilely for her talent? She fought the despair that rose and threatened to close her throat. *He won't accept my talent failures as an excuse. He won't let me quit. And if I fail him—how can I live if I fail him?*

~Do not think about your talent. Just find a circle.~

She started to panic, her breath coming too fast, too hard, too shallow—her chest tight as if banded with metal straps.

~Seek, Tessa. Seek. The Austringer can do this.~ His voice was soft and kind in her head. Her breath slowed, the bands around her chest eased, and she began to clear her mind, to concentrate on the soft brush of the wind in her hair as they flew, to concentrate on that one thing, to push away all other thoughts. Bit by bit, she pulled her attention from the brush of the wind and opened her mind, expanded her awareness away from her body, did the opposite of the grounding exercises she'd been taught. Seeking. Seeking.

She floated in an ocean of no-thing-ness, aware of the clouds, the trees beneath her, the wind, the sun on the back of her head, the ever-present pulse from Adalta. Letting the pulse of Adalta fill her, Tessa concentrated, driving her consciousness down, down. She began to feel it. For the first time since she was seven years old and failed to heal her dying mother, Tessa could feel Adalta. Joy suffused her, and she went deeper, so hungry for the connection she thought she'd never feel again.

~Stop.~

Kishar's voice snapped her back to herself, her head swimming, her feelings confused, her stomach rebelling.

~This is not the time for that.~

~But I could almost feel Adalta, Kishar. I haven't been able to make that connection since I was—~

~You cannot do that, Hunter. What you seek is the opposite of Adalta. A circle is what you search for. You must stay disconnected. You must.~

There was a strange tone in his pathing voice. Tessa could feel that sadness again, this time she thought some of the sadness was for her. And then she was angry. So angry she spoke aloud for the first time in days. "I can't let that go. Do you understand? I can't. I have been trying to get my talent back for eleven years. For the first time in eleven years, I almost had my connection to Adalta back. How can I stop?" She sobbed so hard she choked the words out. "I was meant to be a healer. How can you ask this of me? To let that go. How can you?"

He suddenly dropped a wing and turned hard, forcing her body back against the high cantle. She grabbed the pommel and held on as he arrowed toward the north. He didn't speak again, just beat his wings and glided, beat his wings and glided, ignoring her as they flew as fast as she had ever flown outside a stoop. Flying this way was difficult and tiring for him, she knew, but he flew on and on. Tessa rose and fell in the saddle to his rhythm, tears streaming sideways into her hair. Her sobs turned to hiccups then faded, but the tears still streamed, and the great red sun to the right of them lowered in the sky. Finally, she felt him circle to gain altitude. They were climbing a thermal.

Tessa was cold. All over her body were goosebumps that had nothing to do with being cold. She looked down. Beneath them was devastation. A long, narrow line of skeletal white trees snaked through the forest. She forgot to breathe then gasped, sucking air in. Her eyes followed the line of dead trees north to the edge of a Circle of Disorder. A circle surrounded by more dead and dying trees thrusting bare white branches into the sky. Its surface roiled dark and dry around the sparse, distorted trees and brush that grew inside it.

Kishar flew straight along the line and into the circle.

~Kishar. What are you doing? We can't fly here. It will kill us.~

But he continued. ~This is why I have come. This is why I searched for you. Only you and I can do this. This is why you must stay disconnected from Adalta. Only you have the shields that will let you do the work we must do here. And I am the only Karda left who can fly the circles. Do you see?~

He veered in a sudden sharp turn back toward the line of dead trees snaking away from the circle. ~See what is happening? See how this circle is reaching out? We are among the very few who can even hope to halt this and the only ones who can fly over them.~

Now Tessa knew where the sadness in his voice came from. He was the only Karda of his kind. And she was his only hope. She sobbed again, her chest so tight her breath stuttered. But this time it was for him. And for her failure to understand. She laid her hand on his sleek neck. He turned and glided some distance away from the circle into the living forest to a small clearing where a tree had fallen, leaving a space for them to land barely the width of his wings. He back winged and touched down.

She took her time unbuckling her straps and stripping the rigging and packs from his back. He settled to the ground, and she sat, cross-legged, leaning against his shoulder.

His voice sounded soft in her head. ~Something or someone has awakened this circle. In other places, they are contained, but here, in Restal, the guardian stopped planting, and the containment is failing. Soon the urbat will awaken and spill out. The Lines of Devastation are growing slowly now, and as yet only from this one circle. But unless they are closed off and stopped, they will spread to other circles. Even-tually, they will connect the circles in a net that will strangle Adalta. That is why I am asking you to give up searching for your talent. If we can win this battle, I promise I will do my best to help you recover them before I leave you.~

~Leave me?~ Tessa turned on her knees, looking into his eyes. ~You are going to leave me?~

~I am very, very old, Tessa. And I have been alone for a long time. Too long. And do not ask me why you are not enough for me. I have come to love you. I did not expect this after so many years of being alone. I love you, but you are not of my kind.~

Tessa knew he meant he would die. He was the last of his kind. Her heart hurt. A hole opened inside her that would never heal.

~Another will come to be with you. If we survive the coming battles, I will leave, but I will not leave you alone.~

Her voice a bare whisper, she said, "Are there only us two?"

~No, there is another. The Kern, if he accepts. And the people of Restal, who must start planting again. Altan Me'Gerron and Marta Rowan from Toldar who speak telepathically with each other and all Karda. But only you and I and, I hope, the Kern can enter the circles where the urbat hide. Only, he, you, and I will be able to kill them where they live, to protect the planters who must come. With the circles awake, the urbat will fight to keep them from being contained again and fight to protect the Lines of Devastation.~

"What happens if we don't succeed, Kishar?"

~The Larrak will return to kill Adalta and every living thing on her.~

Chapter Six

The air in the greenhouse was stifling—hot and humid in the mid-day light of the red sun, for once unrelieved by cloud cover. The clockwork fans in the gables pushed a sluggish breeze through, making it bearable—just. Galen swiped a damp sleeve across his forehead. Again. A missed drop of sweat burned one eye, and he blotted it with the back of his wrist, avoiding the fine dirt that coated his hands.

He smoothed the surface of the rectangular seedbed and patted the tiny reddish dots gently into the soil, watered them in with a soft spray from the watering can, and moved to the next tray.

The larger seeds he planted here germinated best in coarser soil. He frowned, tried to swallow the uneasiness that clogged his throat. *How do I know that?* He wrestled a wheelbarrow out from behind the greenhouse door and headed to the large seed storage shed between the two middle greenhouses in the line of greenhouses that spread for a kilometer down the hill toward the river.

Pushing a wheelbarrow. Hauling dirt, seeds, compost. *A few tendays ago I barely knew what compost was. How did I get here?*

But he was curiously happy. Content. He looked down at his hands on the handles of the wheelbarrow, knuckles lined with ground-in dirt, strange tattooed lines across his wrists. The scars on his hands and arms itched with dust and sweat and a new, faint, crawly-ants-feeling just under them that was not unpleasant

He'd never before felt this kind of contentment. If he were honest, he'd never allowed himself to feel much of anything. A vague idea that leaving this planet would hurt leaked into his head. He ignored it— stuffed it down and mulched it well, so the worry weed wouldn't grow.

He enjoyed the work in the greenhouses and fields, even the studying, despite himself. During Guardian Roland's tenure, the fields and many of the great glasshouses had fallen to weeds and disrepair. Only some were usable, furnishing the keep kitchens with out-of-season fresh fruits and vegetables and the resplendent gardens with bedding plants, shrubs, and ornamental trees. The spoiled, self-indulgent, Guardian Roland had spared nothing that would add to his comfort and entertainment. And Restal suffered.

In spite of the political disorder plaguing the quadrant after Readen's attempt to take over, no one wanted the Circles of Disorder to continue to expand. That way lay disaster—the disaster that had created the barrenness on Adalta. Barrenness not healed after centuries of work spreading the new life carried on the colonist's Ark Ship. The push to replant to contain the circles made refurbishing, repairing, and replanting the highest priority, which was how Galen joined the planters in Restal—the need so urgent they scarcely noted his sketchy background. Or didn't care.

Early morning workouts in the arms salon, repairing and reglazing yet another neglected greenhouse, long afternoon hours in study, late afternoons working in the fields clearing away the neglect of too many years, propagating cuttings, and preparing young trees for transplant around the circles left Galen exhausted. He still had not recovered all his strength.

He made it back to the long, low, stone barracks the planters shared with Restal Guard as sunset painted the sky. He usually avoided eating in the hall—he didn't want to run into Marta— but tonight he was too tired to go outside the keep, and barracks food was monotonous.

He saw her as soon as he entered. Marta looked up. Her hand moved as if to touch the scar on his face from across the room, then dropped to pick up her glass. Surprise and concern flashed in her eyes for the barest instant. No one but him would see that. She was as good at hiding emotions as he was. Hard lessons learned in their parallel careers as advance covert agents of Alal Consortium's trade ship.

He recognized the large young man beside her with surprise and unease. The mercenary from the wagon train. The man who had pulled him from the burning cases of the akenguns he was smuggling to Readen. The man who'd spent so many hours riding in the steam wagon with him until they reached the healer hospice in Restal Prime—healing, changing bandages, trying to lessen his pain. The man's look was not friendly.

Galen approached the table and put his hand on the back of an empty chair across from Marta. "Do you mind if I join you? I haven't seen you in some time, Marta." He nodded at the man beside her. "And I owe you more thanks than I can ever pay." He held out his hand.

"Altan Me'Gerron." The man hesitated then reached to clasp forearms in the Adaltan manner of greeting. "You owe me no thanks. Healers don't need thanks."

Galen was startled to feel Altan's healing energy questing through him, searching for pockets of pain or infection. After so long spent with the healers, he should be used to that. But there was no welcoming smile on the man's guarded face, just a sharp nod of satisfaction at whatever he'd felt. Their hands dropped away.

Altan Me'Gerron. That wasn't the name he used when he served as a mercenary guard on the wagon train trip that ended so disastrously for Galen. His hair had been darker, and he'd had a light beard. Galen recognized the name of the heir to the guardianship of Toldar Quadrant. Disguised, Altan had accompanied Daryl when he smuggled himself back into Restal Prime to foil Readen's attempt to take over as guardian of Restal.

Interesting to know Altan was so proficient at changing his appearance. But then Galen's mind had been compromised by whatever Readen had done to him. The familiar rage threatened, and his face started to heat. He ducked his head and took a slow, deep breath. Letting the rage rule him was as destructive as what Readen did.

I guess Marta has decided to follow Father's orders, and seduction is something she can do after all. The man's protectiveness was more than apparent. Theirs was no casual acquaintance. "You don't look well, Marta. Are you ill?" She was pale almost to the point of translucence. He swallowed a surge of shame. This was his fault.

"I'm fine, Galen. May I introduce Tessa Me'Cowyn." She turned to Tessa sitting on her other side. "Galen is an old friend from my village."

The young girl turned from Marta to Galen and back with a look of confusion and suspicion, then half stood and reached to clasp forearms with him, murmuring something that approximated "Nice to meet you." She wore an archer's armguard on her right forearm, and he noticed blisters healing into sword calluses on her hand. He forgot his discomfort in his curiosity and, well, attraction. He also forgot to breathe.

Galen stared, bemused, at the beautiful girl. She was exquisite despite the ragged silver hair she must have hacked at herself. The brown eyes in her heart-shaped face were huge, rimmed with long, dark lashes that lay against smooth cream-brown skin. She looked back and forth between Marta and Galen. Finally, she said—her voice soft bell tones in his head—"Won't you sit with us, Galen?"

And he was able to breathe again. "You cut your hair."

Her brown eyes squinted, and her mouth tightened. "And you're going to tell me how sorry you are to see my—"

His mouth twitched up into a grin. "Looks like you cut it yourself. Good job." His face heated. It wasn't a blush—he didn't blush. It was a flush.

"Humph," was her only reply. But her cheeks pinked. Her eyelids dropped over those huge brown eyes. And when she looked back up at him, defiance smoked in their depths

"You might ask Marta to trim the back where you couldn't reach very well. She's good with a sword."

He saw Marta narrow her eyes. Banter was the way Galen escaped feeling strong emotion. And she knew that too well. He couldn't help it. Tessa was beautiful, breathtakingly beautiful—and enchanting with that ragged halo of silver sticking every which way around her defiant face. He'd heard the gossip about her power-hungry father's blatant efforts to mate her with Daryl—or anyone with power and talent—and her escape on some strange Karda. *Good for you, Tessa.*

The meal passed without much conversation. Altan and Tessa were both in a hurry to get to the arms salon. Galen could barely speak, let alone eat. His eyes flicked between Marta's pale face and the vision with silver hair beside her. He was left alone with Marta way too soon.

Marta leaned back in her chair, the neck of her soft linen shirt falling open under her short jacket. A sizable fire opal held between two gold flying Karda hung just inside, gleaming in the light from the large bronze sconces on the wall and the small candle lantern at the center of their table. He stared at it for a moment—his forehead creased. "Isn't that just like the one Altan wears? Are you playing with fire, Marta? Won't getting too close to him make it harder for you to leave Adalta when the ship moves on?" He kept his voice low though no one sat near enough to hear their conversation.

She dropped her eyes to the necklace, then looked back at him. "I'll face that when the time comes." Her expression was wry. "It's not like I've not left friends before. Or been left by them."

He was silent for a moment, not sure if she was referring to their ended relationship. "I didn't leave you, Marta."

"Galen, you were never with me. I've known you all my life and watched you gradually close yourself off from everyone and everything till I couldn't find you inside that calcified shell you surround yourself with." She fell silent, bit her lip and watched him with a wry twist to her mouth.

He sat with his head down for several minutes then shook himself mentally. Then he looked up. "You don't look well. I've heard Readen held you prisoner before Daryl reclaimed the keep and the guardianship. What did he do to you?" He stopped at the look in her eyes. "I'm sorry. You don't have to talk about it. But did...does he know who you are?"

Galen dropped his head into his hands, elbows propped on the table. Guilt clumped in his throat. He knew perfectly well Readen knew who Marta was. He'd told him, never dreaming Readen would hurt her like this. It was in her eyes, in her pale complexion, in her still-too-frail body. And she'd not gone with the others to weapons training. Before, it wouldn't have been a question. How much did she know about him and his contact with Readen?

The akenguns he was smuggling had been so warped by the fire that burned him, Altan wouldn't have been able to describe them to her even if he thought it necessary. A sudden surge of pain in his scars made him shove his chair away from the table, away from her. He stood abruptly, the chair crashed to the floor behind him, and he left, unable to look at Marta again. He had to get away. He gave up trying to force himself not to run, and he was through the gate in the wall that led to the overgrown tree nursery before his headlong dash slowed.

He slammed the tool shed door back and grabbed a narrow shovel and a sharp weed digger. Making his way to the row where he'd stopped working earlier, his hands brushed the green leaves of a slender hybrid abelee sapling. One of the last few transplanted as seedlings from the greenhouses before Roland let the tree nurseries go. Choked as they were with weeds and stray sprouts, it would take a lot of hard work before they were ready to be dug for planting around the circles.

He jammed the blade of the shovel under a weed and levered it up, pulled it out, shook the dirt from its roots, and threw it on the debris pile from his afternoon's work. Full dark fell, but the plants glowed to his eyes, and he had no doubts as to which were weeds and which were the small cultivated trees. He tried not to think about how he knew that. He tried not to think about Marta. He tried not to think about the disturbing pulses whispering up into him from the ground itself.

Push the shovel into the dirt, lever up the weed, pull it out, shake the dirt, toss it toward the debris pile. Push the shovel into the dirt, lever up the weed, pull it out— —.

He worked steadily, his entire concentration on the job he was doing, on the plants, on the earth—forcing all other thoughts away until the scars on his hands began itching and burning. He leaned the shovel against his thigh and held his hands, palms down, before him. In the darkness, he could make out faint lines like rootlets branching from the tattoo-like markings on his wrists, spreading across the back of his hands to the tips of his fingers, circling them, moving, spreading.

Imagination. He was tired. He imagined it.

He clenched his left hand. It no longer felt useless, restricted by scar tissue. He looked again. Had the scars disappeared? He jerked his hands down beside his thighs and shook them hard.

No. That wasn't possible. He didn't look again, just took up the shovel and pushed it into the dirt, levered the weed up, grabbed it, shook off the dirt, and tossed it toward the growing pile. Grateful for the darkness that surrounded him, that hid him. Grateful for the clean smell of the earth that soothed him. Grateful Marta was still alive.

But the darkness didn't hide him from himself. That wasn't possible. He cast about for something else to think about, and the cream-brown face with the big, brown eyes and the ragged halo of silver hair appeared. He smiled then shook himself and started listing the trees that had adapted best to Restal, the crosses with native species, and the pests that plagued them. She was probably too young. A lot younger than his twenty-two years. She should have a family of big, bruising brothers and a terrifying father—maybe a blacksmith. Yes. That would be best. A blacksmith with massive shoulders and forearms and a fist that could rearrange his nose before he could sneeze.

She was far out of his reach.

A tenday and a half later, Galen loaded a final bundle of bare-root abelee saplings on the last of the long steam wagons and covered them with heavy wet cloths. He filled three lidded buckets with water and wedged them in the side of the wagon. The big water barrels were already full and lashed to the sideboards, one above each of the four wheels with odd brass boxes extending from their hubs.

Master Planter Andra Linden walked up, glanced over the load, then nodded half to herself, half to Galen. Tall and rangy, she wore her grey-threaded, brown hair pulled into a knot on the back of her head—intelligence leaped out of brown eyes that missed nothing. "This'll do. Let's check the others. It was hard to gather enough saplings for this trip. We don't want to have any loaded carelessly and get damaged. The older trees won't be as easy to transplant, and it's going to take us a while to get them dug up and bound. We'll send them after you as soon as we have a big enough load."

They walked back to the other two wagons but found nothing amiss.

She tested a few ropes and finally said, "Have your crew lash the canvas coverings over them tighter, so they don't dry out. Walk with me for a bit, Galen. I need to talk to you."

They moved away from the other planters and trainees, some moving to cover the wagons, some sprawled about under a tree waiting to leave, grateful for the rest. Digging, packing, and loading hundreds of sprouts had been hard work.

Andra was silent for several minutes as they walked the path between two large greenhouses still undergoing repair and dodged workers, stacks of glass and wood, buckets of glazier's putty. "I went over your application—along with the others. Yours was a little bare."

Galen forced himself to keep walking, keeping his stride even with hers.

"I don't care about that. We need people, and it's clear you're very good at what we need. But one thing puzzles me. The space on your application where you noted your talent strengths was blank. But your test results, the written, and particularly the practical, were unprecedented. So I watched you for several days. That's when I called Mother Evya. She watched you for three days, worked beside you, trying to sense your talent."

A stone dropped into Galen's chest, pulsing hot with the rapid beat of his heart. He loved the work he was doing. It filled an emptiness deep inside him and went far beyond his simple need for a cover job. He clenched his fists at his sides. What would he do if they forced him out? Go back to the ship? Admit another failure to his father?

Andra was checking the wagons they passed and didn't notice Galen's tension. "What Evya felt matched what I thought, and it has confused us both."

Galen cleared his throat. "I don't have talent." He could barely get the words out.

Andra looked at him in surprise. "Everyone has talent, however small. The only one ever born without it is Readen. You have talent. I'm not sure how you can doubt that. Though it's true that most people's talent is small."

She walked on. "What Evya sensed in you was a vast and mostly empty Earth talent channel that looked more like a reservoir than a channel, and smaller, though still sizable, channels, or pools, for Air and Water. You have exceptional talent potential, but for some reason, it's mostly quiescent. Your parents probably never noticed your strength, and unless you were tested by a Finder when you were young, you only got trained in the basics."

She stopped and put a hand on Galen's arm. "Evya said the Earth channel felt like—her words were 'burgeoning life, like early spring before the swelling buds burst from their scales.' And she used the words 'unbelievable, untapped potential.' Evya's never felt such a broad Earth channel."

Galen stared at her and stumbled out of a glazier's path. The putty bucket knocked his knee hard. He stopped and bent to rub it. *How am I supposed to react to that?* He struggled to take in her words. Empty talent channels? Untapped potential?

She was silent for several minutes as they paced on. "I don't know how much you know about what happened to Marta Rowan—what she experienced. What she saw." She looked a question at Galen.

"Not much." Galen forced the words out. Marta had come to the arms salon this morning during his regular workout and forced him to spar with her. Not for the first time. She'd been seeking him out regularly, mercilessly prodding him to talk about what happened to him, about the weapons. She knew about the guns, but she wasn't sure how many others there might be. For all he knew she'd seen the results of Readen's tests of them. He ruthlessly shoved down the rage the thought of Readen raised.

"Not many know this but she, too, had broad, mostly unused channels before her ordeal. Now she is one of the strongest talents on Adalta in all three elements. And they just blasted through her—that's what disabled Readen. When it happened, she blew him off his feet. Knocked him out for days after."

Galen stopped and stared at the head planter. How could that be? Marta was like him. She wasn't Adaltan. Like him, she'd been born on the consortium ship. Not even on a planet.

"What are you trying to tell me? That the same thing could happen to me? Marta looks like she's been sick for months. She's only now coming out of it." Galen rubbed his chest—his guilt a sharp, festering splinter.

"Well, she'd also been drugged for days—and tortured. I don't know when you last saw her, but she was working out in the arms salon yesterday. I, for one, don't plan on going up against her anytime soon, if at all. It looks like she's recovering and stronger than ever." Andra turned a corner to the broad path that led to the back of the keep.

Galen followed, his thoughts flitting like a disoriented flock of birds in his head, tangling with her words.

"Latest reports about the circles from the Mi'hiru and the Karda Patrol are that they are growing unchecked here in Restal. Under Roland, the planting nearly stopped no matter how many complaints he got, so the trees and the remedial grasses and bushes are dying. It started about ten or fifteen years ago, I think. No one noticed at first, and the damage has escalated drastically in the last two years."

He almost didn't register Andra's next words.

"I don't have a master planter to go with you this trip. We're stretched too thin, and they're all assigned to other circles. So, I'm putting you in charge of the planters for this expedition." She took his arm when he stumbled. "Evya thinks the more you work with the plants and the soil, the more you'll be able to draw power. And we sorely need a strong Earth talent now with the alarming reports about the circles, especially the one you're headed for."

She laughed—her mouth quirked a little ruefully. "Let's hope we don't need a Kern, too. But with an Austringer found, it's at least possible one will appear. There hasn't been one since shortly after the colonists' landfall when they fought the Larrak, or so the old tales tell. I'm hoping things don't get so bad we need one."

Galen took a step to recover from his stumble, and she dropped her arm. "In charge? I don't know enough to be in charge." Being a covert agent meant sticking to the sidelines, being the observer, never putting oneself out in front.

"You'll have Bren and Captain Almryk to help. Bren has experience leading wagon trains. He knows the route you'll take, and Almryk's patrollers will give the protection you'll need against wandering mercenaries. They think they can take the pay Readen owes them by attacking where they find weakness."

Galen watched her walk away. Well, he'd wanted freedom to travel over Restal. Now he had his chance. Going after the samples his father wanted would be easier if he didn't have to answer to someone else, and he'd be headed directly for where the strange new deposits were.

But what was a kern? He thought it was a word for seed in a language he'd learned for another mission. Andra made it sound like a kern was a person. He'd heard something about the return of a Hunter-with-a-capital-H called Austringer, whatever that meant. Since his father would only laugh, or more probably get angry if Galen reported something Kayne considered a tavern tale from a backward, superstitious culture.

Galen cursed to himself. He'd skimmed over the planet's ancient history. If he'd paid more attention, it would help now. A vague memory of the Kern mentioned in reports of the time shortly after the colonizers had arrived when the Karda first appeared floated from the back of his mind. Quaint and probably highly-fictionalized ordinary-people-turned-heroes-save-the-world stories told around firesides on long cold winter nights hadn't seemed of critical import. There'd been too much else to learn—history, politics, dialect, mannerisms--the list was endless. He should have known better.

He rubbed the ants-crawling-under-his-scars feeling on the back of one hand. The vision of his cupped hands filled with black dirt, and seeds sprouting green shoots twining up his arms flashed through his mind.

The stone permanently lodged in his chest turned over. He'd need to get somewhere to use his Cue. Surely, he could find some mention on his Cue.

"Be you ready, lad?" A short, wiry man, hair bristling up from his head, clapped Galen on the shoulder.

He winced. His scars were healed enough not to feel too much pain from the slap, but he didn't think he'd ever get past shying away every time someone got too close.

"I be Bren. 'Tis me who'll be leadin' the wagons. We should talk a bit about our route."

"Galen Morel?" A lean, wiry guard captain approached him. "Guardian Daryl would like to speak with you. If you would come with me."

Galen looked at the wagons loaded with seeds and abelee sprouts, the impatient horses being backed into place and harnessed, the young planters hoisting packs into supply wagons. He swallowed a surprising grief that now he probably wouldn't be riding with them. Daryl would have him imprisoned. He must have found out about his association with Readen. And maybe even about the akenguns he tried to smuggle into Restal.

He followed the captain to the keep and up to the guardian's study. Two more guards stood outside the door, alert and unsmiling. It seemed Daryl was still uncertain about the loyalties of the people of Restal Quadrant.

The captain knocked, opened the door without waiting, and followed Galen inside.

Tall, mullioned windows, heavy drapes tied back, overlooked the gardens outside. Stacks of books and papers littered the floors. There were piles in front of the cold fireplace of rough-cut red sandstones, on the shelves that lined two walls, and on the massive ornate desk that took up the center of the room where Daryl sat.

Tall, with powerful shoulders and arms that spoke of hard-earned proficiency with weapons, his brown hair streaked by the sun, Daryl was wearing the dress uniform of the Karda Patrol. Galen remembered the funeral services for Guardian Roland had been that morning. The new guardian looked at Galen for several eternities, not speaking.

"Just stack the books on the floor wherever you can find an empty place." He motioned the two men toward the chairs across from him.

His eyes never left Galen's. "I know who you are and what you have done."

Galen froze, halfway to the chair, then moved a pile of books and eased himself down, sitting with his scarred hand in his lap, his right on the table in front of him.

"Let me see both of your hands."

Clenching his left hand, he raised it to the table.

Daryl reached over and touched the tattoo-like lines on Galen's wrist. "It's because of these I am speaking to you. And it's because of Marta Rowan that you were not imprisoned with Readen as soon as the healers let you go. We've known who you are for some time. I also know that part of that time, you were acting under a compulsion that Readen placed on you with his blood magic. We know who you work for and what your purpose on Adalta is."

He didn't raise his voice, but his words were harsh, staccato, and they hit Galen like fists to his diaphragm. "Andra and Evya convinced me you must be allowed to continue studying as a planter and that we need your talent. They don't know who you really are."

Galen's mind raced frantically. How should he react to this? "I can't..." He had to clear his throat. "I can't have talent. If you know who I am, you know I am ship-born, not native to Adalta." Marta must know that he was the one who betrayed her to Readen. He fought to keep his emotions from his face, not to let them overcome him. He had to keep his head clear. The talent issue was not relevant. Who he worked for was. Whoever he worked for.

"Evya is an accomplished talent finder. She might make a mistake about the potential of your channels, but she knows you are an Earth talent. Because of her strong conviction, I agreed to give you a chance. Andra says you know enough to lead this planting expedition. All the master planters she can spare are working other circles. The planters she assigned to your expedition are even younger than you, so there won't be any resentment at being passed over."

Galen felt like he was fumbling, frantically trying to keep up with what Daryl was telling him.

"I'm sending Captain Almryk with his squad of Mounted Patrol with you. You'll need them for protection—too many of Readen's mercenaries are unaccounted for and are roaming the countryside causing problems. But the captain's also charged with watching you. Your trip back to the orbiting spaceship was not unnoticed."

Galen winced, glancing up at the older captain standing beside him, whose face was not the least bit friendly. He'd not sensed anyone watching him when he met the heli-shuttle. How did Daryl know?

"Karda," Daryl answered his unspoken question. "It's difficult to hide from them." He stood and walked to the tall windows, his back to the two men as he looked out across the gardens just coming to life again. "I don't trust you. I don't know you, despite traveling with you for more than a tenday with the wagon train before you were so badly burned. You are not the same man you were then. What kind of man you are now—I don't know. I can only trust the finder's and Andra's assessments of you."

Daryl had been on the wagon train he'd used to smuggle the guns? Galen cursed Readen again. His memories of that trip were foggy and distorted. Not just because of the terrible burns he'd suffered trying to save the weapons from the fire but because of whatever Readen had done to his mind to force him to do his bidding.

"If your talent connection to Adalta is as strong as Evya suspects it is, no matter what your intentions may be, you will not be able to harm the planet. So, I'll let you go with this expedition. As it's leader. This is not a decision I make lightly. The consequences to you should you betray us will be severe, and they won't necessarily come from humans."

When Galen got back to the greenhouse area, he walked the line of wagons once again, checking everything he could think of to check, not wanting to miss anything essential in his inexperience and sure he would.

Did they know about Merrik, the other agent in Restal? Or the ones in the other quadrants? How much had Marta told them? He thought about the pendant she wore. He suspected her allegiance had changed more than he realized. He pulled tight a loose fastening on one of the canvas coverings. He shuddered, thinking about his father's rage when he found out they knew about the ship and his illegal activities. What would his reaction be? Not a pleasant one for the planet, Galen was sure.

What he wasn't sure about was his own reaction, both to being found out and to the thoughts about what his father might do. Or to the strong temptation—maybe even decision—not to tell him.

Sudden pain flared across the scars on his hands and arms. His cheek burned. The tattoos on his wrists clamped like iron manacles, and his knees threatened to collapse as though gravity reached out of the ground and grabbed him. Propped against the wagon, he forced his chest to expand and contract, bringing air to his lungs. Gradually, the heaviness and pain dissipated.

He couldn't move his feet. His boots were buried three inches in the earth. Galen looked around. Only Captain Almryk watched him. His mouth curled in distaste, and he turned away.

Galen straightened and forced fear back through the hole that opened in his chest. He'd faced many strange and dangerous situations on several other worlds—he could face this, whatever it was. He pulled his feet free and strode down the line of wagons to Bren's at the head, ignoring the captain and trying to ignore the fear fluttering inside his head. Trying to ignore what just happened. Trying not to look at his feet, at chunks of dry dirt falling away from his boots as he walked.

They rolled away from the greenhouses not much later—six open steam wagons piled high with sapling bundles; two covered wagons carrying the twelve trainees and their baggage; two loaded with supplies, bedrolls and tents; the blacksmith's and the cook's wagons, and two loaded with sacks of seeds covered securely against the weather.

Twelve Mounted Patrol guards rode along with them, shepherding four extra riding horses, one of them Galen's. He swung up onto the wagon seat, and Bren clucked at the four big mares hitched to it.

Galen noticed Bren's concentration on something, and he felt the faint rumble of steam in the brass-bound, iron box behind their seat. The wheel hubs puffed small white clouds, and the mares settled into an easy gait, and he adjusted his sword and attempted to settle himself on the hard bench.

Bren glanced at Galen's scarred arms and the tattooed wrists below the rolled-up sleeves and blinked. He just said, "This bench is gonna get harder the further we go. You gonna be alright, lad? T'won't be easy ridin'."

"This is better than walking. Though if this bench gets too hard, I may want to trot alongside for a few kilometers. Half a kilometer, anyway. Maybe a quarter. Or better yet, saddle my horse."

Bren laughed. "A few days of ridin' this hard bench and a few nights sleeping on the ground, and you might be ready to trot for a bit. 'Fore we get much further down th' road, we'll be traveling' through rough country."

Chapter Seven

Readen Me'Vere rolled his head back and forth on the rough pillow and rubbed hard on his forehead to clear his head. He was tired despite the fact that he slept nearly all the time. The whispering voice was relentless. The strange dreams with soft words he couldn't quite hear were surely the beginning of madness.

He had to find a way out of this prison. Daryl couldn't be allowed to win. Restal was his. Not his brother's. The very word "brother" seethed inside him, a canker that never healed.

He pounded on the door. The damp walls of his cell were rough stone. Centered on one was a solid metal door with a flap at the bottom where his food appeared. No one was going to waste precious wood on a cell door. One small, high window opposite the door let in dim light.

He waited a long time before a guard came and kicked at the flap in the bottom of the door. They never spoke. He could feel nothing from them. No fear. No anger. Nothing. All the protections put on them made them blank to him. He ached for an emotion to relish as an alcoholic shakes and aches for the wine bottle just out of his reach.

"Paper. Paper, pen, and ink. I need to write to my brother."

He heard the guard walk away. It was a long time before he

returned. The slot at the bottom of the door to his cell rattled, and one sheet of paper slid through. A slender stick of graphite rolled across the stones of the floor, and he snatched it up.

Smooth words rolled from the graphite onto the paper as he wrote. Words to soothe Daryl's anger. Words to exonerate Readen. Words to convince his brother that the Itza Larrak had trapped him. Words to convince him nothing was Readen's fault. Words to explain how the Itza Larrak forced him into doing its bidding. Words to thank Daryl for moving Readen from the cells beneath the keep to this remote prison where the influence of the Itza Larrak couldn't reach.

But he was free now, he wrote. When Marta shocked him unconscious, and the Itza Larrak disappeared, she freed Readen of the monster's evil.

So the words said as they spread his lies line by line across the page. Smooth gray, groveling, graphite lies. His fingers cramped with the effort as the words formed, asking for love and forgiveness, begging Daryl to come to him.

The rage swelled inside his chest till it choked him. A drop of sweat smeared the end of the word forgiveness. Readen smiled and almost laughed aloud. Maybe Daryl would think it was a teardrop. He was that much a fool.

His next meal slid through the small opening just as he finished. He got up, swallowing the hatred swelling inside his chest, and exchanged the folded letter and graphite for his food.

He wasn't hungry—he was never hungry anymore—but he moved the tray to the small table and forced himself to eat. The food and the cup of wine would help erase the fierce pain pounding his head.

Wood. The utensils, the plate, bowl, cup—all of wood, never glass or pottery or metal. And they collected it all every time. They left nothing he could use to make a weapon. Not that anyone ever entered his cell to be threatened.

There were no others in the adjoining cells he could draw power from. The silence was too complete. He wasn't even sure where he was. The wagon transporting him to this forsaken prison had been windowless. Familiar rage swept through him at his talentless impotence.

He swallowed the wine in one gulp. His hand shook, and he slammed the cup to the table and rubbed his palm against his thigh, willing the trembling to stop.

How could he get out of here? Would Daryl believe he'd been controlled by the Itza Larrak all along? He'd always been able to convince his half-brother of his innocence and good will no matter what he'd done. His gullible fool of a sibling always took his word. Always found excuses for him.

For Daryl, loyalty to his older brother was paramount. Daryl's guilt over having strong talent while Readen was talentless had been a potent weapon in Readen's hands. It still could be. Somehow, he had to get Daryl here. Somehow, he had to find a way to talk to him.

Where was Pol? The jailer had been his faithful servant from boyhood. Had he been captured when Marta's sudden surge of talent shocked Readen into oblivion? Or killed? Readen needed to fuel his powers. Pol could be trusted to bring him a victim. Readen needed a victim. A body to scream with pain and fear. To bleed.

He forked a big piece of the overcooked pork into his mouth, and a sliver of bone cut him. Blood welled from the inside of his cheek. He rolled the taste on his tongue. The tiniest hint of power trickled through him, dissipating but not quite disappearing.

Readen sucked in a breath. Glee shivered through him. He could gain power with his own blood. He'd never tried that before. There had always been others to bleed. Now, at last, a way to power.

He worked the sharp sliver of bone out of his mouth and stared at it. It was about an inch and a half long, needle-sharp on one end, pink with his blood. Holding it like the most precious jewel, he jabbed it into his thumb. A glistening red bead of blood formed. Squeezing it, then licking it, Readen felt another faint trickle of power. He threaded the sliver into the hem of his sleeve so it wouldn't get lost. It might not be much of a weapon, but it could draw blood.

He finished the meal with more relish than he'd had for days. Searching the remains for another sliver of bone, he worked out an even longer piece. Putting the dinner tray back in front of the slot, he sat at the table to think about how to use his fragile new tools.

Taking the smallest one from his sleeve, he pricked his index finger, drawing a tiny bead of blood. He licked at it, relishing the warm salt taste, but there was little response, just a hint of power. Useless. Jabbing harder, he broke the tip of the splinter without penetrating his skin.

He almost threw it across the room before he realized it was so small he might not find it again, and these were the only tools he had. He forced down the rage.

The Itza Larrak's harsh lessons had taught him rage could fuel power, but too much rage dissipated it. He took ten long, even breaths, tempered his anger until it became the simmering, solid ground of his life again. Controlled. Ever-present. The necessary nucleus of his soul.

Sitting cross-legged on the floor, he scraped the smaller sliver of bone against the rough flagstone, working it back and forth until he had a sharp edge. The end was too blunt to prick his skin, so he dragged the edge of the bone fragment along his forearm until a bloody line appeared. He licked it and a minute surge of power flickered then disappeared. He leaned back against the cot to think. His tired thoughts whirled and settled in an uneasy half-sleep.

Symbols from the pillars in the cavern beneath the Restal Keep crisscrossed a half-dream. Glistening obsidian, angular symbols, drifted to form words and sentences in the arcane language of spells the Itza Larrak had taught him. Taught him from childhood when he first discovered the immense hidden cavern beneath Restal Keep—and its prisoner, the Itza Larrak.

Symbols engraved on towering columns moved in and out of the cloud that filled his mind, forming and un-forming meanings. Almost, almost, he could make sense of them. Then, suddenly they froze in place, and the message blazed.

He started. His eyes burned. And the meaning flicked away. He jumped to his feet and slammed his fist into the rough stone wall, breaking the skin on a knuckle. A scream roared out of his chest and tore through his throat.

He paced the square of his cell for hours trying to recover what he'd lost, sucking hard on the scrape on the back of his hand. The symbols had been so clear. Their cold promise lurked just behind his thoughts, out of reach.

He sat on the small cot, back straight, feet firmly on the floor, hands on his thighs palms up, and tried to concentrate the way the Itza Larrak had taught him. But all he accomplished was a build-up of frustration eroding his anger with the fear he'd never escape, never get his power back.

The tiny bit of power the blood had given him trickled away, and he made a crucial discovery. He knew he could feed on the fear of others. And he stopped feeling fear when he was a small boy. Now he knew his own fear would erode, even destroy, what power he could garner.

The whispering words of his uneasy dreams, visions of the arcane symbols—the letters that called the Itza Larrak—taunted him, keeping just out of reach, keeping him from sleep.

For three days, he didn't sleep. He didn't eat. He didn't drink. He paced. Seven steps, turn. Seven steps, turn. Seven steps, turn.

Trays of food came and went unnoticed. And he paced, desperate to force order on the drifting symbols.

Exhausted, stumbling over his feet, he fell into the chair at the table and stared at his hands. He took the bone sliver from his shirt, drew it hard across the skin of his forearm along the scabbed line he'd made before. Tiny droplets of blood formed. He scraped it across his skin again, deepening the line into a cut. He drew another line, a diagonal crossing the first, then a third forming an X near the bottom end of the first long bloody mark.

Over and over, he deepened the cuts, absorbing the pain, licking away the blood. He worked long, ignoring hurt and hunger, his thoughts skirting the edges of consciousness. Then he collapsed, head on the table, the splinter dropped from his fingers.

When he woke, the symbols roiling around in his dreams solidified again for a brief moment. His body was stiff, his joints ached. He pulled himself upright in the hard chair and stared at the new scar on his arm. It gleamed like the glittering obsidian dream symbols, hard and black and shiny against his pale, pale skin—a letter in the arcane language of the Itza Larrak.

The sudden rattle at the cell door jerked him around. A hand at the end of a thick hairy forearm, nails rough and split, skin grimy with ground-in dirt, pushed his tray through.

A hand? Always before it had been a wooden stick.

And it didn't withdraw. Instead, it turned, callused palm up. There was a round burn scar in the center of the palm. The hand fisted. Then the fingers extended, fisted, and extended a second time. Then a third.

Readen dove for it too late. Pol's hand was gone.

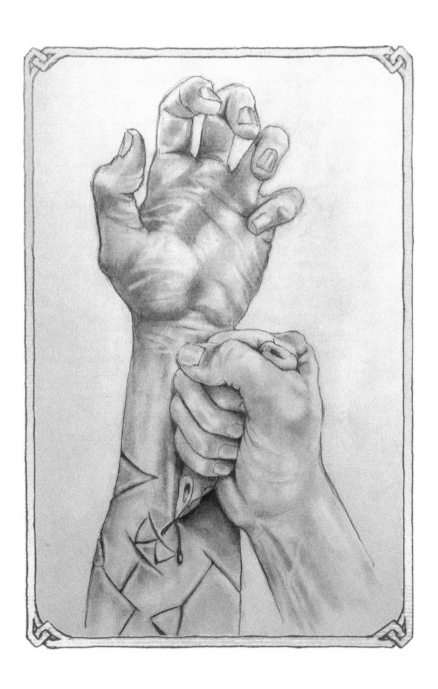

Chapter Eight

Tessa and Kishar circled high above the planters' train of steam wagons, scanning the woods below them and the edges of the barren lands ahead. Barely beginning to leaf out, the trees gleamed pale green, sometimes red or purple with a haze of swelling buds. Pink and white clouds of wild plum thickets made the forest a pastel tapestry, translucent in the early light.

She stood in the stirrups and stretched both arms overhead, clasping her hands and arching her body from side to side to ease her back and legs. Sleeping on hard ground night after night lost its allure after the first excitement of being on her own wore off.

~Warn me when you're going to do that.~ Kishar angled his tail and flipped his wings to get them back into an even glide. ~One of these days, you will catch me off guard, and we will be upside down. I hope you check your straps well. I do not know whether or not I could catch you if you fall.~

~Oh, I know you could. You're too fast to let me fall very far.~ Tessa settled back into the saddle, checked her leg straps, and resumed scanning the forest below. They spotted the occasional band of armed men every day or so, headed northwest toward Readen's mines and his hold, she suspected.

Most of the mercenaries Readen brought in for his attempt to take over Restal Keep were unaccounted for. Bands of them roamed the quadrant freely, taking what they needed, and often more, including women. So far, the groups they spotted had been too far away to cause alarm. That too many appeared to be moving toward the mines and Readen's hold made Tessa uneasy. The steam wagon train carried enough supplies to make it a tempting target.

Both the Karda Patrol and the newly reorganized Mounted Patrol were hard pressed. Too many villages were plundered. Guardian Daryl dispatched all the regular guard he could spare to the larger villages, and every holder was adding to his forces however he could. Tessa wondered how many of those forces were being gathered to support Daryl. How many had been Readen's mercenaries, and how many were hired by those who supported Readen's idea of revolt against the aristocracy of talent?

Readen might be in prison, but he wasn't dead. How many hoped for his escape? How many supporters did he still have? She pushed the useless thoughts and questions away and went back to scanning the forest beneath.

~This is so boring. I'm not sure I like scout duty. Is this what the Karda Patrol does all the time? Endless flying over barren land with the occasional wandering goat herd or dense forests we can hardly see into?~ She leaned forward suddenly and flipped down her second set of goggles. ~Kishar, look to the southwest. Something has disturbed an unkindness of ravens.~ She grabbed the pommel handle and clamped her legs tight as Kishar wheeled in that direction, flying now, not gliding.

~An unkindness of ravens?~ Tessa heard his amusement.

~Yes. Unkindness of ravens, murder of crows, parliament of rooks, blaze of dragons. That's what comes of hiding in old books. Father despaired for me.~ She felt a twinge. That wasn't all he despaired about her.

They both spotted the band of fifteen men on horseback at the same time—headed straight toward the caravan. Men with mismatched uniforms and carrying too many weapons. ~We're high and far enough away they probably did not notice us,~ he pathed and wheeled tightly again, pressing Tessa hard into the cantle of her rigging. She grabbed the pommel handle and leaned forward, pressing her face into his mane, her knees and thighs gripping hard as she rose and fell in time with the beats of his enormous wings. She was now skilled enough at riding that her bottom wasn't constantly pounded and bruised by bouncing in the saddle.

They flew straight to the wagon train and landed on the road downwind and far enough ahead of the lead team not to frighten the horses with the sight and scent of Karda. Tessa scrambled out of her straps and leaped to the ground, taking off like a rabbit chased by a fox, her breath tight in her chest. "Armed men, probably fifteen of them headed our way, not friendly looking," she shouted as soon as she got close enough. She ran past the lead wagon with Bren and Galen and headed straight for the supply wagon, crawled inside and started tossing things around until she found her extra quiver and the large box of her arrows.

She dropped as many arrows as she picked up and forced herself to stop, wiping sweaty, shaking hands on her legs. This was what she'd trained so hard for, but it wouldn't be deer she'd be shooting, it would be people. She clenched her fingers twice then finished loading the quiver with as many arrows as it would bear.

Taking off again toward Kishar, she yelled, "Band of people riding fast from the southwest!" She passed a startled Almryk, spooking his horse. "Better get ready for a fight."

She watched Galen jerk a saddle from the back of Bren's wagon, sling it over his shoulder, and run for his horse, sword swinging at his side. How good a swordsman was he with those scars on his hands and arms? She felt a prickle of worry but forced it away. He was nothing to her. She should worry about the planter trainees, most of them as young or younger than she was. And as inexperienced but without her unexplained expertise at weapons and fighting.

Tessa jumped from Kishar's extended knee to her saddle and buckled the extra quiver to her rigging in front of the horn that braced her knee. She angled the quiver so the arrows were where she needed them for fast shooting.

Daryl told me Galen's the one who was smuggling weapons from the spaceship. He's a traitor, isn't he? Why waste worry on him? Kishar took off from the narrow roadway, rising almost straight up with powerful thrusts of his broad wings.

Tessa pulled the fighting straps she would need for their twisting, turning flight out of her saddlebag, threaded them through the extra rings, and buckled her legs to the rigging more securely. She made sure she could reach her arrows easily and strung her recurved bow. She coiled the bow stringer cord and stowed it in its small pocket on the side of her quiver.

Fists clenched hard to control the large lump bouncing up and down in her chest, Tessa forced herself to breathe, counting each breath, making them long and steady and deep. Then there was no time to think about breathing. Or anything else.

They circled behind the bandits, fifteen of them moving too fast to be friendly. They were nearly on the wagons. Tessa nocked an arrow as she and Kishar glided, owl-silent, wings steady, and she let it fly, catching the hindmost bandit beneath her left shoulder blade. She slipped to the side, foot caught in the stirrups. Her horse galloped off after the others, dragging her behind.

Before she was over the bandits, Tessa shot five more arrows in rapid sequence, hitting her target every time. Kishar spread the enormous talons on his hind feet and grabbed the next bandit in line, spiraling up and away, twisting and turning between the wide-spread branches. High above the forest canopy, he let the screaming man fall. Tessa clamped her legs tighter, fighting to control her stomach. The screams suddenly cut off. Kishar wheeled back toward the wagons, the force of the turn pressing her hard into the saddle.

They flew back around, silent and low. Raiders and guards were fighting around and between the wagons. Tessa chose her targets with care, flying close, aiming between the fighting guards when she was able.

She caught a glimpse of Galen on horseback, attacking the largest of the bandits, and Kishar swerved toward him. Galen struck the man's sword arm cleanly off and turned to block a swing from the woman behind him. He twisted his sword and shoved it through her shoulder just as Tessa's arrow caught the raider in the chest. Galen ducked as

Kishar flew over him, grabbed another bandit, swept in a nearly vertical climb to escape the trees, and carried his captive high and away before letting him fall. His screams cut off abruptly, but they continued to echo in Tessa's head.

When they flew back, Tessa saw Bren standing on his wagon seat, staff whirling in a blur. He soundly whacked the closest bandit, one of Tessa's arrows jutting from his shoulder, and knocked the outlaw from his horse. Galen twisted in his saddle, head swiveling, searching for more bandits, bloody sword across his knees. The remaining raiders took their wounded and fled, leaving their dead and seven horses.

Tessa and Kishar flew far enough away from the horses not to alarm them and landed in the road, both of them breathing heavily. Tessa worked frantically at the extra buckles on her saddle rig, swallowing hard as hot saliva flooded her mouth. A pair of hands freed her from the last strap and caught her before she fell off.

She didn't make it to the bushes at the side of the road before she was retching. Strong hands at her waist steadied her as she heaved the last of her breakfast. A handkerchief appeared in front of her face, and she gratefully took it and wiped her mouth.

She turned and looked into Galen's worried face. How had he gotten there so fast? Wordlessly he led her to the closest wagon and filled a cup of water from the drinking barrel for her. Her knees collapsed, and he lowered her to the ground where she could lean against the wagon wheel. He rinsed out the handkerchief and handed it to her. She buried her face in the cool, wet cloth.

"Your first battle?" His voice was soft.

"Yes," then, "No." The nightmare of the mercenary she killed during the battle for Restal Keep nearly made her retch again.

"I don't think you ever get over it."

"But hopefully you get over the need to vomit every time." She tried a smile and didn't succeed.

His face was so beautiful. She hardly noticed the scars.

His mouth quirked up on one side. "Some never do. Better be prepared."

She stood suddenly and turned away, disgusted with herself for how this traitor made her feel. She'd known he was the one who had tried to smuggle guns to Readen since Marta introduced him as an old friend—Marta was from the space ship and so was Galen. "Thank you." She shoved the wet cloth back into his hand and headed back to Kishar, leaving Galen standing. He made her uncomfortable, made her body heat, made her think things she shouldn't be thinking about someone she shouldn't be thinking about.

Galen stood, feeling the defenses he'd dropped snap back in place with an angry slap as Tessa turned her back and walked away. Oh, well. He was over-protective because he was still in battle mode, and she was so young. But, he had to admit, fearless. She and Kishar flew so low they skimmed the tops of the riders' heads. If Kishar were hit, it would kill Tessa when he went down. Agile though Kishar might be, they could have caught a strike from an upraised sword. He swallowed hard at that thought then gave himself another mental slap. She was just another patroller. Beautiful, yes, and no, she wasn't just another patroller—she was a holder's daughter. And way beyond his reach.

He tamped down the anger that threatened to break his barriers and turned back to check on the wagons and his men. He didn't have time to waste thinking about the forbidden-and-much-too-haughty Tessa Me'Cowyn as if he were a young boy with his first embarrassing crush. And anyway, she was too young.

Three of the young planter trainees were hurt even though they weren't supposed to be fighting. One with a broken finger, one with a dislocated shoulder, and one with a sword slash to her upper arm. Galen, Almryk, and Bren, with his extensive collection of herbs and salves, worked through them. Bren put the shoulder back in place, and the girl's screams didn't last too long—the pain eased after Bren popped it back.

Two of the patrol suffered sword cuts. But one was dead. He'd been the first one caught, too slow to react to what was happening. Galen knew he was new to the Mounted Patrol and not adequately trained. With the defectors in Readen's takeover attempt purged, the Mounted Guard was stretched woefully thin, and this young man was another casualty to be laid at Readen's feet. Galen offered to help Almryk and his squad dig the grave, but as he had for the entire trip, the captain refused to acknowledge him, merely turned away, his eyes cold. Galen went to oversee the disposal of the dead raiders. They were dragged away from the road and left to scavengers and rot.

When they finished, and the caravan was ready to be on its way, Galen carefully worked a sapling from one of the bundles, grabbed a shovel, and planted the young tree at the head of the boy's grave, smoothing the dirt carefully. He sat back on his heels for a moment. Almryk watched, impassive, from the back of his horse.

The wounded were made as comfortable as possible in the trainees' wagons. The horses calmed after they were fed and watered, and the steam wagons moved on, tiny puffs of steam escaping from the brass wheel hubs. The road soon veered away from the trees. They'd been traveling through the edge, the oldest part of this forest. Even the understory trees were immense, and the larger adapted earth species—beeches, elms, oaks, hickories, and conifers rose as high as a hundred and fifty meters in the lower gravity of this planet. Now they rode into the barrens where the land was still unclaimed, unplanted. Galen immediately felt the loss of the trees, the comfort they exuded, the strength.

The ground beneath their feet felt sterile. There was little life in this soil. He'd gotten used to the feel of the soil in and around the greenhouses, alive with micronutrients and microorganisms.

The desolate land, with nothing but scattered pockets of wiry grass and scrub, pulled at him. If not for the wet climate, there would be nothing here but dust and rocks. Weight dragged at his shoulders as he rode until he finally dismounted to walk, leading his horse, feeling as if the land itself dragged him from the saddle, as if gravity pulled at him harder than the others.

As soon as his feet hit the ground, a claiming surged through his body. It fired through the swirling lines of the tattoos on his wrists, down to his fingertips and up his arms, across the scars on his chest and stomach and up to the one on his face. It flamed in wave after wave. Faint in the back of his mind, almost beyond hearing, a joyous voice called, over and over, "You're mine. You're mine. You're mine."

His pace slowed, and the wagons and troops passed, leaving him barely moving along the edge of the hard-packed road as they disappeared over a small hill. He dropped to the ground. His body curled around itself. His consciousness filled with inchoate whispers, fiery demands—then nothing.

Galen woke to the sound of fast moving hoofbeats growing louder. The sensations surging through his scars faded to the faint ants-under-the-skin feeling. Captain Almryk pulled his horse to a stop in front of him, much too close. He was leading Galen's horse, and the sneer on his face showed stronger distaste than usual.

"If you can't stay on your horse, you should go back to riding in one of the wagons." He shoved the reins at Galen. "We're still too close to the forest to be safe from the mercenaries probably still lurking there, and I don't need to be riding back with your runaway horse all the time." He wheeled his mount, kicked it to a hard gallop back up the road, throwing dirt and gravel at Galen.

Galen swung back into his saddle, his body stiff, and rode at a slow canter, thoughts uneasy, trying every way he could to rationalize the strange happening. Dehydration and hallucination. That's all it could be. Though he'd had plenty of water. He thought. Maybe he just hadn't noticed that he wasn't drinking. He reached for the canteen that hung from a ring on his saddle, but his hand stopped. He didn't want to know if it was empty. Or not. Dehydration and hallucination. What else could it be?

They rode through the barrens for days, skirting washes and gullies, fording muddy streams, the horses struggling. Anuma Quadrant, where he was assigned before, wasn't like this. Three generations of neglect had slowed the reclamation of Restal almost to a stop. And it showed. Every time a wagon got stuck, or they had to detour kilometers around a wash or gully growing up to be a canyon, Galen felt anger for the neglect building in his body. Tension surrounded him and never let up. A sense of expectation he didn't understand pulled at him. His body ached—stiff from guarding against it.

They found a spring or small stream to camp by each night. The first planters had been through this area several hundred years before. Trained to survive in the desolate countryside, they had spread their inoculated seeds around the water sources. Poplars, cottonwoods, some hybrid crosses with the few native species that the colonists had found, succulents, grasses, berry bushes, edible herbs—plants for shelter and sustenance for later planters to depend on as they repaired soil and spread seeds and seedlings further and further.

But planters had stopped coming. These oases were beautiful green jewels in a sea of brown dirt, rocks, stiff grasses, and straggly bushes only the hardiest goats and kurga would eat. Welcome refuges after a day of hard, dry travel, they flourished despite the neglect of the years of the Me'Vere guardianship.

Galen found peace in those spaces. His sleep at night was deep, and he woke each morning full of something he wouldn't even try to explain to himself. It was too close to what happened to him on the road. His scars tingled with sharp prickling that faded after a few minutes of morning stretching.

Early one morning after days of this travel, Galen walked to the far side of the oasis where Tessa and Kishar had set their camp downwind of the horses. He paused a short distance away, watching as Tessa moved around, extinguishing her tiny fire, wiping her pots and cups, and stowing everything neatly in her packs. She finally looked up and noticed him, and he walked closer.

"I'm planning to ride ahead this afternoon to see how far we can make it today. You reported yesterday that we're close to the edge of the forest that surrounds the circle where we're headed."

Tessa nodded. "The circle's about an hour and a half straight flight for us. The forest binding it is narrower on this side." She tucked a stray lock of silver hair under the headband she wore in a futile effort to keep her chopped halo contained as she flew.

"It would be good if we found a place for a permanent camp tonight. The saplings need to be in the ground as soon as possible. If you and Kishar could fly ahead and look for a good site, it would be much appreciated. I'll be scouting out the road from the ground. And maybe you could let me know if I'll be riding into a band of men—I could handle a few. But more than a few would be a fight I don't want to have."

Tessa tightened a strap on Kishar's rig then looked at him. Her smile twisted as if she were thinking hard. "Define more-than-a-few for me. I need you to be precise about what you want."

A candle flared briefly in the vicinity of Galen's heart. He cocked a hip, swept his hair back from his forehead dramatically, dropped a hand to his sword hilt, and stuck out his chest. "Five would be a few. Seven would be more than a few. Or maybe nine."

Tessa laughed, and the candle flared brighter. "Nine it is then. We'll keep watch and let you know if you'll be in any danger. From nine. Or maybe seven. Won't we Kishar?"

The big Karda blew out a snort, a Karda laugh.

Galen bowed low to each of them. "You will have my eternal gratitude." He turned, flaring his cloak out around him. Heat burned out of his chest into his face. How stupid could he get? He'd never done anything like that before. *I'm an idiot I'm an idiot I'm an idiot. She thinks I'm an idiot.* But the smile still burned, a tiny candle hiding in one of the many unused spaces in his heart.

It took a while for the flame to burn down to an ember. He noticed Almryk watching him. The captain's hard, definitely-not-friendly expression snuffed the tiny glow.

Galen walked over. "Captain, I need to ride ahead today. Tessa and Kishar will be looking for a permanent campsite, which I hope we can reach tonight. Both moons will be out—the trees are just starting to leaf so the light will be good. We should be able to drive into the night if we have to. We'll be leaving the road this morning, and I need to mark the way for the wagons."

Almryk looked at him, the planes of his face as hard packed with distrust as the road they traveled. "I'll go with you." His words were flat and sharp-edged.

"I don't want to leave the wagon train without both of us. We're too close to the forest where most anything or anyone can hide. I'm sure we haven't defeated all the bandits or mercenaries who might be waiting for us."

Almryk looked at him for a long moment, then nodded. Galen brushed past the captain to pull his saddle from the back of Bren's wagon and headed for the roped off temporary corral and his horse.

Behind him, the man's hatred and distrust burned with a low fire that raised hairs on the back of Galen's neck.

Two hours later, he pushed through a thicket of wild plum and taller cherryapple trees, pink and white with bloom at the forest edge, and pulled his horse up, rummaging in his saddlebags for his Cue. "Good morning, Father."

"Good morning be damned. It's the middle of the night. What do you have to report? What are those deposits?"

The trade ship had kept to Earth's diurnal rhythms for centuries. Galen worked to keep his satisfaction at the irritation in his father's voice under control. But it was satisfying. Petty, but satisfying. "We're still on the road. We should be making permanent camp sometime tonight. But it will be several days, maybe even a tenday or more before I'll be able to try for a sample. You'll have to be patient."

With almost a sense of euphoria, Galen realized he'd never said such words to his father before. He had to clear his throat.

"That's not soon enough. I need to know what those deposits are. And those circle areas. And what about Readen? Have you been able to initiate contact with any of his supporters, at least?" Galen could hear suppressed anger, a jerky undercurrent in his father's voice.

"They were being watched too closely before I left. The only one we might be able to work with is Samel. He's so slippery he'll be back in Daryl's graces by the time we finish this planting and are back in Restal Prime."

There was a long silence. Galen could almost sense waves of anger riding the space between them. Oddly, he felt nothing, no trepidation, no sense of failure, no guilt. "Have we lost contact again?"

"No. Get this so-important planting done quickly. Get those mineral samples. And while you're at it, get samples from one of those circles, too. The geologists are intrigued and curious about them, and the drones we send don't come back, so you'll have to do it."

Galen could feel the blood leaving his face. "No one can go into a circle without dying, Father. What you ask is impossible."

"The cameras have caught images of one of those Karda creatures flying over one in the last month or so. So that's not true. You're being taken in by their backward superstitions. There must be something valuable about them. Find out what it is." Silence loomed over Galen's head for several minutes. "And find a way to contact Readen. Time is getting short. I've moved the rest of the guns down—"

"What? Where?" Nausea almost made Galen retch. Bile burned the back of his throat, and his scars flared with intense pain. His hands jerked at the reins. His horse sidestepped, and he struggled to keep his balance.

"I'll let you know when it's time. That's all."

And the Cue clicked off. Galen sat still in the saddle, staring at the communicator, until his nausea and pain subsided, then closed and locked the small leather journal that concealed his Cue.

He sat still on his horse long enough for it to start snatching mouthfuls of the tender green grass beneath the trees. Then he picked up the reins and moved on through the forest.

Chapter Nine

Late in the night not long before the smaller moon set, Tessa and Kishar guided the wagons to a clearing at the base of a cliff safely to the east of the toxic Circle of Disorder.

Galen watched as she and Kishar moved some distance away to make their place for the night—far enough away Kishar's smell wouldn't disturb the horses. Horses were hard to control when a Karda was near. They were prey, and Karda were predator. The horses of the Mounted Patrol were accustomed to them, but the draft horses weren't. Not yet.

"Tessa," he called, his voice soft, so he didn't startle her. Or Kishar. Galen was still wary around the predator with his huge, sharp beak and those long, sharp talons. "I would like you and Kishar to set up your camp a little closer, so we don't have to space our sentries so far apart. In an attack, you'll be too far away for me or the guards to reach you quickly and—"

"We've been flying and camping alone for much of this season without your protection. Kishar is more than a match for anyone who might come across us—we're hard to surprise. And I am not untrained," she said, her head held high on her stiff neck. One hand brushed the top of the sword at her side, and the other waved at the bow strapped to her saddle.

Kishar cocked his head and looked at him.

"Well, I'm going to post a guard near here anyway." Galen could feel the big Karda's amusement. He turned back to the wagons and the night's temporary camp of a few small tents and humps of tired people rolled up in sleeping bags.

Next morning, he found himself directing the drivers and the young trainees as they set up the permanent camp—unloading tents and supplies, building fire pits, roping off a corral to hold the horses at night. He hoped his inexperience with leading a large group like this didn't show. But the wagoneers knew what they were doing, as did the blacksmith and the cook, so all Galen needed to do was assign the planters to help.

He walked over to check on where Almryk's Mounted Patrollers were setting up their separate area. As always, he could feel the captain's eyes on him. Watching, always watching as if trying to catch him at something. He was getting tired of it, and it was becoming noticeable to the others.

I can't let him undermine me. The thought was fierce—and unexpected. *When did I start caring so much about this?* He looked toward the young planters, laughing and shoving at each other as they gathered up the mallets and extra rope. He felt barrier erosion inside him, a flake falling from his glacier.

He turned to see Bren behind him—his hand half lifted to haul something out of his wagon. He cocked his head to the side and looked at Galen. "You're gonna need to do something about the captain sooner than later, I think." Then he hauled a large pack out, hefted it to his shoulders, and walked away. Galen stared after him.

He went to help with the unloading of the hybrid abelee saplings into the shade of the massive trees surrounding the three sides of the clearing to the east of a granite cliff with a shallow overhang. For hours he worked alongside the young planters, not thinking, just doing. Heave the heavy bundles out of the tightly packed wagon, lug them to the trees, cover them with damp burlap. Heave the heavy bundles, lug them to the trees, cover them. Heave, lug, cover. Heave, lug, cover.

Carrying the last bundle of saplings in his arms like a small child, he knelt to place it on the ground, reluctant to let it go, to lose the peace it carried. He smoothed the damp burlap over it and placed his hands flat on the ground in front of him. Some small, self-aware part of him watched, shocked, from the back of his mind as his scars twisted into roots and vines.

Power surged up into his hands. Through his body. A green and brown and gold wave of—life force?—washed over the long row of sapling bundles stacked in the shade of the trees, flashed, and was gone. He stared at a lone, bare twig sticking out from beneath the burlap. Pale green buds slowly swelled along its length. That was impossible.

Galen jerked to his feet like he was kneeling in hot lava. *What just happened to me? I need to get out of here. I need to get off this planet. I need to get Father's samples and get out of here.* Great, gulped breaths scorched his throat as he stumbled away from the mounds of saplings and into the woods away from the camp, running as hard as he could.

The scars on his arms and chest were afire. The burned side of his face seared with pain. And he ran, unable to think about what he was running from. Finally, his lungs as fiery as his scars, he stopped. One of the massive roots of an oak tree formed a perfect hollow in the ground for him to fall into. Gradually, his breath, stuttering with terror, slowed, and he slept, his head pillowed on the great root.

He woke lying in the grass beside the burlap-covered mound of saplings. A warm blanket of relief settled over him. A dream. It was only a strange dream. But he felt a peace, a sense of being held he hadn't felt since his mother was killed.

The great, red ball of the sun approached the cliff top that bounded the west side of the clearing. Smoke and fragrant smells of cooking reached him. He walked slowly toward the cook's fire, breathing in the smells as though they alone could feed him.

Almryk's suspicious glare accosted him. "Where have you been? You disappeared for hours."

Galen grinned at him. Even Almryk couldn't faze his feeling of calm tonight. "I fell asleep. Unloading the saplings was hard work after setting up camp this morning. I needed a rest. You look like you could use one, too." And he clapped his hand on the captain's shoulder, feeling it tense as he did.

Almryk stalked away.

I need to do something about the captain. Before his suspicions and antagonism spread more than they already have. But he was suddenly starving. It could wait till after dinner.

He waited until he estimated the sun was half an hour from falling behind the cliff and strolled over to the patrol's fire. Almryk was assigning the early watch. Galen waited until he finished.

"Captain, I wonder if I might have a moment of your time."

Almryk turned and raised one brow, and didn't speak for a long moment. "Of course, Planter. As always, I am at your service." His tone was cold, polite—the words spoken with slow, deliberate insolence.

Galen swallowed a surge of irritation. "I have been remiss on this trip about my workouts. If I go too long, I start to stiffen up." He gestured at the scars along his arms. "I was wondering if you might accommodate me this evening with a match."

The older man's eyes lit with a hungry expectation. "Perhaps one of my younger patrollers—"

"No. I think you." Galen knew the man had been too busy fighting his own battle to have seen how Galen fought when the bandits attacked. He'd never been in the arms salon when Galen started back on his weapons work after the healers released him.

Though Galen practiced his forms every night, he did so where he couldn't easily be seen. He turned and walked toward the open area the guardsmen roped off for arms practice. Almryk hesitated for a brief minute then followed.

Galen could almost feel the captain's smirk behind him, and he smiled to himself. Galen had trained with all kinds of weapons since he started walking. The worlds Alal Consortium traded with were often not peaceful, and usually primitive. He practiced sword forms every day of his life. And had fought, not only humans but strange, dangerous creatures, on several other worlds.

He might be much younger than the captain and not much older than the trainees, but he had learned techniques the captain had never been exposed to and had faced adversaries far better trained than the raiders the Mounted Patrol faced.

Almryk opened the large box at the edge of the circle, and they both pulled out heavy canvas practice armor. He started to pull out the weighted wooden practice swords, but Galen stopped him. "Live steel, I think."

The captain hesitated then shrugged, eyes gleaming with anticipation in his otherwise flat, iron-hard face. "Your choice." Pulling on a helmet, he paced to the center of the area.

Galen followed, shrugging on the canvas vest, not bothering with a helmet. They circled each other cautiously, feinting and testing. The captain might have grey hairs salting his head, but he was good.

Galen pressed a little harder. This was a workout, not a fight, but he could see the tension in the captain's grip and shoulders broadcasting his tightly controlled desire to make it one.

Almryk feinted and struck. Galen parried and riposted, resisting the urge to twist Almryk's sword from his grip. He was trying to prove a point without embarrassing the man and making his resentment even worse. If he pushed too far, it could become personal, not political as it was now.

Almryk pulled back and then pressed again, harder. Galen parried and evaded and pressed back, working to make it not look too easy to the watchers but making sure the captain knew.

The ringing sound of steel against steel brought a crowd to the edges of the ring, but the intensity of the fight held them in silence. Galen was sweating, his breath coming fast, as was the captain's.

He struck the captain's sword hard enough to let him know that he could have disarmed him, stepped back, and dropped the point of his sword, signaling the end of the workout. He held out his hand. "Thank you, Captain Almryk. That was a good workout. I needed it."

Almryk hesitated only a brief instant before he grabbed Galen's forearm firmly and nodded. Faint respect flashed briefly across his face. "Yes, I suspect I did, too. Perhaps we should have the planters share workout time with my patrollers."

Galen knew he had made his point. He might not have made a

friend, but the captain knew the planter could have bested him in front of the whole camp—and didn't.

Galen leaned against his shovel and wiped his sleeve across his forehead. This was hard, grueling work. He looked across the open space between the edge of the trees where he and the young planters were working and the Circle of Disorder. Too many skeletal trees lined it, bleached white. Large patches of the remedial grasses and bushes planted under them were dry and brown.

The surface of the circle beyond the trees moved constantly in a heat-like haze. Dust devils whirled across a surface pocked with dull pieces of metal sticking out of the ground. The only vegetation was an occasional small twisted tree or a cluster of thorny bushes with a few small, leathery, brownish-green leaves.

Ugly, oily sensations pricked at the skin all over his body. But his scars and the twining tattoos on the backs of his wrists were cool and unaffected.

He walked back to the wheelbarrow full of hybrid abelee saplings and carefully worked another out of a bundle. Horses were untrustworthy near the circle, so everything they needed for planting had to be hauled on their backs or by wheelbarrow, usually both.

He stepped on the shoulder of the narrow shovel, loosening the soil, digging a hole for the infant tree. Dropping to his knees, he worked the bare roots carefully into the soil, firming and pressing it. Then he pounded in a slender metal stake and tied the sapling to it, loose enough for it to move with a breeze but tight enough to hold it upright in a gale until its roots were well established.

He watched as the leaf buds swelled, and pale green infant leaves began to poke their way out. It made him more than uneasy. Only his plantings did this, or to his further dismay, ones he merely touched. The others had buds, but none leafed out as soon as they were planted. Nor should they. Too often they showed signs of wilting. After all, they were planted in polluted soil. His never suffered from transplant shock.

The sensation of being used intensified when he was planting, working with the soil, feeling pulses of energy move from him into the small saplings. He had to work to ignore it. Push it back behind his walls.

His father had used him for years. Galaxies be damned if he'd surrender to the grasp of something he couldn't name, much less understand, before he'd even tasted freedom.

He arched his aching back for relief and watched as Kishar and Tessa drifted high overhead in their lazy, circling watch, flying far closer to the circle than he liked. Farther away, he could see two more Karda flying low. Hunting, he thought. Hardly a day went by that at least one unpartnered Karda didn't appear at some point. Usually more, but they never flew as close to the circle as Tessa and Kishar.

He listened to the horrific stories the wagoneers and planters told around the night fires about what happened to anyone who got too close to the circles, but Tessa and her Karda seemed immune to their poison. He hoped it wasn't because they were unaware.

But that was naive of him. She was raised with these tales. They might be tales with the sound of oft-told, fireside folk stories, but the very existence of these circles spoke to the truth of what they said. He'd been on a number of worlds, each with their own strange and dangerous idiosyncrasies, but he had never experienced anything like this poisonous emptiness.

"You've been here too long, Planter."

He whirled. He was so lost in his thoughts he hadn't heard Almryk's horse approaching.

"The others have gone back to camp. You'll be sick if you don't leave now."

Galen tossed his shovel in the wheelbarrow and wheeled it back to the live trees, covering the saplings with damp burlap. He looked up at the sky. It would rain again later. The nice thing about being on such a wet planet was there was seldom need to haul water to the plantings. It didn't make up for the all too frequent soakings, but it helped the saplings establish faster. Almryk extended a hand from atop his nervously dancing mount, and Galen vaulted up behind the saddle.

"Thanks for the ride. Sometimes I get lost in what I'm doing and forget about the time. And so far, it hasn't made me ill like it does the others."

"I'd noticed." Almryk's tone was dry.

The two men had established an uneasy peace between them, one with possibilities of friendship, or so Galen hoped. He didn't think he'd ever really had a friend before. Other than Cedar on the ship and Marta, whom he'd betrayed.

From a few bits and pieces he'd overheard, Galen suspected the taciturn captain hated Readen Me'Vere almost as much as he did. Almryk was one of the few who knew who Galen was, so he was willing to answer questions Galen couldn't ask others.

He also suspected Bren knew. Bren, the more-than-just-a-wagon-driver-and-probably-Daryl's-agent, was very forthcoming with his tales of Adalta. Between the two of them, Galen was learning a great deal of history that the pre-mission briefing he'd thought adequate didn't even begin to cover. If he'd paid attention at all. Stories he'd thought were just legends and tavern tales apparently weren't.

He looked down at the tattoo twining around his right wrist. Why was it he, of all of them, didn't get ill when he worked near the circle— longer than the others more often than not?

The intermittent buzzing deep within his pack woke Galen from a deep sleep. Furious, he dug out his Cue. He opened it with the key from a concealed inside pocket on the flap of his pack, and it stopped buzzing. He flipped back the cover and glared at the screen. "Contact me immediately" flashed.

His father. He knew better than to do this. What if Galen had not been alone? Was the man losing all sense? This was the most basic of all the rules. Never, never contact an agent on the ground by buzzing the com-unit. It could compromise him thoroughly. This kind of technology was unheard of on Adalta. And like all high-tech things, forbidden by law and custom.

A pink tinge showed through the trees from the sky in the east. Galen stowed his bedroll in a corner of his tent and headed for the

Mounted Patrol camp on the opposite side of the two big communal tents. Almryk was up and having his breakfast. He handed Galen a cup and, mouth full, pointed to the pot hanging near the fire and the bread and cheese on the makeshift table outside the cook's tent.

Galen filled his cup, and the two sat, sipping quietly in the soft, pre-dawn glow. The rest of the camp was beginning to stir as the smells of the cook's efforts spread.

"I need to do some exploring this morning. Make sure we're spacing our plantings so we'll be able to surround that completely." He gestured toward the circle. "The phytoremediation won't be as effective if we have to space the saplings too far apart. I'm already half certain we need to send for at least two more wagons full."

Almryk rubbed his chin where he'd nicked himself shaving. He wasn't happy. "I've got three patrollers down sick from getting too close to the circle. Can't get it through their thick heads that planters, even those with only a little Earth talent, can stay longer and closer to the circle than they can. I can't spare anyone, much less myself, to go with you unless you want to give some of your planters a break this morning. I can't leave the camp and your people unguarded. My scouts have seen signs that we're not alone out here."

"If there was anything both Master Planter Andra and Guardian Daryl stressed more than the fact that this planting is urgent, I don't know what it would have been. I don't want to slow it down." Galen looked toward the bundles of saplings spread under the trees and back in the direction of the circle.

"I'm new at this, Almryk. And I may not be from this planet, but I can feel the evil here as well as anyone. I know how important this is and what my responsibility is. Miscalculating is not something I want to do. I need to be sure before we go much farther. If the circle is increasing as they say it is, I need to know that what we've brought will be sufficient. Or how soon we need to send to Restal Prime for more saplings and seeds. I need to be able to calculate for sure how far apart to space the saplings. I think I'm guessing right but..."

He shook his head at the question he could see forming on Almryk's face. "And no, we can't use the hardwood saplings. Only the hybrid abelees can cleanse the circles. The poplars the native dalum trees are crossed with were used for a century on Earth to clean up toxic areas. They worked well, just too little, too late."

"Why don't you ask Kishar about the spacing?"

"Why would I ask him?"

"It was the Karda who told us to plant in the first place, centuries ago. When we first came."

Galen looked at him for a long moment. Then he closed his eyes and dropped his head into his hands. "There is so much I don't know."

Almryk stood and slapped him on the shoulder. "You'll learn. And Kishar is your best source for information."

Galen finished the last of the bread and cheese and stuffed a couple of cherryapples from the basket in the middle of the table into his jacket pocket. "I'll ask him. I should be back by mid-afternoon."

He didn't wait for Almryk's permission. However friendly they were getting, Galen couldn't afford to give the captain that power. "I'll be heading south, then around to the west if I get that far. I'll also be looking for another permanent campsite—we'll need to move in another tenday, or we'll be pushing those carts a very long way."

Almryk laughed. "And you'd want help. I don't want to do that. Don't get lost."

"Not much danger of that. The circle is a pretty big landmark."

Galen's mount had a fast, smooth trot, and he rode, weaving through the spaces between the line of dead trees at the edge of the circle. The cool of the morning got even colder as the gray cloud cover thickened, and drizzle began to fall. The soft sounds of his horse's hooves on the layers of damp leaves, the small rustlings in the undergrowth, the early morning chorus of birdsong calmed his anger at his father.

I know better than to contact him when I'm angry. That's an advantage I don't need to give him. An hour later he stopped and pulled out the small Cue. His father answered immediately.

"Finally. I contacted you hours ago."

"Don't ever do that again." Galen's voice was tight with fury. One word from his father and the rage was back. He controlled himself, clenching and unclenching his left hand, stretching the scars, focusing on the pain, tamping the anger, measuring his breathing.

"Do you want to get me discovered? The sound of a Cue buzzing is so alien to this planet anyone hearing it would be dangerously curious and might go exploring in my pack."

Kayne Morel ignored him. "Do you have the samples? Can we arrange to get them picked up? What's taking so long? I can't put off the accounting of Marta's trust much longer. The other trustee is pushing to let her take over her own finances when she returns to the ship. He doesn't want to be bothered with it any longer. As if he ever bothered with it before."

"I'm headed out to do that now. This is the first chance I've had to get away long enough. And I won't be able to get away to meet anyone to pick it up. I'll have to leave it somewhere, and you can send someone to recover it."

"Damn it, Galen. Remember you work for me." He hesitated. "For the Consortium. Get the samples and get out of there. You're wasting time planting trees when you should be concentrating on getting Readen back in power."

For the first time in his memory, Galen could hear a faint, sharp edge of panic in his father's voice. "I know who I work for, Father."

Do I?

The simple question shocked him.

Did he?

Chapter Ten

Readen paced his cell, restless. It would be a wait of several hours until the few minutes his jailers allowed him to walk in the small courtyard outside his cell. The only chance he had each day for stretching his legs with some semblance of real exercise.

Pacing the seven steps that bounded his cell back and forth exacerbated his rage. Twice a tenday, that fat, dirty hand would appear, pushing his food tray through the hatch, sometimes with a deep cut welling blood from the thumb pad. It would rest there, just inside the hatch, letting Readen lick the blood away and rage at his debasement.

Once it pushed a frantically wriggling rat through, once a thrashing squirrel. The rat lasted a day and a half as Readen fed the tiny bit of power growing inside him. The squirrel lasted longer and made more noise.

He shook with the memory of those pitiful squeals. The urge low in his belly for more was near pain. He sat at the table and pulled off his shirt, carefully pulling one of the slivers of bone out of his sleeve and laid it in front of him.

Hardened obsidian scars ran up his arms, across his shoulders, and down his chest halfway to the top of his stomach. Sigils carved into the columns in his hidden cavern beneath Restal Keep were now carved into his body. The cavern of the Itza Larrak lost to him, tons of earth and stone blocking the entrances, brought down by Daryl and Altan.

And Marta. He clenched his teeth so hard a piece of a back molar broke loose, cutting the inside of his mouth.

He started to swallow then caught himself. Salty blood flooded his tongue. Necessary, essential, vital blood. He spat the bloody saliva into the palm of his hand, and rubbed it into the scars on his chest, closed his eyes, calmed his mind. Savoring then releasing the rage.

He began chanting softly, too softly for the ever-present guards outside his cell to hear. "Dalla Itza Larrak Alka Ra. Dalla Itza Larrak Alka Ra." Over and over, tamping down the fear that he would fail again. Fifteen minutes, twenty. Was this the time it would appear? Inhaling a long breath, he continued. "Dalla Itza Larrak Alka Ra."

His body was wet with sweat when the light from the small window high on the cell wall began to darken. A twisting spiral appeared. A cloud of glittering black particles grew denser and denser. A huge form flickered, refusing to solidify—a giant winged beast, a grotesque, vaguely insectoid creature. Ugly, and at the same time oddly beautiful, eerily humanoid, its deep-set yellow eyes pierced the dark cloud. A faint musical rasping rang as enormous metal wings opened and closed—a small, constant movement. Light blinked through their delicate piercings.

The fog of particles alternately coalesced and dispersed, filling the space in the small cell, backing Readen against the rough stone wall behind the table. Sometimes it felt as if the figure were part of him. Sometimes it felt separate. Sometimes pressure and twisting agony invaded his body. Sometimes an emptiness invaded him so profoundly that he struggled to stay upright.

His breath shallow and quick, Readen stabbed the small piece of bone into his wrist, forcing blood out, smearing it on the obsidian sigils incised on his arm and chest. The cloud seethed, and a spectral clawed finger began tracing signs, forming more symbols out of the dark, glittering fog that surrounded him. They burned into Readen's mind, seared his sight until nothing remained but those signs. Then darkness.

His head crashed against the stone floor and shocked him back into himself. His body trembled with glee. He clenched his fist around the sliver of bone, desperate not to lose it. The mists were gone. He pulled himself into his chair. The muscles in his legs twitched with painful cramps. He pressed two shaking fingers firmly over his wrist to stop the sluggishly oozing blood.

Success. Almost success. The Itza Larrak was almost his again. He shivered. His mouth curled up in a half smile. His lips drew back, baring his teeth.

And once again Readen began the painful scratching, feeling with his fingers the proper place on his chest for the next sign the Itza Larrak had shown him. Slowly he collected the blood that beaded on the surface and wiped it over his tongue, sucking his fingers. Faint waves of power thrummed through his body.

He needed to replace all the carefully collected power he expended trying to call the Itza Larrak, including the power from the rat and the squirrel now stinking in the corner. He'd been so sure he'd be successful this time.

It would take days, pain-filled days, to incise those new symbols on his chest and stomach. But Readen drew power from pain as well as blood. Even his own. He smiled another rare, true smile and cut as deeply as the small sliver of bone allowed.

He worked for several hours, hoarding every drop of blood, every twinge of pain until he heard steps crunching across the gravel in the courtyard outside his cell door. He barely had time to hide the bone sliver and pull his shirt over his head before the cell door opened. He'd lost track. Apparently, it was time for his thirty minutes of exercise.

He stretched, popping his back, relaxing his tense muscles, relishing the sting of his shirt brushing against the newly cut signs on his chest, and sauntered out into the small courtyard. He paused at the disorienting sight of a sturdy table with two chairs occupying the center of the open space. They were out of place in the usually-bare, walled enclosure. The four guards always present for his exercise sessions stood, one in the center of each wall. Only this time there were six. Two more guards bracketed the iron door opposite his cell.

And one of them was Pol. Anticipation jolted through him. Pol would only be present if the one who could help him escape were coming.

He began his circuit, jogging the perimeter, staying away from the guards. He'd learned the safe distance. If he'd had more power available—? But he didn't. And they were heavily shielded, probably chosen for their ability to shield, abilities augmented by someone with strong Earth talent. Most likely Daryl himself. Or Armsmaster Krager.

Readen forced himself to keep an even pace as rage surged, swelling in his throat until he had to struggle to draw breath. Krager. *How could I have been so stupid? How could I have trusted the man I knew was Daryl's best friend? How had I ever let myself think Krager would believe my lies about Daryl's betrayal of Restal?*

Krager's supposed support of Readen over the years, from their shared childhood on, had been the lies. The real lies. Readen swallowed hard and smiled. Just the thought of the revenge he would extract sent another trickle of power into his reserves. He'd feed on that trickle of Krager's blood until it became a river.

The barred gate in the wall opposite his cell opened, and a slight man, immaculately dressed, walked through, striding confidently to the table. He stood until Readen joined him then sat, adjusting the empty sword scabbard at his side. A half smile tilted one side of his mouth. "How do you fare, Readen? Have you enough luxuries in this remote prison?"

"I do not appreciate the levity, Samel." Readen used enough of his small hoard of power to force the other man to lean back in his chair at the menace in his low voice. It had never taken much to keep the ambitious, amoral Samel in his place.

"Of course, there is nothing funny about this." Samel looked around and made a twirling gesture with his hand.

Ever the dandy, thought Readen, noting the dapper young man's elegant clothing, his shining red curls dusty from travel. *I wonder what he wants.* He watched, silent, until Samel frowned in concentration and made a slight gesture with one hand.

"I've put up a listening shield. Air talent is so useful." His mouth twisted at the painful surge of malice Readen shot at him. His voice lost a bit of its confident edge.

Readen smiled at him. "Thank you, Samel." Gratitude could be a useful tool.

Samel went on. "The guards won't be able to hear us. I assume you've noticed your guard has changed a little." He shifted in his chair slightly toward the wall where Pol stood. "That's Byrt. He's one of the replacements rotated in a few tendays ago. Daryl is very careful not to leave anyone here long enough for their shields to erode." His eyes shifted back to Readen.

Readen probed. Samel was concentrating on holding the listening shield, not paying attention to the shield on himself. Readen could reach into him, even with the limited power he had now. He pulled his probe back with care.

"Why are you here, Samel? How were you allowed in?" He kept his voice warm and controlled even as the rage inside him flared hot enough to burn through his chest. Samel was the only one of his former supporters who had tried to reach him. This dandy, this vain, too-pretty little man was the only one he had to help him.

The young man leaned forward, red curls swinging to frame the face Readen longed to smash. He longed to have Samel on his table, a sharp knife in his hand. He longed to watch that supercilious expression turn to terror. To hear his insolent voice turn to screams. To watch his naked slender flesh fight its arousal at Readen's caresses. Unwelcome arousal was such a useful weapon.

Samel saw only Readen's practiced, pleasant expression. "Daryl sent me. He wants to believe what you wrote in your letter. He wants me to test you. If he is sure you are sincere, I think I can talk him into moving you to your personal hold." He cocked an elbow on the back of his chair and put his other hand on the table.

Readen noticed its tremor. Samel clenched his fist and spread his fingers over and over. "Krager doesn't believe your letter, of course, but he doesn't trust anyone. Even me. I've convinced Daryl I'm loyal to him and was only serving you until he returned, and I could join him."

In spite of the Air shield he held around them, he lowered his voice, clearing his throat twice. "Daryl is having difficulties. He's not sure about the Mounted Guard, nor about the guard in Restal Prime. Oh, he's sure about the officers and the first rank of enlisted. Anyone who didn't volunteer to be truth tested about their loyalty left very quickly. But the rank and file—those he's not certain of. Too many of them to truth test. Even Daryl's talent has its limits, as does Krager's, and he won't trust anyone else."

Samel straightened in the chair and pushed his hair back. A fine line of sweat dampened his hairline. "A number have left to serve certain holders. Rumor has it the ones of lesser talents are paying well. They're waiting to see what happens with you. To see if you continue the fight against this unfair rule by talent strength."

Ah, Samel's more nervous than he wants me to see. Readen reached for the thread of Samel's fear, drawing it into himself, savoring it, savoring the words about Daryl's difficulties like a fine, dry, red wine on his tongue. He smiled to himself as Samel leaned back and twisted in the chair, draping an arm casually over its back again and crossing his legs, his movements too careful, too studied.

Samel cleared his throat again with a slight cough. "I've always thought Daryl was a little too idealistic, but I also thought he would be more cautious. He's talking about adding representatives of lesser talents to Restal Council. Me'Kammin, Me'Neve, and Me'Mattic are already gathering men, most of them the mercenaries you hired who escaped. They're preparing to fight to keep the tradition of rule by strong talent. They're afraid Daryl's ideas will catch the attention of Prime Guardian Me'Rahl."

He leaned forward. His next words held a gleeful chime. "And that bastard Me'Cowyn, I suspect, is pondering very hard about which side of the fence he needs to fly. He hates you. His talent is powerful, and he won't support a fight against rule by talent. He values his place in that aristocracy, though he rationalizes and uses the word meritocracy. Me'Cowyn's furious at Daryl for supporting his daughter's decision to fly off who knows where with some strange Karda. He's sure her belief that she's the Austringer come back to life is a delusional adolescent rebellion."

An Austringer had appeared? A young girl Austringer? Readen shifted slightly to cover his sudden unease, damning his lack of news. He sifted through his memories for the old tales of the fabled hunter then relaxed. The Austringer had been a threat to the long-disappeared urbat. She would be no threat to him, even if she were an Austringer, which he doubted.

She was the only other person he knew of with no talent, though she'd been born with it, as he had not. Readen's teeth started to grind.

He took a slow breath in through his nose, forced his jaw to relax, and brought his attention back to Samel. "Connor Me'Cowyn is a very ambitious man. She probably is just trying to get away from him."

Samel hadn't noticed his preoccupation. "He wants the guardianship any way he can get it. He thought that marrying his daughter to Daryl would be his way to more power. It's a shame you held her as a hostage. He'd probably have supported you if you'd offered to marry her." He stopped, started to say something else, swallowed, and laughed. The laugh pitched too high. Me'Cowyn would only give his daughter to someone with a lot of talent. Never to talentless Readen.

Their conversation stopped for several long minutes. Samel picked at a loose cuticle on his index finger until it bled.

Readen's nostrils flared, and he drew in a long breath of Samel's unease. He kept his voice low, pleasant, his words casual. "Why does Daryl trust you to tell him whether or not I'm sincere?"

"Because he thinks I was only supporting you to spy for him. And I'm a strong Air talent. Truth testing is no challenge for me. No one can lie to me." He smiled. "And no one can tell when I'm lying."

Readen's face was impassive, his eyes steady on Samel's face.

Samel leaned back from the table. "And I can truthfully tell him I sensed no lie in you." He smiled.

Readen watched like a fox stalking a covey of quail as Samel's smile twisted into a smirk, and his body began to relax.

Readen pounced. He drew on every last bit of his power reserves, forcing Samel's eyes to lock on his. The words he spoke were as palpable as if they hung in the air between them. "I'll expect frequent reports from you on who opposes Daryl, what their resources are, what their plans are—and what their reactions are when you tell them to expect me back."

Samel's frame shrunk even smaller. He winced as he picked at his bleeding cuticle and stuck his finger in his mouth, sucking to stop the bleeding. Readen could almost taste the salty, rusty flavor on his tongue. Samel's eyes flicked everywhere around the small enclosure, trying to escape, but always snapped back to the eyes of the man across the table as if magnetized.

"And I need you to convince Daryl my remorse is genuine. Tell him how sorry I am. Tell him I'm distraught. Tell him I need to explain what happened. Convince him I'm on the verge of suicide at what I was forced to do, at my mistakes. Convince him I was manipulated by the Itza Larrak. Tell him whatever you need to get me released to my hold."

He almost said, "I need to get out of here." But the words didn't escape. They smacked of hopelessness and weakness he couldn't let his toady see.

"I need a girl. A strong, pretty, young girl—or a boy—someone no one will soon miss." The younger the sacrifice, the stronger the power they gave him.

Samel's white face froze. His body was a stone statue.

"Find a way to communicate with me regularly. I need to know what is happening until I'm ready to leave here." He waved a hand. "You may leave now." He broke the connection.

Readen watched as Samel, his body stiff, his natural grace compromised, walked to the barred gate and waited for the guard to open it. Readen had expended every bit of the power he had hoarded from his own blood, from his own rage, from Samel's fear. It would take more than a tenday to gain it back, but the small compulsion on Samel had taken.

A compulsion delicate enough to escape notice, powerful enough to get what Readen needed. Samel would sense nothing more than that Readen was persuasive.

He fingered the medallion that hung on its silver chain around his neck. He would be free soon. Free and the Itza Larrak with him. The power and exultation he experienced as a ten-year-old boy when he first found the Itza Larrak filled him.

Filled every space inside him but one tiny corner.

The corner that hid the fear.

The fear that the Itza Larrak didn't belong to him.

He belonged to it.

Chapter Eleven

Tessa stretched, popping the kinks out of her back, and looked up at the sky. The sun was still making its way up through the trees, but she could see the sky was clear for a change. ~Good morning, Kishar.~

The big Karda opened one eye and pathed, ~When you have had your breakfast you may come back and wake me.~ The eye closed.

~Lazy, lazy, lazy,~ she said and headed for the cooking fires.

Smoke from the fires rose straight up through the still dawn air—sharp, grey columns against the pink sky glowed behind the bare black branches of the forest to the east. Galen and Almryk sat at the table, talking. Galen's face was in profile, only the unscarred side visible.

She slowed and almost turned back. The slanting light of the morning highlighted the sharp planes of his face. That was all that kept him from being too beautiful. That and the horrible scar that marred his other cheek.

Galen finished the last of his tea, grabbed a cherryapple from the basket in the center of the table, and headed in the direction of the horses. He hadn't seen her enter the tent. She stared after him, unable to look away from the easy, loping way he moved, sword at his side like an extension of his body.

"Good morning, Tessa."

She jumped and smiled at Almryk who appeared at her side. "And a good morning, it looks to be. I'm tired of flying in the wet. Kishar's rigging is going to mold if this constant mist and drizzle keeps up, and so am I. I'm glad to see clear sky this morning." She watched as Galen's tall figure disappeared behind a line of guard tents. She turned back. Almryk looked at her—his eyes narrowed. "Is the tea still hot?" She hoped the heat in her face didn't show.

His hand touched her shoulder briefly. "I better get back to my men. They're finally starting to stir. I wonder how many idiots will be sick today. I can't convince them it isn't a test of courage to see if they can stay as close to the circle as the planters. If enough of them get sick, I guess they'll learn."

He hesitated. "Galen is scouting along the circumference of the circle today. Trying to estimate the number of trees they'll need to finish. He's not sure they have enough, and the circle is still growing where we haven't planted. Check on him occasionally, will you? I didn't have anyone to send with him."

Tessa nodded. Head down again, she breathed in the steam from her cup and ignored the tightness in her throat, fighting a surge of happiness that she had an excuse to see him again today.

~Check the breast strap, please, Tessa. I think the dampness has allowed it to stretch too much.~ Kishar knelt and turned his head to watch as Tessa hauled the saddle to his back and started unfolding the myriad of straps attached to his rigging. He rose to his feet.

~Maybe we need to hunt something large today. Are you getting enough to eat?~ She double-checked each strap as she buckled it. ~Let's head up toward the mountains and that herd of deer we saw at the beginning of the tenday. They were fat enough. If we can get two, we'll hang one and pick it up when we head back in for noon-day meal. The cooks gave me wistful looks this morning.~

She felt his surge of hunger, pulled two cherryapples and a large orange out of her pocket, and tossed them one after the other to him, grinning as he snapped them out of the air. ~See what a good friend I am?~

They took off straight up from the ground, Tessa rising and falling in sync with his wing beats to keep from being tossed back and forth in the saddle as his huge wings snapped up and back, scooping air and driving them higher. Tessa looked down. They cleared the huge trees at the edge of the camp close enough to scatter diamonds of morning dew from the leaves.

They gained altitude quickly, and Tessa felt Kishar angle his tail and drop a wing, turning north. It was too early in the morning for thermals to have formed, and they needed to hunt, so Kishar flew straight and low toward the foothills of the mountains gleaming pink in the early light.

Tessa had time to think. Her father had been throwing her in the way of Daryl Me'Vere since she was fourteen. He'd matured into one of the handsomest men in Restal. The troubles with his brother, Readen, and the battle to take back the keep had added depth and character to him.

But Daryl didn't make her stomach lurch as in a swift wheel and swoop by Kishar. He didn't make her lungs starve for air as if she were flying too high above the clouds. He didn't make her body flicker with heat as if the hot core of the planet were seeping out her skin. Galen did.

As unobservant and single-minded as her father was, she was glad there was time to learn to school her expressions, to get rid of those feelings before she saw him again. He'd notice. If she weren't staying aloof and far away from Galen, everyone would know by now how she felt, and not just suspect like Almryk.

Tessa always watched to be sure Galen was leaving the evening sparring before she went to work out, or more often, she practiced her forms alone and away from camp—not all the patrol members appreciated the fact she consistently beat them. She never took her meals when he was in the cook's tent. Since moving into camp, it had become more difficult—as the expression on Almryk's face showed this morning. She'd have to work harder to hide what she felt.

Kishar was silent about Galen, and Tessa didn't ask why. She knew the Karda watched Galen in camp as much as he could. And they scouted the areas where he worked more often than any of the others.

~Your thoughts are far away, Austringer, and yet they are loud in my mind. Your shields are sloppy this morning, and you have missed that herd below us to the east.~

Tessa had to grab the handle on the front of her saddle and clamp her legs tight as he wheeled in a hard turn. She pulled the extra set of goggles down over the ones on her face and searched the ground. The trees were scattered here, mostly small evergreens. They'd flown beyond the edge of the forest into the foothills. She spotted fifteen kurga grazing ahead of them, pulled her strung bow from the straps under her leg, and nocked an arrow from her quiver.

They circled until their shadow was behind them, and the kurga didn't hear Kishar's owl-silent wing beats until it was too late. Tessa shot three times in as many seconds. Three kurga fell just before they reached the herd. Kishar snatched a fourth fat buck, and the herd scattered, heels kicking up clods of damp dirt as they raced over the hill and disappeared before she and Kishar circled back.

~Good hunting today,~ he said as he dropped his prey, its neck broken, and landed.

Tessa pushed her goggles to the top of her head. ~And a lot of work for me while you gorge yourself. Before you start, could you help me throw these ropes up into that tallest tree? I can get them higher from your back. I'm not doing all this work to feed a medgeran.~

Tessa hauled one of the kurga up by its heels, pulled off her gloves, and began field stripping it, piling the viscera neatly for Kishar to finish off. By the time she finished all three, Kishar had eaten the fourth and the remains of her work.

She tied all three together by their hind ankles, climbed onto his back, and looped the end of the rope through the saddle handle. He backed up till the carcasses were far enough from the ground to be safe from anything but one of the largest bear-like medgeran. The notoriously elusive long-haired creatures usually stuck to the higher hills, but it was better to be certain than hungry. Then he circled the tree three times, winding the rope around. Tessa jumped down and secured it with a clove hitch.

~That is one messy, smelly job I am not happy to have learned. It would be better if Father never knew.~ Her eyes crinkled, and she grinned at the thought. She swiped a forearm across her damp brow, careful not to smear her bloody hands on her face. ~These should make the cooks happy to see us this afternoon. Maybe you can talk them into baking you something sweet for tonight.~

Kishar's pleasure at that thought sounded like a child's giggle in her head. He was like a little kid with sweet things.

~I will save a small piece for you for your excellent shooting. We shall rest a few moments.~ They took off, and he dropped down when they'd flown well away from the place where he and Tessa had made something of a bloody mess.

Tessa unfastened a big water canvas from his rig and lifted it to her shoulder, squirting streams of water into Kishar's hooked beak. Then she fished a cup out of her pack and settled down beside him to drink, leaning against his shoulder. ~I'm not a very big girl, and that was hard work. Resting is good.~

She closed her eyes and let her head fall back against him. There was nowhere so safe and comfortable as this. She drifted off into no-thought. The breeze picked up, humming through scattered short-needle pine trees around them, rippling across the every-color-of-shiny-green grasses of spring. The sun shone off and on and was warm on her face as the mostly burned off clouds drifted across the sky.

~Kishar.~ She hesitated. ~Almryk told me my proficiency with the bow was something extraordinary. He said he has guards who've been working with the bow for years who don't have my skill. And I've only been practicing for a relatively few tendays—little more than half a season. He didn't believe me when I told him that, though he didn't say it. I never miss the target anymore, even when they move it as far and fast as they can. I haven't for quite some time. I had to stop practicing with the guards and planters. They were starting to give me funny looks.~

He didn't answer, and she was quiet for a few minutes. The euphoria at escaping her father's plans, the excitement of learning to survive on her own, the ecstasy of flight with Kishar, his incredible friendship—it had all begun to smooth out. And her self-doubt was brilliant at finding holes to sneak back through.

~Before we left Restal, Cerla, the Mi'hiru who trained me how to care for you, wouldn't believe you hadn't chosen me to be a Mi'hiru. She said only the favored, like the Mi'hiru and a few guardians, can path to their Karda. And, of course Marta and Altan who can path to all Karda. Why is it I can?~

~I wondered when you would ask me these questions.~

~You've kept me very busy. Too busy to think, I think.~ She felt the soft rumble of his laughter and leaned her head back against his shoulder, brushing away strands of his mane the breeze blew across her face. Too often faint sadness lay under his laughter, but not this time.

~It is because you are the Austringer. The first to appear for five hundred years. Because your talent was blocked, if your father's arms-master had been able to teach you longer, your prowess would have shown up sooner.~ He turned his head to look at her with one large eye.

She sat up straight. ~I can outfight any of the guard or patrol I spar with, only I never let them know. I've heard Marta Rowan is very good.~ Her voice got small, and her last sentence was more question than statement.

She dropped her head into her shaky hands. Aloud she said, "I'm a freak. I have no talent. No one knows why I can do things—fighting things, sword, bow, hand-to-hand fighting, even the staff—better than anyone without having to undergo years and years of training. All I have to do is work to develop the right muscles. It makes the patrollers I spar with angry if I tell them I'm just learning. I only said that to two of them They thought I was lying."

By the time she finished her sentence, she shook so hard the rings and fittings on the saddle behind her clinked. She stood and almost ran to the far side of the small clearing, falling to her knees beside a rough, twisted evergreen. She held her hands out in front of her--flaky, brown dried blood covered them.

I'm a killer. I have gotten so used to blood I forgot to wash it off. She swallowed hard. *My talent will never come back. Too much blood.* A vision of the mercenary lying on the floor of her rooms, his blood running in the seams of the stone floor knocked her off balance like a storm-driven gust of wind.

~Your thoughts are shouting at me, and you are hysterical.~ Kishar's words scoured through her mind, shocking her out of her terrible vision. Never had he spoken so harshly to her. ~There is a good reason for what you think makes you a freak, and when you are calm, I will tell you that reason once again, Austringer. Come. We will find a stream where you can wash. We will be late for our patrol.~

Their morning patrol passed without incident, though Kishar wouldn't fly anywhere near the circle until Tessa had herself under control again. He talked to her softly and persistently about why she was so proficient with arms. Why she always knew where they were. Why she knew, no matter how his flight twisted and turned, what direction they flew, how far they'd flown, and how far it was to wherever they were flying.

~You are the Austringer. It is the block on your talent that is the reason you are resistant to the sickness of the circles. Your abilities appeared at this time because you are needed. The evil that is reawakening will raise the urbat. They are what we must kill. They are what is evil. Killing them is not evil—it is healing. To think it is evil, to come to believe so, will corrupt you, and you will be vulnerable to the Itza Larrak. They must not be allowed to win.~ Over and over he reassured her until her heart settled, and she could breathe deeply of the clear, clean air over the forest.

She was thoroughly ashamed of her outburst, and he had to talk her out of that, too. ~You are the Austringer, but you are also a young human woman. Cleanse those thoughts and doubts about yourself from your mind. Seek deep for the knowledge and surety that is inside you, for the understanding of what you are and what you are becoming. Face the fears that surfaced in you this morning. It is good that they do so now and not later. See them clearly and do not let them destroy you. Do not let them turn you away from what you know you must do.~

All morning, she could feel his mind holding hers in a safe embrace. Until clarity returned. Until her strengths returned. Until she felt the forging of new determination inside her, cauterizing the shame of having no talent and the insidious doubts that invaded her.

Just before lunch, they flew west and north until they found Galen as Almryk asked. Tessa had to pull her second set of goggles down, and it took them a while to find him. He had stopped for the noon meal and hobbled his horse in a tiny clearing near a spring where the grass was green and tall. They flew over him, Kishar waggling his wings when Galen gave them an I'm-all-right wave.

From their height, she could see a line of skeletal, dead white trees winding south in the direction of Me'Fiere Hold and the large circle far to the southwest of it.

~I'm hungry, Kishar. And the cooks will be so happy to get the kurga we killed. They might sneak us some cake. Let's head back.~ Kishar wheeled, and they flew to gather up the remaining three kurga carcasses, hanging them from the carrying harness Tessa stowed in her pack that morning. Kishar held them steady in his front talons as they took off straight up, barely noticing the extra weight, both eager for cake.

They were back in the air and near the end of their second hour of the afternoon patrol when both Tessa's and Kishar's heads snapped around to the south. Kishar wheeled in a stomach-flipping turn and arrowed straight across the south-eastern edge of the circle to the forest beyond, heading south by southwest. Tessa leaned close over the front of the saddle, her attention focused on the terrible urgency that had her heart trying to fly out of her mouth at the wrongness. It came from Galen.

Tessa could see nothing through the forest canopy spread beneath them. She spotted the line of dead trees snaking further south. ~What's that, Kishar?~ The thin line was vivid against the dark green of the surrounding forest.

~A Line of Devastation. It comes from the circle. You saw another at the northernmost edge. It will be impossible to find Galen from this high in this part of the forest. We must go down.~

She had to grab the saddle handle and hang on, leaning forward, his flying mane snapping and stinging her face. This was old forest with widely spaced trees, and there was room for Kishar to maneuver, sometimes folding his wings to skim between branches. Sometimes he changed direction by twisting around, wings a tight V above her, and shoving off from a thick branch or trunk with his hind feet.

~I can feel him, Kishar. There is something terribly wrong with him. He's sick.~

She urged him on faster and faster until they found Galen a couple of kilometers south of the circle, a few hundred meters from the line of dead trees. He was sprawled on the ground, his hobbled horse placidly grazing nearby.

Tessa tore the straps from her legs and jumped from Kishar, running hard. She skidded to a stop next to Galen and fell to her knees, feeling all over his body for a wound. But there was nothing. She rolled him over as gently as she could, laying her head on his chest. He was breathing, but his breath was shallow. She could barely hear his heartbeat, weak and slow. Wrongness surrounded him, trying to seep into him—the same virulent, greasy evil as the circle. His skin was so very cold.

She looked up at Kishar, whose head was bent close to Galen's. Then the Karda turned toward a lumpy leather bag lying a few feet away as though it had fallen or been thrown when Galen fell. He snatched it up in his talons and took off, weaving his way through the trees until Tessa could see him no more.

She knew she smelled of Karda but managed to catch the reins of Galen's hobbled mount. Galen had buckled the bridle around his neck, and the reins were loosely looped and tied to the saddle. She jerked at the buckles holding the saddlebags, tossing them to the ground, and frantically pulled things out till she found a blanket and his flask of water. She ran back to him, covering him tightly.

Tessa maneuvered his head into her lap, holding it up, and tried to force water into his mouth. It dribbled down his neck, and she stopped before they were both soaked. Terrified and shaking with frustration, she swore an oath she'd only ever heard. All she could do was hold him, trying to warm him with her body heat, smoothing her hand over his forehead over and over. Tessa held him as close as she could, rocking back and forth, stuttering sobs catching at her breath, squeezing her chest with pressure that wouldn't release.

When Kishar returned and back-winged to a stop, the horse squealed and fought his hobbles.

~Where did you go, Kishar? I don't know what to do. I can feel the wrongness surrounding him. I can feel it working its way into him. What happened to him? What can we do?~

~Remove his clothing, all of it.~ He reached down with his hooked beak and jerked the blanket away.

~All of it?~

~Hurry. Start with his shirt and vest.~

Tessa laid Galen's head back on the ground and knelt beside him. She unfastened his sword belt then the buttons of his shirt. But he was too large, his body too stiff, for her to roll him over. ~Help me, Kishar. He's so heavy. Snag his vest and help me roll him over.~

Together they managed to get his shirt and vest off and roll him back. Tessa stared, horrified, at the raised, red, puckered scars covering his arms and most of his broad chest. Kishar nudged her hard with his beak. She worked at Galen's boots until Kishar finally grabbed them with his talons and jerked them off. She pulled off his stockings and hesitated at the fastening of his breeches, heat rising in her face.

~All of them,~ Kishar repeated. ~Cover him with the blanket as soon as you can, but there must be nothing between him and the ground. You must be quick. We do not know how long he's been lying here.~

Tessa's whole body was burning by the time she had him undressed and hastily threw the blanket over him. He was lean and muscular, beautiful—his skin smooth where there were no purple scars. *Oh, how can I think of that now? He's so ill.* Shame tried to choke her.

~Nothing must come between his body and the earth.~

She knelt by his head, lifting it and trying again to get some water inside him, but it dribbled down the side of his immobile face.

~You must roll him over again. He must be face down.~ Kishar helped by pushing with his beak, and they managed. Tessa laid the blanket over him again and sat by his head, her legs crossed, smoothing his hair away from his face, again and again, letting it fall back each time, giving her the excuse to keep touching him.

She laid her palm over the rough, irregular, furrowed scar that disfigured one side of his face then jerked away. It pulsed faintly. She felt it again. It was definitely pulsing. She reached under the blanket to touch the scars on his arm and chest. They, too, pulsed just enough for her to be able to feel it.

~His scars, Kishar. They're...they're pulsing ever so faintly.~ She laid her hand on his scarred cheek again. ~I can feel it.~

~Good. That is good. Now we wait.~

Kishar talked her into leaving Galen long enough to take her bow and hunt. Tessa walked through the immense trees, her feet quiet on the damp leaves. The mature forest was not too thick for him to fly through, but he would be severely hampered trying to hunt. *Why does Kishar say it is good that Galen's scars are pulsing? And insist Galen be naked on the ground? He is so ill, his body so cold.* She shook her head and walked faster. If she thought about his body and what she had seen before she threw the blanket over him, she would set the forest afire.

Two hours later, the sun lowering and the forest growing dark, she staggered back into the clearing, a small deer slung over her back and shoulders, her hands holding its crossed hind hooves in front of her. She dropped it, and herself, to the ground. ~You can do this tomorrow, Kishar. I don't know if I even have the energy to start a fire.~

But she did, and while Kishar ate, she managed to cut a hefty hunk out of one haunch of the deer. ~Thank you for gathering wood for me. I know it's awkward for you, but I'm not sure I could have managed~ When the fire burned down to glowing coals, she used green sticks to prop the small roast over it.

~I must leave before it is completely dark. They will be wondering what happened to us, and we will need supplies. We will be here for a while. I will be back early tomorrow.~

Tessa froze. ~You're going to leave us?~

~Extinguish the fire as soon as you have cooked your meat. It would not be good for it to be visible at night. I will make a wide circle as I leave to be sure there is nothing or no one dangerous near enough to reach you tonight. You will be safe.~

He lifted straight up and was out of sight in seconds before she could beg him to stay. She ate the meat half raw and kicked dirt over the tiny fire until she could see neither smoke nor glowing coals. Then she curled up as close to Galen as she could, covering him and herself with the blanket from her pack, one hand on her short sword, Galen's longer one on her other sider. She could feel the pulse of the scars on his arm through the blanket. It was getting stronger. She felt very slightly less afraid.

Very.

Slightly.

Chapter Twelve

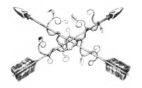

Sometime in the dark hours of the night, Kishar touched down in the center of the small clearing, lumpy bags strapped to his saddle and hanging off both sides. It jerked Tessa from her half-awake state. ~I have told them where we are, and that Galen cannot be moved yet. I do not think Captain Almryk will recover soon from hearing me in his head. Apparently, he has not had the experience before. I may have left him with a bit of a headache. I think he wanted to call me a packhorse in retribution. Somehow, I feel like one.~

Tessa could barely see his dark form as she ran to his side. ~Galen's the same. He hasn't moved, and he's burning with fever. I couldn't cool him. I didn't have any way to carry water.~

Kishar stood still as Tessa pressed herself into his shoulder and reached up to tangle her hands in his mane, her body shaking with fear for Galen and relief that the Karda was back. Then he walked over to where Galen lay, bent his knees, and dropped down near him. Tessa wiped her face with a forearm, taking deep, shuddering breaths.

~I'm sorry. I've been so scared. He hasn't changed at all. His chest barely moves, and I can only feel a faint breath, and sometimes not even that. Oh, Kishar! He's going to die. His scars are so hot I can feel them through the blanket. And when I look, they are fiery red all along his arms and chest. I can see them even in the dark. Look at his face. His scar is changing. Look at the shape of it, Kishar. His scar is changing.~ Her pathed words were a shrill, panicked scream scalding the inside of her head.

The scar that marred Galen's cheek from temple to the edge of his jaw pulsed in the darkness lit only by starlight. It glowed faintly but clearly in the shape of a tripartite abelee leaf, three delicate serrated lobes round and slightly pointed—every vein stood out sharply. The veins of a leaf, not the veins of a human face. No longer an ugly scar.

~Ah, yes.~

The hope in his voice shocked Tessa out of her panic, and she took a long, shuddering breath, burying her face against him. Kishar never showed such emotion, his mind always the solid mountain of calm that grounded her.

~He has come. The Kern has come.~ He bowed his neck and closed his eyes.

Tessa felt his whole body relax.

~He has come.~

Kishar was so still, so obviously moved, so full with hope, that Tessa couldn't make herself disturb him with the questions flooding her. She pulled away from him, untangling her hands from his mane, and began unfastening the canvas bags from his saddle and harness. A small, two-person tent, ground cloths, more blankets, rain gear, food, large canvas pouches of water, food, more food. Her mouth watered at the smell of fresh bread emanating from a bag that held two small cooking pots, a water kettle, a crock of soft cheese, and bundles of herbs and greens she knew Bren must have gathered only a few hours ago.

Kishar didn't move. Didn't take his eyes from the still body lying prone before him in the long grass.

Tessa lit the small lantern she found and unfolded a ground cloth on the side of Galen opposite Kishar. She set up the small tent, working awkwardly around Galen's unmoving body and the unmoving Karda. Kishar had been so insistent that Galen lie directly on the ground she knew better than to try to roll him onto the ground cloth, though she couldn't help but think he'd be more comfortable

She knelt, lifting the edge of his blanket to spread the cloth close to him, and stared. She couldn't breathe. Heavy darkness closed in the corners of her vision. Her body shivered with icy cold.

A network of faintly glowing green-gold tendrils, barely visible, curled up from the soft, loose soil beneath Galen into the scars on his arm. Green and gold light pulsed through them. The scars changed as she stared, hypnotized, into markings running from his fingers to his shoulder. Root-like tattoos spread from the strange tattoo-bracelet circling his wrist down to his fingertips. Scars morphed into slender, branched markings from the wrist up toward his shoulder—brown, tinged with green at the tips. Tessa dropped the blanket. Her fist flew to her mouth to block the unborn scream that lodged—a sharp-edged stone—in her throat.

Shaking, she backed away, fell, scrambled to all fours and out of the tent. She stood, crossing her arms against the pain in her mid-section, and stumbled on the clutter of half-unloaded packs, almost falling into Kishar.

~What is it, little one?~

The concern in his voice stopped the shuddering that wracked her. Her voice shook, and she spoke aloud to him for the first time in tendays. "Something is happening to him. He's…He's… Oh, Kishar, I don't know what to do. I don't know what's wrong. Come see." Her hands shook so hard she could barely grasp the edge of the blanket to lift it from Galen's arm.

Kishar stared for a long time, the feathers on the crest of his head raised upright, and he clacked his fierce predator's beak once sharply. She started to ask him what was happening, but the overpowering emotion she sensed from him nearly knocked her to her knees.

~Centuries. Long, long centuries alone. It is nearly over.~

Tessa knew Kishar didn't mean for her to hear those words. He never lost his control. But the overwhelming hope they held washed over her. And grief—sorrow she could drown in. Somehow, carried on the edge of his emotions, she grew calm—her terror dissolved into the wonder she felt growing from him.

Slowly she moved away to the scattered supplies and began organizing them as best she could in the pre-dawn darkness, covering them with a ground cloth against the wetness of the dew. She couldn't bear to disturb Kishar with her questions and fears right now. She closed her eyes and let his deep sorrow, his wonder, and his fierce, aching hope swirl around her. She could wait.

Kishar, his night-dark form almost invisible, had not shifted from the open side of the tent. His head rested on his forelegs. His gaze rested intent on the still body within. His breath was shallow. Tension quivered through his every feather. Tessa found one of the extra blankets and curled up on the edge of the ground cloth on Galen's other side. She knew she wouldn't sleep, but there was nothing more to do now, and she needed rest.

Despite her worries and roiling emotions, she managed to sleep, but it was a sleep filled with shadowed creatures. Huge, dog-like monsters with short, stubby wings half-ran, half-flew in great leaps through the darkness. Tongues hung from wide mouths ringed with shark-like teeth, strange triangular metallic scales armored chests and shoulders of bodies half flesh and fur, half-metallic gears and articulated limbs. An eerie keening sounded as they raced, mud and leaves flying behind, thrown up by cruel metal claws.

There was no change in Galen all the next day. He lay still and straight beneath the blanket as she watched him across the fire. Late in the evening, Kishar took off to hunt and to make a supply run to camp. Tessa had to talk him into leaving. ~You have to eat, Kishar. And we need water. I have enough for me, but I don't have enough water to even make you a hot mash, and you need more than that.~

Kishar took off, and Tessa moved a folded blanket into Galen's tent and knelt beside him with a cup of water. Turning his head, she let a small stream of water drop into his mouth, relieved when she saw his Adam's apple move as he swallowed, grateful when he drank the whole cupful. She huddled next to him, wrapping her arms around her knees, and waited for morning.

For a long time, Galen watched light flick across the outside of his eyelids, unthinking, only feeling. His mind hung, suspended in a wash of time, aware of the infinitesimal movements of the skin of the planet below him. He sensed the vast land sloping away to the east from the harsh up-thrust of mountains in the west. Of the weight of the ocean beyond them.

Then there was a slight, slow movement of air through his nostrils. His breath. An annoying pain in his hip. A rock. And that was all, until, gradually and steadily, one muscle at a time, his body began to wake, to feel, and he wondered with a distant kind of wonder, who and where he was. For a long time, his mind refused anything more than the welcome weight of his body, tethered again. And the warmth of a body pressed next to him.

Then there was a hawk scream inside his head.

~Tessa! Ware! The urbat come.~

It was Kishar's voice. Inside his head. How—?

Galen felt sudden movement beside him, heard the swish of a sword leaving its sheath—of two swords—and the warm body tore away from him. The shrill, keening, hunting howl of several animals grew louder. He rolled to his back and opened his eyes to see the canvas of the tent over him and managed to sit and then push to his hands and knees—his body, his mind sluggish. The blanket slid away, and cool air brushed his skin. He was naked. He looked down at his hands. There was something wrong with his hands.

The howling snarls came closer, and Galen crawled out the open side of the tent. There was a high wail of agony, and he watched Tessa slash a stubby wing from one of the horrible metal and flesh creatures of his dream. Amber ichor spurted in a thick stream. Even before the monster fell, another attacked. Tessa's sword rang against the metallic scales covering the creature's shoulders. She dropped to her knees and shoved a second sword, his sword, into its throat below its jaw where odd, scales of armor gave way to soft flesh. Another monster came out of the trees, and another behind it, half-running, half-leap-flying with too-small wings.

Tessa jumped back to her feet. Her swords flashed in a blur, tearing into the third monster. She fought with both swords, her back to a massive oak. She sliced its muzzle off, and on the back-slash, she took its head. Muddy amber ichor flew—her sword had found the spot where the armor ended, and its head began.

She stumbled over a root, lost her balance and one sword. The last creature howled in triumph and spread its wings to leap before she could recover her stance. Kishar screamed high above them, diving for the ground, but he'd never reach her in time. Galen saw her terror grow as she realized she was helpless.

Then the urbat twisted. Its head swiveled toward Galen. Red eyes glowed with savage recognition, and it leaped toward him. Without thought, Galen pushed his hands into the soil beneath him and shoved. Green-gold waves of energy surged across the ground toward the snarling urbat, and the earth around it erupted, knocking the ugly creature off its feet. Thick roots twined up and stabbed into its body, piercing skin and armor. Vines twisted around it. Long, vicious thorns snagged it and dragged the struggling creature down. Agonized cries sliced the air, and it writhed, fighting to free itself. Slowly, inexorably, the soil trapped it. Its last cries were strangled, shrill whines, and it disappeared beneath a tangle of thorny green briars and muddy earth.

The green-gold waves spread out over the entire clearing. Black, rich earth rolled over the other three slain monsters, covering them until only slight mounds were visible. A soft fur of tender new green grass shoots pushed up from the raw earth, growing rapidly until the mounds, too, disappeared, indistinguishable from the rolling ground of the clearing.

Galen looked up to see Tessa staring at him, her face pale, eyes wide. And frightened. Of him.

~Tessa.~ Kishar's voice sounded sharp in Galen's head. Tessa shivered. ~Go to him. Prop him up. If he falls over, it will break both his arms.~ He landed as close to Galen as he could.

Galen looked down. He was on his knees outside the tent. Both arms were elbow deep in the ground beneath the grass. He looked up. Tessa ran to brace him with her body. His body shook—hers trembled. No thoughts would come. All he could do was stare at her face, the only real thing in this inexplicable world. Tessa's face, an unruly halo of short silver hair, brown eyes wide, pupils dilated with fear. He couldn't speak. Couldn't move. Couldn't think.

~Kern.~ Dimly he heard the voice in his head, and somewhere in his mind, he knew it as Kishar's. ~Can you pull your arms out of the earth?~

How could he be hearing Kishar's voice in his head?

"His eyes, Kishar. Look at his eyes." Tessa's breath whispered against Galen's face as she knelt beside him, her arm warm around his cold shoulders. "They're green like new spring grass. There are no whites, only green."

~Hold him up, Tessa. I will have to dig him out. He's barely conscious. Don't let him fall,~ Kishar pathed in a calm, nothing-unusual-happening-here tone. And the voice was definitely Kishar's.

Galen felt Tessa's arms tighten around him, and he relaxed against her. They almost fell before she braced herself. He tried to twist around to see her face again, but she was too close. He leaned his head against hers. He was aware of nothing but her arms, her touch, the feathery feel of her hair against his cheek. Something very young in him wanted to laugh and tell her, "I'm naked, and you're holding me."

Kishar dug carefully with his long talons, and Galen felt the earth loosen around his arms until he could draw them out and sit back. Tessa moved away into the tent. He missed the feel of her arms. His teeth chattered hard enough to rattle his head, and he shivered till he felt a warm blanket settle over him.

"Can you get back into the tent, Galen?" Her voice was small and shaky as she tugged him to his feet and turned him around, her face averted and red enough to catch fire. "I'll get more blankets." And she disappeared. He stood there—lost, bereft, empty—until she appeared again in a few minutes, blankets piled in her arms.

"Is it alright if he's not directly touching the ground, Kishar?"

His ears wanted to drink in the sound of her voice until he drowned in it. He watched as she folded a pallet and pulled him over to lie down, pushing gently on his shoulders, careful to keep his body discreetly covered. She spread more blankets over him.

"You are shaking with cold." Her whisper was soft as downy feathers brushing his mind, and she helped him lie back. "Sleep, Galen. Kishar says you need to sleep now."

He reached out and grabbed her hand, and she sank down beside him. He pushed the edges of the blankets aside until he could reach the bare earth and held his hand there, his fingers laced with hers. His last thought before oblivion arrived was, *What if there had been more than four monsters? Tessa would be dead, and her body savaged.*

Next morning, his body felt as though someone had driven a herd of horses through the tent then stomped on him with heavy boots. But his head was clear. He rolled out from under the blankets. Where did those come from? His head hit the top of the canvas tent. And where did the tent come from? He pushed open the flap. A sudden breeze made him shiver. He looked down—he was naked. He found his clothes folded neatly at the head of the rough pallet of blankets and dressed with difficulty, hunched over in the small tent. He sat to pull on his boots.

Tessa crossed in front of the tent, her head down, eyes searching the ground between him and a small fire pit. Its freshly lit fire blazed up like the feeling that rushed through his body at the sight of her. Where did she come from? The last thing he remembered was gathering the samples from beneath the line of dead trees that snaked out of the circle. If this was a dream, it was so life-like he was glad it wasn't a nightmare. The creatures he'd dreamed about last night would have eaten him by now.

Tessa walked, her silver-haloed head searching the ground, over to Kishar—where had he come from?—and the Karda dropped something that clanged into the canvas bag she carried. They were both making their way slowly across the small clearing, kicking at the grass, occasionally picking something up and dropping it in the bag. Early morning light from the red sun silhouetted the tops of the trees that arched from the edges of the clearing. He caught a movement out of the corner of his eye. His horse, still securely hobbled, grazed on the other side of the fire, as far away from Kishar as he could get.

Galen remembered arriving at the clearing, dismounting, slipping the bridle around his horse's neck, and hobbling him. He remembered going to the strange line of dead trees to collect the mineral sample his father was so desperate to get. Then—nothing. He could remember nothing else. *How did I get here?* He shook his head. One hand scrabbled at his hair trying to scratch loose a memory.

"Oh. You're awake." A flash of wonder mixed with fear sheared away the gladness that first lit Tessa's face as she saw him. She dropped the clanging bag at Kishar's feet and walked toward him, slowing to a stop several feet away. Her puzzling fear was like ice, sizzling as it hit the heat of his body. *Why is she afraid? Of me?* She usually looked at him, when she couldn't ignore him entirely, with a mixture of suspicion and disdain. With the occasional pink tinge to her cheeks that never failed to light something inside him.

Galen creaked to his feet like a rusted machine in need of oiling. "Obviously something happened while I was—well, wherever I was."

She raised a hand as if to take his arm then dropped it as he walked to the fire.

"I trust you brought something to eat when you came to visit." He was used to hiding his feelings with hard words and sarcasm. He was accustomed to her suspicion, but the fear he saw was almost unbearable.

She pushed past him to the fire and began knocking it down into coals and low flames, keeping her face turned away from him. "I was waiting for you to wake to make tea and something for us to eat." Her voice stuttered on the word us.

Galen fought to suppress a grin. Now he knew how he'd come to be naked. Then he sobered. She'd seen the scars that marred his body. No wonder she couldn't look at him. She must be appalled by his naked body, disgusted by the ugliness that disfigured his arms, his chest, his face. The body that once entranced any woman he chose was no more. His fingers brushed his cheek. The scar felt oddly smooth this morning.

She pulled a battered teakettle from the small wooden box beside where she knelt. They both reached for the canvas water pouch at the same time, and his hand closed over hers. She jerked away.

"Just hold the kettle still." The tone of his voice was colder than the chill water he poured.

She flinched, and water splashed over her boot.

Tessa rummaged in the box and the bag of food and began to fix something—he didn't care what—for their breakfast. Walking to where Kishar was still searching through the grass, he picked up the canvas bag and looked inside. It was heavy with triangular pieces of metal, gears, and pulleys of all sizes up to about fifteen centimeters in diameter, rods of the same strange, dull metal. Dull globs of dark yellow ichor clung to them in places. He stared, unable to pull his eyes away from the contents of the bag.

His vision blurred green-gold over the images beginning to form in his head. Tessa fighting monstrous, dog-like creatures, slashing into them with her swords, strings of dark yellow ichor flying. Tessa—Galen dropped to his knees at the memory of Tessa, her back to the wide trunk of an oak, fighting the vicious, black-armored beings with two swords, losing one sword, unable to bring the other around in time…

He held his head in his hands, fighting to stay conscious, willing himself away from the horrifying scene before he remembered—remembered what? Head spinning, he looked back at the figure of the silver-haired girl working quietly at the fire. He sucked in a deep breath that almost split his chest in his relief. She was alive—unhurt.

Galen closed his eyes and laid both hands flat on the ground in front of him. They sank slightly into the dirt, and a wave of reassurance rose up, moving through his body, easing the fear, loosening his joints, soothing away the pain and stiffness, clearing his mind, tucking away the memory of something he had done that refused to surface.

He stood, trying to deny the vision, and looked into Kishar's eyes. "Please tell me what is going on. Did something attack here last night? And why can't I remember anything that happened to me after I rode into this clearing and hobbled my horse to—" He remembered his intent to gather samples for his father, and he didn't finish that sentence. "To have a look at the strange line of dead trees running south and west of here out of the circle." Well, that much was true. And it didn't seem strange to be talking to the giant Karda. It was just one more strange happening on this world of strange happenings.

~Hold the sack open for me.~ There was a small pile of the odd metal pieces next to the bag at Kishar's feet.

Galen fumbled the bag open, his hands shaking, and the Karda dropped the pieces in one by one.

"What are these?"

~The remains Adalta spit back up after you buried the urbat.~

Kishar's matter-of-fact tone puzzled Galen. Then he realized he heard Kishar in his head. And it itched. He scrubbed his face with both hands. He'd have to think about that later. He couldn't handle another strange experience.

"Buried what?" Vaguely he remembered his dream of the vicious creatures rising from the malevolent ground of a circle, pawing slimy cauls from their muzzles. And the vision of the creatures attacking Tessa. Creatures half flesh and half metal. He dropped the bag. "I buried them? Why do I not remember that?" Something rolled up from his stomach and stuck in his throat. "Why was I not fighting them? It was only Tessa. Where was I?"

He spread his hands before him. Blackness closed in on the edges of his sight. His hands—the scars on his hands were gone. Fine tattoo-like branching roots spread to his fingertips from the intricate bracelet that encircled his wrists. He shoved his sleeve to his elbow, baring one fore-arm. A brown and black tattoo of a slender trunk split and split into finer and finer branches extending up smooth, unscarred skin. He touched the scar on his face, slightly raised in a pattern he could feel, but it wasn't the ugly, twisted furrows of his scar. He felt a shift in his eyes, and Kishar and the clearing faded behind a pale haze of green and gold. And he remembered. He remembered who he was.

The Kern.

The Seed.

Who he had always been.

The Kern.

Words exploded in his head like seeds bursting from a pod.

No. No. No.

Chapter Thirteen

Galen rode into the main camp late that afternoon soaked to the skin by the steady rain that persisted all day. Exhausted, confused, refusing to think about what happened the day before, the dream-monsters-come-to-life he'd seen. And what he'd done to them. All he wanted was a hot supper and to escape to his tent. His scars were back with their faint ants-under-the-skin feeling. Gone were the strangely beautiful tattoos his mind couldn't rationalize.

He was puzzled to see most of the planters and guards gathered around their fires, half full push-carts and planting tools scattered haphazardly around the camp. They should still be out at the edges of the circle planting saplings.

Four men were digging a large hole at the edge of the clearing near a row of canvas-covered mounds. Almryk stood near the rope corral, staring at the digging men. Galen rode up beside him, dismounted, and started unbuckling his saddle bags.

Almryk didn't look at him. He turned away from the men and the strange mounds, his face pale and sober. "Leave your horse. Brett will take care of him. We need to talk. And you probably could use something hot to eat." The two of them trotted, slipping and sliding through the mud, toward the cook's tent.

Something's not right here. Almryk never lets anyone get away with not taking care of his horse.

"Kishar and Tessa? Have they made it back? They should have been here hours ago." Galen swallowed against the wild fluttering in his chest that threatened to close off his breath. He needed them. He needed someone who knew what happened to him—what he had done. He needed Kishar to make good on his promise to help him understand. He needed to know Tessa was safe.

"They are scouting. Kishar was adamant that they take off immediately when he saw what happened. They told me you'd been ill." His voice was odd, jerky and distracted. He swiped a hand across his forehead. "Hearing a Karda in my mind is a new experience and more than a little disturbing."

Galen's gait hitched, and he skipped a step to catch up. Kishar talked to Almryk, too? The two men settled at one end of a long table. One of the cooks brought two mugs of hot tea.

Almryk looked away, spread his hands wide on the table, and chewed on his lip. "We had to bring everyone in to camp late this morning, in a hurry. Things are a little disorganized."

Galen looked around. "Everyone? Did you send some out again? They don't all look to be here."

Almryk scrubbed at his face, rubbing dirt into his skin. "Galen." He opened his mouth several times to speak before he could get the words out. His face twisted with the effort. "The ones you see are all that's left except for a few in the big communal tent."

"Left? All that's left? Why did the others leave?" Galen stopped, suddenly chilled with horrified comprehension. He looked intently at the captain's face. "They didn't leave, did they? And the ones in the tent?"

"Wounded and sick. Very sick." Almryk's words were a rockfall of boulders that punched Galen in the diaphragm.

Galen sucked in a breath and looked toward the digging men and the canvas covered mound. "They're digging a grave."

"Four guards and seven planters. There's not enough of them left to even tell who is who, except for the uniforms. They were slaughtered. Torn apart. If I hadn't ridden out with them this morning at the last minute, we'd have lost more." Almryk put his hand to his mouth and swallowed several times. His voice was so low Galen could barely hear him.

"The urbat." Galen's flat words left a taste of bile on his tongue.

"Kishar and Tessa say that's what the monsters are. They're extremely hard to kill. They're armored with metal scales, and they can fly in short hops."

Almryk's fists opened and closed at his sides, coiling and uncoiling over and over. He was close to losing control. "We're lucky most of the planters are at least adequate with the sword. And that we made arms practice mandatory for them, too. They were the monsters' primary targets. The urbat attacked early this morning, and the planters weren't yet scattered around the circle's edge, thank the Lady Adalta. If three unpartnered Karda hadn't arrived—they tore into the monsters, and the rest fled back to the circle where no one could follow. That saved us."

He bowed his head then looked up. His rough voice leaked grief and frustration. "If not for that, and if the men had already been scattered around the edge of the circle working, they would all have been killed. We also lost ten mounts. One of the Karda was wounded." He scrubbed at his face. "We killed eighteen, and I estimate another thirty escaped."

Galen shook his head as if he could rearrange his brain to assimilate what he was hearing. It was several minutes before he could speak. "You've set sentries."

"Yes, in pairs and mounted on our fastest horses. Our remaining fastest horses." Almryk held his mug in his hand for a minute as if gathering strength from its heat. "An inner perimeter of my best archers are in tree stands around the edge of the camp. Kishar and Tessa are scouting between camp and the circle. Kishar says the beasts came from the circle. Hopefully only this one circle. Three of the unpartnered Karda left with one of my guard strapped in a makeshift harness to alert Guardian Daryl and the Mi'hiru at Restal Prime as soon as possible. As you can see, Tessa and Kishar are not the only ones up there circling."

Galen looked up. There were more Karda in the sky than he had ever seen in one place outside a prime, flying just under the cloud cover, gliding like ghosts through the blurring drizzle.

"I expect we'll have visitors in three or four days. When they have need, Karda can fly very fast."

Galen pinched the bridge of his nose between forefinger and thumb. He'd gotten used to being the leader of this expedition, but he never expected anything like this. It had been so peaceful. It was supposed to be just planting and guarding against circle sickness and maybe a bandit attack, not this. He looked up. "I'm sure you've taken reports from everyone, but I need to hear them, too. I'll go see the wounded for myself first, though."

He fought not to stumble over his feet as they walked through the drizzle toward the big tent where the wounded were. Too much happening too fast, throwing him off balance. "I hope whoever comes brings healers."

He stopped just inside the tent and stared. There was an ugly brown haze, faint but discernible, hanging in the air, thickest wherever the wounded lay. "What's that?" His stomach roiled with the stench of it.

Almryk hadn't stopped but walked to the nearest cot, covering his mouth and nose with his hand.

"I don't know. And you don't ever get used to it."

Galen shuddered and breathed through his nose. He'd rather have the stink in his nostrils than the taste on his tongue.

Almryk stopped at the pallet where Mirium, one of the youngest members of the Mounted Guard, moved restlessly, her head twisting back and forth. Behind her closed eyelids, her eyes rolled with panic as if caught in a nightmare.

Galen knelt and leaned toward her, bracing with one hand on the ground. Instantly the haze around her body thickened—a dark, sickly, greenish-black aura concentrated on the bandages on both arms and one leg. The stench was close to unbearable. He looked up at Almryk. The captain was pale and held a cloth pressed over his mouth and nose. Galen squatted back on his heels and clasped his arms around his knees.

Oh, stars lost and damned. What is happening to me? What am I supposed to do? Something reached up to claim him, firing his scars. *No. No, I will not belong to you. I will not let you claim me.* He looked at the young woman lying on the pallet, knowing he could help her. Knowing if he did, it might cost more than he wanted to give.

He closed his eyes and put his left hand flat against the ground. *I do this for her, with your help, but I do not give myself to you.* He didn't know who or what he was talking to, but he had to say it.

He laid his other hand over the bandage on her arm. She immediately went still, her body rigid. Her eyes opened and stared straight up, unseeing. A familiar surge of strength moved up from the ground through Galen. The palm of the hand lying on her wound began to heat. The scars on his hands pulsed and morphed into fine rootlets reaching out to his fingertips. He braced himself against the darkness infecting the girl's wounds. His root-and-tree tattoos pulled the thick miasma up his arm and across his chest. They flared iridescent green and gold where his sleeves were pushed up.

The stench became a physical thing, blocking his nostrils, curdling in his stomach. Pain from the wounded girl flamed through his transformed scars across his chest and shoulders to his other hand flat on the earth. He couldn't pull his right hand from her. He couldn't stop his opposite hand from sinking into the dirt. *I have to move it. I can't let it consume me.* He concentrated on the pulsing tattoos, shaping a milking motion, pulling the sickness out of her body, through his, and into the ground. He shivered with a fevered heat, trying not to swallow the oily, metallic taste flooding his mouth.

The girl convulsed, her back arched, her face contorted. Her lips drew back from her teeth in a grotesque parody of a smile, and she shook. Her cot danced on the ground. Galen braced his shoulder against it, but he didn't lift his hands.

Then she relaxed. Her eyes closed, and she curled over onto her side away from his hand. A little snore sounded from her nose. Only the slightest frown of pain marked her face. The fever in his body swept down into the earth. He fought the encroaching darkness and panic, forced himself to hold still, forced himself to breathe, forced himself to count each breath until he felt clean again.

With effort, he pulled his left hand free of the dirt that wanted to hold him and reached out to steady himself against Almryk. He felt the captain flinch away.

"What did you do? Oh, Great Adalta. Your eyes." Almryk's own were wide and staring. He moved away a few steps. "They're green. All green. Who are you? What are you?" His eyes shifted to the trefoil leaf tattoo marking Galen's face where his scar had been, to the root-and-tree-like markings on his hands and forearms, and he took another step back. "What are you?"

Galen heard his words, but they didn't register, and he moved to the next cot, kneeling. It happened again. And again, with the next wounded planter, with the guard after that, with the one after that. Each time, it was harder to pull his hand free of the soil. But he moved through all the injured until there was nothing left of the horrible stench. The oily dark miasma that choked the air in the tent dissipated. The wounded were still wounded, but the malevolent sickness was gone.

Galen stumbled out and ran for the trees, heedless of the rain now falling hard. He didn't stop until the camp was out of sight. He bent over, hands on his knees, and his stomach emptied again and again until his belly muscles screamed. He leaned into a tall white oak, pressing his face and body against the deep furrows of the trunk, spreading his arms, trying to embrace a circumference large enough for three men to reach around.

He wanted to sink into it. He wanted it to open and take him inside and explain what was happening to him. It was a long time before the panic subsided. He began to sense the tree-like tracings on his skin morphing back into tight scars and peeled himself away from the immense tree, anger burning the last traces of his panic.

He walked slowly back toward camp. *I can be stronger than this. I will not let my body, my self, be taken over by some force of this planet, this Adalta.* He refused to let himself feel the tingling that skittered down to his fingertips and up across his chest through his scars. *I will not be a freak, a slave to this uncanny force.* More alive than ever to the sense of the forest around him, the father-voice that lived inside him taunted: *But you are. You may no longer be the too-pretty freak extension of your father's will, but you are, none the less, a freak.*

The next afternoon the sun was heading too swiftly for mountaintops to the west. Tessa reached back to untie her sheepskin vest from behind the cantle of the saddle and twisted around to pull it on under her rain gear. ~We should head in, Kishar. It'll be dark soon, and we've been up here for hours and hours. I'm hungry. You caught a deer this morning, but I've had nothing except an apple and some bread and cheese since breakfast. And now that the wounded are mostly recovered, they are having the burial ceremony at sunset.~

She shut her eyes against the memory of what she and Kishar had found when they returned the day before, too late to do anything about the attack on the planters. *If we hadn't stopped to hunt, we might have been in time.* It hurt. The loss of so many guards and planters was an agony lodged in the muscles of her body.

~I thought I heard something growling. Your stomach?~

Tessa shook away the might-have-beens. ~Why Kishar, you made a joke.~

~Never.~

Tessa flipped up her extra set of lenses. ~My eyes are about to pop out of my head. We've seen nothing out of the ordinary all day. The circle looks even deader than usual.~

~It's too calm.~ Kishar's pathed words sounded too calm to Tessa. He was worried.

She raised her arms over her head and stretched, popping the vertebrae in her back as she arched it one way then the other.

~If you don't start warning me when you do that, you are going to get dumped one of these days, and I won't even try to catch you.~

Tessa grabbed the handle on the pommel of her saddle and clamped her legs as he flipped into a sudden turn. Her stomach lurched toward her throat. She laughed as he leveled out and headed back, away from the lowering sun just beginning to color the underside of the clouds that had dripped all day. ~You say that all the time and I've not fallen yet.~

They flew across the edge of the circle and approached the camp. ~Look, Kishar, to the south.~ A phalanx of Karda flew toward them in

SHERRILL NILSON

a close V formation, riders barely visible atop the huge winged forms. ~I've never seen so many flying together like that. There must be at least fifteen of them.~ She let out a long breath. ~Oh, they're so beautiful.~

The sun gleamed off red and gold and bronze and mahogany wings as the Karda circled and glided down toward the camp to the east, the formation never losing its tight pattern as tails tilted and wings dropped in concert to make the turn. They peeled off, one closely following the other to land in the long narrow opening in the forest near the camp, barely long or wide enough for them to lope to a stop and make way for the next.

Kishar circled high above them before he dropped swiftly and landed right in camp in time to welcome them as they trotted in. Once again, as they had in the mews in Restal Prime, as each Karda approached Kishar, they bent a knee slightly and lowered their heads in respect.

Is he their leader? I've never even heard they have a leader. But then not even the Mi'hiru knew anything about the social organization of the Karda. Not even where they came from other than in the mountains somewhere, the inaccessible mountains. The only fledglings ever seen were the two rescued by Altan Me'Gerron and Marta Rowan the year before.

Ten Karda Patrol and two Mi'hiru had arrived. She recognized Cerla on Badti and blond Steffa on Suala. Her eyes widened as she saw Guardian Daryl Me'Vere and Armsmaster, Krager. Then they opened even wider, Her muscles tensed. She spied her father's Karda, Arib.

No riders dismounted. The Karda stood like statues, eyes focused on Kishar. Tessa knew he was speaking to them, though she could hear no words. Their attention never wavered, but she could feel anger, fear, and a fierce and exultant battle-glee rising, an almost visible cloud of emotion radiating from them. Then the tension broke, and riders began to dismount, unloading supplies and pulling off rigging.

Connor Me'Cowyn wound his way through the crowd toward Tessa as soon as he'd unloaded and cared for Arib ,his big bay. "Tessa." He put his arms around her and held her tight, his head resting on top of hers. "I've been so worried about you. You took off tendays ago without even saying goodbye."

"You were so angry."

"And I still am." He patted her arm and smiled at her. "But relieved to know you are well. We'll talk after this meeting. I understand there has been an attack here, and Daryl asked me to come as a representative of Restal Council. I'll find you after. You can fly back with those of us who are leaving then." He held her away from him, hands on her shoulders, and looked her up and down. "You'll be glad for a new wardrobe after having to wear these rags for most of the season."

Tessa pushed at his chest, extricating herself from his embrace. She looked up at his face. Nothing had changed.

He looked around and laughed. "I'm sure you will be happy to be away from these crude conditions. I don't know how you managed. I suspect there will be several here glad to see you leave and no longer their responsibility. You must have made a great deal of work for someone." He patted her arm. "Go and see to that strange Karda you ride, and I'll see you later. It will be good to have you back at the hold. Aldra has missed you." He strode off to help raise a second large, communal tent near the cook's where the more seriously wounded still lay, close under the cliff that rose to the west of the camp.

Tessa swallowed. Her face felt like marble. Her body stuck in place until Almryk bumped into her, jostling her frozen statue.

He was pointing and organizing areas for saddle rigging, supplies, the area for tents among the trees. "Go see what you can do to help the new Mi'hiru settle their Karda in, would you, Tessa? I'll send someone for you when Daryl is ready for the meeting." The captain turned away to grab a rope and tie it to a stake with a taut line hitch.

Tessa watched for a few minutes and noticed Almryk avoiding Galen. But there was too much confusion for her to do more than note it. Confusion roiled both inside and outside of her. The clearing, not overly large to begin with, was going to be very crowded if all these people stayed. *What am I to do if my father is one of them? What will I do if he tries to make me go back?*

It took a couple of hours before the camp sorted itself out, and Tessa kept herself occupied with organizing the expanded mews. Then she helped Cerla raise a tent for Steffa and herself—they would be part of the reinforcements staying with the expedition—when Kishar called them away. Cerla left Steffa to finish tying their tent down.

~We must join them,~ pathed Kishar as he nudged them in the direction of the new communal tent where Daryl was settling himself at a table with Almryk, Armsmaster Krager, Galen, and her father.

Tessa made note of the guardian's shadowed eyes and a new gauntness in his body. They joined Daryl's Abala and the Armsmaster's Tarath at one side of the tent, which was large enough, if barely, for the three Karda. Obviously, they were to be part of this briefing. Tessa's steps were reluctant, unsure. She resisted the temptation to hold on to the older, stocky Mi'hiru for support.

Then she heard Kishar's voice, in the frequency she knew could be heard by all and with the unmistakable tone of a leader-who-would-be-obeyed, ~I bring the Austringer and the Kern.~

Galen jumped up and stepped away from the table, hands up, palms facing out, his face saying, No, No, No. Tessa stopped where she was, half-in, half-out of the tent, next to the retreating Galen, her face coloring with the same distress.

Her father's face turned red, and he glared at Kishar. He put his hands on the table, pushed up from the bench to start toward Tessa, but Daryl clamped a hand on his arm, forcibly holding him back.

Armsmaster Krager nodded respectfully to Kishar and said, "The others have met you, but I have not. Tarath tells me you are one to be reckoned with, one to be respected. I am Krager, armsmaster to Guardian Daryl of Restal. We are here as you asked."

As Kishar asked? Tessa looked at her Karda, bemused. *Who is he that all these people came at his call? I thought Almryk... They're treating Kishar as they would the prime guardian. Only more so.* Her thoughts scrambled. She looked at Galen, standing next to her. His face mirrored her confusion. The harsh angles of his scarred, yet still-beautiful face hardened like the sharp rocks of the cliff beyond them.

Kishar looked at Connor Me'Cowyn, who leaned on the table, half off the bench. ~Holder Me'Cowyn, if you are not used to hearing a Karda in your head—if it disturbs you too much, you may be excused.~

Connor's raised his hand to his head. Last time Kishar spoke to him when he first arrived at the Restal mews to find Tessa, the Karda's voice had knocked him out.

Tessa had never heard anyone speak to her father in such arrogant tones, as though the man were so far beneath his regard as to not matter at all. Connor's forehead creased as if the pathed words were painful but finally nodded to Kishar and sat back at the table, his face stiff and still, his shoulders tense.

Daryl looked away from Connor to Kishar. "Kishar, you know what these creatures are and where they come from. How dangerous are they? Can you give us an idea of how many there might be and how best to fight them? I have read about them in the old histories, but I thought they were destroyed in the battles when our ancestors arrived. Most people think they are nothing more than scary stories."

He ran his fingers through his hair, rubbed the back of his neck, and blew out a sharp breath. "Obviously the history books are wrong, but why have we never seen them before? Where have they been? And why are they appearing now?"

He glanced at Tessa standing at Kishar's shoulder, nodding respectfully. "You called her the Austringer when you first appeared searching for her, and you name Galen here the Kern." He gestured at Tessa and the stiff young man standing next to her. "What horrors are before us that these legends take life again?"

Harsh words broke from Galen. "I cannot be this Kern, whatever that is." He raised his hands and started to say something else, but Daryl shook his head at him. Galen backed away, body rigid, to the edge of the tent, strain pushing droplets of sweat out of his forehead. He glared at the ground in front of him as if challenging it to move. His anger pushed against Tessa. And something else. Fear. He was afraid.

"Of course, he's not. He's nothing but a planter, probably with a little Earth talent, but no breeding." A harsh note of dismissal threaded Connor Me'Cowyn's words. "Does anyone even know where he comes from? I've never heard of his family, so he can't possibly have enough talent to be the Kern."

Daryl ignored the holder, looking at Galen for a long minute, then turned back to Kishar and raised a brow. "Right now, we need cool heads and clear thoughts. And answers." Daryl had changed from the head-in-a-book young man he had been before Readen's revolt. He was growing the authority and gravitas befitting a guardian.

Kishar began. ~The circles are spreading, and here in Restal, they reach out to each other with Lines of Devastation. So far, we have seen them only here in Restal, but if we do not stop them, they will begin to reach out of other circles.~

Tessa watched each of the newcomers stir at Kishar's words, clearly puzzled at their meaning.

He went on. ~My ancestors fought these creatures, the urbat, and the ones who controlled them, the Larrak, when the Larrak arrived on Adalta centuries before your ancestors came. My ancestors were successful, but the planet was nearly destroyed, stripped of most land-based life. The aliens' ship fell into the ocean with many of the Larrak. The rest were imprisoned. Forever, we—the ancestors—thought. The Karda retreated to their home in the mountains.

~Nearly a millennia later, the Larrak's bonds eroded, and they escaped. We were forced to fight again. But the Ark Ship arrived, and this time we had your help. The legends of the human fighters Cailyn and Donnal, the Austringer and the Kern, were born. All but one of my kind were destroyed in the final battles before the last Larrak, the Itza, was imprisoned again.~

"Ah, and you are their last descendant." Awed respect infused Daryl's tone.

There was a long pause.

~No, I am he. ~

Chapter Fourteen

Almryk stood opposite the side of the table where Daryl, Krager, and Connor sat. "The urbat, that's what Kishar names them, have no organization at all, less even than a pack of wolves. The only thing that might contradict that is the fact that they went after the planters first. Given a choice between a guard and a planter, it was always the planter. But it appeared to be instinct, not planning. They didn't work together. Sometimes they attacked each other, fighting over a downed victim."

Almryk had to stop for a minute at those words. "We were forced to defend the wounded." He cleared his throat. "And the dead."

The thick silence in the tent following Almryk's words blocked Tessa's ears to everything but the fast thrum of her heartbeat. She forced herself to take deep breaths despite the tight bands clamping her chest. This might be the hardest test as Austringer she would face —it was in front of her father.

If she didn't stand fast before him, it would be a failure she could never recover from. Tessa would never have the authority she would need. She stepped toward the table. Galen moved with her, his shoulder brushing hers. She resisted the urge to grab his arm for support. *Because I think he'll break or because I think he'll break me?*

"That matches what I noticed. Three of them attacked our camp near the Line of Devastation. I killed the first two, but then I lost one of my swords."

Her voice lost its quaver. "I couldn't have gotten the second around in time to defend myself. The monster was ready to leap at me when Galen stepped out of his tent and—" She swallowed again. "It snapped around and started straight for him. Then Galen did—what he did and..."

Connor stood. "Tessa, come with me, my dear. You're upset. Two swords, indeed." He looked around at the others and laughed. No one took up the invitation to laugh with him. "I'll take you back to your tent."

Did he not even hear what I said?

"You shouldn't even be here. I told you I'd come get you after this meeting. You're too young, and you don't—"

~Do. Not. Interrupt. The Austringer.~ Kishar's words roared through the tent. It almost sounded to Tessa like he'd spoken aloud.

Connor slapped both hands to his head and dropped hard back to his seat on the crude bench.

No one moved for a full minute. The only sound was a faint groan from her father, his head down and clamped between his hands. She was afraid he might topple off the bench, but Krager steadied him. Connor finally looked up, fury building in his face, in the taut cords of his neck, in the white knuckles of his tented fingers pressed hard on the table.

"Who are you to tell me how I may treat my daughter?" The heat in his voice threatened to singe Tessa's hair even from the other side of the tent. His legendary Air talent temper was red hot and flaming.

She stepped back, bumping her shoulder into Galen, feeling Cerla press against her other side.

Tarath and Abala stood in one fluid movement on either side of Kishar, the feathers on their crests bristling.

Kishar ignored Connor's outburst. ~As Almryk and Tessa say, it is clear from the two incidents that the urbat as of now have no leader. That is good. The Itza Larrak, the last Larrak, may appear at some point, but their disorganization tells me it is not leading them yet.

Unfortunately, however, they could not have risen if the Itza Larrak were still firmly imprisoned. He has escaped the bonds put on him centuries ago.~

Connor rubbed his head again and started to stand. Both Daryl and Krager laid a hand on his shoulders, visibly forcing him down. He opened his mouth then shut it. Tessa saw Daryl's hand squeeze hard, and her father's jaw clamped as he met Daryl's eye. She shifted the sword on her hip, blew out a frustrated breath, and forced her attention back to the discussion.

Daryl spoke. "We were too late, then, when we closed the entrances to Readen's cavern. I assume that was its prison." The guardian's dismay leaked through his impassive expression, his shoulders dropped briefly then firmed again.

~There are other safeguards, but from what Marta Rowan reported, Readen may have the keys to its freedom. Whether he knows that or not is still in question. I assume your brother is safely imprisoned and closely watched?~ Kishar eyed Daryl as he pathed.

Tessa could see the pain behind Daryl's set expression. At his affirmative nod, Kishar continued. ~Thus far, only a few urbat have appeared, and we have killed many of them but with a heavy cost. There will be others. I have had no reports about urbat rising from other circles. Have you?~ He inclined his huge head toward Daryl.

Who asked, "What do you mean by rising?"

Tessa felt Galen stir. His voice was soft, his head down, eyes on the table, as the words squeezed themselves out. "They rise out of egg-like carapaces buried in the circles as if it were birthing them, even to the birth cauls they shed. They were pawing them away from their eyes."

The mix of emotions from the table would have made Tessa laugh if Galen's words weren't so shocking. Kishar cocked his head. Daryl's mouth opened then snapped shut. Krager's usually-stoic face radiated suspicion. Almryk stared straight ahead, not moving.

Disgust rolled across Connor's face and spilled through his voice as he asked, "Who is this man and why is he here?"

"You've seen them. Did you bring them?" Daryl's words to Galen were diamond across glass.

Galen's shoulder jarred Tessa when he flinched. "I didn't mean to say that out loud." He braced his hands on the table and dropped his head as if it weighed as much as his entire body. "No." His voice was muffled. "I dreamed them."

Head still down, he held his wrists out in front of him and pulled his sleeves back, uncovering his tattooed bracelets, staring at them. "I dreamed them when this happened."

The deep, sad note of resignation in his voice made Tessa want to wrap both arms around him and hold him until it went away. The tension in the room was a smoldering fireball on the verge of exploding. She felt Cerla move behind her to Galen's other side and glanced at her with gratitude. Cerla's head dipped with the slightest nod, her eyes forward on the guardian.

~He is the Kern. He knows these things without being told.~ Kishar's matter-of-fact tone snuffed the tension as if he blew out a candle.

But Galen didn't relax.

Tessa wanted to cry for him.

"How can you know this? Who are you? You've claimed my daughter as the Austringer, and now you claim this man no one knows is the Kern? Two legends come to life?" Connor's short laugh spilled scorn.

Daryl looked at Galen, head cocked to one side. "Andra told me before we left that you had the potential to be the Kern. I didn't take her seriously."

Almryk spoke up. "I don't know who he is or care what you call him, but let me tell you what he did. What I and the others in this camp witnessed." And he did. He told them of the healing, the burying, the earth moving, all of it. "And anyone who has seen Tessa shoot from Kishar's back will not doubt that she is something extraordinary."

Endless silent moments passed. Then the ordinary rustling noises of seven tired, worried, and frightened people sitting and standing around a table discussing an impossible situation no one understood started again.

Daryl swung his legs over the bench and got up to pace back and forth. "I don't think we have a choice. We must accept that they are the Austringer and the Kern and go on from here. If we don't accept it, we risk losing an important weapon against what might be coming. What is probably coming. That's the issue here. Not whether or not these two are legends come to life. Either they are or they aren't. We'll find out when the fight starts, I'm sure. And remember, Marta and Altan have the capabilities that Cailyn and Donnal had. They can both speak with all the Karda. So we have four legends come to life."

He paused and looked at Connor whose fire-red face and flared nostrils showed not a glimmer of acceptance. "The Karda Patrol and the Mi'hiru are watching the perimeters of the other circles in Restal as closely as they can and have seen nothing other than the effects of the neglect we were already aware of. The other Planter Corps expeditions are going well, if slowly. There have been no attacks or sightings reported by any villages near circles, not even a hint of anything more strange than usual. Not—" His words faltered. "Not since we imprisoned Readen."

He hides his pain well. But it's there never the less. Having a sibling should be a joy, not a torment.

Daryl continued. "I've sent Mi'hiru messengers to the guardians of the other three quadrants and to the prime guardian in Rashiba Prime as well as to Me'Bolyn and Me'Nowyk of the Coastal Holds. I've heard back from Guardian Merenya of Anuma. Apparently the Mi'hiru and Karda Patrol wings there have been closely monitoring the circles since she left Restal. They've reported nothing."

He leaned over the head of the table, hands flat. "Hugh says the same. He has also sent Mi'hiru messengers from Rashiba to the other three quadrants to alert them, but he's had no word back except from Anuma. He thinks that's good news. I'd prefer a definite no-news myself, and hopefully, that's coming. This is the only circle where urbat have been sighted."

Abruptly Almryk stood, his posture straight, at attention. "Sir. I have failed you as I failed those who were killed or wounded. I knew there was danger. I might not have known what the danger was, but you made it clear the guard would be needed here. I am tendering my resignation. I'll not leave unless that's your wish. There is still a fight to be fought. We have not seen the last of these creatures. I'm sure. But I am not fit to be the captain in charge."

The lines in his face cut deep. His eyes, as he looked straight at Daryl and then at Armsmaster Krager, were bleak, leached of feeling, his body held so taught Tessa felt any movement would crack him into pieces.

~No.~ The sorrow in Kishar's pathed words reverberated in Tessa's bones. ~If there is fault, it is mine. I knew they were rising. It is why I came for the Austringer. I did not expect them to move without the Larrak. Those losses are a weight heavy on my heart, as they are on yours, but blame does not lie at your feet.~

Daryl leaned forward with fierce certainty. "Almryk, your leadership is not to be faulted. Your courage is unquestioned. Would you deprive us of an experienced officer in the middle of a battle? I refuse your resignation. Your place is at this table. We need you."

He straightened, looked at Kishar, and continued. "I brought twelve Karda Patrol, two Mi'hiru, and two healers, all experienced. The head of our Planter Corps, Andra, has pulled more planters, all with at least some fighting skills, from the greenhouses and the other circles. They'll be here as soon as possible with more abelee trees—all she dared take away from other plantings. Guard reinforcements will be with them. Not as many as I'd like but all I can spare. What we need from you, sir is to know how best to fight these creatures. What we can expect from them."

~It is not I who will instruct your forces, but the Austringer.~

Tessa drew in a sharp breath and time slowed. She watched as puzzled faces turned by infinitesimal inches toward her. Then she focused on one angry, disbelieving face, her father's. He moved around the table toward her.

A small, hot spark lit deep in her heart as the world sped back to normal. His mouth opened, and his words began to register.

"This is ridiculous. I will not put up with this absurdity any longer. Look at what she's done to her hair, look at the unsuitable clothes she's wearing pretending to be some farcical female warrior from a fairy story. She's even wearing a sword she cannot possibly know how to use. She's trained for having children and running a household not flying around as some mythical save-the-world-warrior. She is returning this minute to Me'Cowyn Hold. I'll decide what to do with her then. This Karda, whatever it pretends to be, is forcing her into some parody of..."

Every word he spoke was louder than the last. Every word fell like another dry branch on the fire inside her blazing hotter and higher. Every doubt, every insecurity, every failed attempt to make him see her as herself fed the flames. Through a searing, blue-white haze, she saw Daryl put a hand on his shoulder, trying to hold him back.

Connor jerked away and grabbed her arm, pulling her toward the tent entrance.

She didn't move. It was as though fire forged through her body, burning away the dross and leaving white-hot steel. She twisted away from his grasp and shoved him, hard.

"I am no longer your daughter." She heard her words ring loud, like a fire bell. "I am the Austringer."

She looked around at a frozen tableau of shocked faces. She focused on Galen's. The scar on his face shimmered briefly into the tripartite abelee leaf, pale green, sharp and clear.

"I am the Austringer." She shoved a finger in his chest. "And you. You are the Kern. You cannot deny it. Together we fight the urbat. Together we defeat the urbat. Together we choke off the Lines of Devastation that threaten to strangle Adalta."

She moved to stand by Kishar, ignoring her father's shouted, "Come back here now!"

Tessa stood, breathing hard as a protective circle of Karda formed around her. The laws of Restal were clear on the rights of holders. They had absolute control over their inhabitants, and that included, especially, family. Her father had, by law, the right to force her to leave with him. Disowning him as her father meant nothing to him.

Daryl and her father argued—or rather, her father shouted, and Daryl argued—outside the formidable guard of Karda surrounding her.

"You can't stop me. I will take her home. She is mine. My family, my property under the laws of Restal. Now, let me through."

"Connor, do you think you can fight your way through to her. Look at what is in front of you."

The Karda guarding Tessa, including Me'Cowyn's Arib, stood like stones, crests raised, wings mantled, all eyes on the angry man.

"And remember the most ancient law, the first law we were given as colonists here—the rule of the Karda is absolute. It's too easy to forget that because it is so seldom invoked. We too often think of them as ours to command. But they serve us at their pleasure and by their laws. We do not control them."

~Clearly the holder has forgotten those laws. He's forgotten that Karda must be asked, not commanded.~ Kishar's words were as soft in her mind as the sudden silence from the two men was sharp. Tessa could hear her father's harsh breathing as he assimilated Daryl's words and fought to control himself—a too-seldom used skill.

"By Kishar's naming her Austringer, and by her acceptance of that, she is outside the human laws of Adalta. That's what those half-forgotten legends teach." Daryl's voice was low and insistent, calm and forceful.

"She is no longer simply your daughter. You can choose to ignore that and continue to try to force her home, or you can choose to accept and be proud that a daughter of yours has accepted the mantle of the Austringer. Come back to the tent, have some food, and think about it. You will do no good here, and you could well alienate the Karda entirely. You do not want to do that. Think, Connor, think."

He put his hand on Connor's shoulder. "Think about what is important here. It's the urbat. The fight against these monsters. You can choose to be ruled by your pride and court disaster or extend that pride to honor your daughter and her part in this fight."

Next morning Galen slipped away in the confusion of Daryl's party's departure and the Mi'hiru and patrol reinforcements getting settled, saddled his horse, and rode toward the site of the massacre. He was halfway there before he realized he hadn't asked directions—that he hadn't needed to.

The further he rode, the quieter the forest became. Damp leaves muffled his horse's hoof beats. No birdsong, no rustling of rabbit or fat, roly birbir in the undergrowth, no rustling of leaves. Galen didn't even notice as his horse slowed from canter to trot to walk, stopped, and dropped his head to crop the green grass where the sun reached through the trees surrounding them.

His thoughts were not-thoughts. They were a whirl of confusion and denial as he tried not to face the strange facts of what was happening to him. What had been happening since the fire that so horribly scarred him.

But denial was no longer possible, and he had to admit the confusion was self-made—in fact, it was less confusion than stubbornness. Galen didn't want to call it cowardice. His thoughts were stuck on the threshold of choice.

He could choose to return to the ship. He was of no more use here as an agent—too many people in power knew who he was, and he had lost the respect he would need to be a negotiator between ship and planet.

If he made that choice, his strange wrist tattoos might disappear. His scars would stay just that, simply scars. He might never experience the terrifying changes to his body again. The strange and powerful abilities Galen didn't want to claim might disappear. The new and unexplainable knowledge about plants and soils filling his head might fade.

He might be normal again. He didn't think his father could ever rule him as he had in the past. That hold was broken.

But fight against it though he had, the door to caring, to feeling, had cracked open and wouldn't easily close again. Doors that locked as a child when he discovered his mother had died on a hostile planet and no one told him for months. And if that door didn't close, how would he ever survive on-ship? With his overbearing, cold, autocratic father, broken hold or not.

He reached back into the small pack strapped behind the cantle of his saddle and pulled out his Cue. His gelding's head lifted, and he snorted softly then went back to tearing at the grass. Galen shifted in the saddle, turning the unit over and over in his hand, staring at it. He wished he could talk to Marta.

If what was happening to Galen was anything like what happened to her, how had she kept her sanity? How had she reconciled her honor with the change in her loyalties? He supposed he could call her a turncoat, a traitor. His father certainly would when he discovered her bond with Altan was not just the political ploy he'd asked for. Traitor. Turncoat.

He shivered at the very thought of the words. They might be used to describe him, but he could never use them to describe Marta. She was too honorable. Her choice would have been made for her when she discovered the smuggled guns.

His eyes clenched shut. Kayne Morel might be able to accept that from Marta. It would mean questions about his management of her father's estate would be moot if she didn't return to the ship. No one would even care. But if Galen's loyalties shifted, there was a place deep inside him that knew, however much he wanted to deny it, that his father would not hesitate to have him imprisoned on the ship—or killed.

Kayne Morel would never be able to admit that his son had deserted him, so the death would be an accident. His father was so good at lying, even to himself, he could probably twist his mind into believing it was. But Galen would still be dead.

A vision of Tessa, raggedy silver halo of hair flying around her head as she and Kishar soared up through the trees, pushed its way to the front of his thoughts. He would never see her again if he went back to the ship.

But if he stayed on Adalta, she could never be his. She was a holder's daughter. Holders were the closest thing to an aristocracy this planet had, one step down from guardians. No matter their differences, ultimately, she was Me'Cowyn's only heir. Galen could never reach that high. His mouth twisted, stretching his scars. *Even if I am some legendary hero of old.*

Despite what the others said, despite the strange things he'd done, he couldn't believe he had what they called talent. It was hard enough to believe that such magic existed, much harder to accept that he could have it.

Leather creaked as he eased back in the saddle, crossing a leg over the pommel, and flipped the unit open. When the ship dispatcher answered, he immediately transferred Galen to his father.

"Where are those samples? Have you managed to get them somewhere remote so we can pick them up?"

"I am well, Father. And you?"

"Where are they and what's their composition? Crystalline? Some unknown organic compound? How easily mined? My intuition is telling me this is an extremely valuable find. I must have the samples. Every drone sent to gather them failed to return. You must get them for me."

"I don't know the answers to any of those questions. I was able to gather several samples—a dark, heavy material that could be an allotrope of carbon—and that's the last I remember. When I woke up, someone had found me, disposed of the minerals, and told me I nearly died." That part was true.

"I'm not trying again." That was also true. "If you want them, you'll have to send someone with haz protection. And it better be the best. The stuff is beyond dangerous." Again, true.

"Could it be used in weapons?"

"How would I know that? I barely remember collecting it, and I certainly didn't have the time or the equipment to analyze it. I was dying. And we don't make weapons, remember? You're already pushing things by smuggling in the weapons you have. Making new ones out of something we don't understand would bring the Federation down on us like a massive solar flare. If you think you have problems now, just try it. It will be worse than someone discovering the money you stole from Marta."

Kayne ignored that last statement. He was getting even better at ignoring questions and facts that didn't fit the plans he had choreographed. Desperation leaked into his voice. "If you couldn't get samples from those veins, how about samples from those circle areas? Did you get those?"

Using his most patient tone, one he knew infuriated his father,

Galen paced his words slowly in an I-know-you're-stupid-but-even-you-should-understand-this tone. "Father, those veins are offshoots of the circles. If they are so toxic, think how much more toxic the circles must be. I am not about to venture there. They are deadly."

"Well, what use are you to me where you are now? Get yourself reassigned somewhere closer to civilization and get back to me. The Planter Corp is no longer a useful cover for you. I'll have Merrik arrange to meet the team I'll send to gather the samples we need. With all the right equipment. Yes, I heard you about the toxicity. They'll be well protected. As soon as you get back to what they call civilization there, find Merrik. He knows where the akenguns are hidden. You can get them to Readen's supporters. And try not to lose this shipment, too."

And the Cue went dead. Kayne's disembodied words remained frozen shards of ice in Galen's head.

He propped his elbows on his crossed leg and dropped his head into his hands, resting his forehead against the closed Cue. He'd avoided making any irretrievable choice and sent his father off on a tangent before he could think to make more demands.

How long did he have before he was forced to make his choice? Or it was made for him? Not long. He slid his feet back into the stirrups and headed for the site of the massacre.

He rode through tall hardwoods and conifers that gradually grew shorter and younger, the under-story trees and bushes thicker until he finally reached the first of the abelee trees. His nose pinched against the same stench he'd smelled in the tent of the wounded.

The gelding shied and danced, refusing to go further. Galen dismounted, slipped the bit from the horse's mouth, and tied the reins to a tree, giving it grazing room. He hoped it would still be there when he got back.

Trampled grass made a clear path to the edge of the circle. Tools, barrows, saplings were flung everywhere, ripped and shredded. The stench was awful. He crooked his arm up in front of his face and buried his mouth and nose in the inside of his elbow, breathing shallowly. He counted twenty-three dead urbat, dark mounds on the torn-up ground marred by rusty spots of dried blood and thick strings of amber ichor.

He knelt and put his hands on the ground. When Tessa was attacked, he'd buried the monsters unconsciously. And he'd buried his arms to the elbow in the earth. No one was here to dig him out this time.

Nothing happened. For a long time, nothing happened. Not even the ants-under-the-skin feeling in his scars. He rocked back on his heels and put his hand over his nose and mouth, taking short, shallow breaths.

He stood and flexed one cramped leg at a time, shook out his hands and tried to remember what he'd done before. He'd only been half-conscious—if that. It was Galen's terror for Tessa that moved him then.

He walked around the clearing, hand clamped over his nose. The same dark miasma that had welled out of the wounded lay in a thin noxious layer on the ground. Thicker above the blood and ichor and around the scattered bodies of the urbat.

Why did he think he needed to do this? To bury these creatures? It wasn't just the smell. Planters could recover the tools and saplings and leave the grotesque bodies to decay. Or guards could be dispatched to burn or bury them. He walked away, west, toward the Circle of Disorder.

A mild wind blew from the south, carrying away the stench as he neared the desolation. He walked until the toes of his boots nudged the very edge of the circle, closer than he had ever been. He didn't feel sick like he should have. A dust devil swirled in his direction, roiling the surface as it veered sharply away and passed along the circle's verge.

He stared across the barren ground. A few small, grey, twisted bushes grew in isolated clusters. Outcroppings of dark, dull, angular rocks broke the surface here and there. It was as if the circle were an alien, living thing. A grotesque, ugly, torturous cancer feeding its way into the surface of Adalta.

Galen ran his gaze around the edge of the ugliness, along the row of newly planted abelee saplings. Abruptly his vision shifted as if it changed dimensions, and he could see the ugliness shrink away from the rapidly growing roots anchored in clean soil—fingerlings spreading out into the circle. Tiny straw-like cilia sucked up the poison, wicked it away the same way he moved the sickness from the wounded. Cleansed it. Drew it up to be transformed into leaf and branch. Fed on it like beneficent parasites consuming the disease that festered on the body of Adalta.

He took a few steps into the roiling dust. Then another. Then another. He didn't feel sick. He felt protected, as if he were inside a bubble of health in the midst of the sickness. His strange focus moved further across the circle, following the beaten path the urbat had taken. It was as though the disorder became transparent.

His vision finally stopped—he couldn't tell how far away—on a disrupted patch where large, empty carapaces lay scattered on the surface. The discarded shells of the urbat. Two of them were still buried partway in the ground, not empty. Two misshapen monsters, half in and half out of the shells, had died aborning.

He whirled and ran out of the circle, running until he reached the site of the massacre, muscles quivering and cramping, his heart beating as if he'd run for kilometers. He collapsed to his knees, hands rubbing at his eyes, afraid to open them again. He knelt there for a long time until his heart and his breath slowed, and his mind cleared.

Opening his eyes the merest slit, all he saw was the green grass beneath him. Nothing more. He sat back on his heels and looked around. His vision was normal. The sight was ugly—the clearing marred by the bodies of the urbat, blood, and ichor and the strange dark miasma—but it was normal. He could only see the surface.

He took a deep breath and choked on the stench. That was a mistake. But he could clean this up. He had to. Hands on the cool green grass, he drew on the power pulsing in his wrist tattoos. He gathered it in as if he were reaping grain from a lush, ripe field. Hands flat, he pushed.

His scars fired as the design of root and branch spread out from his wrist tattoos, down his fingers, up his arms, across his chest. His cheek burned as the ridged scar morphed into the trefoil abelee leaf symbol. Glowing green and gold rootlets spread from the tips of his fingers down through the grass into the ground.

This time he felt it, felt himself pushing the wave of healing toward the dead urbat. Felt himself controlling it, directing it until all twenty-three grotesque bodies were nothing but humps of green grass. The blood—gone. The ichor—gone. The stench and the miasma—gone.

Grass with the shining sheen of new growth covered the clearing—now littered with metal scales, rods, pulleys, gears—all the pieces of the urbat's metal skeletons, cleansed.

He leaned back on his heels and shook his hands free of the dirt that clung to them. Oh, blessed mysteries of the far-flung stars. He filled himself with the sweet scent of new grass, with the soft clattering tune of abelee leaves singing in the breeze, with the wet, cool smell of clean, fertile earth.

I am the Kern. I am the Kern.

He rolled over and lost the contents of his stomach.

Chapter Fifteen

The heavy canvas bag clanked as Galen dropped it in front of Tessa's tent. "I don't know why you were collecting the metal parts of the urbat, but I brought you these." His voice came out controlled, harsh as the rough bark of an oak. "Kishar told everyone you and I know how to fight these monsters. Maybe one of you should tell me, so I don't look a fool when someone asks me what to do. And I'd like you to tell me about talent."

His lips were so stiff he didn't know how he got the words out. His voice rasped. His mouth was dry. He cleared his throat. He wanted to tell her who he was. He looked away from her as if it would be easier if he didn't see her face. "I need to ask Kishar what he's done to me. Why —how—I can do what I did in the clearing when I woke up and saw the urbat attacking you." His words snapped in the air like dry twigs.

He looked back, his next words a rough whisper. "I need to understand what's happening to me so I can use it."

Tessa reached down carefully as if she were afraid he'd shatter if she touched him and picked up the heavy bag. "Let's take these to the blacksmith. I do know what to do with them." She moved around him, and after a minute he followed, his stride stiff, his body tight, not moving with his usual easy grace. "I'm not the best person to tell you about talent."

He winced.

She looked down, her shoulders tight. She crossed her arms around the heavy bag and curled over it. "It has nothing to do with you and everything to do with me."

Galen knew what those words meant. He'd used them, trite though they were. Just another blow for him to take.

Neither spoke again until they reached the canopy over the hot forge where Beryl was shaping a horseshoe. He was a short man, with a round, unlined face, and a massive chest. Sleeves pushed back on arms pocked with scars from the forge fires. Tessa set the sack down, and they waited for him to finish.

Cold tension stiffened Galen—a counter to the heat of the fiery beats of the blacksmith's hammer on hot iron. He breathed in the hot smell, hoping it would defrost him.

Beryl gave the shoe a last couple of taps and dunked it in the barrel of oily water next to his anvil. Steam billowed and hissed. He dropped the horseshoe in a bin of others and turned a crinkle-eyed grin on Tessa. "Brought me a love gift, have you, Tessa? You're finally comin' round to admit your strong feelin's for me, are you?"

"I can't hide them any longer, Beryl. If it weren't that I'm deathly afraid of your wife, I'd be putty in your hands."

Her easy banter caught Galen by surprise. What had made her so tense? Was it him? He stuffed all his tension behind one of the screens he'd perfected over the years—the affable one, not the cold, arrogant one—and plugged his seeping tension leak.

"Come in out of the wet, darlin'. I see you brought along a protector." Beryl stuck out a surprisingly small hand for such a big man and grasped Galen's forearm. "Galen, lad. Loosen. It's all in fun. We need a little fun around here before things get even worse. And they will. They always do."

"You're such an optimist, Beryl. It's a pleasure to be around you. I could almost lose my pessimism if I weren't so attached to it. I hope you know what to do with Tessa's treasure. She's keeping what she knows to herself, so you'll probably have to play the guessing game before she lets us know her secret."

Beryl pulled a blue metal gear out of the bag, tossing it lightly from one hand to the other, measuring its weight. Then he held it up close to his eyes, sniffed at it, and stuck his tongue out to taste it.

"Don't do that." Galen's words came out sharp, like a slap.

Beryl almost dropped the metal. He looked up, his good-natured face serious. "And why not?" His tone was soft, curious, and there was a note of sadness as he studied the gear. "Is this what I think it is?"

"If you think it's part of an urbat, then, yes. It is."

"I don't think I want to know how you got these." He looked to Tessa. "These are like what you brought me earlier?"

"I know what to do with them now, Beryl. Spearheads, arrowheads, and somehow, you have to figure out how to put an edge of this metal on our swords. The urbat are hard to kill. This metal will make it easier. Especially for people who aren't trained to fight."

Both men looked at her.

She looked back at them, open hands spread in an are-you-that-dumb motion. "There are lots of villages near circles."

Galen figured Beryl didn't want to think about that any more than he did. The blacksmith tossed the gear in one hand, looking at Tessa, his face grim. "Won't ask how you know. All this Austringer and Kern stuff is beyond me. I'm just a horse-shoer and wheelwright. Don't have the right talent to be much of a machinist. Arrowheads and spearheads I can manage. And I'll try modifying a sword or two, but you may have to send them to the prime to a master metalsmith for that. I don't think I have the skill or the knowledge."

"Do you have the equipment?" Tessa asked.

"Aye. It isn't equipment I lack, but I'm no swordsmith. And that's what it will take, I'm afraid. Sorry to disappoint you, lass. But...." He tossed the metal piece toward the sack and spread his hands wide. "You'll have your arrowheads and spear points as fast as I can make them. They'll be razor sharp. And I'll try working on a sword."

They left him looking through the bag of metal, a hard look on his face. Those dead and wounded planters and guards had been his friends, too. "I have family in one of those villages." His last words so soft Galen barely heard them.

"Let's find Kishar and see if we can answer some of your questions." Tessa grabbed Galen's hand then dropped it just as fast.

Oh, no, no, no. The heat of her hand burned, and his face flushed. She marched ahead of him to where Kishar lay, eyes half closed, drowsing under the big canopy the Mi'hiru had erected as a temporary mews. They stopped short of where he rested, hesitant to disturb him. Sometimes, not often, but sometimes, Galen could sense his age and a haunting ancient sorrow about him.

Kishar looked up, blinking open his secondary eyelids, and nodded at them. "You have come with questions, Kern."

Tessa dropped to a cross-legged position at Kishar's shoulder. Galen stood, feet apart as if braced for something unpleasant, then forced his posture into that of the planter with nothing more on his mind than digging holes and sticking saplings in them. He pulled on the mantle of his role like a well-worn shirt. He was so used to wearing a role he wasn't sure there was a real Galen.

He looked around, making certain no one was near enough to hear their conversation, his shoulders hunched just the slightest bit. His voice felt forced as if it came from a great distance inside him. "What am I, Kishar? What am I becoming? I can move earth with little more than a thought. I can see—"

He stopped, his face a shifting, tortured mask. "I can see inside the circle. I can see what's under the surface. I can see the roots of the abelee trees moving in the ground. I can stand closer to the circle than anyone and not get sick. I'm going insane."

Galen stalked away from them and stood—not noticing the drizzle starting to fall. Fists pressed hard against his thighs, he took several deep breaths and walked back as if pushing against a wall. "I am not who you think I am, and this is not the first world I have been on. I was born in space somewhere on a trade ship which has been home to my family all the way back to the diaspora."

His words came faster and faster as if he were expelling poison from his body. "My ancestors were among those who refused to leave their Ark Ships when they arrived at the planets meant to be their homes. They became trade ships traveling between planets." His eyes looked back and forth from Tessa to Kishar.

Then, his words slower, automatic: "Many got so used to life on the ships—their journeys took generations—they virtually couldn't leave. It's a kind of agoraphobia. They can't bear the openness of life on planet. They panic."

He stopped, narrowed his eyes at Kishar. "You knew." He didn't think his shoulders could hold any more tension. His arms were stiff. Fists clenched so tight they ached.

~Yes, I knew, Kern. ~

Galen looked around at everything but Tessa and Kishar, his mouth opened, closed again. He started to scrub at his hair then his hand dropped back to fist at his side again.

"You knew." It was as if his body collapsed in on itself as he dropped to sit, cross-legged, at Kishar's head. His voice came out harsh, accusatory, as if he couldn't forgive the Karda for knowing who he was.

Neither Tessa nor Kishar responded. Galen sat, his face hidden in his hands. His back curled in a stiff arch of shame and sorrow. He couldn't make himself tell them more. About the weapons. About conspiring with Readen.

He looked up. "So how can I be what you need me to be? I am alien to this planet. As alien as those circles and the monsters that created them. How can I have talent? I can't be this Kern you call me." He was so very tired of this struggle. Tired of the guilt that rode him with a too-tight harness.

~Kern.~ Kishar's pathed voice cut into Galen like the honed edge of a sword. ~I have known what you are since your boots touched the surface of Adalta when your shuttle set you down with the weapons you were smuggling to Readen.~

Galen raised one hand, his mouth open to speak. But he couldn't.

~You are the most potent Earth talent in five hundred years. What you are has slept inside your self-built emotional cage for long enough. That cage burned away with the fire that scarred you. Now you must choose. Will you step out from the ashes of your cage or will you be like those of your kind who are unable to leave the constrained safety of their ships for the freedom of life on-planet? It is your choice. Do you remain on Adalta and become what Adalta needs? What you are meant to be? Or do you return to your ship and rebuild your cage to fit the half-life that will be all that you have?~

Emotion tore endlessly through Galen—fear, doubt, anger, resentment for what he had become. What he had forced himself to be to avoid feeling, to avoid knowing himself as the failure of a human being that he was. And after a long moment—hope. Then he folded. His body and his shell collapsed. He leaned forward, knees so close to Tessa's he felt their warmth. He couldn't look at her face, or the disbelief and disillusion he was sure were there.

"Tell me about talent. Help me learn about what I am." His voice was soft, supplicating, thick with feeling he didn't know how to express. If he had ever hoped for her regard, that hope was gone now. She knew him for what he was.

She was silent for so long he was afraid she wasn't going to answer. He looked up to see something— acknowledgment, perhaps, then something like distress. Tessa swallowed. Finally, her voice even and calm, she spoke. "I told you I'm not the best person to teach you. The reason I am Austringer is that my talents are blocked. They have been since I was seven. My father would be more than angry to know that I've told you this, so please, don't tell anyone."

Galen was astonished to see shame in her expression. His thoughts turned from himself to her. He half reached for her hand then drew back. She was wounded, too. Maybe, just maybe, they could help each other. The thought of helping someone else with no ulterior motive was so foreign to him his heart fluttered like a hawk caged so long he couldn't recognize an open door.

"That's the reason I can safely fly over the circles. People get sick near them, I think, because something sucks talent out of them. I'm not sure why you don't get sick when you work closer than the other planters. Possibly because you are so strong, and your emotional blocks have made shielding automatic for you. Or because Kishar says your Earth talent is less a channel for power to move through as it is a great reservoir that you can draw from."

He watched as, head down, she folded her hands together in her lap, clasping them so tightly they surely hurt. "How can I teach you about what I don't have? What I want so desperately without bitterness scouring my tongue?"

I'm not the only one who is confused about what is happening. The thought somehow helped. He leaned forward as she began to talk, her voice a breath of whisper he had to strain to hear.

"Talent is the elemental power we draw from Adalta. The elements of Water, Earth, and Air. It's my understanding that all three of your channels are stronger than ordinary, though your Water and Air channels don't come near what your Earth channel is. It is so strong you scarcely need to try to draw power. It is just in you. You would have to work hard not to have it. You've done something with it that's..."

She hesitated. "Frankly, I think it's frightened you. What happened?"

For the first time since he'd brought her the bag of urbat metal, tension drained out of Galen's shoulders. His grin felt lopsided with relief, and he tentatively allowed her a glimpse of what he thought might be the real Galen beneath his protective mask—the person he hadn't seen in a long time. He drew up one knee and propped a forearm on it, fingers playing with a long stem of grass. "I've never been so scared before in my life. And I've been in some pretty scary situations. But there was always something I could fight. This time what scares me comes from inside me."

"I know you pulled the urbat sickness out of the wounded, and I saw what you did to the urbat that attacked me. What else has happened?"

Galen looked back and forth between Tessa and Kishar, shifted off the rock jabbing into his butt, rubbed at the frown lines on his forehead. His usual careful remoteness dissolved, and he didn't know what to do with his hands.

Finally, he held them in front of him, palms down, staring at the scars and the tattoo on his wrists. "I stood with my toes nearly in the circle for a long time. The longer I stood there, the more I could see. See into the circle. As if it were transparent. I felt no sickness—even when I walked some distance inside. I still don't. Then I went back and buried the urbat and retrieved all their metal parts."

He looked straight at Kishar and in a belligerent tone said, "And I don't know how I did it. The first time I tried, nothing happened. But when I came back from the circle, I scarcely needed to try. I just pushed, and I don't know if I could do it again because"—his voice was loud, almost a shout—"I don't know what I did."

Tessa gave him time, bringing her knees up and clasping her hands around them. When he looked back, she started again, her tone even and calm. "I think we need to start with the basics. I can tell you about the talents, what they can do—or rather, what you might be able to do with them, and Kishar can lead you in grounding and connecting exercises. That's not something I can help you with." She kept her head down, hiding her expression from him, speaking to the ground.

"Everyone has talent. The strength of talent and the way in which it expresses is unique to each individual. I'll give you the short list. Air talent—telepathy, clairvoyance, clairaudience, weather sensing, sometimes weather control, though there are strict rules about that. Sword work and archery draw on Air talent as well as Earth. An Air talent can set privacy shields and truth-telling spells. It is necessary in forming disguises."

Galen started at that. How helpful that could be—would have been. He shook his head and made himself listen again.

"A very strong Air talent can create an invisibility shield—it's helpful to have either Water or Earth for that to work well. All Mi'hiru have Air talent—no one is picked by Karda without a strong Air channel. When combined with Earth, it is what allows you to create and control fire, heat magma stones. Exceptionally strong talents can throw fire bolts. And you don't want to get in the way of one of those."

Tessa shifted, crossing her legs again, hands clasped tight in her lap. "Water talent—healing, and of course, control of streams both above and below ground, water-witching, rain- and weather-sensing." She stopped and cleared her throat. "All healers are strong in Water. The best ones have a good bit of Earth and sometimes Air, too. Empathic senses, foretelling. And no Mi'hiru is chosen who doesn't have a strong empathic sense. That's how they communicate with the Karda. Only a few of those chosen by a Karda can speak telepathically, but with Water and Air, they communicate, as I understand it, using empathy and projected images.

"Good farmers have a mix of Water talent and strong Earth. Earth talent can bring an innate sense of growing things and the ability to encourage and foster growth in plants.

"You already know you can move the ground. That's useful in mining—most of the workers in the mines have Earth." She looked up for the first time since she started talking. "All of the Planter Corps have Earth. The more Earth, the more successful the farmer or planter. It helps in weapons work—especially the martial arts hands-on fighting. A strong Earth talent who grounds herself simply can't be overthrown without someone getting hurt. An Earth-Air combination is necessary for good sword work. And of course, it's necessary to create fire, from lighting a lamp or candle to the extreme of tapping the heat core of Adalta. That takes someone incredibly powerful in both Earth and Air. Like Altan Me'Gerron, Daryl, or the prime guardian. They can throw fire bolts, but Uncle Hugh can tap the magma core almost at will."

She pulled her knees to her chest and wrapped her arms around them again. "Each person has his unique blend of talents, strengths, and what they can do with them, and we are taught from childhood not only how but also the ethics of using them. Experts spend years studying the three talents, what they can do, and how they can be combined."

She went still then shrugged her shoulders. "That's a nutshell description of something far more extensive and incredibly complicated than what I've told you." She looked away but not before Galen glimpsed the pain embedded deep inside her.

"I'm sorry. You can't have much sympathy for my struggles against the very thing you have lost." He reached out a hand to touch her knee.

Tessa stood so quickly Galen almost fell backward.

"I need to—" And she was gone.

Chapter Sixteen

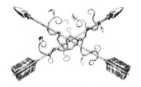

~Galen.~ Kishar's sharp tone hit Galen's wandering thoughts like a gale-force wind scouring grit from the side of a mountain.

"Ouch." He rubbed his head. "That hurt." *Oh, for the days when I still thought telepathy was impossible.*

~I do not know what planet your thoughts were on, but it was not this one. To paraphrase one of ancient Earth's more astute statesmen, you have nothing to fear but fear itself. Connecting yourself to Adalta is not going to hurt, and you are not going to get lost.~ His crisp diction was even more pronounced than usual, an indication of his frustration at three days of Galen's lack of success. ~I won't allow it.~

"That has not been my experience so far." Galen rubbed his arms and flexed his fingers, remembering the all too often times the connection to Adalta had knocked him to his knees.

~She was trying to get your attention—to break through walls you have spent too many years building to protect yourself. That is the only reason you have the power to do what you have done in the past few days. But that power is not going to last forever. You are going to have to learn to replenish it. Grounding and connecting to Adalta is the only way to avoid those painful experiences. And you will continue to have them if you do not learn soon.~

Throttling down what he recognized just in time as an adolescent huff, Galen temporized. "How do you know ancient earth sayings"""

~Daryl likes to read to Abala.~

Galen fixed his gaze on an abelee tree and concentrated on the twirling leaves singing their chattering song on the slight breeze, feeling his way through the silver-white branches, down the trunk, into the roots. He could see the way they connected to the trees around them, grafting a net that surrounded and contained the circle, transmuting its malevolence.

Not letting himself get lost in those connections again, he felt for the soil around them, sending his attention down past the broad mat of grass and tree roots, down through the soil, into the bedrock. He rested there, sensing the streams of water, from tiny trickles to torrents, that filtered from the surface to feed the aquifer a thousand meters below.

And finally, the connection to Adalta surged through him. He stripped off his shirt, uncurled from his cross-legged position, and stretched out prone, arms and legs spread, face and chest scars pressed into the thick grass beneath the trees.

He sucked the scent of damp earth in through his nose. Power flared, wrapping around his wrists, tethered him, flowed through his scars, and flooded into his body from the planet beneath him. He sensed the streams of water that ran through Adalta like its life-blood.

All separateness from the planet disappeared. He felt the burrowing of earthworms. He felt the infinite movements of micro-organisms in the soil, the patient, inexorable push of growing roots. His blood was the water that streamed through Adalta, the oceans that covered most of her surface. His breath flowed with the immense clouds, heavy with moisture, overhead. His bones resonated with the tectonic shifts deep below her surface. For an eternity.

Slowly, the ants-under-the-skin tingling in his scars and a persistent needle-like pain in the tattoos around his wrists surfaced in his mind, forcing him back into his body. He rolled over to his back, brushing grass off his chest, staring up through the fluttering leaves of the abelee trees. A mist-laden breeze touched his face, and he blinked, breathing deeply. Thoughts echoed in his mind as if they came from a long distance. He didn't want to think. He wanted to drift forever in the immensity that was Adalta.

He lifted his arm. The tree branch tattoos faded. His scars reappeared. His tattooed wristbands were darker and moved and twisted as he looked at them. His fingers brushed across the puckered skin of the scar on his cheek.

He turned his head and looked up at the fierce head of the Karda next to him. ~Does anyone ever get so lost in Adalta they don't come back?~ He wasn't even startled that he was pathing, not speaking aloud for the first time. ~I am heavy as the planet and light as the clouds over our heads.~

He felt Kishar's deep chuckle and sat up, brushing grass out of his hair. ~Tessa said I would need to draw power. I don't know what that means. It didn't feel like drawing up anything. It felt...it felt as though I were Adalta.~

~You are the Kern. No one else could know how it would feel to you. You had to experience it yourself.~ The big Karda blinked his under-eyelids slowly and turned his head away.

After a while, he said, ~Others do have to draw power consciously. Apparently, you do not. When I look inside you, I do not see channels. I see three great reservoirs of pure power. Air, Earth, and Water, and the reservoir for Earth is immense. I think your scars, your tattoos, enable you to store power inside you. I knew the moment you finally connected. Adalta trembled with her gratitude.~ He was silent for a long time.

Galen lay back, one knee cocked up, his hands behind his head, looking up at the pale green chattering leaves above. Then he heard the light whisper of Kishar's voice in his head. ~It was an honor to be present for this, your full integration with Adalta, Kern.~

Tessa watched through the trees as the glowing green-gold tendrils reached up from the ground and surrounded Galen in a fine net that pulsed with his breath, growing stronger and brighter. It hovered above his prone body for a long time, then disappeared into him. He lay still for a long time before he finally rolled over to speak with Kishar.

It hurt. It didn't matter that it had taken him days to connect. That he'd had to work so hard. Fighting the envy his connection to Adalta aroused in her was hard. And it hurt. Kishar had all but abandoned her while he worked with Galen.

Tessa stopped herself from stomping back to her tent like an angry, itchy, medgeran growling its way out of winter hibernation. She pulled Kishar's saddle rig out and hauled it over to the Karda's mews tent. Dropping it to the ground in a heap, she rummaged for saddle oil and a couple of rags in the box of supplies. She started wiping the leather down, letting the straps out to the longer length required for Llalara, the Karda substituting for Kishar while he worked with Galen..

Knowing she was reacting like a two-year-old didn't help. Knowing working with Galen was something Kishar had to do didn't help. Knowing other people spent their entire childhoods studying the talent manipulation he was trying to learn in a few days—their entire lives if they had anything approaching his talent strength—didn't help. Knowing only Kishar was strong enough to contain the wild explosions of power that escaped as Galen tried learning control didn't help. She scrubbed at the broad breast strap with enough ferocity to burn holes in the thick leather. That didn't help either.

"I think you have that strap defeated, Tessa."

The cool humor in Cerla's tone didn't help either. Cerla was one of those people so uniquely homely they are beautiful. She carried her stocky body both with the assurance of the beautiful and with the ease of one who knows she's not and doesn't care. Glad as Tessa had been to see her when she arrived with the other Mi'hiru, sometimes Cerla's sharp humor and too-sharp insight irritated her. And that didn't help either.

"We need to rig up. It's time for our patrol."

Tessa rubbed a hand across her forehead, leaving a sticky, oily trail she then had to clean off with nothing to use but the less oily of the two rags.

"I think you have time to wash up, and I'm sure Llalara will appreciate it if you do."

Tessa stifled the impulse to snap at Cerla. Not only did the Mi'hiru sound amused, but Tessa could also hear sympathy in her voice. Rage wove a tight, hot band around her head. She closed her eyes, took a deep breath, then another. The situation wasn't Cerla's fault. It wasn't even Galen's. Or Kishar's. They hadn't caused her loss of talent. She walked to the back of the mews tent, poured hot water into a bowl from the kettle hanging over the small pile of glowing magma stones and washed her hands and face. The sharp scent of lavender in the soap penetrated her fog of anger and self-pity. A vision of her father in one of his rages flashed.

I'm acting like him. I don't need to add that shame to this depressing bouquet of self-pity. She straightened, took a deep breath, and let it out through pursed lips. She had a circuit to fly, people to protect. Self-pity was too heavy a burden to carry and too dense a cloud to fly through.

"We'll fly the north quadrant this afternoon, Cerla." She looked up as the four Karda and riders of the last patrol circled down and landed, cantering to the mews. "Unless someone has sighted something that needs watching. They aren't in a hurry to come in, so they probably haven't."

Llalara's long cantering take-off didn't even provoke Tessa's usual impatience as they cleared the tall red oaks at the end of the runway. Their leaves were starting to show russet at their edges, and she watched a few loose ones fly as Cerla and Badti rose up ahead of them. The little sorrel Karda with white-barred wings and tail headed north, Cerla a dot on his back. Tessa shifted in the saddle as Llalara leveled off. Her legs still felt stretched and achy. Llalara was almost half again bigger than Kishar. But Tessa felt light. Lighter than she had in days.

She closed her eyes and let the mist-laden breeze cool her face and her mind. Patrolling from the edge of the circle and not too close for the Karda's safety required far more attention than flying directly over it on Kishar, though she trusted Llalara's experience.

She flipped down the extra lens on her goggles and blinked as her focus adjusted. It had been more than a tenday since the urbat attack, and there had been no other sightings. The surface of the circle, while it could never be called calm, was at least clear of any movement other than the constant roiling of dust. Here and there, stunted scrub and warped trees with scant leathery grey-green leaves moved and twisted —illusions caused by the swirling dust.

She grabbed the pommel handle as Llalara ended a long, circling rise up a thermal and tilted her wings to glide to another. The Karda's longer wings and slower strokes still threw Tessa's balance off a little, and she was grateful for the tight straps of the rigging. And that the ache in her thighs from riding the larger Karda was easing. She flipped her extra lenses up to concentrate on the area closer to her.

The well-guarded planters strung out along the edge of the circle, no longer worked alone. Llalara and Badti waggled their wings at the group they passed by. Guards and planters waved back. Tessa noticed the barrows were nearly empty of saplings. A few planters stowed shovels and digging forks under the tree canopy, pegging down the tarp that would cover them for the night. Tessa sighed. Her patrol wasn't over. They'd be flying till sunset, and it would get harder and harder to fight the boredom and pay attention without Kishar to talk to.

She flipped the distance lens back down and scanned the circle to the west for as far as she could see. A larger than usual whirl of dust was barely visible on the horizon north by northwest of their flight path. Tessa frowned. Llalara felt her sudden tension and circled higher, beating her wings to gain altitude. Badti and Cerla whirled in a sharp turn to come up beside them.

"Do you see something?" Cerla's yell broke the stillness of the upper air as she raised her binoculars.

"To the northwest. Just on the horizon. Do you see it?"

Cerla scanned for several minutes. "It looks like a dust devil. We've seen enough of those. I don't know how the circles are so dry when everything else is so wet. It's like they shed water."

"It's too big not to check it out, and I don't think it's just a dust devil. Let's head back, fast. I need Kishar." She slipped her goggles to the top of her head as Llalara angled her tail, dropped a wing, and wheeled back to the south, flying straight and fast. Tessa swallowed her impatience. Even at her fastest, Llalara was slow compared to Kishar. They landed in a thunderous rush of back winging and cantered straight to where Kishar and Galen lounged under the edge of the tall abelee trees west of camp.

She was stripping the straps from her legs before they reached them. "I think I've seen more urbat," she called. "But they were too far away for me to tell if it's urbat or just a big dust devil."

Kishar cocked his head toward Galen. Tessa saw his face pale as he listened to the Karda say something she couldn't hear, and he backed away, hands in the air. "Oh, no. No. I don't think that's a good idea. Not a good idea in too many ways."

"What?" Tessa looked back and forth between the two. "What's not a good idea?"

He looked at her. "He says I'm to fly with you." He was still backing away, hands in the air, shaking his head.

Tessa fell off Llalara, hitting the ground hard on her bottom. "You... You can't. You can't carry both of us. You can't." She heard Llalara snort as the big Karda walked toward them, straps dangling.

~And why, I wonder, would you think that? Come back, Galen. You might as well start learning to help Tessa with the rigging. You'll need extra straps.~

It took long enough to rearrange the rigging to carry two for Galen to calm. Both of them finally strapped in, Kishar had to take three steps to get up off the ground. Galen's body was lean, but he was also tall and muscular. Not by any means a lightweight. Tessa felt the heat of him behind her. And his awkwardness.

"When Kishar's wings are beating like this, you have to post, like on a trotting horse, or you'll throw him off. Lift your butt when his wings go down, relax when they go up."

"I can tell I'll be sore. He's a bit wider than my horse." His body began to move in sync with hers, his hands resting lightly at her waist.

~Where are we headed, Tessa?~ Kishar asked.

~About twenty-five degrees north of west. We're not high enough to see anything yet.~ She pulled her goggles down over her eyes. "I don't know if you'll be able to see anything without goggles, Galen. Not till we get closer."

~That's not the direction they came from last time.~

She jumped. His words had been in her head.

Tessa didn't reply for several moments. ~You're pathing.~ She felt him tense and lean away from her.

~Sorry, I thought I was thinking to myself.~ Out loud he said, "This is going to take a little getting used to." She could hear the frown in his tight, clipped, words. And anger. "How do I keep you out of my head?" His tone was accusatory.

Like it was her fault. Like there was something she could do about it. Like he punched her in the diaphragm. She couldn't answer. She swallowed, grateful he couldn't see her face.

Kishar spoke. ~You are both going to have to get used to communicating like this.~

"No. We don't." They spoke in unison—angry, staccato words.

She felt her face heat. Why was Galen so angry? At her? She straightened, leaned forward, and his hands fell away from her waist. The silence between them got longer. And longer. Finally, she forced her voice into a calmness she didn't feel. "How do you know the urbat didn't come from this direction?"

"I could see the trampled path they took. It led further to the south, and they rose up not far from the edge of the circle."

"What were you doing so close to the circle?" She was frazzled. Angry. Sad. Afraid. She could trust Kishar in her head. But trusting Galen was something else.

"Tessa, I can step into the disorder. I can walk the surface safely."

"Oh, my Lady Adalta. Whatever possessed you to try? Have you no sense of self-preservation?" Her words snapped like the twang of her bowstring, and she twisted in the saddle to give him an are-you-insane look.

"You shouldn't be surprised, Tessa. You and Kishar have been flying over the circles for this whole season, at least. If you can do that as the Austringer, you shouldn't be surprised that I'm able to step onto the circles. Everyone keeps insisting I must be the Kern and like the legend says, 'He walked the dark spaces, immune to the evil that lay within."

Oh, now he was all calmness and patience. Humoring her. Quoting the legend he professed not to believe. Her face heated. She spit out, "Can you see anything yet?"

Disconnected flashes of his thoughts—a flash of urbat, irritation at Kishar, a flash of her stumbling out of her tent in the early morning, a tower of flame and a surge of anger at his failure to control it—flooded her. She lost her balance, throwing Kishar off, and he veered. Galen's sudden alarm burned her. She sucked in a sharp breath and felt him do the same. She closed her eyes, trying to push him out, push the images away. They weren't hers. They weren't her thoughts.

She slapped her extra lenses down, swiping him with her elbow as she turned in the saddle to look more north and west.

"Ouch."

~While I realize being able to hear each other mentally is disturbing, could we rein in the tension and pay attention to what we are looking for? You need to set mental shields on your thoughts, Galen.~

Tessa's eyes raked the horizon for the dust eddy she'd spotted earlier. She closed her eyes for a moment, concentrating. ~Shift our heading slightly more north, about a degree, Kishar. Did you hear that Galen?~

Tessa had a mental flash of a shutter opening slightly then slamming shut, stabbing her head like a sharp metal shard. She shifted her goggles to the top of her head and rubbed her forehead. ~It hurts when you slam your mind shut suddenly like that. Please be a little more considerate.~

The shutter slammed open again. ~I am learning, Tessa. Have some patience, please.~

She winced. "I'm going to have a monstrous headache if you keep that up. Or your shields will shatter. I would appreciate it if we spoke aloud until we have time for me to teach you pathing etiquette."

~How can I tell...~ He pathed, then stopped and said, using his voice, "How am I to tell the difference?" *If one more insane thing happens to me on this insane world, I am going to hang myself from the nearest tree.*

Tessa clamped her lips on a laugh. There was nothing funny in the tone of his thoughts. They tolled despair and echoed loneliness in her head. She knew he didn't intend her to hear them. She felt like a voyeur. She pulled her goggles down again and searched the horizon.

"There." She pointed. "Straight ahead."

Galen's breath stirred her hair as he leaned forward. She heard him mentally counting. "They're just rising." His voice was whisper soft. "I count eighteen almost free. And there are four beneath the surface still struggling out of those carapaces. One already looks dead, and I think only one other is going to make it. Several are alive but too deformed to be a danger. They'll probably die, too."

The ugly creatures were pawing at the cauls that still covered them, stretching out stubby metal wings, rolling and rubbing themselves dry in the dust. Kishar circled silently above them, and Tessa pulled her bow from its resting place under her leg and uncovered her quiver. She slipped the bow stringer over one end of the recurve bow, stepped into the loop at the other end, and pushed the bowstring into its notches. She stowed the stringer and nocked her first arrow.

"Kishar, can you set me down close to them?" Galen asked.

Tessa twisted around at his words and almost poked him with her hand full of arrows. "Are you crazy?"

~I'm sorry, Galen. I can fly over the circle, but I can't land. And you will have to practice jumping off me when it's not so dangerous.~

Tessa's elbow jabbed against Galen as she drew the first arrow back. "Sit back out of my way." And she started shooting. Without arrowheads made from the strange metal of the urbat skeletons, her arrows couldn't pierce the armor. She switched to shooting at the hindquarters with more success, aiming for the un-armored spot where the spine met the pelvis. Even as fast and accurate as she was, the urbat swarmed too close together for her to hit many before Kishar overshot and wheeled back.

The monsters milled around in confusion, half-leaping, half-flying on their stubby wings trying to reach Kishar. She felled six more of them before the urbat dashed into a thicket of twisted trees too tangled to shoot through. "They were too fast and too close together, Kishar. Even I couldn't hit all my shots."

Galen snorted.

Tessa's words snapped. "I never miss."

Kishar circled, and his powerful wings carried them higher. ~We'll have to get back to the camp and warn the others. There are fewer than there were last time, and we'll be prepared.~

~Wait, Kishar. Go back. Look, Galen. Can you see what they're doing? Can you see, Kishar?~ The monsters had swarmed out of the thicket and were attacking their own dead. Tessa fought a surge of nausea.

"Oh, black hole, take me. They're eating their own dead."

"No. They're not, Galen. Look closer. Do you see what they're doing, Kishar?"

Kishar tucked his wings and arrowed toward the ground, swooped up just above the milling urbat and back-winged, hovering in place.

He flew up again, and they made a tight circle just above the urbat's flying range. ~They are stripping the metal from the flesh and burying it.~ His pathed voice sounded as puzzled as Tessa felt.

Kishar started beating up away from the urbat. Galen lost his balance and grabbed, pulling himself hard against her. She clamped down on the sudden surge of heat.

Chapter Seventeen

The eighteen urbat they'd discovered in the circle was a fraction of what attacked. Three long, hard tendays and several battles later, Galen shoved his sword above him with both hands, catching the urbat in the throat as it half-flew, half-jumped at him. Ichor sprayed, soaking his head and shoulders with noxious liquid.

His blade twisted as the monster fell, and he struggled to wrench it free, swinging around in time to catch a second urbat on its armored shoulder with the flat of his sword, all his weight behind the stroke. The urbat rolled, unhurt by the blade, but its belly lay exposed to Galen's second swing as it struggled to get upright. Its short wings beat the ground. Galen killed it and turned to the next beast.

His scars sang with power, and he shoved the heel of his hand toward the beast leaping at him, stubby metallic wings whirring. Thick tendrils with long thorns sprang from the ground where the urbat landed, tripping it, wrapping themselves around it, pulling it down into the ground, cutting off its high, sharp howl.

The thrum of an arrow buzzed too close to his ear, and he turned to see another urbat fall, crippled and struggling, an arrow lodged deep in its spine. He shoved to entangle it, bury it alive, and he turned, searching for another. Tessa's arrows filled the air each time Kishar made a pass over the fighting, never missing. Galen buried her victims, one after the other, feeling exhaustion creep in as his reserves drained, every effort more tiring.

Guards and planters fought hard, swords and spears, shovels and hoes searching for unarmored spots on the beasts, aiming for legs, throats, muzzles, wings, anywhere unprotected to slow or cripple the urbat.

Galen's sword hung loose in his hand as he forced green-gold power toward the crippled monsters, trapping them with thorny vines, sucking them down into the earth. The stench was horrific. Blood and thick amber ichor slicked the ground. The fighters struggled to stay upright as they dodged slashing teeth and razor-sharp talons.

The urbat fought viciously, ignoring the guard, targeting planters, until they finally turned and retreated to the circle. The final howl of the last beast cut off, and it disappeared as Galen buried it in a thicket of thorns and earth. The sudden silence was tangible as it hung over the terrible scene on the ground. The human fighters backed away, sickened by the oily stench of rotten meat and the dark haze that hovered over the battleground that had been the center of their camp.

Then they put away their weapons and went to carry the injured to the half-collapsed medic tent and the dead to the edge of the forest where too many others lay. Galen cleared the strange poisonous sickness from the wounded, pulling it out of them through himself and into the ground. Too weary to worry about the strangeness of this anymore, to0 exhausted to worry about losing control, he just let it happen. He was too tired to think about it, about what he was doing. He locked those thoughts away, determined not to let them leak. If they escaped, he wasn't sure he would ever be able to stop them, and he would become a gibbering, raving monster.

He walked to the edge of the clearing and dropped to his knees. With the last of his reserves, he shoved the heels of his hands hard into the dirt. A bright green fur of new growth rolled away from him, and the blood and ichor, the stench, disappeared beneath it leaving the ground littered with pieces of metal skeletons. Rods, gears, hinges. Dark metal glinting in the sun on an eerie empty field encircled by weary fighters whose eyes avoided Galen. He started to stand and had to brace himself with one arm to keep from falling over. He wasn't sure he could get up again if he fell.

Tessa and Kishar landed, and Galen walked over to them and leaned his head against Tessa's leg. He threw one arm over Kishar's neck, almost too weary to stand. "There are too many." He heard the despair in his voice. "They just keep coming. There are hundreds more out there. I can feel them waiting for something. This is only the beginning."

He felt the knuckles of her hand, still clutching arrows, press against the leaf tattoo on his cheek, and he wrapped his hand around hers. It shook with tension. They were still for a long time. Then Kishar shifted, and the moment broke.

"Will you leave? Go back to your ship?" Her voice was soft, halfway between accusation and fear.

"No. Will you leave? Go back to your father?" He looked up. Her face with its ragged silver halo was all he could see. Her face with its fierce frown of defiance. She snorted and jerked her hand away to stow her arrows.

"I think we need a council of war." Almryk's voice sounded with as much weariness as Galen felt.

He turned to face the captain. "How many wounded are there?" How many killed? he left unasked.

"We were luckier this time. Or better prepared, I guess. They killed three guards and one planter." Almryk shook his head sharply. He was wearing his anger like a shroud. Anger at himself. "I knew Orlon wasn't a good fighter, but he wouldn't stay back, and I... There are only eight wounded. When you— They're being tended."

"When I cleared the poison from their wounds and the nasty smell from the field?"

"Yes. That."

"Almryk." Irritation sailed over Galen's head on Tessa's voice. "Galen isn't some monster or freak any more than I am."

Almryk paced around in a tight circle three times, coming to a halt in front of Galen. "I'm sorry, my friend. It's just—when those tattoos pop out on your arms and face, and your eyes turn all green, and things start coming up out of the ground and grabbing—" He looked up at Tessa. "And then the hailstorm of arrows falling out of the sky that seldom miss, never hit anyone accidentally. None of this feels real. Nobody gave me lessons on how to act around legends come to life."

He stepped away and walked around in a circle again twice before moving back to Kishar's side. Emotion whooshed out of him like he'd let go of a balloon full of air. He reached for Galen's arm and pushed up his sleeve. "This time, your tattoos, or whatever they are, aren't going away." He tilted his head to look at the trefoil symbol on Galen's cheek and smiled a crooked smile. "That's going to get interesting."

Galen pulled his sleeve back down. *The thing about Almryk is that when he decides to accept something, it's done. It's like all that embarrassment or fear or whatever he felt never was. Thank the stars.*

Tessa dismounted, and the four of them walked toward the makeshift mews.

"I think we need to get help. And I think we need to go to the keep. Daryl needs to know what's happening, what we're sensing," said Tessa.

"You can sense them, too?" Galen asked.

"Only enough for a quick warning when they start to get close. I don't like the feeling. It's ugly. Nauseating. Like the circle feels, only somehow, it's different. Clusters of sickness, not just one sickness."

"What are you talking about? Or do I even want to know?" Almryk kicked a stone, hard.

They watched it roll to a stop, and Galen said, "There are more of them out there in the circle waiting for something. They're encased in their shells beneath the surface where we can't get at them. I don't think even Tessa's arrows can reach them. Maybe I could force them up. Maybe. But then there'd be only me to fight them. No one can come with me into the circle, and there's no guarantee trying to do that wouldn't trigger something, and they'd all rise."

Almryk stopped. "Into the circle." The hard, flat tone of his voice halted the others. "You can walk into the circle. Did you somehow forget to mention this to me? Did you somehow neglect to tell me that you can do another thing no one else has ever done outside the legends? Did you think it wouldn't be important for the captain of the guard responsible for the safety of this expedition to know this?" His voice rose higher and louder with each word.

He walked away a short distance, his back to the other three. Galen watched him draw several deep breaths, and then he turned back. "Perhaps we should all sit down somewhere and have a little talk. Maybe bring each other up to date on the latest amazing legendary feats we can perform. Okay. I don't have any. Now, what about you?"

"When would I have told you, Almryk? You've been avoiding me like I'm a monster you're not sure you should let live." He kicked the same rock halfway to the mews tent. "Yeah. Well. I guess I kind of am."

He held up one hand and looked at the raised root-like tattoos twining down to his fingertips. They were not fading away as they had before. *I wonder what Father will say if they don't disappear? How will he explain them away?* A fierce hope punched him hard in the chest, and he stopped walking. *Maybe I don't ever have to see him again.*

Kishar swatted at him with a wing, nearly knocking him down. ~You're not a monster. How close are you to getting the planting done? ~

Galen saw Almryk shake his head and smothered a smirk. Almryk did not like hearing the Karda in his head.

"We can't cross the two Lines of Devastation, and we need more saplings and more supplies before we can move around to the other side of the circle. I want to try to figure out how to cut those lines off. Then we might be able to finish before the weather turns too cold. If there are no more attacks. If I can cut the lines. If. If. If."

They reached the mews tent, and Galen helped Tessa unbuckle Kishar's rigging, coil the straps, and carefully stow it in the area of the mews tent Kishar claimed for himself.

~If you can sense the urbat beneath the circle, can you tell if there are more that will rise soon?~

Galen could hear pain in Kishar's voice, and he looked at him sharply. "You are wounded."

Tessa's breath hissed, and she started running her hands down his legs and over his wings, circling him until she found a deep gash in his left hock.

~I dropped down too close to the fighting. I know better. The urbat look clumsy in the air, but they can reach more than twenty feet high with those stubby wings. And their talons are long and sharp.~ He hissed, and his nares flared as Tessa brought water and clean cloths and started washing the wound.

"Galen." Tessa's voice was low and come-quickly urgent with a sharp undertone of fear. "There's something broken off in here."

Galen could smell it then. The noxious, rotten, oily smell of urbat. The flesh was swollen and turning putrid too quickly for this to be a simple gash. "I think perhaps you might want to lie down, Kishar."

"Can you heal it?" Tessa's voice was too tight, too controlled.

"I don't know anything about healing, Tessa. I wouldn't know where to start. I can draw out the talon that broke off in there. Or at least draw off the poison. I can try." *If I have enough reserve. If I am not too tired to control myself and make things worse.*

He looked at her. Anguish pulled at the muscles of her face. "It always works for the others, Tessa. But you and Kishar were still in the air this time when I cleared the field. Maybe that's why it didn't work for him."

"I'll get a healer. They're probably finished with the other wounded by now. If she has to, she can cut the talon out, so the gash can heal." Almryk left at a run.

Kishar fell to the ground in a controlled collapse—his injured hind leg stretched out. ~I think perhaps you must hurry, Kern. I have been poisoned before, and the poison will work on me too rapidly.~ He stretched out his head on the ground, rolling slightly to one side. ~Don't let me kick you.~ His voice was weakening, and he closed his eyes.

Galen knelt at Kishar's hock, well away from his taloned feet. He looked up at Tessa. She was frozen, staring down at Kishar's wound with a bleak, lost look. ~Step around here, Tessa, where he can't kick you. He's probably going to convulse.~

She didn't react. He reached across the Karda and pulled her around to his side. ~Didn't you hear me? I don't want you to get hurt when he starts convulsing.~

~Convulsing?~

He put one hand on Kishar's flank and the other on the ground.

Tessa shook his shoulder hard. ~What do you mean convulsing? What are you going...~

Galen ignored her, concentrating his attention on the worsening wound, pulling at the putrefaction. The sickness pulsed through the tree-like markings up his arm and across his body and he willed it into the ground through his other hand. His head swam with needle-like shards of it, and he started to lose control as it threatened to overwhelm him.

Then Kishar's body convulsed, throwing Galen back. A long, wicked, metal urbat claw pushed out of the wound in the Karda's hock and slid to the ground.

Galen's stomach heaved. He barely controlled the retching. He rolled over, tore his jacket and shirt open, and fell flat, prone on the ground, arms spread, fingers digging into the dirt, face buried in the grass, heart thumping too slow. He could hear activity around him. Words that made no sense. Almryk and the healer dressing Kishar's wound. Tessa's anxious voice. Her hand touched his back.

He relaxed into the ground, into the sweet, clean power that surged up into him, engorging the leaf and root and branch markings on his body and face.

He lay there for a long time, then rolled over and looked up at the sky. Tessa's face filled his vision, the sun making an aureole of her silver hair.

The corners of his mouth lifted with the joy of her. He watched her concern wash away. Her wrinkled brow smoothed, and her mouth curved up into a smile that linked with his in an intimacy he'd never felt before.

An intimacy he'd never allowed himself to feel before.

Everything shifted.

Everything.

Chapter Eighteen

Tessa staggered as the rope she was holding jerked, and the dining tent came down, billowing into an untidy pile of canvas. She joined the guards and planters and began folding the pile into an orderly bundle. Moving camp was a tremendous undertaking. With so many killed and wounded, and so many on guard duty, even the Mi'hiru and Karda who were not on patrol were helping.

Tessa needed to be flying patrols, but the healer insisted Kishar take one more day of recovery from his wound. Kishar agreed, and she wouldn't leave him. So she was helping take down the tents and packing the wagons. Half a tenday and they'd be at the new campsite. Another few days and they'd know if Galen could figure out a way to cut the Lines of Devastation snaking their way out of the circle.

Then the two of them would fly to Restal Prime, to the keep, to report to Daryl and the master planter and arrange for more supplies, seeds, and saplings. It had been a long, long growing season. They needed more guards and planters. She shook away the sadness that thought stirred.

She badly wanted a bath in a real tub and someone to do her laundry. Much as she relished the freedom she had out here, clean laundry was showing up increasingly often in her thoughts. With even the barest hint of Water and Air talent, she could swish her clothes around in a tub, and they would be clean. Instead, she had to scrub and scrub and do it when no one was watching. After dark.

Maybe she should admit her lack of talent. It was that lack that made her the Austringer, so why keep it secret? It was her father's ambition that made it imperative that no one suspect. Just the thought of bringing it out into the open, as a sacrifice, as something to be proud of, as what made her the Austringer, peeled years of weight off her shoulders. Then years of shame piled it back on. Her face flamed —the thought of being the focus of look-down-the-nose or well-meaning pity from others piled on even more weight. Her shoulders sagged.

She packed her belongings in the wagon space she was assigned and made sure her second quiver of arrows with their new points of urbat armor scales could be reached in a hurry. Galen reached around her to stow his packs, and she took a deep breath. He levered his bundles into the small space that was left and walked away, not looking at her.

Over his shoulder, he said, "Tessa, come with me to the edge of the circle. I want to know if you can see what I see. Though I'm not sure see is the right word for it. The patrols haven't spotted anything, so it should be safe. I've saddled a horse for you, and there's an hour or so before the cooks have dinner. Most of the packing is done, so I think they can spare us."

The sun was approaching treetop height to the west side of the camp and heading for twilight as they rode out. "I might get saddle sore, but horseback is better than those hard wagon seats are going to be."

Galen laughed. "Just one ride on Kishar and I thought my legs would never recover. You'll feel like you're riding on pillows when you're horseback. Flying is not for the weak of limb. How long did it take you to be able to ride him in comfort?"

She looked at him with surprise. "I've been flying Karda since I was a little girl. If I ever got sore, I don't remember it."

"Oh, yeah. I forgot. You're a holder's daughter." The good humor left his face, and he was silent for the rest of the ride. Confused by the hint of something—bitterness? sadness?—she tasted in his words, Tessa didn't try to talk.

It was nearing dark when their horses began to sidle and balk. They were close to the edge of the circle. They tied them securely and close to each other for comfort, slipping the bits from their mouths so they could graze. Galen finally spoke. "You're probably not used to walking any distance. Let me know if I go too fast for you."

Tessa bridled. "I'm quite sure I can keep up despite the fact that, as a holder's daughter, I was carried everywhere, my dainty feet never allowed to touch the ground."

Galen missed a step then laughed through teeth clamped so tight muscles jumped along his jawline. "I suppose I could carry you most of the way. Though I might be crawling with you on my back before we get there."

She didn't laugh. "That's the least my father would expect of you." She tasted her own bitterness.

He looked away. They both watched a bright crimson leaf from a black gum tree twirl down through the still air and walked on.

The great red sun was making a last glorious stand enormous under the clouds to the west as they reached the edge of the circle. "I'm usually high in the sky when I'm this close. It smells more wrong down here." Tessa's words were soft with unease as if she spoke too loudly, the circle would wake.

Galen stepped closer to her, his shoulder touching hers. She didn't move away.

"I've gotten used to it, but you're right. There is a wrongness to the air this close."

She looked up at him. He closed his eyes and was still. Tessa closed her own eyes, took a long deep breath through her nose, and sent her consciousness out across the circle, as far as she could reach. She felt Galen's hand reach for hers, and their fingers linked. They stood together for a long time, seeking for what they both were afraid to find. Finally, she felt him shift, and he turned to walk back to the horses, tugging at her hand.

Tessa resisted, still facing the ugliness that was the circle. "There are so many. I don't sense them this well when I fly over, even far inside the circle." Tessa felt the quiver in her voice, so small in the quiet air of twilight. Long shadows stretched from the circle's twisted shrubs and low trees that reached toward them.

"Come away, Tessa. We need to compare what we sensed."

She shivered. "I'm not used to being so close. It's different flying over it. How do you bear it, day after day? It makes me nauseous."

"Planters can stay near the circle longer than others, and it seems I'm immune, at least so far. And I try to look at what I'm planting, not the circle, and seldom so closely as we just did."

They walked in silence. Tessa pulled her hand away from the warmth of his. It was foolish to be so frightened of something she flew over every day. "Why do you think that is, when the Line of Devastation made you so ill I thought you were going to die?"

"Kishar says the reason the circles are so deadly is that they feed on the talent that, as he puts it, anchors us to Adalta. Somehow too much exposure to circles burns away talent channels. Without talent, people sicken and die. You and he have shields that prevent it—your talent is locked safely behind your mental block. I am able to fill myself with talent and then close off the conduit. Rather than constantly drawing on it, or being tethered by it, I carry it with me. And planters can work near the edges because they are tethered, in a way, to the trees and grasses they are planting to remediate the corruption of the circle."

"What would happen to you if you weren't able to refill yourself? What if you left the planet?" Tessa's breath almost stopped. It came shallow and quick. *Don't answer that. I don't want to know.*

Galen was quiet. The last of the light was disappearing. They walked slowly through the trees just beginning to show their harvest season color. The abelee leaves hung still in the windless calm that marked the moment of transition between night and day. Finally, his voice so soft she strained to hear, he said, "I don't know."

They rode back in silence, Tessa's horse following Galen's so closely she didn't need the reins.

Almryk met them at the roped off corral and helped them unsaddle and groom their horses. "Kishar said to tell you he's fine, now, Tessa. And he's anxious to hear what you found. As am I."

Galen took a final swipe with the brush, tossed it in the tack box, and slapped his horse on the rump. It took off at a trot toward the feed trough, Tessa's mount close behind. They stood the saddles on end under a low canvas shelter and headed for the travel tent where the cook's fire sent out the mingled smell of wood smoke, roast venison, and onion.

They filled plates and carried them to where Kishar lay, legs tucked under him, head raised, a short distance from the other Karda.

"I don't think we want anyone to overhear what we have to say," Galen said and dropped to sit cross-legged, balancing his plate on one knee.

Almryk settled beside him.

"It's too bad you can't join us telepathically, Almryk."

The captain shuddered. "I have no desire to be a legend, and I don't get lonely being the only one inside my head."

Galen laughed.

Tessa sat as close to Kishar as she could get, leaning into him, ignoring her plate of food on the ground beside her. "Somehow I'm not very hungry."

~Letting it get cold won't improve its flavor, little one. Eat.~

She hunched over her knees. ~What I sensed, Kishar...~

~Eat. It can wait until you've eaten.~

She swallowed against the slight nausea she'd carried from the circle and forced herself to pick up her fork.

Galen finished first, cradled his mug of hot tea in his big hands, and began to speak, his voice low and reluctant, as though if he didn't have to say the words, what they revealed wouldn't happen. "I stopped trying to count them. There are hundreds of the egg-things out there. Hundreds."

Tessa took a last bite. It was all she could manage. "I sensed the same. But...they were different. Remember, Galen? Kishar? Some of those we saw when we flew out there didn't hatch—if that's the right word. They looked like they weren't finished and broke out of their shells too soon. They were crippled. Or dead. And there were some of the egg-things that didn't open at all. Those were like what I sensed this time."

Almryk looked up, a tenuous hope in his expression. "You mean they were dead? Damaged?"

Tessa shook her head slowly, and thoughtful lines creased her forehead. "No. Not damaged. Unfinished. They felt unfinished. I didn't feel any that were ready to come out. Be born. Or hatch." She looked at Kishar. "That's good. Right?"

~Do you agree with that, Galen?~ Kishar's pathed voice didn't hold the reassurance Tessa wanted to hear.

"My impressions are more visual than Tessa's. But I didn't see any that were opening. My senses were of great numbers, but in what stage I couldn't tell. Although I think there are empty shells out there that outnumber the ones that have attacked us. I didn't get any sense of where those clutches of urbat went. I think they've left the circle."

Tessa rubbed her eyes with the heels of her hands. The day had been long, the evening fraught with tension. Her food lay heavy in her stomach, and dread pulled at her. "Waiting. They are waiting."

~Yes. They are waiting. For the Itza Larrak. Were it not free and near to manifesting again, you would not be able to sense them, Tessa. You might not be able to see them, Galen.~ Kishar's voice was soft with an ancient weariness. ~It was our hope that the years of planting special trees and grasses and bushes used on Earth for phytoremediation would eliminate the threat. That hope is dying, at least here in Restal where the planting has been sporadic for the past several generations.~

No one spoke. Then Almryk said, "How long?"

No one answered.

They traveled through soft, steady rain all the first day of the journey to the new site. Camp that night was wet, but the tents started out dry, and her ground cloth kept the dampness from Tessa's sleeping blankets. The cooks were able to use the remains of the venison in a hearty stew, and the biscuits were light, hot, and drenched with honey.

The second day it rained more, soft and steady. The tents were damp, the ground squishy beneath the waterproof cloths, Tessa's bedroll only slightly damp. Dinner was scant and consisted of stewed dried meat and vegetables. The biscuits didn't rise quite so high.

The third day rain was still steady. But now it was harder, at times pelting them with small hailstones. The sky growled with thunder intermittently, and the wind blew harder. The wagons slogged through mushy forest humus. The horses struggled to keep going, as weary and dispirited as their human companions.

They were traveling not far from the edge of the circle where the forest was younger, the trees smaller and closer together. There was no road, and they had to make their way through the trees, detouring often when they grew too close for the wagons to pass through.

The Karda were a bedraggled and grumpy lot. Feathers wet, manes and tails dripping, beaks snapping, they trudged with lowered heads on mud-clogged feet. It was difficult for them to fly in steady rain, and lightning grounded them several times. Walking through the mud was an unpleasant but inescapable alternative, and they took to the air every time the rain slacked off.

Tessa's tent smelled of mildew. Her bedroll smelled of mildew. Her clothes smelled of mildew. She suspected even her hair smelled of mildew. But late in the afternoon, she and Kishar, Cerla and Badti startled a herd of deer toward an outlying patrol, so dinner was much better.

The biscuits obeyed the wishes of the cooks, and the honey was still plentiful. Bren's foraging turned up a big cluster of her favorite greens. And in the night, Tessa woke to silence. No patter of rain pelted her soggy tent. At daylight, the camp woke to the rarity of cloudless, turquoise skies.

A day of rest spent with bedding and damp clothes spread on lines crisscrossing the camp, eventless patrols, and one more day of travel took them to the campsite Galen and Almryk had scouted. They spent yet another day setting up the communal tents, establishing camp, and flying more eventless patrols.

The next morning, Tessa stumbled to the cook's tent, half-awake after a restless sleep, muscles stiff, hands red and blistered from the unaccustomed work of hauling at heavy, damp tent ropes. Grateful for the hot egg toast instead of the cold biscuits and cold, chewy meat that had been morning travel fare for the past few days, she wrapped both hands around a hot mug of tea.

She stared into it as if it held the secrets of the universe, relishing the warm, fragrant steam that rose around her face, grateful to be dry, grateful to be awake and free of the visions that plagued her all night.

Galen slid his long legs along the bench next to her. Almryk sat across, both with plates piled high. After several minutes of eating as if they'd starved for days, Galen laid his fork across his empty plate. "Tessa, I think you and I need to head to Restal Prime. Daryl needs to know what we've found, and there are villages near the circle that need to be warned about what might be coming."

Tessa propped an elbow on the table, pinching the bridge of her nose between thumb and forefinger.

"What is it? What's wrong?" Galen's voice was warm with concern, his hand warm on her back.

She kept her voice low. "That's what I dreamed about all last night. More than dreams, I think. Fears?" That last word rose, and she looked at him as if hoping he'd tell her what she'd had were just dreams. Because she was tired. Because she'd worked as hard as the strongest planters helping to set up camp yesterday.

Almryk said, "I don't know how we'll fight off another attack without the two of you and Kishar."

Galen sat straighter and looked into the distance. "They have never attacked on our days of rest. It's the planting that disturbs them."

He looked at Almryk. "Stop planting—we're running low on saplings and seeds anyway. Concentrate on setting up defenses and training the fighters. Before I leave I'll throw up a thorny hedge around the camp. Daryl will send more soldiers and planters as soon as he can."

Tessa scrubbed at her face. "We'll need to carry as much urbat metal as possible."

~I'll get a couple of my pack Karda to carry the metal to Restal Prime and the villages along the way.~ Young Karda hated the job of being pack mules. Kishar sounded gleeful.

"We'll instruct as many villages as we can get to on our way to the prime what they must do to prepare." Tessa looked across at Almryk. "Will they believe us?"

The captain chewed on the side of his lower lip for a minute. "You'll need Daryl's authority. I hate to say that. It will take time we may not have. But it will be hard enough to convince the village leaders even with it. They're tired of too many years of neglect from the guardian and nervous about Readen's aborted revolt. Even if Daryl's sent warnings, they won't want to believe them. They'll just want to put their heads down and work, grateful for the tax relief Daryl's promised after so many years of Roland's greed. They won't want to face the prospect of a threat from an enemy they only know of from history and legend. One we'd thought destroyed."

Galen sat up straighter. "Finish your breakfast, Tessa, and let's go talk to Kishar. I think you're going to need the energy if we're to get to Restal Prime soon. We'll be flying hard and fast. If we can find a Karda who'll carry me."

Chapter Nineteen

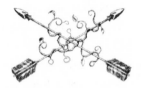

Llalara moved into a glide, and Galen stood carefully in his stirrups, stretching, keeping his gaze on the horizon, afraid to look down. His thighs burned from the long stretch across the Karda's broad back. Horses were smaller, their gaits different from the movements of flying. And they didn't make his stomach lurch with every terrifying shift. Didn't make him feel he was about to fall despite the straps of the saddle rigging buckled firmly around his legs. Straps that rubbed them raw.

Without reins to occupy his hands, he didn't know what to do with them. They moved from resting on his legs to grabbing the pommel handle. When Llalara shifted from a glide to powerful, thundering wing beats, it threatened to toss Galen tumbling through empty air to the ground so far away. Or so it felt.

~Llalara says to remind you that we are highly empathic creatures. She can feel your pain and discomfort. She says if you let yourself relax, flying will be more comfortable. For both of you.~ Galen heard the amusement in Kishar's voice.

~I am a creature of Earth, Kishar. Of dirt and rocks and plants and water. Even when I'm horseback, I can feel the connection to Adalta. Up here...~ He shuddered. ~I am cut adrift.~

Tessa's voice startled him. ~Galen, start watching for a long enough meadow for Llalara to land. There's one just to the west ahead. It's getting late. Kishar and I will hunt and find you later. There's a herd of deer below us.~ She hadn't spoken for some time. He looked over at her. She was rubbing her head, and a large handkerchief in her other hand half-covered her face.

She always knows where she is and what's around her. Does she have a picture of the entire continent in her head? He watched her and Kishar shear away and go vertical. Kishar stooped for the ground faster than Galen could have imagined. He blinked, and Kishar and Tessa disappeared into the forest below.

He put his hand on Llalara's neck and, feeling more than a little foolish, tried to project a picture of a long, narrow meadow from his mind to Llalara's. The big sorrel tilted her wings, turned slightly west, losing altitude, and it wasn't long before a break in the trees appeared not far from the circle. Llalara touched down, broke into her three-beat, horse-like canter, and slowed to a stop.

He fumbled the straps off and slid to the ground. His legs threatened to collapse under him. He grabbed a stirrup strap and hung on, bending and straightening first one leg then the other, willing circulation back into his trembling thighs and aching calves. Even his toes hurt.

Saddle and saddlebags stripped off, Galen fished out the brush, the curry comb, and the small bottle of light oil for Llalara's feathers. After so many days of rain, they needed extra care.

He went to work, and the big Karda leaned into his brush as he scraped sweat off her body, then brushed it and her mane and tail till they gleamed. He sensed her gratitude and finished with light brushes of oil to the shafts of her flight feathers.

He turned away to start making a camp, and she butted him with her head, lifting one long-taloned foot. He laughed. He'd forgotten her feet. He checked each one, paying particular attention to the hard, horny pads on each digit that fisted into a hoof when she landed. They were fine—smooth and unbroken. "Thank you for reminding me, Llalara. I won't forget again." He stepped back, and she shook herself all over. Small downy feathers flew. Galen sneezed.

He followed her to a tiny cress-choked spring seeping from a scree of chalk and flint rocks at the side of the meadow and dropped saddle and saddlebags in an open space. He found a circle of blackened stones for a fire and a raised flat place cleared of rocks for their tent. This meadow had been used before. *I hope that means we're far enough from the circle to be safe.*

By the time he had the tent up, a fire going, and a kettle of water with a double handful of dried vegetables set to simmer, he heard a thud behind him and whirled to see a deer lying on the ground, and Kishar landed. Galen hung the carcass from a tree limb and field stripped it, carving out a roast for their supper, while Tessa unsaddled and groomed Kishar.

Dinner of roast venison, stewed dried vegetables, and peppery watercress from the spring, finished, pots and utensils cleaned and stowed, they sat, side by side under the ground cloth Galen rigged as a porch for their tent. The drizzle that started midway through their meal hissed and spat in the coals of the fire.

Galen got up and walked away, using the excuse that he needed to relieve himself. He walked up the meadow and back twice in the darkness, his Earth sense telling his feet where to step, where there were rocks, where there were puddles. The tiny point of light in front of the tent flared. Tessa had tossed in more wood and stirred the coals to life, turning the silver brush of her hair to gold.

Tessa.

A tiny point of light shining in the bleakness of his life. *But that's all she can be. I can't let this go farther. It will only bring her pain.*

He turned away and walked the long distance to the circle. Just to check. Just to be certain there were no urbat near. Just to get away from that point of light.

Tessa woke, legs entangled with Galen's, her head nestled in the hollow between his shoulder and his neck. Warm and comfortable. Too warm and comfortable. Despite the blanket over her head, she felt exposed and vulnerable. He didn't want her.

She pulled herself away. hoping he didn't wake and find her wrapped around him. He didn't want her, and he was pulling himself away from her. She felt frozen. Cold inside. Embarrassed that he had guessed how she felt when he didn't return the feeling.

She reached mentally for Kishar. Something was wrong. She felt the Karda's alarm before she heard his words.

~Tessa. Galen. Ware! Urbat come.~

Her heart raced. She knew the Karda were not in the camp. He and Llalara must have gone hunting and spotted the urbat. She scrambled for her clothes. Her fingers fumbled her sword.

Galen sat up. ~How many, Kishar? And how far away are you?~

~Twelve. No, fifteen. They're almost on you. They will get to you before we can.~

Tessa had never heard fear in Kishar's voice before. She heard it now.

Galen snatched both sword belts, grabbed her arm, and jerked her to her feet and out of the tent. She pulled loose and dove back for her bow and quiver. *Thank Adalta, my arrows all have the new arrowheads. Now, if they'll only work as well as I hope.*

They ran for the edge of the trees toward a low thicket of evergreen bushes. Galen shoved her through, following so close behind his breath was hot on her neck. Sharp-edged needles tore at Tessa's bare arms and snatched at her hair. He pushed her down and crouched beside her.

She maneuvered around enough to string her recurve bow and sling her quiver over her back. She pulled four arrows out and stuck them in the ground in front of her.

"Galen. They'll find us here. They'll smell us. We need to find a tree to climb." She tried to push up, but he held her down, her face almost in the wet leaves on the ground.

"The trees here are too big. No low branches to climb. And urbat can fly. Be still."

Galen wrapped each hand around a branch of a shrub close to the ground. The resinous smell of pitch filled her nose. The air around them was hazy. She could see their tent through a thick curtain of twisty green and brown.

The urbat came. Clawed feet threw dirt and leaves behind them. They ran noses to the ground, yellow eyes glittering, searching.

In eerie silence they circled the clearing, tearing into the tent, tearing into their packs, ripping up bedding. They crisscrossed the space, chasing scents.

Tessa shook, biting hard on her lip to keep the mewling sounds of fear inside her as three of the beasts snuffled the ground around the thicket where they hid. Galen pressed his face into Tessa's neck, holding her still, pushing her to the damp humus, his legs wrapped around hers, his body hard against her.

She could see one of his hands tight on the trunk of the bush. Green and brown tendrils swirled from his tattoo marks around the stem, pulsing with a faint glow. The resinous smell grew stronger, burning her nose. The urbat moved on.

Sudden shrill shrieks sounded from the sky, and Kishar and Llalara swept into the clearing. All Tessa could see were long legs and slashing talons as the Karda hit the urbat, carrying two of them up into the air. She heard long, high howls that cut off with a disturbing abruptness.

The green screen around them vanished, and they pushed out of the thicket. Tessa's bowstring sang as she shot arrow after arrow, finding vulnerable spots with each one, piercing eyes, stabbing between scales into the flesh beneath. The new arrowheads sliced through the armor, but the urbat were hard to kill.

Galen moved past her, his swords a blur, slashing, shoving a point between the scales of armor, stabbing the other into unprotected necks and bellies.

Kishar swooped in, back-winging, and grabbed a leaping urbat. She watched it struggle and twist in the Karda's long, lethal talons, its howls shrill with panic. Kishar tore its head off, dropped it, swooped back around, and grabbed another.

Llalara swept into sight and snatched another urbat. Two more leaped, tearing into her, dragging her down. Tessa's breath stopped, her heart almost bursting, her hand frozen mid-pull, unable to release the arrow. Llalara screamed and struggled, her enormous wings flailed, tossing three of the monsters across the field. More urbat attacked her, ripping and shredding her wings. Tessa released her arrow and shot again and again, but there were too many.

Llalara stilled, and the urbat tore her apart.

Tessa kept shooting.

Galen dropped to his knees and shoved at the ground toward the downed Karda and the urbat swarming over her body. Dirt and grass flew, thorny vines shot up, twisting into the urbat, pulling them down, trapping six. The three remaining howled their triumph and fled in the direction of the circle. Too late for Llalara. Out of arrow range.

Tessa stumbled at the weight of Kishar's terrible grief. He circled, helpless, above and screamed rage. When the last urbat disappeared into the ground, he spiraled up into the aerial dance that honored the fallen Karda.

Tessa and Galen dropped to their knees and watched, faces wet with sweat and ichor and tears. Galen knelt and pushed more dirt over the body of the Karda. Grass, shining with the green of new growth, spread over the mound. Faint clangs sounded and the metal rods, gears, and wires that were all that was left of the buried urbat surfaced all over the clearing.

Kishar continued his sad, beautiful dance in the air above them.

Galen spoke. "This was my fault. I shouldn't have gone to the circle last night. I shouldn't have tried to sense what was out there. All it did was alert them. It was me they were after. I think they know when I'm near. They were after me, and Llalara paid."

Tessa reached to touch his shoulder and he moved away.

It was long after the sun had set when the two of them, wet, tired, and hungry, finished grooming Kishar in one of the roomy stalls reserved for Karda at Folded Wings Inn. The small village was not far from where the Line of Devastation snaked out of the circle and not far from the boundary of her father's hold. Galen arranged with the sleepy stable boy for extra feed and a hot mash for the wet, tired, hungry, and silent Kishar. They were still several long flights from Restal Prime.

Two other Karda were stabled there. Kishar broke his silence to inform Galen and Tessa they were carrying a Mi'hiru named Nyla and Justiciar Donavan from Restal Prime. ~I will be back before dawn,~ he pathed. He put his head down, and Tessa touched her hand to his mane, stroking it.

~I'm sorry, Kishar. So sorry. If we'd started fighting before you...~

~No, little one. You need carry no blame. Nor does Galen, Llalara was young, and the stories of the urbat are old. Too many centuries have passed since we fought them. The blame is mine.~ He stilled for a moment under her hand, then he lifted his head and stalked out, the two other Karda following. Tessa knew they would dance their aerial mourning for Llalara for hours into the night.

Light from the windows of the inn bounced off the wet cobbles of the courtyard between the inn and the stables. "I'm not sure this is a good idea." Tessa's steps were reluctant despite the steady drizzle. She couldn't get much wetter. Or colder.

"You coughed all afternoon, Tessa. And Kishar needs to grieve with his friends. This village is way on the outer edge of your father's hold. If anyone recognizes you, they won't have time to get word to him before we leave in the morning." He turned and pulled the hood of her short riding cloak forward. "You need something hot to eat and a warm place to sleep out of the weather. We were lucky to salvage enough of Kishar's rigging to get us here."

Tessa wanted to swoon at the redolent smells of cooking that met them when Galen opened the door to the crowded common area. Justiciar Donavan, slight and slightly bald with a round, almost sweet face, held forth at one end of a long table of villagers in a deep voice.

Mi'hiru Nyla took notes beside him. With her head bent down, all Tessa saw was a tight, braided crown of red hair. A few heads turned to the two tired travelers then turned back to listen to the justiciar. She followed Galen to a small table as close as he could get to the glowing magma stones in the large river rock fireplace.

He handed their cloaks to the serving girl, who rearranged the drying rack near the fire and hung them to dry. Tessa sat, half falling into the chair, and let him order for both of them. Blessed warmth scented with the smell of wet wool, the hot-metal tang of flickering magma stones, and too many bodies surrounded her.

She shivered even in the heat of the room. Galen was right. She'd be too sick to fly if they had to spend another night on wet ground wrapped in damp blankets that were half rag, with no tent, no food. Sick with a cold. Sick with sadness.

Tessa inhaled half the bowl of stew before she even tasted it. A basket of thick slices of dark, heavy bread smeared with fresh butter and fruit preserves almost made her delirious. She finally looked up from a bowl of hot peach cobbler with thick yellow cream and dropped her spoon.

He looked up, a spoonful of cobbler suspended in front of him. A large hand appeared and grabbed Galen's shoulder. He stilled. Tessa looked at the guard in her father's colors and felt hands clamping her shoulders. Two more guards behind her pulled her out of her chair.

"You need to come with us, Sir. Miss Tessa, we'll take you to your father in the morning." A second man appeared at Galen's other shoulder. "We'll hold this man tonight. He won't bother you..."

Tessa's chair crashed to the floor behind her, and she whirled, sword in one hand, knife in the other, both pointed at her two wide-eyed guards. She went from seated to standing so fast the guards didn't have time to move. A drop of blood appeared on one man's neck, her sword just touching it.

Galen stood, twisting out from under the guard's hand. "You'll take her nowhere she doesn't want to go." His hand went to the hilt of his sword.

The stones of the floor groaned in the silence. Galen rounded the table to Tessa's side, pulling her away.

The floor shifted beneath the guards. They managed to pull their swords free, but the flagstones tilted beneath them with a loud, grinding noise of rock against rock. Cursing and flailing, they fought to keep their balance. Chairs moved of their own will, the wood curling to wrap the men's legs. The four men froze.

Shock and fear sucked the air from the room. The only sounds Tessa heard were the shuffling of feet and the grating slide of chairs on the stone floor.

The space around their small table cleared, people scrambled toward the walls, half raised glasses and dripping spoons still in hand, eyes and mouths open wide. Tessa, Galen, and the four trapped guards stood alone inside a circle of frightened faces.

"What's going on here?" Justiciar Donavan's voice cut through the silence. "Put away those swords." He stood, leaning over his table, palms flat, round face darkened by a furious scowl. "All of you." The Mi'hiru walked from behind him, her hand on the short sword at her waist, to collect swords from the guards' frozen hands.

Tessa sheathed hers and tucked her knife away in its arm scabbard. Galen walked over and laid his sword on the long table, taking one short step back from it.

Fear and uncertainty shook the first guard's voice. "This is Tessa Me'Cowyn, sir. She's been missing all summer season. I don't know who this fellow is, but she is underage. Too young to be with him."

"No, I am not." She forced herself to speak through her fury and her clogged, fuzzy head. "I am eighteen. And I am not missing. My father knows where I was."

"She is the Austringer, Justiciar Donavan." The Mi'hiru's dry, matter-of-fact tone sounded forced. She gestured at the flagstones heaved every which way, at the twisted tangle of chair legs imprisoning the guards' legs, at the root and branch and leaf markings that replaced Galen's scars. "And something tells me this man is the Kern come to life again."

Tessa's voice was rough. Her throat was sore. Her head ached, and her body shook with fever and chills. She stood as close to the Folded Wing Inn's magma stone fire as she could without frying, and she was still cold. As much from swallowed grief for Llalara as from sickness.

The elders of the village listened to her with faces unconvinced. The stories of the Itza Larrak and the urbat were old, entrenched in their minds as fireside tales. The threat was stale, the danger believed gone centuries ago.

"Targeting planters and other Earth talents is the only organized behavior we've observed in the urbat so far. If they haven't already, Karda will bring in pieces of their metal parts to give your blacksmith. Spears and arrows tipped with their metal penetrate their tough skin and armor more easily than conventional metals." Tessa cleared her throat. "They are very hard to kill."

"But they're gone. The urbat have been gone for centuries. Since humans first arrived on Adalta." The village head man's words were pitched too high, more question than assertion. He was the third villager to say the same thing.

Justiciar Donovan rubbed the side of his face in frustration. "No. They're not gone. The threat is real. Listen to Tessa and Galen."

"We have walls."

Galen broke in, "Your walls won't help. Their wings are stubby and their bodies heavy, but they are able to fly in short hops. They can fly over anything under twenty feet. Your walls are not that high. You need to keep continual watch. It would be wise to work in groups when you're working the fields and keep your weapons close to hand. I'm not sure what they'll do to your livestock. And..." He pounded hard on his next words. "Protect your Earth talents. They are the most at risk."

"There is one other thing." Tessa clenched her fists, pressing them hard against the sides of her legs. Her eyes burned, and her thoughts were so fuzzy she fought to concentrate. "The wounded that they leave have some kind of sickness in their wounds."

"Not just the wounded. Wherever they fight, they leave behind a sick, stinking cloud," Galen said. "It will take your healers and Earth talents, all of them, strongest to weakest, to combine forces to clear it. I'll tell them how."

Galen hoped it would be enough. Kishar had told him it would. Just thinking about the stinking fog the urbat left in their wake soured his tongue. "It won't be easy. Do not—do not let a healer try to do this alone. It will take several Earth talents to support her. Or him. Even if your healer's secondary strength is Earth."

Mi'hiru Nyla added, "Guardian Daryl has the Mi'hiru and the Karda Patrol flying extra watches near the circles and villages close to them. The circle north of here is the only one so far where urbat have been sighted. Stay away from it. If a goat or a lamb, even a wounded deer, strays too close, let it go. Do not go after it."

"I repeat what I told you before the Austringer and the Kern arrived. These are orders from the guardian." Justiciar Donovan's voice was full-force-of-law firm.

Tessa noted, with relief, the justiciar's tone began to dispel the air of disbelief that lingered in the room. She understood. She didn't want to believe either. They fielded a few more questions, then Galen stood, pulling her up with him, her legs shaky. "We need rooms. Tessa needs to rest, as do I." He looked at Donovan. "I trust these guards will not be a problem."

The justiciar walked with Tessa and Galen as they followed the innkeeper up the stairs. His voice low, he warned, "I can protect you from these guards and keep them here overnight, but it would be well if you were gone early in the morning. I'd be hard-pressed to stand up to Me'Cowyn if he comes. The line between holder law and quadrant rule is not a clear one. As you know, the Me'Cowyn Hold is a legacy of the group of colonists who believed women were the property of men, and an unmarried daughter has little legal recourse against her father here."

He stopped and put his hand on the latch to his room. "An angry father might not agree that the Austringer and the Kern are above such laws—if he even accepts that is what you two are. From what I hear, Tessa, your father is angry. Daryl will not support his demand to haul you back to Me'Cowyn Hold. I don't know what your relations with your father are, but just being with Galen unchaperoned will be tinder for his anger. His plans for you are no secret to anyone."

Tessa thanked him for the help. "I'd hate to be the one who tried to take me away from Kishar. And I suspect your two Karda would be as dangerous. But we'll be gone by daylight."

Chapter Twenty

Readen rolled off the hard cot to his feet, unsure what woke him. He moved to the wall under the high window and listened. The night breeze carried faint sounds of screams from the nearby village. Something was happening. Strange, eerie howling and snarling grew closer and closer.

Finally, after hours, the screams and howls died into a dense, pregnant silence. Silence that pressed into him until he clapped his hands over his ears in pain.

The jarring rattle of the key in the lock of his cell broke the stillness, and he jumped as if thunder cracked. Pol appeared wrapped in a heavy cloak. He tossed another on the table and grabbed Readen's clothes. "Hurry. Rescue comes." His eyes were white, and his voice was rough with fear. Shoving pants and shirt toward Readen, he helped him dress and knelt to pull on Readen's boots.

Readen hissed as the shirt rubbed against the tender sigils carved into his chest and stomach. "Who?"

"Don't know. Hurry."

Then the screams started again, closer, louder. Readen waited, harvesting the fear they carried, Pol at his elbow, just outside the cell, unsure, listening as the screams of terror went on and on. Then snarls and howls rang through the courtyard, and monsters crashed through the iron-banded gate.

A mad, seething mob of huge, dog-like creatures poured in, blood dripping from jaws and fangs, eyes red. Half armor, half muscle with patchy hair. Metal gears jutted through the skin at their joints, long, articulated metal tails whipped. They surrounded Readen and Pol, who half drew his sword.

Readen jerked away as one of the monsters grabbed Pol's wrist in his powerful jaws, but the creature held it, not breaking the skin. Pol's eyes rolled with fear. His grip loosened, and the sword slid back into his scabbard. The unnatural dog-like creatures pushed and shoved, herding both men through the splintered door and out into the hallway. Readen slipped and almost went down. Blood. Blood and entrails were everywhere, across the floor, up the walls. Sprays of arterial blood spattered the ceiling. Readen's hated prison guards were in pieces, recognizable only by the shreds of uniform that clung wetly to unnamable parts.

Overwhelming power flooded into Readen's body, fire flamed through his muscles, his bones burned, and he fell, convulsing, to the bloody, stone floor.

Someone was wiping his face with a wet cloth. Readen struggled out of blackness to see Pol's face, distorted with concern, above him. He took a deep breath. Power. He rolled over, gathered his legs under him and stood. Power. Power like he'd never felt before. He looked at the dozens of monsters surrounding him, sitting calmly on their haunches, licking blood off their claws and their strange half-metal, half-flesh, armored bodies.

Then they looked at him, stood, and began to move as one body with Readen and Pol in their center, toward the gates to the prison. He knew there were no humans left alive in that place but Pol and him. He gloried in the power of all that blood and terror.

Only two terrified horses remained in the stables. Pol threw blankets over their heads and murmured to them until they calmed enough to saddle, then the two men mounted and headed north. Readen was free. Powerful again. Free.

And surrounded by monsters.

Days later the urbat melted away into the surrounding forest, and the two men stumbled through the gates of Readen's compound near his mines in the northwest of Restal, starving and weak with thirst and fatigue.

Readen's overseer stood, gaping, in the doorway to the fortress-like hold. Two stable boys ran round the side of the building and skidded to a stop, wide eyes moving back and forth between Readen and Pol. Readen dismounted, muscles screaming. He hadn't been off the horse since his strange rescue except for the most urgent bodily necessities. Pol took the reins and headed for the stable boys.

Readen stalked, stiff but upright, refusing to show pain, into his home. "Don't just stand there. I need food and water and a bath. Get guards up on the walls. Let me know immediately if anyone approaches. I assume my rooms are prepared. And I need two messengers for a long ride. Send them to me immediately."

One guttering candle lit the cold stone walls and floor of the small space, most of it taken up by the granite table in the center of the room, its surface stained dark, rusty red. Small, high windows not unlike those in his former cell let in dim light. But this room was in the cellars of his own hold, many kilometers from the hated prison. Now he could come and go as he wished, eat when he wished, bathe when he wished.

His messengers were on their way to militant Akhara Quadrant to two mercenary companies with an offer he knew they would take. There was the familiar brief flame of rage in his chest at the thought of how much faster his messengers could be if he could command Karda.

For days he'd reveled in the luxuries of his hold, immersing himself in sybaritic pleasure. Three children. Samel had brought two young girls and a boy from the prime as soon as Readen sent word. One was still waiting. He exulted in the power he gained just anticipating the boy's fear.

Readen was always gentle and solicitous with his victims at first. Patient until he felt the beginning of a response, reluctant pleasure at his touch. Then just a little pain, eliciting a few tears. Then loving patience. A little more pain. Patience, pleasure, and pain. Patience, pleasure, and pain. Until the screams began and couldn't stop. Sometimes it took days. Some he could make last for weeks, his rage honed to an edge as sharp as the knives he used.

Readen smiled, remembering, and cut the last line of a sigil into his skin just under the left side of his ribcage. It burned fire, and his body shook with pain and power as the symbol blackened into sharp, glistening obsidian. It transformed as soon as he finished cutting a mark now. His left arm, his chest, now most of his upper belly were covered, stiff with the gleaming signs. He only needed four more. Four more to fully materialize the Itza Larrak. Four more and he would have the army he needed to destroy Daryl and take back control of Restal Quadrant.

He shook himself and motioned Pol to bring the figure who stood waiting beside the door, arms twisted to his back, hands securely tied. One of his guards suspected to be more loyal to Daryl than to Readen who got caught trying to sneak away. The man stumbled to the table, oblivious, dazed. Readen picked up a small, sharp, silver knife and handed it to Pol with a shallow stone bowl. "Bleed him of what you can. Don't let him pass out."

Pol held the man's wrist over the bowl, pricking it with the tip of the knife. Blood dripped in a sluggish stream until the bowl was half full of liquid, black in the dim light. He clamped his large fingers over the cut until it closed. Dipping a cloth in the basin of water on the table, he wiped the blood from the dazed guard's wrist and bound it with a clean pad.

Readen stood directly in front of the guard, forcing the man's head up to look into his eyes, traced a fingernail down his face and his throat, a gentle, sensuous stroke, imagining the beads of blood he could raise with the little knife. "Go back to your cell and wait for me to summon you again." It was nice to have time to play. This one had been especially defiant when they caught him. A tenday ago he had been strong and healthy. Now he would walk to his cell, lock himself in, and wait. Unfortunately, he was beyond fear. He seldom screamed now.

Readen leaned over the bowl in the center of the table and drew in a deep breath. The sharp, metallic smell of the blood helped relieve his frustration. Usually, he had time to play with his blood donors, male or female, heightening their fear, arousing them against their will, sucking in their fear and self-revulsion, feeling it fuel his power.

But he was growing impatient. He might have control here on his own hold, but it was still imprisonment until he could safely leave. Until he could gather back his scattered human forces and had the akenguns safely in hand. Until the Itza Larrak fully materialized and was able to free the urbat to Readen's control. He shuddered in spite of himself.

The monsters that had freed him from prison waited, hidden and silent. A few watched from the forest. The rest returned to their circle. But he could feel their attention, even this deep beneath the hold. They were waiting, out of sight from his staff and the few mercenaries who had made their way to his hold. Readen knew no one would fight for him if they knew he was allied with the monsters.

He closed the door, returned to the table, and picked up the guttering candle before it went out. Light flared as he lit the two iron torchieres on the walls. He blew out the candle. The acrid after-smell masked the copper scent of the dark blood in the bowl. He began to chant. Four times he repeated the strange words, "Dalla Itza Larrak Alka Ra." His fingers dipped into the bowl, scooping blood, wiping it over the sigils on his arm. He dipped, again and again, smearing the thick, red liquid across his chest, wetting each sign. He chanted, "Dalla Itza Larrak Alka Ra," again and again, the words rasping out his throat.

A slight movement of air seared the obsidian scars with pain as if the cuts were fresh. The words grew rough and harsh, his mouth dried, his tongue thickened, but he kept chanting, chanting, chanting. With exquisite slowness a spiral of dark, glittering motes formed, growing, filling the space around him. Readen's voice died. The monstrous figure of the Itza Larrak flickered.

Faceted eyes glittered fierce yellow. Huge, pierced metallic wings rang sibilant, discordant sounds as they opened and closed, the walls beyond them not quite visible through the flickering movement. Long talons clicked on the stone floor as the tall form moved, rounding the table toward Readen, more and more tangible, but never fully materialized. Readen turned, head painfully stretched back to look up at it towering over him.

"Readen, my own son." Its soft mechanical voice filled the space in the small room, echoing in Readen's ears. The voice he hadn't heard since Marta defeated him in the cavern that had been the Itza Larrak's prison.

Readen's head fell back, his arms raised over his head—he could barely contain his joy. Success tasted sweet on his tongue. He was not alone. His ally was back—the ally he'd feared lost. His breath quickened in his chest, fast and shallow.

He licked his lips and spoke, words rushing out in a torrent. "The symbols. The last symbols. Show them to me, and I will be able to bring you forth. You will control the urbat for me. Nothing can stand before me with you beside me, behind me." His body quivered with anticipation. The pain in the scars on his arms and chest was nothing. The Itza Larrak had not been destroyed in the cavern. Readen's mind reeled, drunk with relief.

The monster stilled, its form wavered. Silence grew. Unease wormed its way into Readen's jubilation. Sweat slicked his body. A drop rolled down the side of his face into his ear. He moved a hand to wipe wet strands of hair from his forehead. Neck straining, he stared up at the alien face of the Itza Larrak. It was changing. It's features softened, became more human—oddly familiar.

The figure flickered. Then it spoke. Its words crackled, sharp—piercing Readen's conceit with hot needles. Knives cut at his confidence, shredding his certainty. "I will not be behind you. You are mine. My creation. I created you, forged you into my weapon, put you into your mother's womb to be my gateway back into this world."

The words—created—your mother's womb—gateway—swirled and pounded and bled in his head like wild animals caught in a trap. Pushed by a lifetime of pain and shame his words squeezed out. "My talent? What happened to my talent?"

"Useless to me. I needed you to release me from my prison. Talent was a barrier."

Useless to me. Useless to me. Useless to me. Readen's head was a great bell— the words a clapper pounding back and forth, back and forth, relentless. The bell cracked. This was why his mother died when he was born. The Itza Larrak was why his childhood was so miserable. Why he suffered from the shame of no talent from the earliest time he could remember.

Readen staggered, his knees buckled. The monster's form grew more and more solid, its strength grew. It grabbed Readen's arm and forced him back against the table until its edge cut into his spine. Pain seared as a razor-sharp talon tore through his shirt and cut a line into the soft flesh of his abdomen. Then another. And another. Circling his navel. The Itza Larrak was carving the last symbols into Readen itself.

He grabbed at the monster's wrist, its metal joint so cold it burned. Anger, terror, shock flooded him. Readen knew the Itza Larrak would take over his body if it finished the symbols. He would be lost.

Subsumed.

Gone.

Useless.

He scrabbled, frantic to force the monster away. His body ran with sweat. Salty sweat that dripped in searing runnels, washing through the blood on his chest, smearing over the obsidian symbols. He called on every bit of his power and strength to push the creature's talon away, to stop it from carving into him. It hissed a command in its strange language, the language of the symbols. "Do not resist lest I destroy you. I will finish this. Finally."

Readen's arm swiped painfully against his chest, smearing sweat, blurring the sigils under the blood, and the form of the Itza Larrak flickered. Its shape faded. Hope flashed inside Readen.

The knife-sharp black talon paused, hooked in Readen's flesh, unable to finish the last sigil. The monstrous figure flickered again. Its grip on Readen's arm loosened. Its hand blurred. Readen's other hand scrabbled around the table behind him and found the pink-tinged basin of water he'd used to wash the prisoner's blood away.

With all the strength he had left, he swung it around and sloshed it across his chest and arm, sloughing away the blood that called the creature.

A scream pierced Readen's head—high, shrill, keening that went on and on. Exquisite pain stabbed his ears, doubled him over. And the Itza Larrak dissolved back into a spiral of glowing black motes and winked out of existence.

The basin crashed to the floor, shattering. Readen fell into the chair then slid to the cold stone floor, slicing his cheek on a shard of the broken bowl. He rolled away, curling around the screaming pain. The symbol the Itza Larrak had carved burned to obsidian on his belly.

Complete.

All but one. All but the last one.

All but the last, most important one.

But he knew it now.

He lay on the floor.

A lifetime of anger and resentment seethed inside him.

An entire childhood spent in fury and frustration boiled his blood.

Chapter Twenty-One

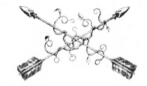

After a long night of several cups of foul-tasting herbal tea and a trip to the bathroom down the hall, Tessa had sweated the fever out and was almost herself again. They left in the still of early dawn just as the sky in the east was showing pink.

The guards from Me'Cowyn Hold disappeared in the night, probably to bring reinforcements. Or even Tessa's father. That wasn't a confrontation either of them wanted.

They flew straight for the Line of Devastation and followed it almost to its end. Galen rode behind Tessa, strapped in with extra leathers. His relief when they finally landed safely amused Kishar. But it was relief tempered by disbelief that the line had snaked so far from the circle. Kilometers. Most of an arrow-straight two-day flight.

~I would not drop you, Kern. Or if I did, I would at least have caught you before you hit the ground and made a mess.~

~And I would be properly grateful, I assure you.~ Galen rubbed his thighs. Riding pillion on a Karda was not for the faint of heart. ~As grateful as I am that this flight has ended.~

Kishar must have had word relayed back to the camp because two un-partnered Karda landed just behind them, dropping bundles of saplings carried in nets, beaks clacking and making sounds suspiciously like grumpy muttering. Young Karda did not like being pack animals.

Galen unloaded the tools and packs from their backs, including a tent and other supplies to replace what they'd lost, and stripped off their rigging. Kishar swatted one of them with his wing, and they took off to circle above, keeping watch.

~Lazy younglings.~ And he made the same grumbling-muttering sound.

~Stand still.~ Tessa laughed and finished grooming him. ~Go dig up some tubers. I can see some growing under that hickory tree.~

~I'll save some for the two of you.~

~Don't bother. I wouldn't want to deprive you of your favorite treat.~

Galen shuddered. He'd tried them. They tasted like sawdust, even when baked and loaded with butter, but the Karda loved them.

Unsure how long it would take him to cut this line—or if he even could, Galen set up the tent and piled rocks in a fire circle, scraping the thick grass away for a safe distance. The grasses in the meadow swayed low with heavy seed heads. Kishar would likely have them stripped clean by the time they left.

He wrapped the long straps around the saddle rig and stowed it in one side of the tent. The rain had ended, but the air was hot and heavy with moisture just waiting to turn into drizzle. Good for planting the saplings, but miserable for Karda and human.

He gathered up an armload of saplings and a shovel and headed for the line, leaving Tessa asleep, wrapped in blankets in the tent, and Kishar back in the air, circling. He stopped about twenty meters from the edge of the line.

Stark white skeletal abelee trees, some standing, too many fallen in a criss-cross jumble, all dead, scattered through the space in front of him across a mat of dead grass. A few of the phyto-remediating grasses and low-growing plants under the trees were still struggling, but most were dead, the air heavy with the smell of rot.

He looked up at the tree he stood under. Leaves turning yellow with the season's change mingled with leaves withered the diseased brown of death with no promise of return. The sickness in the soil moved up through his feet and legs to lodge as nausea in his stomach. He forced himself not to heave. Kneeling, he placed his hands on the trunk where it flared and met the ground, pressing his forehead against the smooth bark.

"Tell me." His words the barest whisper of sound were caught by the breeze and spread to the trees around him.

Immense relief and gratitude, despair and hope, swept through him, and the tree showed him swarms of tiny bug-like things, part organic and part living crystal, streaming from the circle into the line toward the end. There they spread wide and attacked roots, encircling them like sharp-edged garrotes, cutting through them, cutting the life force of the trees and grasses.

It was several long moments before Galen pulled himself away from the tree's embrace and sat back on his heels. Nanobots. A type of nanobot. He felt them cut through the roots and then move on, pushing through the dirt, fusing into a hard conduit for more of their kind, stretching, reaching, extending the line.

Centimeter by centimeter, it crawled with the strange tiny creatures, alive with a primitive, ant-like, mechanical intelligence and the same greasy, evil feel as the urbat and the circles. Simply planting saplings and spreading seeds was not going to stop them.

This was what made him so sick before. So sick he almost died before Tessa and Kishar found him. He could feel them attacking again. Tiny prickling sensations wherever his body touched the ground. The tattoos on his wrists flared with heat. His scars disappeared as root and branch replaced them, spread down his fingers, up his arms, across his chest. Sharp needles stung the scar on his cheek as it morphed into the trefoil leaf tattoo. His eyes burned, and the world took on a green cast.

Anger swelled out of the hard, sick knot in his chest, fierce and burning. It licked the inside of his skin. What could he do? Kishar's voice echoed in his head, telling him over and over how to twist the force of Earth and Air into fire, pushing him, pushing him until he learned. Would that work? Could he burn them away? Cut the line with fire?

He knelt, palms flat on the ground, and called to the molten heat deep in the core of Adalta, pulling it to him, drawing it up through his Earth and Air talent, twining them the way Kishar taught him. The rope of fire seared through his body, fighting his control.

He was flame. He was heat. He was forge-hot fire frying the bots, a scalding scalpel scorching through the earth toward the line, burning a fiery path through the strange bots, spearing across the Line of Devastation. Burning, fierce, blue-white flame cut into the line, searing it, cutting it away from the circle.

He felt the heat lick up against cool, living soil on the other side of the line, pushing against his control. Frantic he tried to draw it back, tried to control it before it reached the live trees on the other side. Before he set the whole forest aflame. It continued to burn, heating inside him till he feared his blood would boil.

Galen threw his consciousness into the soil and rocks beneath him, diving into the coolness beneath the surface, desperate to quench the blaze. Deep he reached, into cool soil, down through limestone and granite. Deep he reached for the river of water hundreds of meters below, trying to draw it to him, to quench his fire before it consumed him, too.

Desperate, still fighting the force threatening to destroy him with searing flame, he slipped into green darkness and fiery orange pain.

Cool mist fell on his face. Every muscle ached. His bones ached. His scars were red and hot. Heat scalded his eyes. Exhausted, he rolled up and leaned against the trunk of a dead tree, welcoming the fine mists that drifted down through the bare branches.

I might need to work on control a bit more.

He looked at the circle where he had burned across the line. He hunched his shoulders, moving as little as possible. Every brush of his clothes against his skin hurt. He concentrated his vision and watched the tiny bots swarm over the cut he worked so hard to make—swarming like a disturbed ant pile over the cooling three-meter-wide swath. Despair threatened to leach the little strength he still had from his bones.

The strange black, half-organic, half-crystalline nanobots were already repairing the damage he had done to their conduit, the damage that had taken nearly all he had to inflict. He closed his eyes again. Weariness dragged him back into sleep.

When he woke again, he could move without wanting to scream. Carefully he stretched one limb at a time. He was naked. Again. His tattoos pulsed as if they were pumping water over his body, carrying away the heat. The canvas above him glowed with sunlight. He was in the tent. It must be late afternoon. How had he gotten there? He must have been able to walk at least a little.

Tessa wasn't strong enough to have gotten him away from the circle by herself. But she remembered to lay him with bare skin directly on the ground. He wasn't healed, but he could at least move around. He found his clothes folded next to him, dressed, and started to pull on his boots. Three Karda screamed in the sky above him.

~Galen, wake up! Look.~ Both Tessa and Kishar shouted the warning at him. He looked out across the circle. A storm cloud of dust rose over a distant pack of urbat headed down the line straight for them.

~There are too many of them for us to fight. We need to get out of here right now. Hurry.~ Tessa's words screamed in his head.

Galen saw her throw the saddle rig on Kishar, her fingers sorting straps, fastening buckles as fast as she could, both their sword belts slung over her shoulder. He grabbed a couple of blankets out of the tent, swiped up his boots, and ran for the Karda, sharp rocks stabbing his bare feet. Tessa leaped from Kishar's bent knee to the saddle.

~You don't have time for your gear. We'll have to leave it.~ Kishar half-flew, half-leaped toward Galen, who grabbed for Tessa's arm, clambered up behind her, and buckled in, trying to keep the awkward bundle of blankets and his boots wedged between them. Kishar took off.

Tessa had her bow out and strung before they were twenty feet off the ground, aiming for the first rank of urbat that snarled and leaped at them, tore through their tent, scattered pots and water canvases, and shredded the bundles of saplings stacked under a tree.

~There must be twenty-five or thirty of them. Let's get out of here.~ Galen hissed with pain. He was helpless to keep the saplings from being destroyed, and his tattoos felt as if the urbat were clawing them from his skin. He shifted out of the way of Tessa's elbow as she shot arrow after arrow. She downed four of them before Kishar flew out of range, the other urbat turning on their own wounded and dead in a snarling mass.

~Let's make one more pass, Kishar. I can get more of them.~ Tessa reached for another arrow out of the quiver by her left knee. ~The new arrowheads are much more effective.~

~Look, Tessa. Look at what's coming.~ Galen reached around and pulled her hand back. Dozens of urbat swarmed over the hill and into the clearing to defend the Line of Devastation.

~There are too many for us to fight by ourselves. I don't have a bow, and I'm not about to get on the ground. Even if it were safe for Kishar to fly low enough for me to jump off, I'm not sure I could move enough earth to handle that many even if I were at full strength, which I'm not. We need help, Tessa. We can't take them all ourselves. Something has happened to wake that many of them. Maybe what I did to the line last night has only made things worse.~

Tessa's body shook with frustration against his chest as she let the bow drop, her thoughts leaking through their connection: *I'm supposed to be the Austringer, the Hunter, and I'm failing.*

Galen tightened his grip on her waist, holding himself as steady as he could, trying to ignore the pain from his tattoos. ~Who do you think we could talk into giving us another tent? We're a little hard on our camping equipment.~ He made his inner voice light and bantering, and he felt her begin to relax.

Both of them falling into despair would solve nothing.

They circled above the urbat, trying to get an accurate count. The creatures milled around too close together, some of them leaping up after them, beating their stubby wings, but Kishar was too high for them to reach. Tessa finally gave up. ~It's like shooting into a swarm of bees. I'm tired, Galen. I can feel you hurting. And somehow, we need to get to Restal Prime to tell Daryl what we've seen.~

She unstrung her bow, stowed it in its scabbard under her leg, and rubbed two fingers against her temple. ~There's a village a half day's flight from here. We can stop for the night, and hopefully get supplies. Again.~

~Did you notice what they did to the saplings I was going to plant? They shredded them into mulch as if they know what we use them for. I'm getting more and more worried about the people we left behind.~

~They've been fighting the urbat for tendays, long before we left. They're experienced, and you told the planters to hold off on planting so as not to set the urbat off. It's a long trip to Restal Prime, but tonight should be our last stop.~

Galen shifted his balance with Tessa's as Kishar wheeled in a circle above their campsite and followed the Line of Devastation south until it ended, several kilometers away. Then they veered southwest, all three of them silent as they flew on toward the afternoon sun.

Tessa waved at the two Mi'hiru who joined them on their approach to the village's landing meadow late in the afternoon. She could see three of Restal's Karda Patrol circling high above the village. Kishar touched down at the edge of the trees that separated the field and the village, and the Mi'hiru's Karda loped up to meet them.

"We came in from the other direction over the village, and something is very wrong there." The taller of the two Mi'hiru spoke before anyone dismounted. "I can't path to Bettan, but he is upset. I was so glad to recognize you, Kishar. Maybe you can tell us what's wrong." Her lined face creased with agitation. She nodded to Tessa and Galen and dismounted. "I'm Amanda. Bettan carries me, and Peyta partners LiLi."

Amanda waved away Tessa's attempt to introduce them. "We know who you are, Tessa. Austringer." She glanced at Galen. "And Kern."

Tessa slid off Kishar's back and had to stop herself from helping Galen down. His movements were stiff and controlled. She knew he was hiding pain and might not appreciate her calling attention to it.

LiLi smoothed wind-scrambled hair out of her face and spoke, looking back and forth between Tessa and Galen, curious despite her agitation.

"The three patrollers with us are keeping watch. We've seen mounted people in twos and threes, mostly men, riding through these woods. We thought bandits might have attacked here, but that's not the sense we get from Peyta and Bettan. They wouldn't be projecting so much fear and dread if that's what it was. And there wasn't a hint of smoke nor a sign of any burned buildings like there would be if it were marauders who attacked."

Amanda looked toward the village, hidden behind the screen of trees. "In fact, there was not a hint of anything or anyone, and no one has come to meet us. Something is very wrong."

Kishar cocked his head toward the other two Karda, then looked back at Tessa and Galen. ~Urbat.~

Tessa could almost feel the blood drain from her head. "Urbat," she whispered. She didn't want to say the word out loud, as if not speaking it would make it not be.

The wind changed, and nothing could make it not be. The sick sweet smell of death blew across them. Tessa gagged and slapped her hand across her mouth and nose.

"How long ago?" Galen asked Kishar.

The three Karda looked at each other, and Kishar pathed, ~A tenday or less.~

"He says they were attacked by the urbat less than a tenday ago."

The wind shifted again, and Tessa could breathe. She watched the disbelief grow into horror on the faces of the two Mi'hiru.

"It can't be." LiLi breathed the words out like they took all the breath she had. "I thought the urbat were only a danger around the circle far to the north." She and Amanda looked at each other and then at their two Karda partners.

Bettan pushed at Amanda with his head. "Oh, my lady Adalta. They can attack anywhere." She leaned into his neck, holding his mane as if it were all she could do to keep standing.

Galen walked out into the meadow and circled his hand above his head. Tessa heard him suck a breath through his teeth in pain. After a brief conversation in signals, two of the patrollers landed, loping toward them.

"Is it too much to hope that whatever happened here was an accident or a sickness?" one of the patrollers said as they dismounted and strode over. He reached to grasp Tessa's forearm. "I'm Brett, and this is

Dillon." He waved his hand toward the Karda who brought them in. "They are Usala and Sanao."

Tessa watched his face go from cocky to pale as he looked at the distraught expressions on the faces of the four of them. "I'm Tessa, and this is Galen, the Kern."

Brett hesitated, and Tessa saw a flicker of surprise flash across his weathered, lined face. He flinched at the scars on Galen's face and reached to grasp his forearm in greeting, eyes bright and curious. "Do you think he's been killed?"

"Who are you wondering about?" Galen asked, holding on to Brett's arm a little longer than was polite. Then he turned and greeted lanky, grizzled Dillon.

"This is the village where Daryl imprisoned Readen," Lili said. Her flat words spread into the sudden silence like a muddy, debris-laden stream flooding into a clear lake.

And the breeze shifted again. All six of them turned and looked in the direction of the village Tessa still didn't know the name of. Somehow that seemed essential—like not knowing was a kind of disrespect. She shuddered. For the dead.

"Ardencroft. The name of the village is Ardencroft." As if he heard her thoughts, Dillon's voice was soft.

Tessa knew she would never hear that name again without feeling deep, deep sorrow and anger and smelling the stench of death.

Tessa watched as the third patroller—she'd never heard his name—flew off in the direction of Restal Prime. She wanted to be up in the clear air with him, away from the terrible smell of death. Away from the terrible sight of too many bodies torn into too many pieces.

She held her breath as she untied the cloth from over her nose and mouth and poured more vinegar on it, tying it back as fast as her fingers could move, feeling the sharp eye-burning liquid drip down the front of her neck to soak her shirt. Her stomach muscles were an agonizing clutch of pain. She didn't even feel the urge to vomit anymore. She was empty.

Tessa looked down at the small wrapped bundle lying in the bed in front of her, one of the last of the bodies they'd found, one of the very few not torn apart. She couldn't cry anymore. There was no more cry inside her. Carrying the child with all the tenderness she could find under her building rage; she made a vow to this unnamed bit of a life too soon cut off.

There would be no urbat anywhere on Adalta that would be safe from her. She would fight them all her life if she had to. She would not die while there was a single urbat left anywhere. If she lived past eighty, and they were not gone, she would still hunt them.

Tessa reached the pit and handed the child to Brett whose weathered face was tight with grief and anger behind the vinegar soaked cloth over his mouth and nose. He placed the child with the others in the large hole Galen scooped out at the edge of the village under the long arms of a chestnut tree. There was no way to tell which of these ravaged bodies was its mother or father, brother or sister.

Tessa looked at her empty hands and pressed them to her stomach against the hot ball of grief and rage that burned against her diaphragm. Then she went back to make certain there were no more.

The six of them went through every house, every shop, every stable, garden shed, and greenhouse in the village. Then they crossed the small creek that divided village from prison and went through that. Every cell, every guard room, every bathing room, every outbuilding. Sick with too much blood and the stench of death, they finished with the human bodies and started on the urbat.

Galen stood in the middle of the dusty street polluted with ichor and blood next to the wheeled cart they used to carry the dead.

He was looking down at the mangled remains of one of the too few dead urbat. "There's not much more than small metal parts from their bodies here, Tessa. They took the large pieces. They stripped the flesh away and took the metal. Remember? We saw them stripping their dead in the circle and burying the metal parts? Do they know it's dangerous when we use it against them? Is that why they take it."

They stood, looking down at the lacerated flesh and fur.

"I don't even want to touch it. If I weren't certain that burying them in Adalta will clean the evil from these bodies, I would let them lie here and rot."

"I know. If I didn't think it would dishonor the dead to leave this filth in the town where Ardencroft's people lived and loved, worked and played, I'd want to leave them, too." Tessa's voice was low and quiet.

"How many were there to fight and kill all these villagers, all the guards at the prison, and still leave twenty-two dead urbat?"

Tessa shuddered. "They didn't listen. Daryl is spreading the word everywhere. I know this village was warned. I found a big bag of urbat metal stuffed on a shelf in the blacksmith's shop. But not one weapon anywhere tipped with it. They didn't believe."

"Judging by the state of the bodies, and allowing for the cooler weather, Readen could have been free for tendays." Galen looked at Tessa. "It's too much to hope he died here, too."

"This must have happened not long after the first urbat attacks on us at the circle. How could this...this...abomination be kept secret for so long? Someone must have known. Must have diverted patrols. Lied."

Ardencroft was part of the Me'Neve Hold. Tessa'd seen him at the Keep too often when she was one of Readen's hostages. Whether or not he'd supplied Readen with overt support, she didn't know. He'd also been one of the more vocal of the holders who refused to believe Marta's story about Readen and the Itza Larrak. He'd believe now.

She looked up to see the lanky Dillon help Amanda haul more urbat remains from between two buildings. *What would provoke a holder into this kind of betrayal of his people? Did Me'Neve even know? He couldn't have. He was one of the holders who supported Readen's revolt—I saw him in the keep when I was hostage—but he couldn't know about this and keep quiet.* She shuddered. Then she went back to the task of burying the dead.

When they dragged the last urbat to the pit Galen gouged out of the earth near the village midden—a petty revenge—Galen knelt and shoved. Dirt piled up over the corpses and furred over with green grass and a thicket of thorns.

She stood with the two Mi'hiru and the two patrollers and watched, wrapped in silence, with faces that radiated raging fury at what they'd seen. Galen still had the villagers' grave to cover, so he knelt, hands flat on the ground, head down, to recover.

She took the cloths that covered her face and his and soaked them with vinegar again. She wanted to burn her clothes. The stink of death permeated everything. She didn't know how she would ever erase it from her mind.

She and Galen walked slowly back to the other end of the little town. The others were already there, two sitting cross-legged, heads down, one leaning against a tree, one kneeling at the edge of the pit despite the smell. They were exhausted.

All five Karda stood behind them, staring across the grisly space. They stood as Tessa and Galen approached, awed expressions of respect tinged with not a little fear marked their faces. Watching Galen move the earth to form the burial pit erased any doubt that he was the Kern.

Galen knelt, and they stood, each human with a hand on his or her Karda, in a half circle behind him. He placed his hands on the ground in front of him and bowed his head.

Amanda spoke in a low voice, "Accept these people, Adalta, as we honor them for the lives they lived. Lives of happiness, sadness, work, play. Lives sometimes of greatness and sometimes of pettiness. Ordinary lives in all their glory and all their meanness. Honor the mother who smiles no more, the father who gives no more lessons, the child who will never build the castles she dreamed of, never plow the fields like his father and his father's father. Use their bodies in your renewal. Make of them flowers, trees, fruits, grains, grasses. Give them new life in this place of death. Make of these deaths, not a waste but a renewal."

"Renewal." Soft.

"Renewal." A whisper.

"Renewal." A breath.

"Renewal." A sigh.

"Renewal."

The whispered words drifted. The Kern's hands pushed, and the four of them witnessed Adalta rise to cover the bodies with a gently sloping mound that sprouted grass, flowers, berry bushes, and in the very center a sapling.

A slender shoot of green rose above the grass. They watched a a rare native darisa tree, grow tall and reach its branches wide. It unfurled green leaves and blossoms that budded and spread in a lacy white veil, a purity of promise that showered petals down to blanket the ground. Tight buds swelled into pale orange globes of fruit that glistened with drops of juice, fell, and offered their seeds to the soil beneath.

And they watched the darisa's green leaves burn bright blood-red, scatter and whirl in the breeze and fall to seal the promise of new life to come in this place of death.

Chapter Twenty-Two

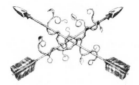

Piles of paper covered Daryl's desk—his father's over-large, over-ornate desk—and spilled onto the floor. Books, some of them old and fragile, covered every flat surface in the room. Three mismatched, stuffed bookshelves stood against the walls of the once elegant study.

Tessa watched Daryl pace back and forth in front of the long, mullioned windows. Galen stood silent beside her. They'd come directly from the mews, leaving their Karda in the care of others, to report to Daryl Galen's failure to cut the Line of Devastation, the escalating dangers coming from the circle, and what they'd found in Ardencroft. What they'd done.

She smelled of the death they brought into the room. She wanted nothing more than a bath, clean clothes, a bed, and at least twenty-four hours to spend in it.

Daryl stopped and looked at her and Galen over the top of a pair of gold-rimmed glasses, folded them, laid them on the desk, and pinched the bridge of his nose. "Samel left two days ago, with a squad of Mounted Patrol to check on Readen. He and Me'Neve are the two I assigned to watch him."

He looked away, his mouth twisted as if he could taste his bitter thoughts. "I'll ask the Mi'hiru to send someone to tell Samel to follow

Readen's tracks and report back. Me'Neve was a supporter of Readen's, but I don't see him allying with those monsters. Krager suspects he's involved with the growing revolt against the aristocracy of talent. Me'Neve isn't a strong talent."

He picked up the pair of glasses and tossed them back on a shifting pile of papers. "He swore his allegiance to me."

His eyes lifted to Galen's, and the planes of his face hardened, the lines sharpened. Neither man looked away until Tessa thought the tension in the room might catch fire.

She shifted on her feet. She was damp, dirty, discouraged, and black-hole-damned if she was going to wait for the two of them to quit glaring at each other. "It isn't Galen you should distrust. Are you blaming the messenger for the message? Readen was your responsibility."

She waited for Daryl to explode on her. *I can't believe I said that to him.* But the past few days had burned more than grief into her. That grief forged her strength and courage into a sharp, flexible sword of determination.

Daryl looked at her, dropped his eyes to the messy desk, and scrubbed hard at his face, pulling strands of hair out of the leather tie that held it back, but his shoulders didn't relax. "Someone put a complicated don't-look-here over the town and the prison, using unfamiliar, unknown spells. Abala tells me it even affected the Karda. I hope I'm wrong, but it appears someone or something is controlling those urbat. It has to be the Itza Larrak."

He paused, toying with his glasses. "I think it escaped the cavern and is not just controlling the urbat but Readen, too. And I think it's been controlling him for a long time."

He shuffled a stack of papers. "These are his letters from prison. He says he's been under its influence since he was a child."

Tessa sucked in a breath. *Is Daryl deliberately trying to excuse Readen's responsibility for his actions? To make him a puppet?* She bit her lip to keep from asking the question aloud.

He looked out the window for a long moment then blew out a harsh breath and looked back at Galen. "Abala also tells me this isn't necessary, but I need to hear you say it. I need to hear you say you are not the person you were. I need to hear who you are now."

Tessa leaned forward, opened her mouth, and anger started to spill out.

Galen put his arm out in front of her. "No, Tessa. He's right. I played a part in this disaster. And it is not to my credit that it wasn't an even bigger disaster. I was bringing weapons that would have decimated any force Readen came up against. If they hadn't been destroyed—"

He looked down at the scars on his left hand. "If Readen hadn't gotten impatient and too far ahead of himself, Daryl might not be the one standing here in front of us."

He pulled his sleeve away from the tattoo on one wrist and clamped his other hand around it, looking at Daryl without blinking. He sucked in a deep breath and blew it out. "I am deeply sorry for my actions. I have no excuse. I can't even say I did it because it was my job. I didn't care about that. I didn't care about what the weapons would do. I didn't care who got them, who would use them, who would be killed by them."

He looked down at his scarred left hand. "I am paying for that. Kishar tells me, assures me, that I am the Kern. What that means, I'm not certain. Only that I do things every day I would have thought impossible, even if I could have envisioned them." He held his hands out, palms up, in front of him and looked down. "I have a…a power so strong it scares the hell out of me. And I can't say I will use it in your service."

Daryl frowned and started to speak.

Galen stopped him, his voice taut and low, his words precise and yet soft, each syllable articulated with a force that sounded as if it originated deep in the center of his chest. "But I can tell you I have, and I will use it in the service of Adalta. It belongs to her. It comes from her. I am her tool." In a voice so soft Tessa and Daryl had to lean forward to hear, he said, "If her tool doesn't shatter."

Tessa could see a muscle jumping in his jaw, and he was trembling so hard she didn't know how he could stand. The bitterness of regret that spilled out of him was tangible. His face flushed as if he were embarrassed by the strength of the emotion that flooded each word.

The men stood, two statues facing each other, then Daryl gave a sharp nod, dropped into the chair behind his desk, said, "All right," and waved them to the chairs opposite him.

Galen sat, settling into the chair as if his bones were brittle, as if he moved too quickly pieces of him would break away and be stepped on, ground to dust.

Daryl's shoulders didn't relax, nor did his expression.

"Daryl." Tessa was still standing. "We came directly here from the mews. It's very late, we are exhausted, and I am sure you can smell the death and filth on us. I feel like it's permanently sunk into my skin. I need a bath. I need clean clothes. I need sleep. And we will need Kishar with us to continue this…"

Daryl turned his head and looked at her, though, clearly, his thoughts were still focused on Galen. Finally, he wrinkled his nose. "Yes, both of you are more than a little ripe, and I'm sure you'd like time to wash some of what you've seen away. We'll meet in the morning immediately after breakfast."

Next morning Tessa stood at the open doorway to the mews, her long cloak wrapped tight against the cold autumn air, and watched Kishar circle to land, his silhouette dark against the deep pink of the dawn sky. He wasn't alone. Two other Karda flew with him, almost dwarfing him in size, riders on their backs.

~You've been hunting and caught more than food, I see.~ She'd thought she could sleep the night and the next day away, but here she was, looking for Kishar before the sun made its full appearance. Nightmares of Ardencroft had chased her out of sleep.

~Who have you found? Was your hunt successful?~ It was an effort to keep the residual nightmare out of her voice.

~Most satisfying. A tender young doe. And I found someone you will be glad to see.~ His flurry of back-winging whipped hair across her face as he touched down. It was time to take the scissors to it again.

The other two Karda came in, one behind the other, loping down the landing meadow to a stop, and Marta Rowan and Altan Me'Gerron slid off them. Tessa went flying to Marta, grabbed her hard, arms around her, holding on as if Marta were her lifeline. She was crying so hard she couldn't breathe. Great, gulping sobs washed out of her, and she felt Marta's strong, sure arms fold around her, holding her tight.

Finally, she pulled back, her head down, and scrubbed at her face. "I'm sorry. I'm sorry. I don't know… This isn't exactly being in yarak."

"Yarak?" Marta looked across Tessa at Altan.

"Describes a hawk primed, ready, and eager for the hunt," he said.

"Oh. Tessa, no, I'm sorry. Sidhari and Kibrath have told us what you've been through." Marta's hand still held Tessa's arm as if she knew Tessa needed the gentle touch of another. Another who had experienced evil and survived.

Tessa pulled away and stumbled around the corner of the mews. Nausea overwhelmed her, and she lost her meager breakfast, retching until her stomach muscles burned. Marta reached around her with a cloth, and Tessa hid her face in it until she could trust her stomach to stay calm. "I'm sorry. I'm sorry. People are going to start introducing me as Tessa-Who-Vomits. I thought I was holding it together. I thought I was getting tougher."

"After hearing the little Kishar told us of what you and Galen have experienced, I think you are doing very well. Come inside and help us get the rigging off them so they can go hunt. Kishar says he found a small herd not too far away. They must be very stupid deer to be wandering so close to the mews."

~Stupid, but tasty.~ Kishar pathed. He nudged Tessa with his big head. She reached up and laid her hand on his sleek neck, absorbing some of his deep calm, and went to help the two visitors care for their Karda.

Tessa was glad to see Marta recovered from her ordeal at Readen's hands. Marta pulled the saddle off Sidhari, gathered up the long straps, and carried it to the saddle rack, refusing help from either Tessa or Altan.

Altan saw Tessa watching her and said, "Yes, she's recovered. And stronger than she ever was. Her talents are immense, and she's learning to control them better every day. It's not easy learning as an adult what we train for from childhood."

Tessa winced. She'd trained since childhood. And every day since she lost her talent, she suffered through it, never able to forget.

"I heard that." Marta tapped his arm hard with her fist. "And whether I'm learning to control them is open to question."

"I've learned to throw up shields in an instant. She exploded a magma stone she was trying to heat." He touched a small scar, still pink, high on his cheek. "She's so strong Father was forced to name her Me'Rowan."

Marta laughed, her smile curled with more than just a twist of irony. "And he wasn't particularly happy about it. Nor was Altan's mother. Will you stop telling that story? Ever? I'm much better at it now. And that scar is hardly visible at all. I think you didn't heal it, just so you can tell people about it."

Marta looked around the mews and was silent for several minutes. Then she hooked one arm through Altan's and reached to hook the other through Tessa's. "I'll come back to talk to the Karda later. Let's go see Daryl." There was just the slightest pause. "And Galen."

It felt strange to think of Marta as Me'Rowan—the Me' prefix identified the strongest talents and members of the ruling class. She wondered what kind of test or ordeal Marta endured to earn that. Or if she'd had to at all—exploding a magma stone might have been enough. Tessa worked to swallow her jealousy, to remind herself again of the responsibilities she could only fulfill without her talent. She turned away. The pain it caused her hadn't stopped. She reminded herself, again, that Kishar promised she would get them back.

The streets were waking. The three of them twisted and dodged the shop awnings being raised, bins rolled out, tables and hanging racks of goods and groceries appearing, ponies and mules, tricycles and bicycles backing carts into place.

Women walked with large baskets on their arms, and children dodged between carts and around unhitched animals being led to the market stables on the outer edge of the walls of the prime.

The smell of hot sausages and sugary egg toast came from a three-wheeled cycle with a smoking griddle on the back, and her stomach growled. It was too confusing and crowded for talk, for which Tessa was grateful.

Armsmaster Krager met them as they started up the stairs to Daryl's study. Tall, taciturn, dark-haired, the sharp angles of his face relaxed into a grin when he saw Marta and Altan. Tessa hadn't been sure the solemn man could grin. She heard a note of relief in his voice when he greeted the two visitors from Toldar.

Daryl introduced the others in the room—Galen and Commander Kyle, Restal's new arms commander, a man of medium height, with a broad, round face, tree trunk legs, and ax-handle arms.

Altan reached across Marta to grasp Kyle's forearm. "It's good to see you again. And good to address you as commander, not captain. Congratulations on your promotion."

"Thank you, Altan. Though it took an attempt to overthrow the guardian for me to be promoted. I'm not so sure I should be congratulated as much as consoled." Kyle spoke in a melodious tenor. "It's good to see you again. And it's good to see you looking your strong self again, Marta. Congratulations on your own promotion."

Galen stood at one end of the monstrous desk, and Tessa saw his body tense. "Marta is now Marta Me'Rowan, Galen," she explained. "That makes her one of the ruling class on Adalta. It is a signal honor." His face was a study in surprise, confusion, and concern.

"I'm not sure whether it's a promotion or a sentence, but thank you," Marta said, her eyes holding Galen's for a long moment.

Then he nodded.

"I'm not sure she's ever going to get over it," said Altan as they took seats in the half-circle of chairs in front of Daryl's desk.

Daryl sat in his chair, looked around the crowded space and down at the desk that took up almost a third of the room. "I should have taken the time to get rid of this monstrosity of a desk." He took a deep breath and said, "Galen, Tessa, I think this story starts with you."

Tessa looked at Galen. He cocked his head at her with the tiniest movement. She looked down at the hands twisting around each other in her lap, looked up at Marta and Altan, and began the story. "You two were still here when Kishar arrived and named me Austringer, the hunter. But I didn't know what that meant until the urbat came…"

Early the next day, Galen left on Keida. Kishar flew alongside to relay messages between them and to hunt. With so many Karda coming in to Restal, they needed to range farther and farther away for game.

They flew for most of the morning. Kishar spotted a landing meadow, and they left Galen there. ~I don't know how long we'll be gone, Galen. We'll take a look around when we leave to be sure nothing will disturb you and be back as soon as we eat,~ Kishar pathed.

Galen watched the two Karda fly away. So much had changed since he'd last spoken with his father. The thought of contacting him now was disorienting. It would take work to pretend to still be the person his father thought he was. It was a switch to be lying to his father, rather than for his father.

He pulled his Cue out of his small pack and stared at it, turning it over and over in his hand, thinking of the data he'd collected and transmitted before he was burned. Thinking of how different the information he now had was. Not so much a difference in facts but a difference in his interpretation of those facts.

A fine mist started to fall, and he moved to the edge of the meadow, stooping under the trailing branches of a spruce into its cave-like shelter, grateful for his long, fur-lined coat. The face of the Cue glowed green in the half-light when he finally opened it and heard the disembodied voice of the dispatcher. "Planetary Findings."

"Galen Morel reporting for Director Morel." Now he'd see what kind of actor he was.

"Galen, where have you been?"

When his father's voice came, it was with the taut, impatient tone Galen had heard all his life. But this time he felt nothing but perhaps pity for a man so lacking a sense of human connection.

"Holed up in some tavern with a woman? Why haven't I heard from you? What the gods bedamned galaxies have you been doing? Merrik is waiting for you to contact him. He needs to know where to take the akenguns."

Galen didn't bother to remind his father that he'd been told where

Galen was and what he was doing several times. It wouldn't make a difference. "Readen's escaped his prison and is headed for his hold and his mines in the north. He may already be there. There are rumors some of his former troops are regrouping and heading that way. I'm back in Restal Prime."

He swallowed, grateful the Cue was no longer able to send a visual of his face. Keeping his tone even, he asked, "Where is Merrik? How many weapons does he have, and where can I meet him?"

"Do you know where Readen is? We've lost visual contact with the entire north of Restal. The blasted roving electro-magnetic fields disrupt what little contact we had. We can see nothing."

Galen's body tensed, and he blinked. He heard desperation leaking through his father's words. "Did you manage to get the samples of ore you wanted? What are they?"

There was a long silence then a short, sharp, "Yes." Another shorter silence. "The ore is a triple allotrope of carbon. Not something anyone has seen before. I can't even begin to estimate how valuable that could be, especially in communications." There was another silence, and Galen thought he'd lost contact until his father continued. "The two I sent to collect it are dead with symptoms that indicate radiation poisoning. But the geologists insist the mineral isn't radioactive. You better stay away from it until we can figure out what the danger is."

I guess Father has forgotten I almost died trying to get his samples. Galen dropped his head and pressed his temples between fingers and thumb. He said nothing into the silence.

Kayne continued, "Dispatch tells me you haven't transmitted any data for some time. You should be able to get around by now. We need more data on the planet's resources."

There was a long pause full of static, then his father's voice went on. "Merrik is in Restal, and he has the weapons with him. Are you familiar with a tavern a few streets from the place where those flying creatures are stabled? It's called The Red Horse. He tries to be there several times a week, or rather, tenday. He's been waiting for you to contact him. I'm assuming you have a way to get the weapons to Readen. This time don't fail." And the Cue went dead.

Galen closed and locked the Cue and tucked it in the bottom of his pack. He leaned back against the broad trunk and ran his fingers through his hair, pulling it back and retying it. He slid down the tree and sat with one knee cocked, tapping it with one finger. That conversation was too short. *He didn't even ask for particulars about how I'm supposed to get the weapons to Readen. Something's wrong up there.*

He tilted his head back against the trunk as if he could see through the dense evergreen branches and the clouds to the ship above. *He wants me to give the weapons to Readen with no assurance, no guarantee, that Readen will honor his part of the bargain. Readen can get along without the mining equipment we promised him. Father must know by now that the chance the machinery he's offering will work here is uncertain. Even if Readen decides to honor their bargain, he won't give Father the ore until he tests the equipment.*

He stretched out his legs and let his eyes close. *If the gods of the galaxies are kind, I may never have to hear my father or see my father or speak to my father again.* That thought triggered an uneasy feeling in his stomach that was almost fear. *Who am I if I am no longer my father's son?* He fell asleep until he heard Kishar call his name.

When they landed back in the mews, Daryl, Altan, Tessa, and Marta met them. ~I assume you called a meeting, Kishar, and that's why they are all here waiting for us. Have you been reading my mind?~ Galen pathed.

He heard a mental chuckle. ~I don't even have to try. You are broadcasting your thoughts so loud I'm surprised Keida isn't able to hear them.~

Galen stripped the saddle rigging off Keida and groomed the little bay while Tessa took care of Kishar. He was so aware of her he wanted to wrap her around him like a blanket. *I can't do this anymore. I can't be this close to her.* He thought about his father. About how like his father he had been, might still be—the seeds were there inside him.

I almost destroyed Marta. I don't want to hurt Tessa. I am an exile without a home or anything else to my name. Except my history as a monster of self-indulgence with a host of strange, unwanted, un-asked-for powers that could destroy me and everything around me if I fail to control them.

Keida flinched. He lightened up on the brush, patted her in apology, and leaned into her, his head pressed against the slight hollow between her neck and withers, arms slack at his sides. He waited till Tessa left, then followed her out to meet the others, with Krager and General Kyle, under a massive spreading elm where a large table of planks on trestles was set up. He stood at the side of the table where she was out of his line of sight and forced himself to pay attention. Not only Kishar, but Kibrath, Sidhari, and Abala, Daryl's Karda, joined them, with several others in a larger circle around them.

Kishar spoke. ~For five hundred years the Karda have tried to hold ourselves separate from human politics, to keep ourselves loyal to persons, not places, not political alliances. We encourage the Mi'hiru to rotate their assignments, so they develop allegiance to no faction. We have watched you establish your colonies, your quadrants, your political, social, and economic systems with little interference. For five hundred years we have served you in gratitude for the aid you gave us in defeating the last rising of the Larrak and the work you do to contain the circles and restore the barrens, bringing life back to Adalta. Now one of yours has joined with the last Larrak, the Itza, and destruction threatens once more.~

Kishar looked at Daryl. ~There is a reason Restal's barrens are more extensive than in the other quadrants, and the land is less alive. It was here the last battles were fought. It was here the Itza, the last Larrak, was driven into the cavern that became its prison, and the guardians of Restal charged with its keeping. A charge abandoned too soon.~ He stopped. His head lifted. ~A charge that was not left only to you. I, too, have failed, lulled by so many years of peace.~

"Peace?" asked Altan. "It has only been in the last few years that there has even been a semblance of peace on Adalta. Too many of the fractures in the original colony are still not resolved. Akhara Quadrant has been a hotbed of war and revolt from the beginning."

Galen noted Altan didn't mention the growing resistance to rule by strongest talent in Restal that had lured many to Readen.

~But it has been peace for Adalta. The planet has not been threatened. Until now,~ Kishar replied. ~Now, once more, we must fight together or lose everything.~

Marta rubbed her wrist. Galen could see the cords of her neck were taut as bowstrings. She looked at Galen "But when we came this time, we brought destruction with us." He looked away, half turning from the group, exposing his scarred cheek. He lifted a hand as if to cover it then dropped it to his side.

Kishar spoke again. ~You were necessary, Marta. It is you who flushed the Larrak out before it was ready. Before Readen was ready. And Galen. Galen is the Kern. We need you both. And the people on your ship will find they need us soon.~

Marta pulled on her earring and bit her lip when Galen caught her eye. He thought about the failing systems on the ship and shuddered. She nodded.

Kishar went on. ~We have resources to assess, allies to be certain of, plans to make, strategies to develop. We must know more about where Readen is and what he plans. We must know if the Itza Larrak has indeed escaped the cavern and where it is. But now, Galen, you must tell us what your father said to you today.~

"I contacted my father as you asked, Daryl. The weapons are somewhere here in Restal. I'm to meet Merrik—"

"Merrik." Marta choked the name out and her shoulders straightened. "He sent the weapons with that...that weasel? That worm crawled out of his black hole and got himself assigned to bring in the guns? Are you sure he hasn't already sold them to someone else?"

"I'm reasonably certain he won't cross Father. I'll be more certain tonight if he's where he should be. I take it you've had dealings with him before, Marta?"

That was evident in the curl of her lip.

Chapter Twenty-Three

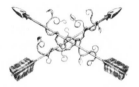

Readen looked around the small, cell-like room. He was as prepared as he could be. A tall, blond man stood, silent, beside him, shirtless, expressionless. The crucial final symbol wept blood, the cuts sure and deep across the flat, hard muscles of the man's chest.

A small stone bowl sat on the table in front of him in the center of his workroom beneath the hold, ready for blood. A large pitcher of water was inches away from Readen's hand. A thick pad of cotton and a length of bandage lay next to it.

This must work. It had been so easy to call the Itza Larrak in the cavern. He'd done it by accident as a child when a cut on his finger opened, and he bled on the arcane symbols carved on one of the pillars. He had learned all he could from the Itza Larrak, memorized so many symbols, struggled to learn the language of the columns, to memorize the spells they held. But he hadn't been taught these particular symbols. Without them, the Itza Larrak's fully materialized form couldn't exist outside the cavern.

But he knew those symbols now. They covered half his body—all of them. Only the final one was incomplete. The one bleeding on the chest of the man standing with vacant eyes beside him. Empty, a perfect vessel. Tall, strong, the sharp, lean planes of his face handsome, he was at the peak of his physical power. An intricate, dark net of energy connected him to Readen. Its filaments wove through the sinews of the man's muscles and his veins, open only at the bloody sign incised into his chest.

Readen checked the spell again for the fourth time. It must be accurate to the tiniest detail.

It must work. He couldn't do what he wanted without the Itza Larrak. The urbat had rescued him, but now they waited—most disappeared back into the circle, a few ranked unseen in the forests outside his hold—grotesque statues deaf to orders from Readen

Readen couldn't let the Itza Larrak take control of his body. He would be lost. His mind trapped, powerless, dead. *It may have created me, but it cannot have me. I will kill myself before I allow it to force itself inside me.*

He thought of his talentless childhood—bullied, ridiculed, motherless, deposed as heir in favor of his brother—the only one who stood up for him. And how Readen resented that.

The creature may have created him. He might only be half-human, but that was the half he must hold to lest he become a mindless automaton, servant to the Itza Larrak, like an urbat.

He checked the connection between himself and the man and the built-in gate that ensured he could disconnect if he lost control of the spell.

Readen picked up a small, silver knife and pierced the vein in the crook of his own elbow with its sharp tip. He held the dripping wound over the little bowl until it brimmed with bright red blood.

He slapped the pad on the cut, pressed until the bleeding stopped, and wrapped the bandage around his arm, using his other hand and his teeth to knot it tight. He stood for a moment, checking his body. It wouldn't do to faint from loss of blood. Adrenaline flooded him, quickened his breath, fired his muscles.

Readen was ready.

One deep breath, two, then he drew the symbol in the air. The black lines hung in front of him. He let just enough of his essence leak through the web of connection wrapping the man to infuse it with a taste of his own being.

He poured his blood, already thickening, blackening, over the sigil on the tall man's powerful chest, smearing to coat every inch of the bloody sign.

He began to chant. One hand grasped the medallion that had not left his body since the Larrak gave it to him as a child. "Dalla Itza Larrak alka ra. Dalla Itza Larrak alka ra…"

The familiar dark spiral of motes formed faster than before on the other side of the table.

The Itza Larrak struck.

Readen stepped back and shoved the empty body between himself and the huge monster. It smashed into the body in front of him and disappeared. High, shrill keening lanced into Readen's ears, piercing and painful. The body of the young man fell to its knees, hands braced wide on the flagstone floor, head hanging. Then it fell over, curled in on itself, shaking, arms and legs jerking. It convulsed, its head arched so far back it almost touched its hips.

It lay still for several long minutes then gathered its limbs under it and rolled to its feet and turned with slow and deliberate movements to face Readen.

Readen forced his feet to stay where they were. He would not back away.

The eyes that looked back at him were no longer human. They radiated triumph, fierce glee, and danger. The creature took a step toward him.

Readen sliced the final mark on his own chest—his safety net. "If you kill me, that body dies, and you will have no way back." His voice was thick with terror he dared not show. "The language you taught me dies with me. The signs on my body, the sign on that body,"—he gestured at the body now inhabited by the Itza Larrak—"will rot away."

Readen stepped back, pulled a chair away from the table, and sat, willing his limbs to work, willing his body not to shake, willing steadiness into the hand he laid oh-so-casually on the table.

"Will you still live? The cavern that was both your prison and your only way to freedom is gone, sealed beneath tons of rock and earth.

Can you reach it? You didn't the whole time I was imprisoned. I don't think you can."

Yellow eyes flashed. One hand flexed, then the other.

Readen concentrated on holding his breath steady, on keeping his mind from skittering away in terror.

Something battered and pulled at his connection to the web between them. The medallion turned cold, burning his chest. He clenched the fist hidden in his lap, willed his other hand to be still, fought to hold the barrier he had constructed with meticulous care.

Time stopped, and Readen fought the silent battle of wills. Sweat beaded on his forehead, and he blinked the sting of salt out of his eyes.

Slow words slurred and garbled as the creature spoke through its unfamiliar human mouth. It said, "You will take me. To the nearest. Circle of Order. Now. This body. Will not hold for long. You will not. Wish me to need. To possess another. You are the closest. I will be. Ready. Next time."

Readen took a breath and swallowed the flood of saliva in his mouth before he spoke, keeping his words slow, his voice steady, his tone deep and assured. "We will leave now."

The Itza Larrak looked at him. Readen fought to keep his eyes steady on the creature's face, refusing to look away. The complete, cold absence of humanity in those once-human eyes was terrifying.

Its voice echoed, harsh, mechanical. Its mouth and tongue struggled with the human form. "You will. Tell me. Your plans. You will. Tell me. Of your forces. Of your allies. Of the ones who would oppose me."

Readen very carefully, very slowly, exhaled and inhaled a long, deep breath, hiding his relief, soothing his terror, never taking his gaze away from the yellow gleam of the Itza Larrak's eyes. He hadn't yet lost this battle. But nor had he won.

Moving slowly so as not to betray the trembling of his legs, his whole body, Readen led the way up out of the cellar room, the Itza Larrak too close behind him. Its gait was jerky and uncoordinated. It emanated a tangible aura of jubilation.

"We'll need horses, food, and equipment for camping. It's a two-day journey to the nearest Circle of Dis—" He stumbled on the last word. "Order. Circle of Order."

The Larrak kept walking, up the stairs, through the rooms of the hold, and out into the courtyard, bypassing the way to the stables. Readen blessed his foresight at releasing the duty guards that night. It would be better if no one saw him with this shambling figure. Only Pol was on the gate.

When Readen and the Larrak were out of sight of the gate, twenty urbat moved silently from the surrounding forest where they had stood ranked and out of sight for days, unmoving. They pushed at Readen, surrounding him and the Larrak, giving him no chance to stop at the stables, to do other than keep walking.

They walked for two days in the monotonous gray light of drizzling rain that never quit. They stopped for nothing. Readen stumbled with fatigue, shook with cold and hunger, soiled his clothes with his own waste. It took everything he had to hold a coherent thought and stay on his feet while the Larrak raped his brain for information.

The Larrak never spoke. The urbat moved in a silence so complete Readen's head ached with it. The only sounds were the occasional sibilant brush of paws through dead leaves and weeds and the faint, rhythmic click of claws on rocks and hard earth.

For a day and a half after they left the village and the settled area of Readen's hold, they traveled through the edge of one of the vast unreclaimed areas of Restal. The urbat walked steadily in a straight line, detouring only for the steepest arroyos. When they finally reached the forest, they followed a twisting line of stark white dead trees that snaked toward the circle.

Because of the negligence of the last couple of generations of the Me'Vere guardianship, the forests in Restal were narrower and the circles larger, so they reached it, two hundred kilometers from the hold, hours after dark of the third day.

They were far inside its boundaries when the urbat allowed Readen to collapse in the brittle, sparse grass under a low, gnarled tree and surrounded him. He was too exhausted to take advantage of being in the circle for a spell to replenish his power. Where his power had been was a vacuum that threatened to suck him in. The Larrak had been stealing it.

He watched with horrified fascination as the Larrak-possessed body walked with shambling, awkward steps into the midst of a cluster of large, round humps. The ground split, a deep crevice opened. The Larrak hung suspended over it, then sank, bit by bit, its hair falling away, its flesh slipping as if it were decaying. Three urbat went with it, supporting it. When it was almost out of sight in the blackness, an angry radiance of unnatural green-orange light shot up, piercing the low hanging clouds, the drizzle steaming away from it. Angular black symbols swarmed like fish in a bowl through its depths. Familiar, they flashed too fast for Readen to make sense of them in his exhaustion and disorientation. He watched the silhouette of the deteriorating human sink into the strange and beautiful swirl of coruscating orange light, held upright by the three urbat. He watched it disappear, unsure whether what he watched was real or hallucination.

The remaining seventeen monsters pushed him into the tight center of their ranks. He fell into exhausted half-sleep. His fingers feebly traced the symbols in the dust that would force the circle to give him strength, his body hyper-aware of the monsters pressed against him, cold, unmoving, and silent as stone. Nauseated, his nose full of their rank, half-machine, half-animal smell, Readen drifted into a limitless lacuna of no-thought.

Sometime later he became aware he was moving in a sickening, swaying motion. Hard bristles rasped against his face. Sharp points dug into his chest. His hands burned. He lifted his head.

He was face down, draped over the back of one of the monstrous urbat. His knuckles dragged the ground to either side, his legs dragged behind, boots scuffing across the rough surface, the leather toes wearing through. He slid to one side. The triangular metal scales of its armor ripped his tunic and tore his flesh.

He rolled to his hands and knees. Shaking his head in an attempt to clear his thoughts, he stood. His legs trembled with the effort of holding him upright. The urbat surrounding him kept moving, forcing him into a stumbling walk.

The Itza Larrak marched at the head of the macabre procession, no longer trapped in the human body, its metallic wings in constant movement, opening partially and closing, opening and closing, ringing with a menacing, melodious murmur. Its long arms and legs ended in articulated digits tipped with sharp, cruel talons. Its dull gray, armor-like skin absorbed light. Huge, strong, the dark presence marched with long, purposeful strides.

Finally, the familiar walls of Readen's hold appeared. The Itza Larrak and the hoard of urbat melted into the surrounding forest. Readen stumbled through the gates alone, his mind scrabbling for hope in a fog of exhaustion and despair.

ITZA LARRAK

Chapter Twenty-Four

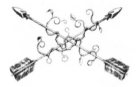

For the next few days, Karda and riders began to drift into the mews in Restal Prime—Mi'hiru and Karda Patrol wings from other quadrants and Rashiba Quint. Galen spent what time he could hiding in the greenhouses and the growing fields, taking his meals in the planters' barracks. He stayed away from the main rooms of the keep. Working with saplings, seedlings, and soils helped drain away some of the sorrow and ugliness from the village of Ardencroft that clung to him like dark, sad shadows. And it helped him own and hone his power, forced him to concentrate on precision instead of relying on brute strength.

He saw Tessa only in passing, and they seldom spoke. The less time they spent together, the better. He ignored the way she carried sunlight every time he caught a glimpse of silver hair. He kept out of her way.

He wiped sweat off his forehead with his sleeve and stood, arching his back to stretch his cramped muscles. He'd bent over trays of seedlings all morning, thinning them out and losing himself in the smell and feel of damp soil and tender shoots.

"Galen, sir." One of the keep pages was at the door to the greenhouse. "Guardian Daryl wants to see you in his study."

Reprieve was over. He rinsed dirt from his hands, splashed water over his face from a bucket, dried off, and followed the boy to the keep.

The page announced him, and Galen stepped inside the study. Roland's ornate, oversized desk was gone—the top of the even larger plain table in its place hidden under rolled maps and troop rosters. Altan and Daryl stood on one side of the table. Two large maps anchored at the corners with books and a couple of rocks was spread out in front of them. A tall, big-boned woman in flying leathers sat in Daryl's chair, a wine glass in her hand, her narrow, browned face lined with fatigue and worry. Tessa stood beside her.

Daryl looked up. "Altan wants to know what you did when you tried to sever the Line of Devastation. Guardian Merenya arrived this morning." He gestured toward the woman. "She tells us they flew around lines like you described branching out of several circles. Some in Anuma."

Merenya stood and held her arm out to Galen. "I'm glad to meet you, Galen. Especially if you are indeed the Kern, as Daryl and Altan think you are."

Daryl coughed. "I'm sorry, Merenya, Galen. I should have introduced you. I'm getting ahead of myself."

"These are parlous times, Daryl. I'll forgive your temporary lapse of manners." Merenya stabbed a finger at the maps, pointing to one circle after another in a meandering line between Restal Keep and Anuma Prime.

"These are the places where we saw lines of dead trees snaking out of the circles. We could tell they aren't simply the circles expanding. They are narrow, crooked bands. One, at least, went for more than six kilometers before it ended."

Though she was travel-weary, her voice held confidence and authority. "The trees hadn't just dropped their leaves. They were dead. Bare white skeletons of trees, some standing, some fallen. Every one of the lines we saw points in the direction of another circle."

Altan rubbed the side of his face. "What I don't understand is, these lines have been forming for some time for the trees to be dead enough to fall. Why have the Mi'hiru and the Karda Patrols not seen them?"

"Karda won't fly close enough to the circles to see them." Merenya broke the silence that followed. "But that's changed. Pagra insisted we fly closer this time, and the other Karda didn't object."

"Kibrath pretty much picks his own flight path, so I didn't notice we were flying closer until I saw the first line of dead trees when we were on patrol near the border a tenday ago. The closer we got to Restal, the more lines we saw and the longer they were. They are why father asked Marta and me to come," said Altan. "One of the reasons."

Galen didn't think he meant those last words to be heard.

Daryl moved a book a little off the map. "So. Galen, Altan, and I are strong talents, as is Merenya. She's particularly powerful in Earth. Marta's just as formidable, and Altan can help her with control. Tessa, too, is a strong talent. Tell us what you found and what you did and what we might do to stop this."

Galen couldn't look at Tessa, but he didn't have to. He felt the pain at Daryl's words jab her from across the table.

Galen told them about the fiery heat he'd sent to cut the line away from the circle. "It didn't work. The next morning, I could still see where the fire had scorched across the line in a band about three meters wide, but the nanobots—that's the closest thing I can think to what they appear to be—were swarming all over it."

There was silence for several minutes, then Daryl asked, "Uh, what's a nanobot?"

Galen looked at him and hesitated, his mind a blank. *How do I explain bots to someone who has no experience or knowledge of robotics?* "Think of them as ants, very small, fabricated ants with a singularity of purpose and a refusal to let anything stop them. I don't know how many I fried, how many more were fried during the night before the earth cooled enough for them to bridge the gap."

He bit his lip and scrunched his face, rubbing it hard as if he could force the right words to the surface. "They are mindless machines, too small for the eye to see. They don't feel pain. They don't feel anything. They don't think. They do the one thing they are programmed—instructed—to do, which I think is to feed on the living Adalta through the trees and grasses. They then join and fuse into a deposit of what appears to be a crystalline allotrope of carbon that to my knowledge isn't found on any planet we've had contact with."

Galen took a half-step away from the table and cleared his throat. "If it can be mined, it would be unbelievably lucrative for the consortium. If it is anything like what I suspect, its value is in technology that doesn't exist here. What it could be used for on Adalta, I don't know."

Galen looked at their blank faces. "That's the closest explanation I can think of about something I don't understand or would ever have believed possible. Carbon doesn't form that way naturally, and they are not nanobots I know anything about. Kishar says they are forming the strands of a carbon web that will allow communication between the circles when they connect. Or an antenna that can reach into the stars."

Merenya's voice was flat. "That does not sound like a good thing." Her tight face and stiff shoulders shouted tension.

"They were created by someone or something. They are not a natural form of life on Adalta. The material they are made of is similar to the metal in the urbat." Galen's tone was just as flat. He wasn't sure he wanted to know what that similarity could mean.

Daryl asked, "If they are too small for the eye to see, how did you see them?"

Altan looked up at the note of suspicion in Daryl's voice then over to Galen, the same question in his eyes. Tessa moved around the table to stand beside Galen, and her shoulder brushed his arm. He shifted away.

"I don't know," said Galen. After a minute he went on. "But then, I don't know how I can do any of the things I do, much of which I can't even control. Not well anyway."

Altan looked thoughtful. After a minute he said, "What if the three of us join our talents with yours? Do you think that would be enough to cut the line?"

Tessa spoke up. "The circles kill by siphoning off talent. The line almost killed Galen before he—before he became fully the Kern. The reason he can get so close to the lines and the circles is that he doesn't have channels—no, that's not right—he's able to dam up his channels to form reservoirs he can fill with talent. It doesn't flow through him as it does others. The three of you would be a tasty snack for whatever it is that controls the circles." Her hands fisted at her side, and she added, her head down, and her voice pitched low, "And my talent is blocked. And useless."

Daryl ignored her. "We have to try. If the five of you work in shifts, maybe you can create enough of a break in the line to stop them." He shifted and looked out the window behind him. "I can't afford to leave the prime until we know more about Readon's plans. And about the Itza Larrak."

Altan frowned and rubbed the back of his neck, thinking. "It's worth a try." He looked around the table at the others. "We have to try. Those lines cannot be allowed to grow unchecked. I'm willing."

"We'll need to be certain we can cut ourselves loose if it doesn't work." Marta's tone wasn't as assured as Altan's. "We don't want to feed ourselves to whatever that is."

There was a long silence, then Galen broke it. "I'm to meet Merrik tonight to get the akenguns from him."

"Krager, Altan, and I will go with you. We need to know who he is." Daryl pushed away from the table, looking at Galen. His suspicion swirled around Galen's shoulders. Galen straightened and looked back.

The room emptied of everyone but Tessa and Merenya. Tessa stood, staring down at the maps and papers littering the table. Eventually, after what felt like a long, long time, Merenya put her hands flat on the table and leaned across toward Tessa. "Tessa, the only people who thought this was a big secret, were you and your father. It happens. From time to time it's happened to others. Your block has just lasted longer than most."

Tessa stared at her. Merenya's words were meaningless sounds she fought to unscramble. Tessa forgot to breathe until she got lightheaded. She gulped in a huge breath, it hiccuped out, and she whispered, "That can't be true. Father is ambitious for me, I know. But—"

"Your father's a proud man. And his family line is dying out. His fear of that has made him blind. His fear has convinced him that your talent is truly gone."

She took Tessa's chin in her hand as she might a small child. "You have talent, Tessa. Probably the very strength of that talent is what has made your block so powerful. Your father's fear has served to make it even stronger."

She dropped her hand and unhooked the travel packs from the back of her chair. "Think about it, Tessa. Think sideways, past your fear—and your father's fear."

Tessa stood, unable to move, unable to think, staring at Merenya's face lined with concern.

For most of Tessa's life, she had been imprisoned by this secret that wasn't secret. For most of her life, she had been locked in the shame of this secret that wasn't secret. *For most of my life, my father has held me hostage to this secret that isn't secret. That has never been secret. That has never been shameful.*

Kishar had told her that her block was the gift that made her the Austringer. There was no shame in it.

She started shaking. Merenya reached for her hand, and Tessa pulled back. She walked away—faster and faster through the halls of the keep to where she could disappear into the busy streets of the city. Merenya's words battered the inside of her head. *All those years given away to a secret that isn't secret, to a shame that isn't a shame.* She wondered if she would ever recover from the burning anger growing in her body. If she would be destroyed in its flames.

From a table in the back corner, Galen watched Daryl come through the door of the Red Horse, toss his wet cloak on the drying rack by the door, slap a merchant on the back as he walked past, and head toward the cheerful man behind the long, polished bar. Altan stood at the other end of the bar—as a surly don't-even-look-at-me-wrong mercenary, his sword in a well-worn scabbard at his waist. Beyond him in the shadows was Krager, half-turned away from the room, leaning his elbows on the bar.

Galen sipped his beer slowly and watched Daryl work his way through the dark room, greeting acquaintances, clasping forearms in greeting, laughing at a word here, patting a shoulder there, obviously at home, well-known to the mostly-male crowd in the ancient, none-too-clean tavern. He could hardly reconcile the quiet, studious Daryl he knew with this friendly, well-liked and well-known man.

A few women, Mi'hiru and patrollers, were scattered here and there. Galen wondered at Merrik's choice of meeting place. This busy tavern appeared to be a favorite of the guard, the patrol, and the Mi'hiru. It would be impossible to hold any clandestine meeting. With Galen's scarred face, an attempt to be unnoticed was even more impossible.

He set his heavy glass mug on the table and turned to catch the attention of the serving woman, hoping she'd take her time to get him a refill. He could only sit here so long staring into his beer before it became obvious he was waiting for someone. When he turned back around, Merrik was pulling out a chair at the table next to his.

Merrik was of medium height with a broad, open face on the wrong side of handsome, nondescript until he took off his cap, and Galen could see the wide ears set too high on the sides of his head. When the woman brought Galen's beer, Merrik reached out and tugged on her skirt. She twitched away. Her practiced smile a bit, no, a lot more forced.

"Bring me one of those, Miercie. And a bowl of stew." Merrik's voice was a mellow, friendly tenor, his smile wide and affable, and he gave her bottom a too-congenial pat.

She slapped it away and headed back toward the kitchen without answering.

Merrik winked at Galen. "She likes me." He scooted his chair side-ways and propped an ankle on his knee. "You haven't been in here before. My name's Merrik." He held out his hand, and Galen reached to clasp his forearm. Merrik smelled of not-too-clean stable.

Galen tilted his chair back on its hind legs to get away from the odor. "No, I haven't. Seems like a good place. Friendly."

"Yes, it is. And busier than usual tonight. With some illustrious customers." Merrik looked away from Galen toward Daryl. He waved at a woman across the room. Her smile back was less smile, more grimace.

Merrik's way of blending in was to make himself so obnoxious no one even wanted to see him. It worked well and, Galen thought, made use of his natural talents. Galen didn't even want to see him.

"I run the stables down the hill and two streets over. Be glad to stable your horse while you're here in the prime. Good feed. Clean straw. Bring him in. We'll take good care of him. Better'n any others." His voice was too loud.

"I'll keep that in mind," Galen said and sipped at his beer, scooting his chair around the table away from the stable smell.

Miercie brought Merrik his beer. "The stable where he works shoveling shit is full of it. Just like him," she muttered to Galen.

He almost choked on his swallow. He finished his beer, handed her a few extra coins for putting up with the worm, and left, snagging his cloak off the drying rack as he went by. One by one, over the next hour, Daryl, Altan, and Krager joined him in an alley around the corner from Merrik's stable, a few paces outside the circle of light thrown by a street lantern. Daryl was his usual, solemn self again.

"If he keeps to his pattern, he'll be drinking for at least a couple of hours, yet," said Galen. "And he'll be moving from tavern to tavern. That's how he collects most of his information. He might be obnoxious, but he's very good at it."

Altan looked at Daryl, smiling. "Did you change your personality in there? Or was that your doppelgänger?"

"He turns into a child again. He doesn't have to change, just remember," Krager said, his voice barely audible. "I just wish he'd do it more often."

Daryl glared at him. "We should start searching for those guns." And he started down the hill toward the stable.

"Wait." Galen reached to grab him but dropped his arm when Daryl looked at him, his fierce scowl just visible in the dim light. "If he's hidden them here, he'll have them trapped."

Altan started to say something, but Galen said, "and not with magic. If they're not in the stable, there will be traps anyway. If we spring them, he'll know someone was looking. And believe me, Merrik trusts no one and nothing, so there'll be traps within traps—so many we won't find them all. He'll insist on taking me to the weapons. And since he hates me, I'll have to work for it. He'll want me to make mistakes he can report to the ship. If the weapons are not in the stable, they'll be where he can watch them. He's going to want to know where I'm taking them, how, and with whom—he'll have a lot of questions before he finally leads me to them. I don't have to answer them. One of the reasons Merrik hates me is that he thinks I'm the spoiled, arrogant son of his boss. Which I am. So not answering will be in character. He'll expect that, but I'll have to play his game until we find them."

"We'll be following—" Daryl started.

"No." Galen scrubbed his hair away from his face. "He'll spot you."

"I've never had much to do with him before, though I've seen him many times." Krager's usual taciturn expression was cold—and flat with self-disgust. "I've never had the least suspicion about him. And I'm suspicious of everyone."

Not long after first light the next day, Galen pulled open one side of the double doors to the stable where he was to meet Merrik and immediately missed the clear, clean morning air. The ammonia reek of sour, urine- and manure-soaked straw was a physical assault to his nose. He wouldn't stable a goat here, and he didn't even like goats. Making certain there were no loose animals to dash out of the filth, he dragged the other door open and stepped inside—about three steps. He wouldn't go any further inside if he didn't have to.

"Merrik?"

"Back here, Galen." The voice came from a stall halfway down the hall. Merrik's head with its uncombed hair poked around the stall door. "Come in for a minute. I'm not quite finished cleaning up. Lend a hand, and we can be on our way sooner."

"How far away are the guns? I can't be gone very long, or someone will get suspicious." Galen ventured a few more steps into the odiferous stable.

"Not far." Merrik appeared with an extra pitchfork, holding it out to Galen, his smile broad and full of good humor. "Who do you have to haul the guns, and where are you to meet Readen?"

"That's not for you to know, Merrik. I'll—"

A slight scuff sounded behind Galen, and then there was nothing but sharp pain and blackness.

Galen felt a tremor in the hard surface he lay on. He tried to roll over to sit, but he couldn't move. Stabbing pain in his head all but blinded him when he opened his eyes. He took a few experimental breaths through his nose and made an effort to get his mind to work through a fog of pain and disorientation. The familiar ozone re-breather smell and the faint tremor meant he was on a heli-shuttle.

He tried to move again. There were straps across his chest and around his arms and legs, straps used to secure someone unconscious —or hold a prisoner. Breathing slowly, he fought panic and waited for his mind to clear.

He rolled his head to the side. Intense pain flared behind his left ear. Then he remembered. The stables. The smell. Merrik.

Fury and fear roiled through his chest and down the arms straining against the straps and into his clenched fists. Merrik would never have done this without direct orders from his father. Galen's father.

The smell of hot plastic hit his nose, and he realized the restraints holding him were on the verge of burning. He pulled back on his talent and willed his anger down. He could feel the scars on his arm pulsing, stinging, wanting to change. He was away from the planet, away from the source of his power. He couldn't afford to waste talent until he knew more.

His ability to think finally returned—the pain-filled haze cleared. He checked his body for injuries. Other than the large bump and laceration behind his left ear, a scraped knee, and a sore shoulder where he must have hit the ground, he was fine. And—most important—he had talent. Full reservoirs of talent.

I should have paid more attention to Kishar's lessons on healing, A head wound on myself is not a good place to practice. But he'd learned enough working on wounded survivors of the urbat attacks to at least ease the pain and strain on his shoulder. And that wouldn't show. Healing his head would, and Galen had no desire to let anyone, Merrik or his father, know the kind of power he had. Power he still had forty thousand kilometers above the surface of Adalta.

He felt the grav-grab bump that meant the shuttle was docking. It was several minutes before he heard his father's voice. "Gently now. Don't bounce him around. He's hurt and sick. Get him into the quarantine pod and to his quarters. I'll contact medic and meet you there."

Galen didn't open his eyes and didn't speak—not sure he could stand yet and not sure what to say. 'Where am I?' would be a bit dramatic—and stupid, so he said nothing. He needed more information. He needed a clear head. After a moment or two, he felt the surface he was on being lifted and carried out of the shuttle, the motion sending sharp spines of pain through his head and shoulder. He needed to hit someone.

All of a sudden, the walkway tilted and bucked as though the immense network of pods that made up the ship had taken a deep breath and let it out with a great shudder. The men carrying his pod stumbled. One of them cried out, "Gravity grab me, not again." And the end with Galen's head hit the ground.

He passed out.

He woke up when they deposited him in his quarters, and the restraints were released. He managed to roll up to sit. He didn't try to stand. His equilibrium was not trustworthy. "Hello, Father." A blurry Kayne stood between him and the door, haz-mask over his face, with four, armed Ship's Watch in the hall behind him, also masked.

"I assume you have a reason for bringing me here in this fashion. You might have just asked."

Kayne motioned the watch outside and closed the door, pulling down his mask. "Would you have responded? Would you have come back to the ship if I had asked? I've been concerned about you."

Galen tilted his head to one side. "What reason do you have for thinking I would not have?" *Concerned about me? So concerned he had me knocked out and kidnapped?*

"I'll leave you here to think about that. Perhaps you can come up with the reason." And he left, pulling the mask back up. Galen heard him speaking to the watch. "He's still disoriented. I'll call medic to check on him. Make sure he doesn't wander off before they get here. We're not sure what he has, and I'm worried about that bump on his head. My agent found him wandering—"

The door closed, and Kayne's voice cut off.

No medic came. Several hours later the lock clicked, and one of the servers he recognized from the cafe nearest his quarters brought a meal, set it down on a table by the door, gave him an apologetic look, and disappeared. Two of the watch were behind her. All of them wore haz-masks.

Galen opened his mouth to speak, but before he could, one of the watch said, "Sorry, sir. Your father says we are not to talk to you. He's worried about your head wound and doesn't want you to be bothered about anything. I'll tell him you're awake."

Galen slept for most of a day. When he woke, he paced. Pacing helped relieve his fury and frustration and the fear for Tessa that clamped a band tight around his heart. She would think he'd deserted her, deserted Adalta. The server came twice more, set his meal on a table just inside the door, her eyes wide, apologetic, frightened, over the haz-mask and left.

Tired of pacing, he sat, like Kishar had taught him, and experimented with sending his consciousness out, widening it slowly to encompass the room, the hallway outside, the rest of the apartments he and his father lived in. There was plant life everywhere on the ship, a major part of the ship's life systems. And he could send his senses through them. They didn't feed him power, but they didn't draw on him either.

It was as if they accepted him as one of them. It was as if his body was locked into the interconnected wholeness of the ship—remote, cool, and self-aware. He sensed its decay with growing alarm. The plant life was aggressive with an intent that both awed and alarmed him. It penetrated the ship's systems, sometimes disrupted them, sometimes held them together, but mostly it waited, poised for what he didn't know. The perception of a link between the biological systems on the ship and Adalta grew until he couldn't ignore it. He didn't know how he knew it was there. But he knew.

A steady throb reverberated through him as he sank deeper into the ship's systems. The ship pulsed sadness, pulsed resignation, pulsed exhaustion. It grieved. It was dying.

Galen was no longer Galen. He was connections. He was a vast, complex network of failing systems interpenetrated by a vast, complex network of growing life. It was a long time before he slept, and when he awoke, he was Galen again. But a profoundly moved Galen.

When his father finally came back two days after he'd left him imprisoned, Galen was lounging in his room, the lights at low, the music at low, his temper at low boil. He didn't sit up, and he didn't allow his father time to speak. "Do you know what is happening to this ship? Do you know how little time there is before it fails?"

"Don't be ridiculous, Galen. And I hope you won't be spreading such a rumor. The maintenance technicians keep up with the minor incidents that occur. It isn't something you need worry about."

"Does that instruction not to spread rumors mean my imprisonment here is at an end?"

"I am allowing you time to heal, son. You're hurt, and you haven't been yourself since your accident happened."

"It is good of you to be so concerned about my health. I notice you're not wearing your haz-mask. Am I no longer contagious?" Galen drawled the words, his tone unconcerned, his hands linked behind his head where his father couldn't see how tightly they were clasped. His eyes fixed on the ceiling above his father blinked slow and sleepy.

"Your sarcasm is wasted, Galen. You will not be returning to the planet." Kayne's tone dripped sorrow.

Galen waited for the words "it's for your own good," but they didn't come—they just hung in the air.

"And your reason for this restriction?" A painful twist inside his chest stopped his breath for a moment. At least he wouldn't need to avoid Tessa. That problem was taken care of. He forced himself to inhale.

"I find I am unable to trust you to do the right thing, Galen." Kayne sat at the table near where Galen lay. "And that saddens me. I have always been able to depend on you, even when there was no one else."

He leaned forward and placed his clasped hands on his knees. "According to the reports I've gotten, after the healers released you,

you made no effort to garner support for Readen and his revolt. You made no effort to further my—the consortium's—aims on Adalta. I'm sorry, but I have assigned Merrik in your place since he tells me you appear to have involved yourself as an actor in one of their primitive legends, and your allegiance seems confused." Kayne's voice was soft, his eyes on Galen's were wide with concern.

Galen swung his legs to the floor and stood, keeping his movements slow, his balance precise so the imbalance that tore at him inside wouldn't escape. He felt as though he was waking from a dream. The falsity in his father's tone of concern and disappointment rang clear. As though his head was above water for the first time. "My allegiance to whom, Father? To you or to the ship's people?"

Kayne sliced his hand sideways, his face twisted and turned hard and cold. He hadn't anticipated this reaction. "Same thing. It doesn't matter. You cannot leave. You may take all the time you need to think about who you owe allegiance to. I'm disappointed in you. If you don't change, you won't be going back. Not to Adalta nor to any other planet when we leave here—with the cache of minerals we need and without your help. Your only hope of ever leaving the ship is as an asteroid miner. They're always tethered."

There. His real father was back.

Chapter Twenty-Five

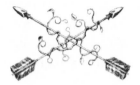

Several men and three women leaned over the large trestle table under a spreading oak just outside the mews. A ring of Karda surrounded them, and an improvised tent sheltered them from the drizzle. Fat drops collected on the tree and splatted loud against the canvas.

A rough drawn map of Restal Quadrant was pinned on the table—the holds, the prime, the mountains and foothills to the west, the Tarana River, the expanses of barrens dotted with villages and their surrounding cultivated fields. The circles surrounded by forest.

Tessa leaned against Kishar's shoulder, listening to Daryl, Altan, Krager, and Kyle discuss tactics and strategy with the Karda. They carefully avoided mentioning Galen when Tessa was with them. Marta and Merenya studied the map, pointing to one feature and then another. Mi'hiru and patrollers flew in and out, reporting to the men at the table, humans reporting to Daryl, Karda reporting to Marta and Altan. They'd been coming and going for several days, scouting the circles, the lines, and Readen's hold.

Kishar stirred, and Tessa looked up to spot a small sorrel approaching the far end of the runway meadow, white barred wings and tail catching the light as they flared for landing. It was Badti with Mi'hiru Cerla on her back. The little Karda stumbled when her feet hit the ground, recovered, and cantered toward them. Foamy sweat flecked her shoulders, and her powerful chest heaved when she stopped next to Kishar, head hanging, wings drooping, nares flaring.

Cerla was bent nearly double over Badti's neck, her fingers fumbling with the straps holding her to the saddle. Tessa ran to help and grabbed to keep her from falling when she slid off.

"We've been flying for three days," Cerla said. "Badti needs food and rest. We only stopped long enough to find water and to rest when we had to, and she's had nothing but dried meat since we left..." She held a hand over her mouth and looked around at the others, her eyes blinking away tears. "Since we left the camp."

Marta ran to Badti, her arm over his neck, led him to the mews, and listened to his story.

"What has happened, Mi'hiru?" Daryl's voice steadied the short, stocky woman, whose whole body trembled with fatigue and distress.

"The urbat. The urbat attacked the camp." She swallowed and bent over, pressing her face into her hands, her words interrupted by gulping sobs. "Hundreds of them. It was a massacre."

"Someone bring her a chair." Daryl half-carried her toward the table beneath the tree and kept a hand on her shoulder when she sat, the others grouped around. He held up his other hand. "Give her a little space." He knelt beside her. "Take your time, Cerla."

"They're dead. All of them. They're dead. They started planting again, and they're dead." Her voice choked. She repeated, "All of them." She looked up, eyes wide with desperation, flicking from person to person as if she wanted one of them to tell her it was a mistake. That what she had seen was wrong—hadn't happened.

Merenya brought a tumbler of water from a side table and knelt in front of Cerla, careful not to touch her taut body when she flinched away.

Cerla looked into the older woman's eyes and spoke as if speaking to only one person would make the words hurt less. "We were on patrol, Badti and I. Maren and Tal flew back early because Tal killed a deer. They wanted to take it to the cooks."

Her eyes didn't move away from Merenya. Her voice was thick with the effort of holding back grief and self-blame. "We finished the patrol. It was only an hour, little more before we were due in, so I thought it would be all right. I know we are supposed to stay in pairs. But it was such a short time. I thought it would be all right."

She stopped and looked around for reassurance. Merenya closed her fingers around the Mi'hiru's hand as if to tether her to something solid.

"By the time we flew back, it was all over. They were all dead. Urbat swarmed over the whole camp." She grabbed Merenya's hand with her other one so tight her knuckles were white. The tendons in her neck were taut wires. The look on her face splintered Tessa's heart.

Cerla's voice dropped to a whisper. "They tore Maren and Tal to pieces. And the planters. There was hardly anything left of the planters. The patrollers, they just—" She stopped for a long moment. "I had to leave. I'm sorry. I had to leave. I couldn't save them. I'm so sorry. I'm so sorry." She collapsed, repeating over and over, "I'm so sorry, I'm so sorry."

Merenya knelt in front of her, arms around her, holding her tight, smoothing a hand over her head and down her back over and over, rocking her like a small child.

No one spoke. No one moved.

Every Karda in the mews appeared, cantered to the landing meadow and took off, one by one into a vertical double helix, rising and falling above the landing meadow, their precise formation appearing out of and disappearing into the low clouds. Haunting, piercing musical cries with discordant harmonies tolled their dirge for the dead and rang in the bones of the listeners on the ground.

"Renewal," Tessa whispered, and heard from the bowed heads all around her—

"Renewal."

"Renewal."

"Renewal."

Cerla was the first to look up. "Before we left, Badti and I, we followed the trail the urbat left. We couldn't get close enough to the circle to be certain, but we think they came from there and went straight back into it." She cleared her throat and put her hand to her chest. Her fingers clamped onto her jacket. Then Cerla went on. "We didn't land, but Badti and I flew over the..."— She swallowed— "the camp several times to be...certain...to be sure there were no wounded."

Merenya's voice was soft. "Could you be certain from the air?"

Cerla closed her eyes, opened them, and again looked deliberately at Merenya as if it made the story easier to tell. "Yes, Guardian. What they left.... yes, I could be certain." She shuddered and looked away.

"We found Lieutenant—I can't remember his name—and Bren on their way back to the camp with the patrol reinforcements and the wagons of new saplings and supplies and landed to tell them. They turned around and are probably only a few days behind me. They were still on the road in the barrens." She stood.

She dropped her hands to her sides and shook them as if shaking away what she'd seen. "I did notice one strange thing. The dead urbat..." This time when she paused, there was a fierceness about her eyes and her voice, and she looked at Daryl. "The dead urbat had been stripped of their biggest bones. The large pieces of metal from their bodies. The only metal left, for the most part, was small gears and triangular pieces of armor, pieces too small for them to carry in their mouths."

It was late afternoon, and Tessa took the stairs up to Daryl's study two at a time. The door was open, and she didn't knock or wait for the young page to announce her. "He's not back, Daryl. Galen's not back yet. It's been days. I've looked everywhere. His horse is in the stables, but he's not anywhere."

Daryl took his glasses off, laid them on the papers he was studying. He looked surprised to see that the sun was throwing long shadows across the formal gardens and making the broad beds of late autumn flowers glow outside his study window. "Tessa. I know. I was afraid of this very thing."

"No. You're wrong, Daryl."

"Tessa, he's taken the guns and is gone."

"I've asked the Mi'hiru and the Karda Patrol who scout the

northern areas. No one's seen him. You're wrong. I've asked Kishar over and over."

"And what does Kishar say?"

Tessa looked down. "He says wait. Wait." She looked up at Daryl. "He's not concerned."

Daryl propped his elbows on the table and dropped his head to rub his eyes with the heels of his hands in an on-top-of-everything-else-I-don't-need-this gesture.

"I know it appears suspicious, but Daryl, he wouldn't just leave like this. He wouldn't betray us. He identified Merrik for you, didn't he? Something's happened to him."

"Ask the page outside the door—whose presence you ignored—to come in."

Tessa wasn't the least bit repentant. She stuck her head out and motioned to the boy to come in.

"Find Commander Kyle, Armsmaster Krager, Guardian Altan, Mi'hiru Marta, and Guardian Merenya, and ask them to come to my study, please, Pers," Daryl said. The boy left at a run, and Daryl stood, turning his back on Tessa to stare out the window while she paced back and forth in front of the big table and its litter of books and papers and maps, pens and mugs and empty plates.

Tessa waited for him to speak, but he just stood, impassive. So, she began stacking the dishes on a side table near the door, dropping pens and pencils into the several holders on the table. She touched a few piles of papers, straightening them, tapping them to align their edges, trying not to think about Galen's absence. But there simply wasn't room for any other thought in her head. Where was he?

Finally, Daryl spoke, his voice low and soft. "How can you be sure he hasn't found the guns and is on his way to Readen, Tessa? He has no real ties here on Adalta. His family and friends are on that ship. He betrayed Marta to Readen, a woman with whom he'd had an intimate relationship, a woman who'd been his friend since childhood." He turned to look at her, leaned forward, his hands on the table. "You can't be certain, can you? All his training is training in deception, Tessa. For most of his life."

Tessa took several deep, slow breaths to control the heat building in her face. "He...He hates his father." Her voice slowed. "And he doesn't have any other family." She crossed her arms and resisted the need to fall into a chair. How could she know, indeed? He'd never told her he felt anything special for her. She'd needed to believe he did. She'd needed to believe there was someone, someone besides Kishar—who'd told her he was going to leave her someday—someone who would mean she wouldn't be alone. Someone to stand with her against her father when Kishar was gone. And most urgently, someone to fight urbat with her.

The Kern was only a legend, after all, and Galen didn't have to fulfill it. Did being the Austringer mean she would have to fight alone? He was the only other person who could enter the circles where the urbat hid. She ducked her head and closed her eyes. She swallowed against the lump in her throat, breathing slowly, in and out, in and out. ~Oh, Galen. Where are you?~ she called silently.

Then the others began to arrive.

"I know it's been days, but I agree with Tessa," Marta said. "He would not betray us. He's finally broken free of his father's hold, and I don't think he would go back. Not willingly. I'll check with all the Karda who are here to see if one of them saw something and ask them to spread the word. Have you searched his rooms? Did he take his Cue with him?"

"What does it look like?" asked Kyle. "I'll send someone to check."

"No," said Daryl. "Better to go yourself."

"Do we want to advertise that he is missing?" asked Altan. His frown and the arms crossed over his chest were clear indications that he didn't agree with Marta. "But if any Karda anywhere say something, we'll find out."

"I'll be careful how I word my orders," Kyle replied. Their shared glance showed he thought Altan's suspicious might be justified.

"It looks like a small, locked journal about ten centimeters by sixteen, a little less maybe," Marta told Kyle, poking Altan in the ribs with her elbow. "You just don't want to believe anything nice about him."

"With reason," Altan muttered.

"I'll go with you, Kyle. I don't know if I can do any good, but at least I might recognize something he'd have taken if he did go back. And we should see if his pack is still there," said Marta.

Kyle and Marta left. Altan watched them leave, biting his lip. He wasn't happy to be separated from her.

"Krager." Daryl, elbows on the table, rested his chin on his steepled fingers. "Who do you have watching Merrik?"

"Masyn, today. Merrik hasn't done anything or gone anywhere. If he gave Galen the guns, I don't know when he could have. And Readen's forces are still at his hold. He hasn't been spotted."

"Keep watching. But in the meantime, we need to start thinking harder about how we are to fight these monsters. They are more dangerous than Readen."

Tessa noticed he didn't say "without Galen." But she saw that thought in the glance he flicked at her.

"I wonder if they have attacked any other villages?" said Merenya. "It seems they attack with overwhelming force and don't leave survivors, but surely your Karda Patrol and Mi'hiru would know if they had."

"The overwhelming force wasn't so at first," said Tessa, rubbing her face to rid herself of her worry over Galen. And her doubts. "There weren't very many of them, and we could fight them off, even when it was just the two of us and Kishar. But they keep increasing their numbers. I think that started when they rescued Readen and attacked Ardencroft." She blinked hard against that memory. "And except for that, we believe they only attack when the circle itself is attacked. Or one of the lines."

"I don't suppose there's any chance they killed Readen, too, when they attacked Ardencroft and the prison?" Altan spoke in an undertone.

But Tessa heard and shook her head, slow and deliberate. "Amanda and Bettan, Lili and Petya flew low circles around the village and prison, low enough to see the tracks of two horses leaving and heading north. Karda's eyes are like hawks'. Lili said the tracks were deep and the horses were moving fast. Probably in a panicked gallop. They were on top of the urbat tracks in some places and intermingled in others. Amanda and Bettan followed them, and…"

She rubbed a hand along the top of her leg. "They should be back by now, but I don't know how far they followed them."

"So far, unless Amanda found something different, urbat come from the circle, attack, and go back to the circle." Altan leaned his chair onto its back legs and stared toward the ceiling. "Since we can't go into the circles, we won't be able to tell where they are, where they will attack, or when. We're not fighting an army that has to make camp, forage for food, set up armories." The front legs of his chair hit the floor, and he looked across the table at Daryl. "Shit, we don't even know whether they need to eat or sleep, much less how many of them there could be."

Krager added, "Or how many other circles they might be hiding in. And there's no way we can find out."

Tessa looked up. "No, that's not true. Galen can walk into a circle, and he can sense them beneath the surface. And Kishar and I can fly over them without harm. I can also sense them from a distance. Not as well as Galen, but I know when they are coming. With enough time, we could probably get a good estimate of how many there are in the circle where we were planting. Where they all probably came from."

No one spoke for several minutes.

"Galen can walk inside a circle." Daryl's tone was deliberate and flat. "He can see beneath the surface?" He looked at Tessa for a long minute. "And neither of you thought this was something the rest of us might need to know."

Tessa looked back at him, her face still, her voice firm. "I thought you knew. He's the Kern."

Merenya broke the long silence in the room. "You and Galen and Kishar are the only ones we have now who have fought them and lived."

"And Bren and some of his drivers," said Tessa. She pushed back from the table and walked out into the hall to a window at the end. For the first time since she'd heard the horrible news from Cerla, she let the tears fall. Tears for her friends. For the people she'd lived with almost since Kishar's arrival. She stood for a long time, her bent head pressed against the cool glass. She watched the light fade into night, grieving for the friends she'd lost and the friends she knew she was going to lose in the coming days, tendays, seasons.

And when Galen gets back, how will I tell him? That Almryk is dead. That they are all dead.

She heard footsteps and turned to see Marta and Kyle come up the stairs. She went back into the room with them.

"If he left, he didn't take much with him. His Cue is still there, and I couldn't tell that anything was missing." Marta reached for Altan's hand and sat.

Tessa didn't know whether to be relieved or even more frightened.

Chapter Twenty-Six

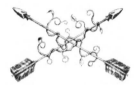

Galen jerked out of sleep, not sure what disturbed him. A soft tap sounded on the door. Then he heard the lock click and the door open and close.

A female voice said, "Lights. Low."

Galen blinked and stood. His head swam, and he steadied himself on the table by his bed.

Cedar Evans looked at him, hands on her hips, a deep line creased her forehead between narrowed eyes. "You don't look like you're about to spiral into death's black hole."

"Hello, Cedar."

Short, petite, curvaceous, black curls running wild over wide, brown eyes, Cedar looked like she always looked, cute and clueless but with dirt under her fingernails. Dirt that had been there as long as he'd known her.

She might be the only person on the ship Galen hadn't managed to alienate. Once Cedar decided to like or dislike someone, nothing changed her. The more distance he tried to put between them, the more she laughed and treated him like she always had. As the friend who could always be counted on to poke holes in his defenses.

She crossed her arms around the small bundle she carried and leaned against the closed door. "Should I be wearing a mask? Are you infectious? I've heard arrogance is highly contagious."

"I'm glad to see you, too, elf. Where are your pointy shoes?" And he was. She was a relief from the cold burn of anger that froze his gut and the hot panic that burned in his lungs at being away from Adalta. And Tessa.

Her head to one side and her eyes squished into a squint, she said, "You haven't called me that in a long time." She walked up to him and shoved him in the chest. He sat back on the bed with a thump.

She dropped down beside him. "What's going on, Galen? When I heard the whispers that you were back, I tried to see you. There's a watch on your door, and I was told you were ill and contagious with some mysterious virus you brought from the planet. No one knew exactly what. I asked Arlan, in medic, and he gave me a lot of ipsnoral shit and never looked me in the eye. So I hacked into his records, and —guess what?—there's nothing there. Nothing but your last visit when he examined your burns. So, I tried to see you again. Even went to see your asshole—forgive me—father." She threw up her arms. "He looked me in the eye and told me quite sadly you were quite ill, and he was quite concerned, and quite sorry that no, I couldn't see you. I was quite aggravated."

She grinned. "That's how I knew you needed rescue." She twisted around to face him and cocked a knee on the bed. "Whatever disease you brought back, I want some. You look great. Even with all the horrible, horrific scars that have finally made your unearthly beauty human."

Galen grabbed her with one arm and hugged. "I am glad to see you, too, Cedar. How have I ever lived without your constant adulation?" He was almost giddy with relief from the fear and frustration at not being able to reach Kishar or Tessa. Giddy and guilty.

"Galloping galaxies, Galen. You really have caught some horrific disease. I don't think you have hugged me since we were eight, and I took the blame for the Great Potato Sprouts Disaster." She pushed back and looked at him. "Are you in love or something?"

He looked away. "No. Yes. Well. No. I mean, it can't..."

Her face lit like she'd said, "Lights. Bright." "Oh, my. You found someone who didn't fall in love with you at first sight. I am so glad I lived to see this day. My life is complete. I can retire to the Great Planet of Beaches and Blue Water."

He ignored her. He couldn't bring himself to talk about the unde-served-unobtainable-out-of-reach Tessa. "How did you get in here? Aren't there guards on the door?" At least Cedar didn't know what he'd done, about the guns. How long was that going to last?

"There was a mysterious commotion of some kind in the 24-Hour Latte in the next pod. Since your guards were the first ones I saw when I came running, I sent them to take care of it. And I have entry to everywhere." She waved her arm at the greenery in the room. "Plants, you know. As newly elected Director of Bio-Systems, I must take care of the plants. Life support of the ship and all that. Let's get out of here before they come back. I want to know what's going on."

She handed him the bundle. "Get dressed. You are now one of my minions, minion. I promise not to look." And watched him change into the nondescript brown shirt and short pants of the bio-systems uniform, leering at his legs. "We better take your planet clothes with us. In case we don't want to come back here."

"I need to show you something," Galen said.

"We'll need to be careful. You may be wearing a bio-systems uniform, but you're still too recognizable," said Cedar.

"I don't think it's something we need to worry about." Galen closed his eyes then opened them before he fell. His connection to the ship was still there. He had to concentrate to feel it, and it made him dizzy. "But I'll know where there are guards." He brushed the wall with his hand. It tingled.

"Where are we going?"

"Warehouse pods."

"Then we're headed the wrong way." And she pulled at his sleeve to turn him to another walkway.

"Not that way. There are guards coming."

"How do you know that?"

"Don't ask, and I won't have to tell you something you won't believe anyway."

They made three detours around walkways with too many people.

Cedar stopped asking after he jerked her around a corner right before four guards came by. Four heavily armed guards moving fast and looking for someone. Him.

Finally, they got to the warehouse pod on the outer edge of the ship where he'd found the weapons. He tried the door. It was locked.

"Here, let me." Cedar hip-shoved him aside and pressed her palm to the lock. Nothing happened. She tried again and blew out a harsh breath. Her lips receded to a thin line. "I can unlock any door on the ship. Bio-Systems can't be locked out of anywhere that isn't personal space."

"Let me try." Galen shifted to the nearest access panel. "I'm sure Father monitors the lock. Can you open this panel?"

She pressed with her palm till there was a click and flipped the cover up. A tangle of roots embedded the circuits and wires controlling the doors on this corridor into one cohesive mess. "It's like this everywhere. Maybe not as bad as this, but it's bad." Cedar chewed at her lip and stared into the box. "I hate to start cutting away at this. It hurts every time I have to do it."

"Wait." Galen concentrated and sent a probe as delicate as he could make it into the tangle. He pulled back before he fried the whole thing. *I should have practiced harder at the fine work when I had the chance. But then I guess killing urbat doesn't require a fine touch, and that was more important at the time.* The unscarred side of his face twisted in an ironic smile. *I'm almost nostalgic for another chance.* Then he thought of Tessa having to fight on her own. He sucked in a breath, closed his eyes, and started again.

Roots curled and expanded as if they were waiting for him to ask. Connections broke apart. The lock on the pod door clicked. He closed the access panel. "Now it will look like the roots did it if anyone comes to check."

Cedar stared at the closed panel as if she could see through the cover if she stared hard enough. "What did you just do? That's not possible." She looked at him. "Uh, Galen, your eyes…"

"Yeah, I know, they're green. It's a long story."

She backed away. "A long story?" her voice was high and shrill. "Your eyes are completely green. Completely. And you made those roots move just looking at them. I'm gonna have to hear that story very soon. I think I'm going to be sick. And why didn't you just open the door to your room instead of waiting to be rescued?"

"Guards. Guards with big bad weapons and who never slept," said Galen. He pushed open the door. "I figured you'd come find me eventually, and I didn't want to wander all over the ship looking for you."

The pod was dark. Not even the ubiquitous gro-lights lit the space. "Lights. Low." Heavy brown, dead vines hung from the planters along the tops of the walls. Leaves littered the floor beneath them. Another small burn of anger kindled inside Galen.

"Oooh," breathed Cedar. "How did this happen? Why wasn't I notified?" She stood in the center of the mostly empty space and turned around and around, hugging her chest, hands rubbing up and down her upper arms as if she were cold, her mouth a quivering, twisted down-turn of distress, his all-green eyes forgotten.

"It's because of this." Galen walked to the small stack of crates in one corner—all that remained of the akenguns. He found a crowbar in a utility closet near the door. He broke one crate open, pulled out an oilcloth-covered weapon and unwrapped it. "Because of these. Father couldn't afford for anyone to find these."

The little that remained of the bouncy, ebullient Cedar vanished. Her mouth tight, she stared at the weapon. "What are those doing here instead of the captain's weapons locker?" She turned to two larger stacks of smaller, unmarked, hard plastic containers. "What's in these?"

Galen pulled one down and undid its straps. It was packed with smaller boxes he recognized. He leaned against the stack of crates and closed his eyes. Something tight released in his chest.

He'd found the shields that protected against the akenguns. He'd found his redemption.

Hand shaking, he pulled a flat, round badge little larger than his palm, about four and a half centimeters thick, off the bandolier it was attached to. His fingers curled around it. When activated, it threw a force field that disrupted the akengun's killing pulse. He didn't want to let it go.

But he put it back and closed the crate. "I have a story to tell you,

Cedar. It doesn't make me look good. Let's find a quiet place where we can talk. Where we won't be interrupted or overheard. Where there is coffee, maybe? I really miss coffee."

She crossed her arms over her chest again, holding tight to her shoulders, and turned slowly around and around, looking at the dead plants. "I hate seeing this. It hurts."

"Yes. It does."

She shot a quick, brow-lifted glance at him and huffed out a frustrated, angry breath. "Let's go. I do know where there's coffee. I only have a few varieties, but they produce some good beans. And I hoard the best. I'm not a nice person."

Before they left, Galen relocked the warehouse pod. Then he fused the lock. It would be blamed on the roots. He could get back in, but it would be difficult for anyone else. And he wanted those shields.

"Thank you for the seeds and soil samples you brought on your last trip, Galen. The soil is amazing. I have introduced some of the microorganisms I found into one of my quarantine pods and even this early in the experiment, I've seen results that make me happy."

She grinned. "And I have good news for you. I believe, from the meteorological scans so far, there is a good chance that the high range of hills on the southern coast of Akhara Quadrant might prove ideal for growing coffee. Once the soil is repaired, I mean."

Galen let her talk, half listening, as she covered her anger and dismay with words. He followed her to the small cafe near her laboratories. To his relief, he sensed no guards. He frowned and caught her when she stumbled making an illegal jump from one walkway to another. She never stumbled.

"There'd need to be covered drying sheds because the rainfall is too frequent, but that shouldn't be a problem. The real problem, I suppose, would be getting people to develop a taste for coffee after centuries of nothing but tea. I wonder if the colonists didn't bring coffee beans with them, or if the crops failed. I will be so interested in talking to the planters and seeing their records when we make ourselves known. This is the only colonized planet we know of that has introduced so much Earth flora."

They made another illegal jump in the web of interconnected walkways. He grabbed her arm again when she tripped. What was wrong with her bionic foot?

"And to have a whole corps of people dedicated to growing—I'm in ecstasy, Galen. I'm sorry. I get carried away, I know." She laughed. "You must have some idea of the reception we can expect down there. How soon do you think we'll be able to reveal our presence and begin to trade?"

Galen noticed, in spite of her mindless chatter, she didn't miss a single pot or planter along the corridors, reaching to touch a leaf here or back-stepping on the moving walkway to keep even with a pot there so she could check the moisture or adjust an irrigation emitter. He doubted she ever got all the dirt out from under her fingernails.

They made a last switch—another illegal jump from one moving walk to another—and entered the small cafe near the entrance to the gro-pods. They were the only people there this time of night, or rather, early morning by now. He saw her quick, automatic check of the plants.

"I think you might find out sooner than you think if what I suspect is right." He poured a cup from an insulated pitcher on the counter at the back of the deserted cafe and took a sip. He sat at one of the small tables and closed his eyes, taking another drink and letting out a long, satisfied sigh. "You can't know how much I miss coffee. My life might be worth living if only we can grow this on Adalta. What's wrong with your foot?"

Cedar was talking to the ship monitor on the wall and ignored him. She finally shut the console and turned sharply at his words. "You said *we*, Galen. Not *I* or *they*. I don't believe I've heard you use that particular plural pronoun for years."

Galen had forgotten how perceptive Cedar was. She missed nothing, and she'd known him since childhood. He raised his eyes from his cup. "You were a good friend, Cedar, if I'd ever let anyone be a friend."

She sat back, biting her lip. Then, "I wanted to be. I kept trying. You were always so intent on pleasing your father you didn't have room or time for anyone else."

He looked away then down at his cup again, lifting it for another sip, savoring the bitter bite, avoiding the bitter bite of her words.

"You look both elated and sad about something." She watched him over the rim of her cup.

A sudden, fierce longing pushed inside his chest. He rubbed it with one hand. Where was Tessa now? What was she facing? Anger choked him. He had to get off the ship. He had to get back. He had to take those shields back to the planet. He had to see her at least one more time.

Cedar's head was down. "Your father has a lot to answer for." Her voice was the soft, low growl of a large and dangerous cat.

They sat in silence, drinking occasionally. Cedar waiting. Galen's thoughts were fighting among themselves. It took effort, but he shoved them back and moved the emotional maelstrom deep inside.

He changed the subject. "You might get to the surface a lot sooner than you had anticipated, Cedar, if what I think is going on here is right."

She took a deep breath, raised her eyes to the ceiling, and held her palms together in front of her as if in prayerful gratitude. "Tell me what you are thinking, Galen. I have a feeling it matches what I think."

"The ship is failing. I don't think it will ever leave Adalta's atmosphere. I don't think it can. In fact, I think it is on the verge of breaking apart. I don't think she's going to let it leave."

"No one wants to admit it. It's a collective blindness. Even the directors and the captain ignore me or placate me when I tell them what's happening to the plants." Cedar let another small space of time go by before she said, "It's a running joke on ship that this planet's people think of it as a living being. Refer to it as she."

She took a sip and looked at him over the top of her cup. "It isn't a joke, and it isn't their imagination, is it, Galen?" Her words were not a question. "You said she, and you are one of the most unimaginative people I know."

He laughed, knowing the expression on his face probably resembled a silly sheep. It was good to be with someone who'd known him all his life, who didn't know and wouldn't care about his betrayals, who could accept him as he was. "There's an insult in there somewhere, isn't there? Let me see if I can figure it out with my lack of imagination. And what's wrong with your foot?"

"I'm sorry. I should have said you are someone who never lets his imagination take control. Or something a little less insulting." She ignored his question and smiled the whole-body-smile of someone who is back with a friend she hasn't seen for a long time and is happy to have him back because, for a long time, she hadn't been sure he was still in there like she remembered. "Do you want another cup?"

"Yes," Galen breathed, relieved. He could trust her, and she had the kind of access no one else had to every space on the ship.

Her back to him, refilling both cups, she said, "I can't tell you how many times engineering calls me to untangle vines or roots from some circuit or junction. After the first couple of times they killed a plant doing it themselves, I insisted I or one of mine be called when they found a problem with the greenery. I've put it in my reports. I've put it in my records. I've reported it in the director meetings. I've made certain engineering reports every incident. And no one cares."

Her face took on a wide-eyed innocent look. "I'm just the little girl director who got her place because her mentor liked her and pulled strings. Most of the time, I let that work for me, and I get what I want. But it isn't working in this case."

She set his cup in front of him and sat again, feet tucked under, her body leaning across the table, her hands flying, punching every word. "I've looked behind access panels all over the ship. And, Galen, every space I look into has been broached by my plants. The roots aren't always actively interfering. After a point, they quit growing and just sit there. I can almost see their growth tips quiver as if they are waiting for something. And at this point, there is nothing I can do about it. It's too pervasive. So, yes, Galen. I agree with you. The ship is failing, and no one on board is willing to admit it. As if the entire ship population has been infected with a collective blind and deaf virus."

Cedar stood and walked to the monitor console by the door, her back to him, shoulders tensing. "Galen, do you know your scars are changing? Just while we've been talking? And your eyes are all green again. Have I had too much coffee? Or did you put something in my coffee?" Her voice shook.

He touched his cheek. The scar was smooth, meaning the tattoo had taken its place. He looked at his hand. The root and branch markings were back. He cursed inside. Apparently, the itching ants-under-the-skin warnings no longer let him know they were changing. His hands dropped to his lap, and he tried willing the tattoos away.

He took a deep breath and let it out through his nose, caught his bottom lip with his teeth, and envisioned absorbing the tattoos into his talent reservoirs. Itching started in his cheek, then his hands, then his arms and chest. Gradually the itch went away.

He felt his cheek again. Felt the raised ugliness of his scars and for the first time, was grateful to feel it.

"You can look now, Cedar. They're gone. And, no, there is nothing in your coffee, and the gossip you hear that people on Adalta believe in magic is true. Remember the first adage of traveling on a trade ship, 'Nothing is impossible, even elves and fairies and Yetis.' Yes, I know that refers to alien life forms, not magic. But in this case, it does."

She finished typing something on the monitor and turned back to face him. Her head tilted to the side to better see the scar on his cheek. Her voice carrying only a slight tremble, Cedar said, "It isn't fair, Galen, for someone so beautiful to have the only blemish he's ever had in his life turn into something lovely. You never even had a puberty pimple. And now you have beautiful tattoos and mysterious magical powers? What's fair about that?"

"I wish people would stop telling me I'm beautiful. It just isn't manly."

Cedar laughed, and the tightness that had come back to his chest loosened. She'd be alright. She'd get used to thinking in this new way.

Her face stilled. "And the magical powers? Tell me I imagined those roots doing what you told them to do."

"Well, yes. That, too. And I'm not the only one." He looked down into his half-empty cup.

"And there's more, isn't there?" She waved a hand toward the monitor. "I've just checked. The ship's manifests show that warehouse pod to be empty, but it isn't. No mention of akenguns, of course. No one's fingerprints are on those manifests, and I can only think of one person who could do that. Besides me, that is."

"I think he forgot you have access to every inch of the space on this ship. No one notices plants. They're just there, and everyone assumes the ship's systems take care of them. It was short-sighted of Father, wasn't it?"

He closed his eyes for a minute. "I'm going to need you, Cedar. I hope, when you've heard all the story, you'll still want to help. There is a war breaking out down there—a war waged off and on for thousands of years. I sometimes wonder if Adalta made herself known so we could find her. Twice. Once to the original colonists, and now to us. She needs our help. And from what I've seen since I've been up here, this ship needs Adalta."

Cedar looked at him, her smile tight. Her face flickered between doubt and confusion. "You believe that. I think you've let those magical, mystical powers chase away your better sense, Galen."

"What's wrong with your foot, Cedar?"

He barely heard her answer. It was so soft.

"No one knows."

Chapter Twenty-Seven

Tessa swiped at the sweat dripping from her forehead with her headband and pushed it back up. "I know you can do this, Kobe. I've talked to every blacksmith and metal fabricator in the prime. They all say they can make the arrowheads and spear points and swords, but you're the only one with the skill for this. It's been done before, and I know you are the one who can do it this time."

She was tired. Tired and hot and sweaty and worried about Galen. The heat from the forge glowed red behind the burly metalsmith who wore a fierce, stubborn frown. Whose mouth looked like he clamped it shut with the heavy tongs he held in his hand.

Tessa was baking. Her patience baked beyond the point of done. Now she knew why everyone she'd asked who could make what she wanted told her, "Kobe." And added, "Good luck."

The fabricator held the triangular urbat armor scale in the tongs and stared at it, concentrating until it glowed red. He sniffed and pulled back, rubbing his nose with his other hand. "Stinks."

It never stopped hurting when she watched someone else use talent the way she couldn't. And Kobe's grouchy stubbornness didn't help. "Yes, it stinks. But when it's worked, the smell goes away."

"Not fast enough. Still stinks." It appeared Kobe considered words precious things to be used sparingly for fear he'd run out.

Tessa resisted the urge to swat him with the flat of her sword. He ignored her for the better part of an hour before he picked up the piece of urbat metal with a pair of tongs. At least he was finally talking to her. Kobe might be the best, but he was galaxy-damned temperamental.

She watched as he turned the rod back and forth, concentrating. He finally picked up a hammer and started tapping the scale against an anvil, tapping and turning, tapping and turning until, white-hot without ever touching the forge, it began to form a solid square shaft.

He dropped the hammer and picked up a long, narrow piece of metal with a deep groove at one end and a handle at the other. He laid the glowing rod over the mold, picked up the hammer, and tapped until the mold filled, end to end, with a thin rod.

Kobe stepped back and frowned, hands on his hips, staring at the cooling metal. "Wire nets, you say?"

Tessa forced herself to quietly let out the breath she was holding. He wasn't even sweating. The heat from the forge and the metal didn't affect him at all. "Yes. Round. About three meters in diameter and as light and strong as you can make them. Hunting nets."

"Ummm." He picked up another metal scale and bounced it in his calloused palm. "Light."

She leaned against a bench on the side wall of Kobe's workshop. *Where's the cold rain when I need it?*

He brushed his hands together and looked at her. "Can't be done. Be too heavy anyhow for one man to throw."

"Kobe, I just helped bury two hundred and thirty-seven people in Ardencroft. And I had to put a tiny infant by itself in the mass grave because there was no way to tell who his mother was. I don't want to have to do that ever again. We need these nets. I know you can do this. It's been done before, and every other metal worker in Restal Prime says you are the one who can figure out how to do it again."

He shook his head, frowning down at the cooling rod of urbat metal.

She sighed, wiping at her dripping forehead with her sleeve before the salty sweat rolled into her eyes. Again. "Well, give the metal back to me. I'll find someone who will at least try to do what you can't." She reached for the canvas sack at his feet.

"Humpf. Leave it. Come back tomorrow."

She left before he could change his mind. The cart outside his shop was empty now. She'd started out with ten bags of the metal collected from Ardencroft, leaving metal with every blacksmith, swordsmith, and fabricator she could find. Climbing up on the seat, Tessa clucked to the pony who looked as hot and tired as she was.

"When Galen comes back." Tessa glared at the carefully neutral faces across the table from her in Daryl's office and repeated, "When Galen comes back, he and I and Kishar will start monitoring the circle where we know the urbat are awake. Galen and Llalara—"

She stopped and swallowed. Not Llalara. Llalara was dead. "He and whichever Karda chooses to carry him can monitor from outside the circle, and Kishar and I from inside. What we do will depend on what we find. On our way, we'll take word to the two villages west of the circle that haven't been warned and give them what urbat metals we can carry so they can begin fashioning more effective weapons."

"I went to see Kobe again." She rolled her eyes. "And thank you for letting me be the one to approach him. It has been such a joy. He's finished the first net and says, with help, he can have twenty more in a couple of tendays. It doesn't need to be skilled help, just hands. Young people would be best, he says. Their fingers are more nimble."

There was almost a sigh of relief.

"I'll see to that," said Commander Kyle.

Daryl made a note on a paper in front of him. "Something will have to be done about the lines that are extending from the circle. They can't be allowed to connect." Daryl leaned on the table with both arms, staring at the marks indicating Readen's hold in the North, the mines beyond them, and the lines reaching out from the circles toward each other much too fast.

"I know Galen failed the first time, but he's still thinking about them, and—" Tessa stopped and just stood, staring out the window. Her voice small, she said, "He'll be back. I know he'll be back. Somehow he'll get back."

She looked around at the faces turned away from her. Merenya, Altan, Daryl, Commander Kyle, Armsmaster Krager. No one would look at her. No one but Marta.

"Kishar says two Karda saw a—what do you call them, Marta? A something shuttle? He says they saw one take off straight up into the sky with someone who had to be carried on. He was probably unconscious, they said. Galen, I mean."

Marta reached out and touched Tessa's shoulder. "It's all right, Tessa. Galen didn't volunteer to return to the ship. And he's resourceful. He'll figure out a way to get back. I don't believe his father has support for his plans for Adalta from the other directors. I don't think any of them know what Kayne's doing. Galen will find a way to get back."

"But will anyone up there believe him? Over his father, I mean. You say his father is one of the most important people on the ship. Why should they believe Galen instead of him?"

Daryl straightened and said, "It doesn't matter, either way, Tessa. We have battles to fight here, whether he comes back or not. The urbat are not our only problem. We need to act before Readen manages to gather up what he can of the supporters who scattered when we defeated him before. We have guards around his hold, but not enough."

He leaned back in his chair. "We have no idea if the Itza Larrak managed to get out of the cavern and is with Readen. If it is, we need to know how to fight it, what its abilities are, if and how it controls the urbat." He went back to studying the map. "I don't want to believe Readen is with this monster willingly. I'm sorry, Marta. I know…"

He stopped. His jaw tightened, and he looked down at the table. He shrugged his shoulders as if to shake something off and looked at Tessa. "Tessa, while you wait for Galen's return, you and Kyle keep the pressure on Kobe and the other fabricators. Altan and Marta, I suggest the three of us fly north. We need information about where Readen is and where the urbat are."

Galen spent the day hiding and pacing in Cedar's quarters. She wanted him to go to one of the other directors with her, but he wanted nothing to delay his trip back to the planet with the shields. He'd let her tell the directors and the captain about the smuggled guns. He needed to stay out of sight and work fast.

Now he stood on a small ladder outside the warehouse pod, poking at the planter above him. The brown uniform of Cedar's Bio-Systems workers was too small and pulled across his shoulders and in even more uncomfortable places. *How is it that this section, which is as out of the way as it was possible to get, is so busy when I need it to be empty?* Two techs came around the corner, glanced up at him, and passed on.

His father was looking hard for him, but Galen's communication with the ship helped him avoid Kayne's men so far. But who knew what they'd been told about him? Everyone he sensed carried hidden arms. Kayne couldn't afford to alert the Ship Watch. He didn't want Galen caught by anyone official.

He concentrated on the lock he'd fused the night before when he and Cedar left the warehouse pod. The sharp smell of burnt oil and hot metal scalded his nostrils. Galen jumped down from the ladder and opened an access panel beside the door, and three more people walked around the corner. He kept the scarred side of his face turned away from them. Cedar had smeared it with heavy makeup, and it was "night" on the ship, so the gro-lights were off, but his disguise wouldn't fool a close look.

One of them laughed. "Smells like you better fix whatever you're working on before the techs get here, or they'll kill another plant for you."

Galen ducked his head closer to the workings inside the panel and waved a pair of secateurs over his head. "On it," he muttered. The lock opened, and he shoved his foot over to hold the door closed till the three passed, then slammed the access panel shut, grabbed the ladder, and slipped inside. The crates of weapons and containers of shields stacked against the back wall were undisturbed. "Lights. Low," he said.

The door opened again behind him. Cedar and three of her crew—ones she was sure she could trust— rolled mobile pallets off the walkway and inside, quick and quiet, loaded with racks of plants in pots.

"I'm sorry I'm late, Galen. It took forever for the directors' meeting to end. I got permission for this experiment and managed to get papers for it so you can leave. Your name is now Peri Wilton. He volunteered to lock himself in his quarters till you're on the surface and the shuttle comes back. He wanted me to hit him over the head, but I didn't. Not that I haven't wanted to at times."

Cedar ran her fingers across the tops of the small plants. "I hope they don't die before you can get back to them."

"You look like you're sending your best friends on a suicide mission, Cedar. I promise to do my best, but they aren't my priority. Let's get busy. This is going to take a while." He pulled a container from the stack and started unpacking the shields, pulling them off the webbed belts.

Cedar upended a plant, tapping it loose from its pot, dropped the shield in, and put the plant back. The five of them worked for two hours, hiding the shields under the plants and replacing them on the racks. They stacked the large containers back as they were, now filled with nothing but boxes of the empty bandoliers.

Finally, Cedar brushed off her hands, went to a small closet for a broom and dustpan, swept up the dirt they'd spilled, and dumped it in a bucket. Galen retrieved the ladder and spread the soil in the planters of shriveled brown plants ringing the top of the walls.

"I'll discover the dead plants in this pod tomorrow," said Cedar. "I'll raise such a stink about it, your father won't be able to get in here until we finish. Which, given the fact that I'll need to test the soil, check the irrigation systems and drainage, look at the environmental systems records for the last several months for what went wrong, and whatever else I can come up with. Which means we'll be in here working for several days. I'll be able to have this pod quarantined for quite a while to be certain whatever killed these plants doesn't spread. It will take a while to rule out everything but neglect."

She smiled an I'll-get-him smile. "Since none of the crates in here are on the manifests, I'll open them and raise another stink about what I find."

"He'll stop you."

"No. He won't. I'm Director of BioSystems. When I shut something down, it is shut down." She stood, feet apart, arms crossed, staring at the crates of weapons in the other pile. "And your father needs to be shut down."

"You'll never find his fingerprints on anything that might lead to this." Galen kicked at the stack of crates.

Cedar smiled. "I've been Director of BioSystems for a while now and acted for the director for several years before that. It took a long time for the old man to retire. While you were off exploring other so-exciting worlds, I explored the ship's systems. Since I was ten. Not much can hide from me."

"I can't believe you call Glenn Voigt 'old man' to his face and get away with it. He scared me to death."

"When you grow up following him around like a gosling follows a goose, getting in his way, and asking millions of questions about the things he loves, you can call him anything you want. He knows he's the person I respect above all others."

She hooked her arm through Galen's. "And don't sell him short. He's still a force to be reckoned with on this ship. When he and I get through with your father, Kayne will be compost. Let's get these plants to the shuttle bay."

Cedar looked at the three workers. "You guys picked up these plants in gro-pod seven and are sending them planet-side with Peri, here, for an important experiment."

The youngest of the four mock-saluted. "You're the big boss, Cedar. If you say this is gro-pod seven, then that's where we are."

It took most of an hour to load the plants back on the mobile pallets and get them to the closest cargo shuttle bay. Cedar waved her paperwork at the two guards stationed at the door who refused to let them through. "What are you guarding, anyway? And who authorized you to be here? Go find whoever it was and have him come explain to me why you are trying to keep me from loading a shuttle with the first experiment I've been authorized to make on this planet."

Galen watched with amused amazement as she bullied, coerced, beguiled, and charmed shuttle techs, fuel techs, loaders, and whoever else came near, got the plants loaded, him on board, the bay emptied, and the cargo shuttle launched, in less time that the trip to the planet would take.

He set the coordinates for a forested area with a clearing large enough to land the shuttle, and Karda as well, as close to Restal Prime as he thought he could and not be seen. He blessed the low cloud cover that blanketed that part of the planet this morning with mist and fog.

Six hours later he landed, and before he got the last of the plants unloaded, a Mi'hiru on a bay and a magnificent, gleaming gold Karda with an empty saddle rigging landed in the field and cantered to the shuttle. The two Karda jostled each other to stick their heads inside with great curiosity. "Amanda. And Bettan," Galen said. "How did you know I was here? How...?"

"Kishar sent us. He's had probably every Karda not still in the mountains watching the skies for you." Amanda's eyes were nearly as big as Bettan's as she looked over the shuttle. "Wow. A real spaceship? Can I see inside?"

"You can not only see inside. You can help me carry out the rest of these flats, so I can send it back. And it's not a spaceship. Just a small freight shuttle. How many people know about the ship now? I take it you've been let in on the secret."

Amanda was too busy examining the shuttle to answer.

Galen turned to the beautiful gold Karda that had flown in with them. "And who is this?"

"This is Ket, Galen. He has agreed to carry you."

"Greetings, Ket. I've never seen a Karda like you before."

The Karda inclined his head in a regal nod. Ket was a gold, but his coat and mane were pale with a metallic sheen that glowed—he looked mystical and unworldly in the swirling fog.

Chapter Twenty-Eight

Readen stood under a massive spreading oak at the edge of a clearing in the woods outside his hold, staring up through the leaves. One hand shadowed his eyes. The other rubbed up and down the side of his leg, fingering the seam of his trousers. Three Karda, not much more than specks in the sky, circled above. "They come every morning, for three days now, and circle up there for hours."

"Shoot them down." A hard, unreal, quasi-mechanical voice came from the Itza Larrak, who stood under the trees out of sight of the flyers.

"They're too high. The weapons can't reach them."

"Then ignore them. They can't see much from that high."

Readen glanced back at the towering figure. Its iridescent wings never stopped moving with the soft, rasping, ringing metal-on-metal noise Readen could hear in his sleep, a constant melodious-mechanical buzz. He shivered.

"They can see everything. Their vision is akin to that of hawks or eagles. It's telescopic. They could probably see a mouse running across the clearing at midnight from that high."

The Itza Larrak's voice lowered and dripped with scorn and fury on the word Karda. "There have been Karda flying over the whole time we've been here. What bothers you about these three?"

"They have riders."

It took a step out from under the trees and raised its head toward the flying Karda and riders.

"Don't come out into the open. They'll see you."

The yellow eyes dropped back to Readen. "Do you imagine they do not know we are here?"

"They don't know about you, and if word spreads that you are back and with me, I'll lose every supporter, every trooper I have. They'll leave by tomorrow. A front's moving in from the mountains. The Karda won't want to fly under it. It would put them in range. Samel tells me Daryl knows about the akenguns. Galen told him."

"Ah, yes. Galen the Morel. The valuable being you lost."

Readen closed his eyes, his head tilted up to the sky. Impotent fury scoured his concentration, sharper than any talon. He forced himself to relax, one hand on his chest, fingers tracing the hard outline of the medallion under his tunic, feeling for strength. It could amplify his spells, but it couldn't amplify his patience.

He counted four deep breaths before his anger dissipated, and he could form words. "As you say. But I still have the guns." He directed his focus toward keeping his body still and his words even and devoid of emotion. It helped him regain control.

The prisoners were due in a few days.

He felt a carnal smile stir deep in his belly. How many young "power sources" would arrive? Readen knew better than to hunt them near his hold's village, even when disguised with an illusion. He'd exhausted that source a long time ago.

He couldn't get away to find a victim himself. He didn't dare leave the Itza Larrak and the urbat, and he didn't dare take them with him. They were too unpredictable. The large question mark of who was in charge hung in the air over the Itza Larrak every time Readen looked at it.

In the past tenday, four urbat had been caught in the open by Karda and dropped from on high into the middle of the clearing. Readen still tasted the stink on the back of his tongue.

Readen had killed one Karda that flew too close over his hold. The tolling notes of the Karda mourning song as others flew their aerial dance of grief bathed him with power for an entire day after that. It was worth the loss of one weapon's power reserve. He was finally able to reinforce the shields he held to protect him from the Karda and their riders.

Hiding in the back of his mind was the thought that his shields would need to be a great deal stronger to protect him from the Itza Larrak if it decided it didn't need him.

"Perhaps you could take a weapon and fly high enough to get within range." Readen turned to face the Larrak. He bit the inside of his mouth hard enough to taste salty, coppery blood. He held his arms tight against his sides, his feet apart in a show-no-fear stance.

The monster stared long into the sky. Its eyes followed the circling flight of one Karda in particular, a large mahogany bay whose wingtips winked bronze in the sunlight. "Give me your weapon."

The tension in Readen's shoulders bled away. The Larrak took the weapon from him. It was small in the behemoth's talons as the monster turned it over and over, studying it. Readen took it back and demonstrated how to trigger its killing charge. The akengun was awkward in the Larrak's large hands with its long, sharp talons.

It marched to the edge of the clearing. Weapon held tight against its chest, it took six long, graceful leaps. It spread its wings with a resonant boom, grabbed the air with hard down-thrusts, rose up and circled the clearing, ever higher and higher.

The tight trio of Karda above separated into a wide triangle around the rising Larrak. A green firebolt streaked from one of the riders and exploded. An iridescent bloom streaked around the curve of the Itza Larrak's pearlescent shield. Then another rider sent a bolt that exploded against the shield leaving neither scratch nor gouge. Readen watched the dark figure's wings, half again as long as the Karda's, power it higher. It hovered in the center of the triangle of three flyers, ignoring the bolts flaring against its shield, and readied the weapon.

Light flashed with an intensity that blinded Readen. When he could blink wet tears past the fiery color bursts that seared his eyes, he watched the Larrak fall in a tight, twisting, rapid descent, one wing useless, its tip shredded, the thin metal mangled. It spiraled ever faster toward the ground. The akengun had exploded against the inside of the creature's shield.

Eerie howls vibrated in Readen's ears, and six urbat ran from the shelter of the massive forest trees. Stubby wings beat hard, and they rose in a tight formation to position themselves directly under the falling Larrak. It plummeted into the midst of them—one wing folded tight against its body, the damaged wing spread half open. The urbat on the outside of the formation beat their wings in a blur to slow and cushion the monster's fall to the ground. When it climbed off, two of the urbat didn't get up.

Surrounded and supported by the four remaining urbat, it limped to where Readen waited. Its yellow eyes glowed orange, tight with fury. One delicate, metal wing drooped. Its twisted tip dragged behind it. It held one arm, taloned hand missing, clamped tight against its damaged, misshapen chest. Thick, yellow ichor seeped from the severed limb—amber fluid that reeked with acrid, oily vapors. Readen gagged at the stink.

"I return in seven sun cycles."

The harsh voice grated, and Readen took a step away with one foot before he stopped himself from running back toward the hold gates. He'd never heard such implacable frost in the Larrak's voice. The words speared his ears like icicles.

"We will move then. I cannot be trapped inside your forest to wait for the enemy to return in force. I will not wait for them to attack. I will control this struggle. I will not let them choose where to engage. You must be put back in power over the humans in this quadrant."

The harsh, mechanical voice continued. "I cannot allow the restrictions on the circles to continue. The lines must be allowed to connect. I must be able to communicate with the others of my kind, and this planet must be made ready for them. I have waited long for this. You will not be allowed to fail."

It turned and motioned for the four urbat to follow. Its uninjured, taloned hand braced on the back of one of the monsters, it limped away. Six more flanked them, clawed paws silent on the forest floor.

Readen stood, unmoving, until it was out of sight.

Connect the circles.

Communicate.

Others of its kind.

The coldness in the Larrak's words spread through Readen's chest, and he wrapped his arms around himself. *What have I aligned myself with? What have I done?*

It would be a long seven days for Readen. *Think. Think. This is the last Larrak. They are not indestructible. They can be killed.*

He took several long slow breaths through his nose, letting them out his mouth, feeling the spiky ball of fear poking his diaphragm begin to soften. There was an extensive library in his study with some fragile old books of the early history of the colonies. They were incomplete, and the information about the Larrak was sketchy, but there must be something he could use. This was the last Larrak. Something killed the others. There must be stories somewhere about how.

For days Readen buried himself in the histories while he waited for the Larrak's return. Individual fighters who had been with him before trickled into the hold—hardened, battle-scarred men and women with tight eyes that never stopped moving and tight mouths that seldom opened to speak.

The urbat stayed out of sight. The Itza Larrak returned in the half-light of dusk the evening of the seventh day. Readen was in the forest waiting, pulled by a tension he couldn't resist.

The Larrak was whole. It didn't limp. It had both hands. Readen wasn't certain, but he thought it was slightly smaller in stature. He looked behind it through the open forest. One urbat followed. Ten had left with it, and only one returned. Only one.

He sucked a breath through his teeth. When he'd followed the shambling body of the young guard the Itza Larrak had appropriated, it had come back out of the circle whole. And several of the urbat that had gone down into the strange opening with it had not returned that time either.

The Itza Larrak and the urbat were alien to this planet. Did that mean...? Could that mean...? Did that mean there could be no more? Readen's eyes moved across the pile of carefully salvaged metallic urbat bones stacked to one side of the clearing and stopped. He looked closer. Every time one died, the others tore its body apart. He'd thought they were eating the carcasses. But they weren't. They were harvesting them. Salvaging the metal. Alien metal. His eyes unfocused. He stared at a hole in the clouds above. A slow, deliberate smile stretched his mouth.

The urbat numbers were finite.

They could not reproduce.

There would be no more when these were gone.

Chapter Twenty-Nine

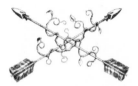

Galen closed the cargo shuttle ramp. Its rotor arms whined and lowered, and it took off in a small storm of leaves and twigs and dust. Amanda, Bettan, and Ket watched with open mouth and beaks until it disappeared into the cloud cover.

"Wow," breathed Amanda.

Galen looked at the shining gold Karda with the same wow feeling. Ket was stunning. Galen was a little embarrassed to ask such a glorious creature to run a mundane errand, but he said, "Ket, if you would take word back to the prime that we need a cart to transport the shields, Amanda can help me—"

~I am not a messenger.~

Galen looked at the silken, shimmering gold Karda. *I guess I shouldn't have asked.* ~I beg your pardon. But I could use someone with hands to help me with unloading these pots—like Amanda.~ He pulled the saddle rig off and stood it on end to air. It appeared he and Ket could communicate telepathically.

And it seemed Amanda had heard Ket. She looked back and forth between Galen and Ket. "Wow. I can hear Ket in my head. I can't even hear Bettan. Wow."

Ket's head turned slowly, and he looked down at her, blew a harsh breath out of his nares and turned back. All Karda had something of an arrogant look, with their big, hooked, predator beaks and fierce eyes, but Ket took arrogance to a new level.

"Umm. We'll go. I didn't know what you'd need. So...umm. We'll be back as soon as we can."

"Thank you, Amanda. And Bettan." Galen bent in a half bow.

The Mi'hiru and Bettan took off.

Galen stalked to the pallets loaded with plants and started upending the pots, one by one, stacking the akengun shields to one side and repotting the plants. Cedar would expect an accounting of every one. ~Perhaps I should have asked them to bring another volunteer Karda back.~

Ket shook himself all over. Down and dander flew, and Galen sneezed. ~I thought all those lessons I had to take in human communication were just exercises, not something I'd ever need to use.~

I wouldn't have thought it possible to mutter telepathically. Galen pounded on the bottom of a pot so hard he knocked the dirt from the plant's roots and had to resettle it after he removed the shield. *Karda have lessons?*

~This is very confusing.~ Ket bated his wings. ~There is not room in my life for this. I have responsibilities. I only came from the mountains out of curiosity, and suddenly I find myself volunteering to carry you.~ He was silent for a moment. ~I am perturbed.~ His wings settled back to his sides. ~And that saddle itches.~

Late the next morning, Galen woke huddled under Ket's wing after a damp, cold, and hungry night. Amanda and Bettan landed, heralding the rattling appearance of a small wagon loaded with large baskets. He rolled away from the Karda. "Thank you for the shelter."

Ket's head lowered in a regal nod, turned his back, and walked away to the edge of the meadow to dig for the Karda's favorite tubers.

Bettan loped to a stop, and Galen reached a hand up to help the Mi'hiru dismount. "I hope you brought food, Amanda."

She grinned at him. "I did. And a heavier jacket for you. You look cold and miserable. Or rather Lannys brought it and drove all night to get here. Galen, this is Lannys. Lannys—Galen."

The tall, lanky woman tossed back her dripping rain cloak and jumped down from the wagon seat, rolled her shoulders, and bent over, stretching out her back. When she straightened, her eyes widened, and her mouth dropped. "Oh, where did you come from? I've never seen such a beautiful Karda."

Ket's head came up. A tuber hung from one side of his beak. Its green top drooped out the other. His neck arched, and he preened, dancing around so she could get the full view.

Galen snickered. Ket was like a little kid showing off for his favorite aunt. "This is Ket. He's condescended to carry me back to the prime. Ket, this is Lannys."

Between wide-eyed glances at the beautiful gold, she pulled a small canvas sack and a folded jacket out from under the wagon seat. "It's not a hot meal, but it should do for us until we get back to the prime. I didn't think you'd want to stop and build a fire to cook." She looked at Ket and inclined her head. "I'm sorry I have nothing for you, but Amanda indicated you were not used to dried meat and would probably prefer to hunt for yourself."

Ket nodded his head at her and looked at Galen. ~I will return as soon as I find something.~

Galen watched until the Karda, its pale, metallic gold coat and feathers gleaming in the early morning light, soared out of sight.

He turned to grab a crate from the wagon bed. "Let's get these shields packed up so we can leave."

Tessa walked out of Kishar's stall, moving carefully, shoulders back, willing her feet not to fly into a full-out run. She passed the stall with the great gold Karda. *I've never seen a Karda like that. I'll have to ask Kishar about him. He's spectacular just standing in the stall. I bet he's dazzling in the sun.*

She looked at Galen, busy brushing the Karda's shining gold coat, his back to her. He didn't turn around, and he didn't speak. Her body was cold then hot, hot then cold.

The big doors at the end of the mews were closed against a biting, wet autumn wind. She used the smaller side door, slipping through and literally slipping on a patch of ice outside. She muttered a word she didn't even know she knew and wrapped her heavy cloak tighter. The wind whipped around the corner of the mews and clutched at her with freezing claws.

Since he got back, Galen ignored her as if she didn't exist. He walked away when she came near, never let her catch his eye. Her face heated in spite of the icy sleet her hood didn't keep out.

The walk up the hill to Kobe's forge would be cold, but at least there it would be warm. He'd sent word he'd finished the first nets. The Karda and Mi'hiru needed to start practicing. Throwing hunting nets of metal wire was going to take a lot of practice, especially for those throwing them from the back of a flying Karda.

She approached an alley around the corner from the forge and stumbled as someone grabbed her arm. She fumbled under her cloak for her sword, and a harsh voice said, "Tessa, it's alright. It's Cael. It's alright."

She went still.

"Can I let go now?" he said.

Tessa nodded.

"Will you follow me?"

She hesitated.

"We'll go someplace public, but someplace no one will notice us. Or at least no one will tell anyone they noticed us."

Tessa had seen nothing of Cael since that awful day she killed her attacker after the battle ending Readen's short-lived revolt.

"It's important, Tessa. I need to tell you what I know. Krager is away, and I can't wait for him to get back."

She nodded again, and he turned back down the hill. They walked a long time to a small tavern in the shadow of the outer walls of the prime, far from the keep's stables and the Karda mews. The few people inside this early in the day were sunk in their ale-worlds and in no condition to notice anyone. They took a table in the corner away from the rough bar. Cael held up two fingers and called to the half-asleep woman behind it. "Two hot ciders."

He was silent until they had the mugs in front of them and the woman disappeared through a ragged curtain into the back. He took a long drink and exhaled, relaxing his shoulders. "I thought I'd freeze waiting for you."

A long, appraising look later he said, "I've heard all kinds of stories about you." His mouth quirked up in a rueful smile. "You've changed since I left Me'Cowyn Hold. Since your father caught me sparring with his little girl."

"Father chased you away, didn't he? When he caught you teaching me sword work. He was so angry."

"You could call it that."

"That's why you're a mercenary. Father probably told everyone he knew not to hire you. Where have you been, Cael?"

"Doesn't matter." He lifted the mug of cider again, but it was empty. "What does matter is what I have to tell you now."

"You're still working for Readen? How could you, Cael? He's evil."

"You don't need to tell me that, little one. I know even better than you what he is." Cael's voice turned into a low growl that made the hairs on Tessa's arms stand up. "So, listen. I can only be gone for a few more minutes before Lieutenant Rees misses me, and I don't want that. Readen is at his hold. And there are two, maybe three, hundred monstrous creatures, half-machine, half-dog or something, hidden in the forest just to the north of the hold. They're hidden behind a don't-look-here illusion, but I'm pretty good at piercing illusions. They give me an itch.

"About a tenday after he arrived, he went back out the gates with a young soldier who didn't move right. He walked like he didn't quite know how to move his parts, not like he was drunk. I slipped out and followed. When they were out of sight of the walls, a whole phalanx of these monsters appeared. I couldn't see them too well, but there was a moon, and I saw enough to scare me back inside the gates."

"I know. I've fought them. They're urbat, and they come from the circles."

Cael's mug hit the table with a dull clunk, and he sat without moving. There was a long silence.

The woman came over, picked up both mugs, and brought them back, steam rising from the hot cider. Tessa wrapped her cold fingers around it and sipped, waiting for Cael to absorb what she'd said.

SHERRILL NILSON

"I'm telling you something you already know." He leaned back in his chair. His eyes were hooded. Deep lines scored his face.

"No. We didn't know for sure where Readen went." She looked into her mug. "And we don't know how many urbat there are. And I didn't know they could survive for so long outside a circle." Those last words were soft and quiet.

Cael put both hands on the table in front of him. "When Readen came back, he brought a monster with him. No one saw it but me. I was watching for him. It was dark, so all I could tell is it's tall—half a meter taller than Readen—not human, with metallic wings that never stop moving. I think it can fly. It's in the woods with those creatures. I think it's the Itza Larrak."

Tessa's hands cramped around her mug. "I have to go. I have to tell Daryl and the others."

"And I have to get back to—"

"Surely, you're not going back, Cael. Readen is horrible. If he discovers you're spying on him..."

"Who else is going to be able to tell Krager and Daryl what they need to know? First, there is someone high up in the aristocracy who sometimes come to see Readen. I don't know who it is—he hides behind an illusion, so it's someone with stronger than normal Air talent." He passed Tessa a grubby, folded paper. "Here are the dates I know he was there. And the other reason I stopped you was to tell you why I was sent here—to be an escort. One of Readen's mercenary lieutenants has abducted three children, and he's taking them to Readen."

Tessa's stomach lurched, and she wrapped her arms around herself, remembering the girl she'd found wandering the keep after Readen had finished with her.

"They need to be rescued. And I need to be certain I can get back to Readen with a plausible story about how I escaped a successful rescue attempt."

"Cael, no."

He touched the back of her hand with one gentle finger. "I'll be in touch when I can."

And he left.

She trudged up the hill as fast as she could on the icy cobbles, working to put away her fear for Cael. Kobe's smithy was on the way to the keep, and she would find Daryl or someone as soon as she was back to tell them about the children. Or rescue them herself if she had to.

The heat and the rhythmic ring of hammers on metal reached her before she neared the smithy. Outside the entrance, a rack held nets of fine wire hung like draped skirts from hooks, small weights fastened about a meter apart around their edges. Tessa spread one as wide as she could. She couldn't believe how light and supple they were.

"Oh, Kobe. They're perfect. You're doing a fantastic job. These are going to work. They're really going to work."

"Humph."

"I'm leaving soon, Kobe. The supply officer, Lieutenant Zandyr, will keep tabs on all the metalsmiths and the progress they are making. I know you don't need supervision but humor him. All right? Don't hurt his feelings and tell him to take a flying leap off the nearest Karda."

Another "humph" was all the response she got, but she didn't think she imagined the glint in his eye and the slight upward quirk of his mouth.

"Send half the nets you have to the mews so the Mi'hiru and the Karda Patrol can practice throwing them and half to Commander Kyle. His troops need practice, too."

She left to visit each of the metalsmiths she'd dragooned into making and refashioning weapons with the urbat metal, letting them know she was leaving the prime soon. Then she headed back to the keep to report their progress to Kyle and to tell him about Cael and the children. Krager was gone, and Daryl wasn't back from scouting Reader's hold.

~They return.~ Kishar's voice woke Tessa who was wrapped in her cloak and tucked under his wing.

Three immense Karda loped out of the gloom, one after the other. Daryl, Marta, and Altan were back. Finally.

Tessa bent forward and arched her back. Her fingertips brushed the ground, and she felt soft pops along her spine. A short nap on straw in a cold stall was not comfortable. She straightened and ran to catch the saddlebags Marta threw down, helped her unsaddle Sidhari, and hoist the rig to its stand inside Sidhari's stall. "Someone is bringing hot mash for your Karda," she told the three riders. "They can hunt in the morning."

"We flew back as fast as we could." Daryl rubbed fingers through his windblown hair. "They're tired and hungry. We're tired and hungry." He looked at Tessa. "I understand you need to know what we found, but it'll have to wait till morning. I don't think any of us could give you a coherent report tonight." He turned away to finish brushing Abala. "Is Galen back?"

All six heads, human and Karda, turned to hear her reply. "Yes. He's back. And he brought shields against the akenguns."

"Yes. Yes. Yes." Marta danced in a little circle. "Shields."

Altan frowned at her. Tessa could almost hear his grumbled thoughts. Altan was not going to be Galen's best friend any time soon.

Tessa put her hand on Daryl's sleeve, stopping him mid-brush stroke. "This can't wait till tomorrow, Daryl. I need to talk to you now."

He tossed the brush into a cabinet on the wall and followed her to the tack room.

"What is it, Tessa? What can't wait until tomorrow?" Daryl pulled himself up to sit on an empty saddle stand and leaned back against the wall, his eyes closed.

"Cael was in the prime yesterday."

"Who is Cael, and why should I care he was here?" He didn't open his eyes.

"Oh, dear. I was sure...And Krager is gone on patrol..." She bit her lip.

Daryl sighed. "You were sure what, Tessa? I'm tired, and I don't have time...."

Her words fell out in a rush. "He said he was here to ride escort on a wagon back to Readen. One of Readen's lieutenants abducted three children, Daryl, for Readen, and you need to be sure when you rescue them that there is a good reason Cael can escape that won't get him killed by Readen when he goes back there. Back to Readen, I mean. And I couldn't tell Krager because he went with a patrol to check out Me'Neve Hold before you got back." She finally stopped for air.

Daryl opened his eyes and stared at her. Then he leaned forward and shook his head as if he couldn't be certain what he'd heard. "Who is Cael?"

"I thought you knew. He was my father's armsmaster until Father kicked him out, and he's with Readen to spy for you. Or for Krager. I thought you knew." Tessa paced to the door and then paced back. "You have to save the children. And Cael. You have to save them."

She stopped herself. *I'm flailing around, bating like a young hawk that's fallen off his perch. I'm not acting like a hunter in yarak.* She took in a breath and let it out slowly, bringing her thoughts back to order. "Cael's worked for you, or rather for Krager, for several years, as one of Readen's men. He wouldn't have contacted me if it hadn't been for the boy and the two girls. One of them is only ten. They are children, Daryl. What Readen did to Marta is nothing compared to what he has done to others, and these are children, Daryl. Children."

Daryl's face was white, as though there was no blood left in him. He raised a hand to his head. It shook so violently he dropped it and clutched the wood of the saddle stand so hard it cracked. "When . . . when is Krager expected back?" His voice was soft and thick as if he were speaking through a heavy blanket.

"Today. Any minute."

"Thank you, Tessa. Meet us back here in two hours." And he walked back into the alleyway of the mews and into Abala's stall.

Tessa knew he would be with his Karda until they left.

"What do you mean, it's disappeared? It's a road. It can't disappear." The lieutenant's high-pitched voice stabbed through the trees to where Tessa perched on a broad limb ahead of the stopped wagon. It was a tall, closed box of a wagon, with two small vents high on the side she could see.

Six uniformed horsemen, well-armed with swords and crossbows, surrounded it. The lieutenant was shouting at the eighth member of the party, Cael, not in uniform, riding back down the road from his scouting position far out to the front of the wagon.

"Well, the impossible has just happened, Lieutenant Rees. The road disappeared. It just stops right in the middle of a thicket of blackberries. With thorns. I rode around it to see if there is a way to bypass it. There isn't. Not for as far as I could see. The trees and brush are too thick for the wagon to pass." Cael eased back in his saddle and waited.

Rees's horse dropped its head to snatch at the grass beside the road. He sawed hard on the reins, and the horse crow-hopped. Rees rowelled it hard enough in the flanks to draw blood and hauled its head around until it stopped bucking and stood, quivering.

"You're gonna ruin that horse's mouth, you keep hauling on the reins that way, sir," Cael's voice was quiet, even lazy, but Tessa could hear the anger in it.

Rees didn't. "Never mind how I treat my horse. Show me this place where the road supposedly disappears." And he started up the narrow track, Cael and four of the uniformed horsemen following.

The driver of the wagon wrapped the reins around the brake handle and hopped down. "I'll be back in a minute. I need to take care of some business." He stepped off the road far enough to be hidden from view and dropped his pants. He was right under Tessa. She clapped a hand over her mouth. It wasn't funny. It wasn't funny. She curled down over her stomach to stop the giggle from burping out, and the tip of her bow knocked against a leafy branch.

The driver jumped, tripped on his pants, and fell over on his side. Krager slid from behind the tree and slit his throat. Tessa looked away, back toward the road, and shot twice. The other two men toppled off their horses, one after the other, arrows sticking out of their chests. Nothing broke the silence but the sound of blood-spooked horses' hooves on the road. One rider's boot slipped out of the stirrup, and he dropped to the ground. The horse sidled away and moved to the verge, blowing hard. Then it lowered its head and started eating grass.

Tessa rappelled down the trunk of the tree as fast as she could, jerked the rope down, coiled it, and looped it over her shoulder. Krager ran to the back of the wagon, Tessa right behind him. She could hear sword clashes and yells coming from up the road. Krager pulled out the crowbar stuffed through his belt and popped the heavy latch out of the wood. He opened the door and jerked back.

A short, jagged board smashed down close enough to his head for him to almost lose some hair.

"Stick your head back in here. I'll take it off." The high voice was thin with panic.

Krager rolled his hand at Tessa in an it's-all-yours-now motion, sheathed his sword, and stepped around to the front of the wagon, catching the reins of the harnessed horses and watching the road ahead.

Tessa pitched her voice low and slow. "It's alright. You're alright. We've come to take you home. You can come out now."

"I'll hurt you if you get close to me," the thin voice said, and a long, skinny leg slipped out and found its footing on the step. The rest of the girl followed—her hair wild around her head, her eyes looking everywhere, caution in every tense movement. When she saw Tessa, she dropped the piece of wood and stood, shoulders heaving, tears streaming, her body jerking with hiccupped sobs she tried to swallow.

She turned back to the wagon and beckoned. A young boy and a younger girl crawled out and huddled behind her. The girl looked up at her and asked, "We're safe now, Becca? They're not going to hurt us?"

Becca swiped at her eyes and wiped her dripping nose on her sleeve. "We're safe, Angie. I know who this is. It's the Austringer. She came to my pa's forge. We're safe." Her voice quivered, full of wonder.

Tessa dropped to one knee, and the children swarmed her, getting as close as they could until she felt like she had eight legs, not just two.

It was only a short while until Altan and Marta rode in a slow walk back down the road to the wagon. Fifteen minutes later Daryl followed, deep in conversation with Cael, whose arm was in a makeshift sling torn from his shirt. Wet crimson seeped through a rough bandage wrapped around his bicep. He held a pad in one hand, dabbing at a large contusion weeping blood above his left eye.

He grinned at Tessa through a grimace. "Do I look like I'm left for dead?"

"The other four?" asked Krager.

"Taken care of," Daryl replied.

"And the lieutenant?"

"Taken care of."

"Where's Galen?" Tessa asked.

"Putting the road back." Marta looked behind her. "It's amazing to watch. I've never seen anything like it. He just made them grow. Right in front of us. They just kind of wove their way up out of the ground. A whole thicket of blackberries. I even picked some." And she held out a hand with fingers stained purple. "They were delicious. I wish I had a basket."

"Me, too. We could have pie," said Altan.

Krager scratched the top of his head. "I guess I get to be the one to drive this wagon back."

Becca spoke up. Not a hint of hesitation slowed her words. "We're not getting back inside. We're not."

Krager looked at the three children still clamped to Tessa. "Then you'll have to ride up top with me. Don't fall off."

Tessa knocked on the open door and stepped inside Commander Kyle's office. He sat, his chair tilted back on two legs, fingers laced on his chest, studying a small stack of large medals on his desk with a look of smug relief.

Galen faced him on a hard chair, face drawn, faint purple shadows under his eyes. He started to smile at her but looked away. His eyes moved to Kyle, to the piles of paper on the desk, to the door, back to anywhere but her. He stood, motioned Tessa to take his chair, and stepped back to stand with his scarred cheek a fence between them.

Tessa looked from Galen to Kyle and down to the pile of medallions on the desk. She decided to ignore Galen. Curiosity trumped her hurt. "What are these?" She looked back at the commander. "You're looking very smug and happy, Kyle."

"Shields." The smile on his face wasn't just smug and happy—it was a long, slow, relaxed and relieved smile.

"They don't look big enough to shield much of anything."

"Tell her, Galen. I want to hear it again."

"You wear them on your chest, and they protect against the aken-guns. They project a shield—I don't know how to explain it." His voice was flat. He looked at her then his eyes shifted away. His face was expressionless.

He won't even look at me. It was difficult to keep her tone level. "Strong Earth/Air talents can throw up a force field that stops pretty much anything you throw at them. You mean something like that?" She sat on the edge of the chair so aware of him it was as though she could feel him against her skin. Her hands in her lap held each other like they'd fly away if she let go. She crossed her ankles and shifted sideways.

"Yes, and doesn't that make me feel stupid? I know so little about the—I guess you could call it technology of talent. But yes. A force field specifically designed for akenguns." He spoke, his face turned to Kyle, not to her, his tone even, forced, disinterested. Disinterested? In something that could save their lives?

Tessa looked at Kyle then back at Galen. She managed to squeeze out more words without allowing her voice to quaver and squeak up and down the scale. "Does this mean we can protect our Karda from these guns? Can the Karda wear them on their breast bands?" She forced his cold behavior to the side, anger starting to harden. *I'll think about this later.*

"Yes." His voice was so brittle she felt it shatter against her. Shards of it ricocheted inside.

She left.

Chapter Thirty

It was late morning, and Abala, Sidhari, and Kibrath weren't back from hunting with Kishar. The Karda needed to range farther and farther for game every day. Tessa finished checking Kishar's rigging and went to the front of the mews. Daryl stood at the table under the tent nearby shuffling through papers and pinning spread maps with small stones. Altan paced back and forth behind him, his eyes on the sky and the approach to the landing meadow, the hood of his heavy cloak thrown back. They couldn't start their planning meeting until the Karda returned.

Marta was in the mews checking and oiling the straps on Sidhari's rigging and talking with the Karda who where there. Galen was grooming Ket's shining coat. He hadn't spoken a word to anyone else all morning—wouldn't look at anyone.

Marta looked from him to Tessa, cocked her head, coiled the strap she was oiling, and said, "Tessa, let's take a walk before we go crazy waiting for the hungry beasts to catch their breakfast."

They pulled their heavy cloaks around them, pulled the hoods up against the freezing drizzle, and walked from the mews to the trees at the side of the landing meadow littered with large bundles. They watched Mi'hiru and Karda patrollers swoop down, throw Kobe's nets in whirling circles, catch on a bundle—sometimes—carry it off, and dump it back down. Sometimes. But they were getting better.

"How they can throw those nets and not foul their Karda's wings, I can't imagine, Tessa. It takes amazing teamwork. You're used to Karda. You've been around them all your life. I don't think I will ever lose my wonder."

They walked on under the sheltering trees, silent, watching the aerobatics.

Tessa didn't think she could speak past what felt like feathers in her throat, and Marta was fine with just walking and not talking. Finally, Tessa managed to get a sentence out. "You've forgiven Galen for what he did to you, haven't you?" She looked over at Altan, still pacing behind Daryl. "I don't think Altan has."

Marta glanced at her and took seven steps before she answered. Tessa counted them.

"Galen and I pretty much grew up together shipboard. When we were eleven, he lost his mother. She was killed on a mission. The ship was leaving the planet's system, and he went looking for her. When he couldn't find her, it was my father who told him, not his father, even though he'd known it for months."

Tessa stopped dead. "What a horrible thing to do to him. To a child. What a horrible man he must be."

Marta looked back at her, and Tessa moved to catch up with her.

"His father is a master of manipulation. Nothing Galen ever did pleased him. Oh, his words might say he was pleased, but his actions said the opposite. I watched Galen grow colder and more remote until he developed such a defensive shell nothing could get in to touch him. And he didn't try to get out to touch anyone else. I tried. I thought we were close, very close for a time."

Tessa listened, not breathing, her stomach roiling. Head down, she watched her feet move through the dry grass laden with sleet pellets. She didn't dare look up to let Marta see her face, to let her see how much she envied that closeness, how much she wanted what Marta had had.

Marta stopped and turned to Tessa. "But there can't be a couple when half of it isn't there. He was becoming more insulated, more arrogant. He was so handsome before—he was beautiful, you know, but cold. So cold. I ended what had become nothing more than pretense before we left the last planet." She kicked a short branch aside and kept walking, silent long enough for Tessa to start breathing again.

"What Readen did to Galen was as bad as what he did to me. Maybe worse. He took Galen's mind away. He took Galen's control, and his control was what defined him. Readen took his insides away, and he took his looks away. He left him scarred inside and out. Then Adalta kidnapped him."

That startled Tessa. "Adalta *kidnapped* him?"

"You've known talent all your life, Tessa. You cannot know how it feels to someone who hasn't—I felt assaulted all the time. Even now, when I know about talent, I get a jolt sometimes, when I feel the power Adalta gives me. I don't know that it will ever feel—natural, like it does to Altan, to those born on this planet who've known that power all their lives." The bitter wind blew her cloak open, and she pulled it tighter around her.

"Then Kayne had him kidnapped and imprisoned him, proving to Galen that he is nothing but a tool to his father, that if he is not useful, he is nothing." They watched the practicing fliers clear the runway, and Abala, Kibrath, and Sidhari landed, one after the other, and loped down the runway. Kishar touched down so close to the table Daryl threw himself flat, arms wide, to keep the maps and papers from blowing away.

Tessa started to speak, and Marta held up her hand. "You have to understand. Adalta set you free from your father when you became Austringer, but she captured Galen like she captured me. He didn't know what was happening to him. He couldn't know. It is so outside anything he ever experienced he must have thought he was mad. And even worse, the fire that gave him such hideous scars also burned away what was left of his self-image and ripped him open to emotions he's barricaded against since he lost his mother."

They reached the end of the landing meadow, turned back, and walked in silence for a long time. Finally, Tessa asked, "Why are you telling me this?"

"Because I know you care. And I can tell Galen cares for you." She stopped walking and turned to face Tessa with a wry grin. "Plus, the Karda told me to. They think you both are being stupid. Despite being the empath I am, I was blind to how bad Galen is till I watched him around you, but the Karda see it. Galen doesn't feel worthy. He's hyper-aware of your aristocratic heritage as a holder's daughter and heir, while he belongs nowhere, has nothing to offer you. He's loaded down with disgrace and shame about what he did. He is shattered, Tessa, held together by the thin thread of his need to redeem himself. So, you have to hold on to him. Don't let him force you away."

She started walking again. "You two are the Austringer and the Kern. A pair. You have to fight together like Altan, me, and the Karda. Your excuse, your reason." Marta's voice came down hard on the word *reason*. "Your reason for confronting him is that the two of you have to join in yarak. Keen, fit, focused on nothing but the hunt, focused on killing urbat, focused on destroying the Itza Larrak. The urbat must be destroyed, and you and Galen are crucial to that battle. He can't do it shut down like he is now." She squeezed Tessa's arm and left to walk back to the table scattered with maps and papers. Hooking her arm through Altan's, she pulled him close.

Tessa looked down the length of the landing field and watched the flyers swoop in, toss their nets, jerk the rope up to trap the bundles. Marta had thrown her net and jerked Tessa out of her fear and distress about Galen. *What he feels or doesn't feel about me isn't important, but he is.* Her chest ached like Marta had pulled out a festering splinter. *I can't let this go on. Not just for him, but for me. If he doesn't care for me, I will heal if I let myself.* Finally, she pulled herself out of her thoughts, shaken, but with her head clear as blue sky—with only an occasional little white cloud.

Merenya and Galen came out of the mews and walked with her to join the others at the table under the trees. Merenya maneuvered Galen next to Tessa so she was pressed against his cast-iron-tight shoulder.

"First of all," Daryl said when they were all around the table, Karda ranged behind them. "There can be no more doubt that the Itza Larrak is back. Marta, Altan, and I, all three—excuse me, Abala, all six of us—saw it, so no one can say it's a product of your pain-induced hallucinations, Marta."

Altan sucked in a breath and blew it out. "I threw firebolts at it, and they just splashed across its shield. I've never had to throw more than three to break a shield. How many bolts its shield can endure without weakening we don't know. When the explosion happened, it left us blind for several minutes. The Larrak walked away from its crash-landing, and its shields were still holding against me. I tried." He scrubbed one hand through his hair, pulling half of it out of its leather tie. "So did Daryl."

Tessa felt the same frustration, like a pebble in her boot.

Marta looked away from the table toward the mews and said, in a low, if-I-say-this-too-loud-it-might-happen way, "It was a close call. If he'd been able to use the weapon, we'd be three large heaps on the ground by now."

Merenya slapped the table and papers flew. "But now we have shields. We have aken shields, thanks to you, Galen."

Galen gave her a half-salute.

Tessa's stomach only flipped a tiny bit.

~You need to know about the Larrak's powers,~ Kishar pathed to them all.

Tessa looked at the fading smiles on the faces around the table. What little hope Merenya raised around the shields, he just killed.

~This is what those who fought the Larrak before taught me. Its power comes from only one circle, and it controls the urbat that come from that circle. It projects shields, as you saw, and not only on itself but on others for some distance around it. And it is able to push a field of fear for several meters in front of it that will send seasoned fighters to their knees in terror. It takes a constant, prolonged barrage to weaken and destroy it with weapons like firebolts, but it can also be weakened psychically. A team of Air and Water talents can be taught to drain it. But they must work continually until it is dead or escapes their range.~

Merenya cocked her head, her hand up, palm out, in the I'm-listening-to-my-Karda gesture. "Pagra reminds me that means they will not be available for the battle and will need protection as well. That will take several strong talent wielders away from the fight."

There was a loud cheer, and a wild "Screeeee!" from the landing field celebrated someone's success with the nets.

Kishar went on as if he hadn't heard. ~It wields mental powers of illusion and emotional control. It is able to heighten the ferocity of its forces and instill fear in its opponents. With the shrinking of the circle over the last centuries, its powers will be diluted, but do not make the mistake of thinking that makes it weak. Fighting near a circle gives it extra strength.~

"Perhaps I don't have the right to ask, Kishar." Marta's words were hesitant. "But why is it that this Larrak was not killed before? Why was he imprisoned instead? The war was won, why risk its escape?"

There was a long silence, then he said, his pathed words quiet, their pace deliberate, ~You, Marta, have the best right to ask.~ He held his head up to look out at the flyers practicing in the landing area. ~I was very young. All of my kind were dead except myself and one other. It was Abalan, the brother of my father who imprisoned the Itza Larrak with the last of his life force. He killed the only other Larrak left, and he was dying. It was he who charged me with the duty to watch and to kill it if it escaped its cavern. All the other Larrak were killed, all the others of my kind perished with them. Abalan— ~ He turned his head and looked at Abala, Daryl's Karda. ~You are named for him, Abala. It is a proud name. Abalan made me swear to wait, not to try to kill it until I was old enough to be certain I would not fail. To leave it in its prison and watch. I was so young. Young, brash, cocky, over-confident of my strength.~

His head came up, and again he looked out at the landing field, at the Karda and their riders swooping in to throw their nets, pull back up to dump their catch, circle around and try again. ~I was like so many of those out there. Some of them will die in the battle to come. Some know that. Some know but ignore it. And some, the younger ones, like I was, do not even think of it in their eagerness to fight.~

His voice in Tessa's head was heavy with grief. ~I was furious at Abalan. So confident of my strength and abilities. But he swore me to accept his charge. If I had not accepted, if I had defied Abalan and tried to kill it, I know now I would have failed. The Circles of Disorder would continue to grow. The Lines of Devastation would connect in a net—an antenna of power that would allow the last Larrak to call across space to more of his kind, and they would have come.~

Tessa fought to breathe.

~They would have come to feed on the life force of this planet because that is what they do. They land on a planet, use it to build more of their kind, and leave it dead and barren. The Karda would have been no more. Your ancestors, the colonists who helped save us, would have perished.~

Kishar shifted. He looked at the rapt faces around the table, human and Karda, and said, the tone and tempo of his words firm and strong, ~But that's the past. We must anticipate what Readen plans now. He will not be content to stay locked behind the walls of his hold.~

He turned his great head to Daryl. ~What are his defenses? Is he gathering forces to defend or attack? How many urbat wait outside his hold?~ He stopped speaking and looked to the overcast sky full of Karda and riders for a long moment. Everyone at the table drew a long breath and blew it out, shaking off the heavy pall of Kishar's tale.

Until Marta said, "If it drops its shields for an instant to use an akengun in the air—if it shoots from above, the shields attached to the Karda's breast collars won't protect them." Her words spread silence around the table like a wave of soul-dampening fog as Karda and riders looked at their partners.

Finally, Tessa looked at Galen. "But we riders will also have shields. Will they be enough to protect our Karda?"

Galen didn't move. For just an instant he didn't look away from her face, as if surprised it was so close to him. The ridged scar on his cheek flipped from scar to tattoo and back. Green flicked across his eyes. He looked away from her to Marta. "They are designed for fighting in units of nine, with shields on every third soldier that extend the protection to each side to cover soldiers next to you. So, yes, they will, at least their heads and bodies. I'm not sure how much of their wings it will protect."

The silence came back.

Merenya finally spoke, looking from Daryl to Altan to Marta. "What kind of preparation were you able to see?" Her voice was thick as if it took effort to push her words through the heavy silence.

Daryl shook his head. "Not much." He pulled a map out of the pile and smoothed it in front of him, anchoring its corners with stones against the breeze that rattled sleet against the few dry leaves left on the tree above them. "We couldn't get any clear idea of how many urbat were there. They are hidden by a don't-look-here so even my men on the ground can't tell. We know much of what was going on in the hold. Some of the mercenaries he used when he tried to take the keep here are trickling in. They weren't enough last time, and they won't be enough this time. He'll need to hire more. Probably mercenary companies from Akhara, and that will take time. Winter is almost here. It will be spring before he can get them to Restal."

"Late spring," said Galen. "There will be mud early."

"He keeps the urbat hidden from his human forces," Altan said. "I don't think he can pay them enough to fight with the urbat."

"Now is our chance to destroy the urbat and the Itza Larrak, or at the least, weaken them," said Daryl. He crossed his arms and clamped his hands in his armpits. "It will be difficult to attack Readen in his hold He's been preparing against attack for years, and we would have to fight the urbat just to get to him."

His voice was quiet, and Tessa thought she could hear a note of relief that he wouldn't be fighting his brother yet. She looked from him to Galen. How alike their situations are. Galen has no one but his manipulative father, and Daryl has no one but his manipulative and evil brother. It should make them closer allies, but it hasn't.

Merenya pulled her hood tighter around her face and asked, "I think it would be best to separate them and fight one at a time. And it will have to be the urbat. And the Itza Larrak if it is still able to fight. Can you estimate how many there are?"

Galen cleared his throat. "No. Even if we could, it wouldn't help. There is still an untold number of urbat unhatched in the circle. And maybe other circles as well."

Kishar pathed, ~He does not control the ones in other circles. Not yet. Not until the circles are connected.~

Tessa stamped her feet. Standing around this table in the cold was getting more than just uncomfortable. Icicles dripped off the edges of the awning that protected them from the cold, sleety drizzle, but not the biting wind. She pulled her cloak tighter, wrapped her hands in the folds, and hunched her shoulders. *Does no one else feel the cold? I think my ears are about to fall off and shatter on the ground.*

Daryl cupped a hand on the back of his neck and rubbed. A thinking crease deepened between his eyebrows. "With the Karda, we have mobility they don't. Yes, the Itza Larrak can fly, if it was able to regenerate its wing. I think the tip of one was blown off. And the urbat can fly, of course, but only for short hops. Readen has no Karda."

Merenya looked at him. "What kind of magic does Readen have? How powerful is he?"

No one spoke. Daryl dropped his hand, and pain deepened the thinking crease.

She asked again. "I assume since he doesn't have talent, and as he was expecting three young children, that his power derives from blood and death. Maybe sex. What can he do?"

"No one thought he could do anything. Whatever abilities he has he kept hidden. If he practiced them, it was where no one could see him," said Daryl. He steepled his fingers in front of him, tapping them on his lips as if to hide the tightness in his white-rimmed mouth.

"Shields," said Altan. "Wards. Coercions—he tried to put one on Marta, and he did put one on you, Galen. He had wards on the keep, and they weren't elemental like talent is."

"But he steals talent." Marta frowned and pinched her bottom lip between finger and thumb. Then, "That's what he was trying to do to his old tutor, Malyk, in the cavern, and to me. Readen uses pain, fear, and finally death to steal talent. I wonder if he can use the talent he steals." She pulled at the small gold hoop in her ear. "I mean, if he steals from an Air talent, can he use it? Was that how he could manipulate you, Galen, with coercions like an Air talent can? If he steals from a Water talent, he could manipulate emotions. With Earth and Air, he could create wards, couldn't he?"

Galen's shoulder tensed against Tessa's. She held herself still. Sometimes it felt as though she were propping him up. Like they were propping each other up. *I don't think he's aware of it.* She had to concentrate to keep her attention on the conversation. She was teetering back and forth between listening, worrying about Galen, and a quivering yarak excitement, wanting to be on the hunt, impatient with these delays, the endless talking, even as she knew it was necessary.

"You're the one who broke his wards on the keep before we attacked, Altan. Is what Marta says possible? Were they made with stolen talent?" Daryl asked. "Father forced him to attend talent lessons under Malyk with me, so he knows the technology. Although, if he paid no more attention to those lessons than he did to our ethics lessons, maybe he doesn't know much." Those last words were low as if spoken to himself.

Altan looked away, staring without seeing at the activity on the landing meadow. "It's possible. I didn't stop to analyze them. I didn't care what they were. I just wanted to break them. They weren't anchored like talent wards are. I'll try to remember."

"But," Marta said. "Readen uses symbols. The ones carved in the pillars of the cavern. He was drawing them in the air above me." She shuddered. "He uses symbols and spells he's learned from the Larrak to direct the talent he uses pain and death to steal."

Altan drew her to him and wrapped his cloak around them both. His tone was thoughtful. "That might make him slower to react."

Daryl said, "I'll ask Malyk to put his prodigious intelligence to work on that problem. He's never recovered his physical strength after Readen's torture, but his mind is sharp as ever. I will send an envoy to all the holds, even Me'Neve. They need to be informed by more than rumors, and I need to know who will join the fight against the urbat and the Itza Larrak. And how many troops they can send. According to the information Cael had, Me'Neve will soon be on his way to Readen, and we need to know how many he takes with him. I figured out the person who has been visiting him under an illusion is Samel. Krager arrested him three days ago. But he'd already delivered the guns."

There was a long silence.

Krager said, "Winter is nearly upon us. There won't be time to fight two separate battles. We'll have to fight Readen in the spring, and by that time he'll have reinforcements."

"The only place he can hire enough mercenaries is from Akhara. They won't be able to cross Toldar," said Altan. "Father will be watching, so they'll have to come up the coast to the pass in the north. It will be blocked until late spring, with snow and ice, and then mud, and they won't be able to hide. We'll know when they get here. I'm sure Kishar can manage to find Karda to watch for them."

"A running battle in the spring in the mud won't be fun," said Krager. "And if we manage to destroy the Itza Larrak, we won't have the Karda and Mi'hiru to help us."

There was another long silence. Tessa looked at Kishar, eyes wide, then she looked away. *When the Itza Larrak is destroyed. That's when Kishar will leave me.*

Galen looked at her for the first time. Concern flicked across his face, then he looked down at the littered table, and that fraction of a flash of connection was gone leaving her to wonder if it had ever been.

Then Altan spoke. "With your permission, Daryl, I will send a message to Holder Byrhn. His hold is just across the border into Toldar, and I have father's permission to send to him for help. This threat can't be allowed to spread. It isn't just a threat to Restal. There are two other holders on the border close enough to send help, too, depending on where we decide to draw the urbat."

"Toldar has my thanks, Altan,' said Daryl.

Marta studied the maps. "We can make them come to us. The prime's walls are strong."

Tessa's head jerked around. Her voice was fierce. The words burned up through her throat. "And leave the urbat to range free out there?" She waved an arm toward the trees beyond the landing meadow, almost hitting Kishar. "I don't want to live to see another Ardencroft, and you don't either." Galen's hand brushed her back, and she took a breath.

Marta's face twisted with distress. "Oh, forgive me, lady Adalta. Tessa, you're right. I wasn't thinking."

Merenya's voice was calm, and her measured words allowed some of the heat in the frigid air to dissipate. "And we don't know yet what horrors the Itza Larrak is capable of."

"If I decided to make a defensive stand here, every holder in the quadrant would have the right to challenge me for not protecting our people. And staying here would lose us the advantage the Karda give us," said Daryl.

"Karda and Mi'hiru have never fought in the battles between quadrants. Only against raiding parties of marauders and in the colonists' battle against the Larrak hundreds of years ago." He looked at Kishar. "We will have to discuss about how best to use you. And the best terrain to take advantage of your abilities."

Daryl's voice was quiet as he shuffled maps and papers around on the table. He looked at each, in turn, human and Karda. "So, how do we do it? How do we get the urbat to face us? They have no reason to organize against our forces. They can raid at will in smaller groups, and we can't react fast enough to deter them."

"Attack their safe zone," said Galen, laying a finger on the edge of the circle to the north. "If you send a large force of the Planter Corps where the road between his hold and Restal Prime passes near the circle, the urbat will be forced to defend it. They attack every time the planters, or I, get close to the circle or a line. The Austringer and I can hunt them inside, and you can attack when they come out."

Tessa's head was down, her eyes on the maps. She felt as if she were shrinking. He said Austringer, not Tessa. *He won't even say my name.* She took in a breath and fanned a small, determined spark smoldering inside her. *I am tired of flipping back and forth between a moonstruck child of eighteen and a woman—no, a warrior—of eighteen.*

She spoke, her voice hoarse with tension. "If we send enough planters to make a real threat to the circle, we might be able to draw the urbat and the Larrak. They can move in and out of the circle, but so can I—and the Kern. Galen's arm tensed against her shoulder, but she leaned against him and wouldn't let him shift away.

Merenya said, "I think we should also make an effort to cut at least one of the Lines of Devastation. I've been thinking about what you told us you did, Galen. If we work in relays, firing it, keeping up the fire for as long as we can without wearing ourselves out before we have to engage in battle, we might succeed."

"If it draws urbat and separates the Itza Larrak from Readen, or brings him to us before he's ready, that can only work to our advantage," said Krager.

~It is vital that the planting around the circle resume. The Larrak will move to defend it. And you must resume work near where the line leaves the circle. That will slow the line's growth and ensure the Itza Larrak comes where we want it to come,~ said Kishar.

"It will take time and resources to get more planters there. Do we have that time?" asked Krager.

~There is no choice,~ said Kishar, his voice taut and determined in Tessa's head. ~That circle is this Larrak's locus of power.~

"Andra has already called in the Planter Corps Rakes working at other circles," said Galen.

Marta laughed. "Rakes? The Planter Corps is divided into Rakes? Someone had a sense of humor. Are the planters Tines? Are their leaders Handles?"

Galen's mouth twitched. Tessa felt the tension in his shoulder shift. "There aren't many saplings ready, but there are tons of phyto-remedial seeds for bushes and grasses that will raise the alarm if I boost them. They can be packed in on horses and mules. We can send planters in with the Mounted Patrol and enough supplies to set up temporary camps until supply wagons can get to them. He rubbed his face, his gaze flitting from one person to another, finally settling on Daryl. "Will Readen join the urbat? Will he be with the Itza Larrak?

"He can't afford to be seen with it. The only one who has seen him with the monster is Cael. His witness is not enough."

Tessa couldn't decide if the look on Daryl's face was agony or relief. It seemed the silence following those words would never end.

Then Galen said,

"But the planters will need a lot of protection."

"Prime Guardian Me'Rahl is coming, with troops. Me'Fiere Hold is between here and that circle. He'll have no hesitation about sending troops with the Planter Corps. Nor will any other holder. They might not all join me to fight Readen, but they'll not hesitate to fight in this battle. Not after Ardencroft."

Chapter Thirty-One

Galen wriggled out of his bedroll and looked out the tent opening across the meadow toward the line of dead trees, stark and white against the gray sky, that extended into the distance. Four Karda dug for tubers near the edge of the living trees behind them, and Tessa hunched over a small cooking fire. Kishar was flying over the circle, keeping watch.

The squad of patrollers there to protect them if they were attacked were already gathered around their fires.

Merenya lay back flat on the dead, brown grass, and Altan sat, head down between his knees, breathing hard. They were exhausted. Galen was so tired his bones ached, but he poked Marta's sleeping bag in the general direction of her back. "Our turn, Marta. Let's go."

He hurried to sit beside Merenya. She looked up and nodded—her teeth clamped on her bleeding lip. He closed his eyes and extended a tendril of talent, hooked into hers and followed it to the swarm of nanobots attacking the roots of the trees and grass and bushes.

Her power pulled away, and he twisted Earth and Air together into fire, heating the ground into lava, continuing the flow where she stopped. He felt the wild heat of Marta's talent join his, and the spear of heat intensified, threatening to trap him, suck him into its furnace.

The steady presence of Merenya calmed him on one side, Altan monitored on Marta's side, and Galen relaxed into the work. He relished the way the Earth and Air forces twisted into a blue spear of intense heat, relished the feeling of control.

He was learning. They had been burning away at the line of bots for a day and a half, never stopping, never letting up, switching around from monitoring to burning, from burning to monitoring, sleeping and eating when they could.

Time stopped. There was only bright blue flame, searing, scouring the swarming ant-like bots. For endless hours and minutes, there was only the burning blue fire and the relentless river of nanobots.

But...But the swarm thinned. Marta's energy surged, and Galen sharpened his attention. The river of bots slowed. An infinity passed. Then there were no more. He waited. There were no more bots.

A long time later, someone tapped him on the shoulder. Then tapped again, harder. He struggled to pull back his fire. Watched. Waited. But there were no more.

Galen fell backward on the ground, arms and legs spread, soaking up the power he needed to refill his reservoirs. He opened his eyes, blinked, and rolled to his side. The sun shone low through the bare branches to the west, throwing striped shadows across the dead area of the line. He had been working since it was straight up above.

He levered himself up to sitting, and Altan reached over his shoulder with bread wrapped around cold venison and cheese. He had never smelled anything quite so good.

"I think if Galen will watch through the night and tomorrow, and if there are no more of these bot things by the next morning, we can leave." Merenya's voice was scratchy and tired.

"There's no guarantee—in fact, there's a high probability they'll come back," Galen said. "But maybe it will be some time before whatever it is that produces them can make more. We'll fly to the circle. Kishar can let me down into it, and I'll know more. We need to practice what you showed me, Altan. Climbing down a rope and back up while he hovers. He's good at hovering."

~Thank you, Galen.~

Galen wondered how he could know Kishar was smiling tele-pathically.

~Humph~ It wasn't hard to tell when Ket was grumpy. Just hard to know what he was grumpy about.

The next morning, blanket wrapped around him, Galen sat near the edge of the still dormant Line of Devastation under a big cottonwood, a hot mug of tea cupped in his hands. He watched two wings of Karda Patrol pass over, many with two riders, carrying planters to the camps on the edge of the circle near the line. Two riderless Karda loaded with fat packs swooped low, waggled their wings, and flew on.

It was cold. Frost on the branches and the leaves that hadn't fallen caught the light of early morning and threw glitters back at the sun clearing the horizon to the east. He hoped what they'd done caught the attention of the Itza Larrak and drew out the urbat. A troop of Connor Me'Cowyn's men, about fifty, passed them during the night to join the guards from Me'Fiere Hold already there to protect the planters. The urbat would attack soon. According to the Mi'hiru carrying messages back and forth they were on the move with Daryl's forces harrying them relentlessly. There was no sign of Readen.

Once Galen had the planters settled and at work, he and Tessa would start. Find the urbat. Kill them. Burn their nests. His eyes went to Tessa, squatted on her heels at the fire.

"You look at her like you are a starving man, and she is a sizzling cut of venison and a bottle of wine," said Marta. She joined Galen under the big cottonwood. Gold leaves fell around them in flurries.

Merenya and Altan sat several meters away, cross-legged under a dead tree near the Line of Devastation, eyes closed, hands flat on the ground, bodies still as if frozen in place, as if they were part of the rock and soil. Merenya's head tilted back as though a string pulled on her chin from the clouds. They were monitoring the line for movement. If they sensed anything they'd call Galen. It was still dead, but they would observe for at least another day to be sure it stayed that way. At least long enough to call the Itza Larrak.

Tessa sat in front of the tent, the one they all shared, tending a pot over a bed of coals and chopping potatoes as close to the fire as she could get. Galen glanced at her, and her shoulders came up as if his glance poked her in the back. Her head turned toward the Karda digging for the tubers they loved at the edge of the clearing.

"Mind your own business, Marta." Galen's fingers traced along deep fissures of the bark on the massive tree trunk. He concentrated on the gentle brush of his fingertips against the rough bark, trying to close his ears against the words he knew were coming.

"Why, Galen? Why can't you allow yourself to be with her? She is lovely. She cares deeply for you. And she needs you. She can't go back to her father. And if I read things right, Kishar will leave her when this is all over. So. Why?"

He flinched as though she'd poked him with the pointy end of an arrow and didn't speak. He couldn't look at her. His eyes went to Tessa again, then to Kishar. Marta was right. Kishar was going to leave. How could Tessa survive that? Finally, his voice tight in his throat, he said, "Two completely different cultures, Marta. You know how often ship-planet relationships fail."

"Well, since I am in one that is working very well, no, I don't know." She pulled the gold chain from under her tunic and looked down at the pendant she wore always. Two gold Karda wings bracketed a glittering opal. Galen watched a rainbow of fire flash across her face. She clasped her hand around it and tucked it away again. Altan wore one just like it.

"You didn't..." He looked away from her into the line of skeletal white trees, some standing dead and some down in a tangle of bare branches and uprooted trunks.

"I didn't what, Galen? Betray my training, my ship, my friends? Well, yeah, I did. And yet here I am. In a happy, well-adjusted, devoted, loving—"

"Yeah, yeah. Altan doesn't look that well-adjusted. If he weren't concentrating so hard on monitoring the line, he'd be burning hot holes in my body with his laser eyes."

She laughed and pulled up her knees, locking her arms around them, watching Altan.

"You've got drool dripping off your chin, Marta."

She turned her head toward him, resting it on her knees, and looked at him sideways. "So, why, Galen?"

He scrubbed at his face and looked away again. "I betrayed the ship, and I betrayed myself when I agreed to go along with Father's insane plan to smuggle weapons to Readen and rape this planet. Then I betrayed my father and Readen when I not only failed to deliver the weapons but turned around and joined the enemy. I went even further, stole the shields, delivered them to Daryl, and enlisted Cedar to uncover Father's machinations and expose him to the other consortium directors."

He rubbed at the scar on his cheek. It morphed into the tri-foil leaf tattoo. More and more often, every time he got near an emotion his scars morphed back and forth between ugly ridges and beautiful tattoos—and itched like crazy. His eyes were probably glowing green, too.

"I have nothing. I have no home, no family, no resources other than these strange talents that are so strong I can't always control them, and I'm set to burn myself to ash at any moment. What kind of future is there in all that to offer Tessa?"

Marta stood and brushed off the seat of her split riding skirt. "Ipsnoral shit, Galen. I think you need to get over yourself. And, incidentally, in case you want to listen,"—she leaned over, so her face was just inches from his—"your attitude is getting in the way of your job. Which is to work with Tessa to destroy the urbat, and you know, be all heroic and manly and save this planet."

She walked away. "Now get up. Join the fun. It's our turn to monitor."

In the late afternoon half a tenday later, Tessa and Kishar circled high and wide above the distorted wasteland inside the circle. It was cold. And wet. The sheepskin vest and thick, wool divided skirt she wore under her rain gear were adequate but not warm. She pulled her knitted wool cap tighter over her ears and pushed her hands between her thighs and the saddle.

Distance goggles covered her eyes, and she kept her attention focused on the ravaged land below, searching for telltale dust plumes that heralded a moving pack of urbat or boulder-like lumps on the surface that signified a nest of leathery eggs.

All three planters' camps were in sight at some point on their patrol, spaced to come to each other's aid in a hurry. Tessa hoped she didn't have to report urbat coming at all three at once. She could hope she wouldn't have to report urbat coming at all, but it wouldn't do much good. If hopes were horses, there would never be a shortage of fertilizer, and the world would reek like a dirty stable.

The latest message from Daryl, brought by one of the many new Karda who came at Kishar's call, estimated the number of urbat moving their way from Readen's hold as high as two hundred. She, Kishar, and Galen, with Ket listening intently, sat long into the night trying to come up with an idea of how many they had killed, and how many more they had seen in the circle. It was discouraging. They estimated they'd destroyed only a hundred and forty since the attacks began, but there had been dozens in the attack on Ardencroft, Cerla reported hundreds had attacked Almryk's camp, and they had sensed many hundreds in their explorations inside the circle. That was not encouraging.

She shifted in the saddle, sifting through the nauseating scents of oily evil that reached her from below, searching for clusters where the sickness intensified, marking them in her mental map of the circle's landscape. They were there, but fewer and farther apart than what she and Galen had sensed before, and they were quiet, no more urbat were rising yet.

She spotted too many places littered with freshly broken shells that had held urbat asleep for centuries. Every place she found those was also littered with a few misshapen, half-hatched dead urbat. Sometimes more of those than empty shells, as if the force that kept them alive had degenerated over the long years.

The area she and Kishar patrolled was the western quarter of the circle. They were on the top arc of their patrol when she sensed something pulling her attention far to the north. ~Can you feel that Kishar? ~ Kishar's wings twitched, and she grabbed the pommel handle to keep her balance. ~Is something wrong?~

~No. Our endless circle over this evil, empty space is hypnotizing. Your question startled me out of my thoughts.~

They flew in silence for several minutes. Finally, he said, ~Yes. I do sense something. We've seen nothing moving since we started early this morning. Let's explore.~ He flipped vertically into a wingover that left Tessa's insides at least a kilometer behind, and they headed north, staying a few hundred meters inside the edge of the circle.

They flew for an hour, and Tessa was about to suggest they give up when he announced, ~There. Ahead about a kilometer and a half and ten degrees to the east. Something is there.~ He tweaked his wings and tail, and their course changed.

She watched a thick column of haze rising into the air come closer. ~Uh, Kishar? I don't think we want to fly into that. That doesn't feel safe. It stinks of burnt hair. Oily, burnt hair and other nasty things.~

His wings cupped the air in mighty downbeats. They flew higher, then he wheeled in a tight circle around the haze, pressing Tessa back against the high cantle of her rigging.

Below them was a narrow, deep, black fissure that stretched along the flat ground for fifty meters. Far down into its depths, a small glow of ugly, cold orange fire throbbed, bright, dim, bright, dim, like an alien heartbeat. The edges of the hole blinked with the slow fluttering of a sleepy eye. Tessa sensed nothing living anywhere near.

~All right. I've seen all I want to see, Kishar. Have you?~ Tessa wanted to be far away from the corruption that surged and ebbed in the crevasse. Soon. Like—now. ~I was already cold. This is turning me to ice. Whatever this is, it reeks of evil. My hands are shaking.~ Her voice was shaking.

~Yes, I think it best if we were far away from this. I need to think about what we see here.~

They flew a direct line back to the camp, covering territory they hadn't covered before, west of a center line bisecting the circle. The terrain was much the same. She spotted four large pockets of intact eggs with as many as forty eggs apiece. They were scattered widely, and there were three large clutches of empty, broken shells and half-hatched, misborn urbat. She made mental notes of it all, adding them to her tally.

It was a relief to finally spot troopers guarding the planters who worked in tight groups at the edge of the circle. They landed near the tent where they stored the Karda's rigging.

Mi'hiru Philipa knelt at the fire at the edge of the dripping awning, stirring a large kettle of hot mash for the Karda. She helped Tessa pull Kishar's rigging off, and Kishar loped to the edge of the landing field to take shelter under the drooping branches of a large spruce tree with Cystra, Philipa's small, delicate Karda, and Amanda's Bettan.

"Go stand by the fire for a bit, Tessa. Your nose is blue. You need to warm up. I'll wipe this down and get it stowed for you. Amanda will carry a bucket of hot mash to Kishar."

Tessa was grateful. She was cold inside and out. She shivered, staying as close as she could get to the fire and still be under the awning. Rain came down harder, mixed with sleet that rattled against the canvas, but a widening band of bright blue pushed up against the garish pink and silver-gray clouds to the west.

She looked around at the camp. One-person and two-person tents marched along opposite the mews and bracketed the landing meadow. The big cooks' tent took up much of the center space. Beyond that were the tent storing the bags of seeds and the rope corral for the horses. The camp was nearly empty.

Her toes, nose, and fingers were beginning to thaw when she heard the chatter of voices, and Ket appeared, his gold coat gleaming in the wet, and behind him Galen and the planters, the sacks slung across their shoulders flat and empty. The sun had dropped low, and the cooks' tent glowed gold with lantern light in the darkening evening. She stepped back from the fire into the gloom of the mews tent and watched.

Galen moved from planter to planter, hand on a shoulder here, fist-punch to an arm there. He clasped forearms with several who gathered around when he sat. He and Tessa would start their campaign against the urbat the next morning, and he was giving last minute instructions to the planters. She watched till the others drifted to the line in front of the cooks' fire. Galen looked up and found her in her hiding place. Even from this distance, she watched an emotion she couldn't decode flash across his face. He looked away.

How could they fight urbat like this? If something didn't change, they'd get themselves killed before the first day they had to fly together inside the circle was gone, and probably Kishar, too.

He headed for the spruce tree where Ket joined the other Karda in its shelter. Tessa went to intercept him. Determination lifted her chin. Trepidation lifted both hands to smooth her spiky hair, unsuccessfully. Her feet were cold. Her hands were cold. Sweat beaded on her forehead and trickled between her breasts.

She stopped in front of him, feet apart, blocking his path, ignoring the sleet.

"I don't care where you came from. I don't care what you have done. I don't care that you have some dumb idea that you aren't good enough for me."

Her words ran together, rattling like the sleet on dry leaves. "I love you. I love you, and I want you to tell me that you don't love me. If you can tell me that, I'll... Well, I'll accept it and work with you until we have done what we have to do, and then I'll go."

She glared at him, grabbed his face, pulled his head down, and kissed him, a long, hard, searching kiss. When it ended, her lips soft against his, she repeated, "I love you. Tell me you don't love me." Her head tilted back, her eyes not leaving his.

His breath came so hard she could hear the air rasping out of him. He shuddered and leaned his head into hers, resting against her forehead. His hands clamped onto her shoulders so hard it hurt. She tried to swallow, but her mouth was dry, and a ball of feathers stuck in her throat and wouldn't go down. *He's going to tell me he doesn't...he doesn't...* She couldn't finish the thought. If she finished the thought, she'd ... She didn't know what she'd do.

"Oh, Tessa." His words were whisper-soft.

Her arms dropped to her sides. She couldn't feel her hands. *He doesn't love me. He's going to tell me he doesn't love me.* Her knees were giving way.

His hands tightened, and he held her up.

~I can't tell you I don't love you. I want you more than I have ever wanted anything before. I can't be without you.~ His mental words curled through her body like tender shoots and took root in her starving soul. ~I can't be without you. I love you, Tessa.~

They stood for a long time, resting against each other. Then Galen wrapped his arms around her, pulling her against him. "I promise to hold you forever. I promise to protect you forever. I promise to let you protect me. I love you. I love everything about you," he said, his breath soft against her ear.

"I love your spirit. I love your courage. I love the way you hold your bow as if it's your best friend. I love the way you treat your arrows as if they were your children. I even love your awful hair."

The coil of feathers clogging her throat went poof! and was gone.

Chapter Thirty-Two

Readen paced near the gates of his hold's crowded courtyard, his leg muscles so stiff and taut his boots beat staccato on the stones. Paired off troopers filled the center space practicing with swords, knives, and hand-to-hand fighting. The walls rang with the clang of metal against metal and shouting men and women. Every few days, more mercenaries trickled in, one, two, four at a time, as the word of his escape spread. Not enough.

"Where are Cael and Lieutenant Rees?" Readen realized he'd spoken aloud—he was talking to himself. A little worm of worry wiggled in the back of his mind. He smothered it with a deep breath. Self-doubt, self-questions were not something Readen allowed—not since he was a child. Anger and arrogance had long since smothered them. He raked back the hair that fell loose in his face, smoothed and re-tied it at the base of his neck.

One of the big iron gates swung open, and a man rode through. Cael. Lieutenant Rees wasn't with him. Cael's arm was in a sling, and dried blood flaked the left side of his face. The long-anticipated wagon did not roll in behind him.

Fury turned Readen's sight red.

Cael slid out of his saddle and hung on the stirrup leathers, leaning against the horse's shoulder. His face twisted with pain and weariness. His eyes narrowed with caution when he saw Readen. "We were attacked. They took the prisoners we were bringing to you, killed the other guards, and left me for dead."

Readen didn't speak.

Cael shifted his feet.

Finally, Readen said, "Where is the wagon, and why are you not dead?"

"They blocked the road a half day from the prime." Cael shifted his feet again. "They shot from behind the trees and killed the driver and two guards. Then five of them attacked, more than we could handle. They overpowered me, knocked me out, and I fell on top of Lieutenant Rees's body. I think they thought we were both dead."

He staggered ad grabbed hold of the stirrup strap. "When I came to, I heard them talking. I don't think they cared if we lived or died. They were just after the prisoners. Who was in the wagon, Readen, sir? I hope their loss…" His words dribbled to a stop, and he swayed. His eyes flickered with fatigue.

Readen called two troopers. "Take him to someone who can heal him." He turned to Cael. "I'll talk to you later." He watched as the two men escorted him away. The delicious thought that he might use Cael to restore his power skittered away as soon as it appeared. He blinked. His head twitched.

"Your messenger is back."

Readen closed his eyes and forced himself not to jump. He turned. The Itza Larrak's mechanical voice sounded eerie coming from a tall, dark-haired soldier, the illusion Readen had finally persuaded it to wear. It had taken hours to convince it that the mercenaries would not fight alongside it and its urbat. They would leave, all of them. There would never be enough money to pay them if they knew Readen's allies were the monsters of their legends.

His mercenaries were hard, experienced fighters, disciplined, tough, and proficient at arms, but Readen's hold would empty if the Itza Larrak dropped the illusion. The urbat must remain hidden, and the Itza Larrak must appear to be a simple soldier.

It came every evening wearing the illusion. When it crossed the cobblestones toward him, Readen saw, not for the first time, a slight hitch interrupt its smooth gait. It spoke, its unnatural, metallic voice rang too loud. It was as impossible as ever to discern the Itza Larrak's thoughts. "Now, tell me when you will send your messenger to bring more troops. You do not have enough."

It had said those same words every night when it appeared. Illusion and a don't-look-here spell assured both it and the urbat avoided discovery by hunters and villagers, and the patrols from Daryl Readen knew were out there. Readen knew those spells, but the Itza Larrak's were far more powerful.

"I've sent messengers to Akhara with the authority and the funds to hire two companies of mercs."

The tall man with the empty face and yellow eyes looked at Readen. "Follow me."

It was all Readen could do to walk beside it. If he showed the least fear, any advantage he held would start the long slide of erosion, and he would be lost. He lengthened his stride. The Itza Larrak stopped on the road outside the gates, well into the forest and dropped his illusion.

"This cold weather does not affect my urbat yet, but it will when it turns colder. We must start planning where we send them. The country between this hold and my circle must be under my control. Your force will accompany us."

Readen's gut clenched, and he hid his clenched hands behind his back. "As I have said before, my men will not fight with the urbat. They cannot even know I am allied with them. They will leave and probably join the fight against you."

"Then we should kill them now."

Readen tilted his head and looked up at the sky. "No," he said, struggling to keep his voice slow and controlled while he swallowed screams of frustration. "No. We need them. I must stay here. Mercenaries are still arriving, a few at a time, and my hold is well fortified. When spring comes, and the companies of fighters arrive from Akhara Quadrant, they will be ready and eager to fight. But our forces must remain separate."

He clenched his hands tight behind his back and faced the Itza

Larrak. "That's when our true fight begins. But now we turn the urbat loose."

The Itza Larrak stopped and stood, a silent statue of rough, light-absorbing obsidian, in the center of the road, staring to the southeast. The tall trees of the ancient forest rested in the stillness of noon. The listless brown leaves left on their black branches shifted in the warm air that smelled of earth and humus. The rain and sleet of the last few tendays had ended in a temporary lull.

Readen shifted his feet. The Itza Larrak stopped with no explanation. He waited. It stood, immobile, a surreal carving of black. If Readen were to imagine a human expression on that too-insect-like face, it would be worry. Not a sentiment he ever felt from the Itza Larrak.

The Larrak started walking. Readen watched it misstep once. If he weren't hyper-aware of the Itza Larrak's every move, he would have missed it. It wasn't a tired stumble. It was more like a clock that skips a tick then starts again as if it will go on forever the day before it winds down.

"We march to the east."

The harsh, mechanical voice startled Readen out of his thoughts. He tucked his chin, took a slow breath, turned and looked up into its face. "Why do you wish to change our plans now? The only thing to the east of us is a circle. Going there offers us nothing. I want Restal Prime. That is what we agreed upon. We agreed to use the urbat against villages all over Restal, weakening Daryl's hold and scattering his forces to assure our success in the spring."

"One of my lines has been cut. They are attacking my circle—" The Itza Larrak's voice skipped a beat. "They must be stopped."

Readen looked at it, forcing his face not to change. The Larrak was unaware of its hesitation. This immense—and he had thought inde-structible—presence in Readen's life faltered.

A mad mix of relief, uncertainty, and anger wound through him. His thoughts flashed from the mother he'd only heard stories of, to the frustration of having no talent, to jealousy of his brother, to a child-hood of bullying and intimidation. He needed the Itza Larrak long enough to secure his control in Restal. But he didn't need the Larrak to control him. If it failed, what would happen to the urbat? What would happen to him?

He watched it stride away, its gait as fast as a trotting horse. Silent ranks of urbat moved out of the forest, falling into ordered phalanxes behind it.

It didn't falter. Perhaps it just took time for it to adjust to its material body. Or perhaps it was failing, and Readen would be free of its control. But he would also lose his most valuable, his crucial ally.

He looked down at his hands, at his fingernails. They were thicker, longer, and dark. Almost black. He thrust his hands behind his back again where he could continue to refuse to see them,

I must learn everything the Itza Larrak still has to teach me, all its spells, everything it can teach me about the power in the circles. I must learn to control the urbat. Then I must learn how to kill it.

Chapter Thirty-Three

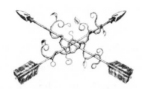

Kishar took off almost straight up and circled Camp One. Galen wrapped his arms around Tessa and looked down to see Ket gallop to the landing field and take off after them.

~Kishar. What's Ket doing? He can't follow us. I told him over and over. If he gets too close to the circle, he'll sicken and die.~

Kishar was silent, probably talking to Ket telepathically in the Karda frequency humans couldn't hear.

Finally, he spoke to Galen. ~He'll be fine. He is not stupid. Young and foolish, but not stupid.~

"He headed back." Galen rested his head in the curve between Tessa's neck and shoulder, the suede of her sheepskin vest rough against his cheek.

~Adalta has ruined me. I've gone from caring for no one to caring for…so many. Too many.~

Tessa laughed. The joy in her voice rang bells in his chest.

He wanted to celebrate.

They circled up a rising thermal, and leveled off into a long glide, powering on in a flap-and-glide pattern until they were far inside the desolation of the circle. Eventually, Tessa pointed.

~There, see it? Just there and a little to the east. That's the closest one I found. It's also the smallest.~

~Probably good to start with the smallest.~ Galen suspected his attempt at casual was a flop. He reached across Tessa's leg and shook loose the coil of rope tied to the pommel of the saddle. Loops were knotted every seventy-five centimeters along the twelve-meter length trailing below them. Tessa flipped it to fall from under her quiver and left leg.

Below them on the barren, rocky ground lay a scattering of large, leathery, egg-shaped carapaces. Some of them were translucent enough Galen could see the urbat, fully grown, fully formed and curled, fetal-like inside, encased in cauls the color of anemic and rotten egg yolk. He wiped his palms on his leg. Sweaty hands wouldn't help.

Yes, he knew he was safe from the poisonous influence of a circle. Yes, he, Tessa, and Kishar had practiced this over and over. But still. Urbat were big, vicious, and fast. And they could fly. Not very high. But still.

Kishar leveled off and hovered at the edge of the nest. Tessa freed one stirrup, and Galen slipped a foot into it, grabbed the rope, swung around her, kicked free, and dropped, feet dangling, his face pressed against her knee, his heart dangling by a thread from a cloud. Tessa touched his face, and Galen started down.

The rope jerked and swung, gyrating wildly with every powerful down stroke of the hovering Karda. The world whirled round and round. His hands slipped too fast, the rope rasped his palms. He locked his legs around the line, took a firmer grip, let himself down hand over hand, and jumped the last three meters.

He landed on his hands and knees too close to the thorny, black branches of a low bush. Oily dust roiled around him, and he pushed his face into the crook of his elbow until it settled. *I need to find something to tie around my head next time. I don't want to suck this dust into my lungs.*

He glanced up at Tessa and Kishar above him—Kishar's wings almost vertical in a tight circle. Arrow after arrow slammed into the eggs, and Galen ran toward the nest, dodging fountains of yellow-orange ichor that spurted out of every hit, dodging the bodies thrashing in their death throes, dodging scattering shards of shells.

She never missed. He pulled the quiver from his back and jerked arrow after arrow out of the bodies, throwing them, their heads clotted with gelatinous yellow mucus, into the empty quiver.

Kishar circled wider and higher, and Galen surveyed the dead and dying half-hatched monsters. No plant life he could call would survive in the circle, but he could burn and bury them. He called Earth and Air from the pool of talent inside him and shaped them into arrows of cleansing, searing blue flame. One after another after another the hulks shriveled into stinking black ash.

Then he knelt, shoved, and rolled a wave of polluted black dirt to cover the nest. Galen coughed, tried not to breathe, pulled up the front of his jacket to cover his face, and ran as fast and far from the nest as he could to wait for Kishar to come around, trailing the rope. He looked down at his red, scored hands and shuddered. *This is going to be painful. I need gloves.*

He slung the quiver of recovered arrows across his back, looked up, and waved his hand. Kishar did a wingover one-eighty and dropped down into a low hover over his head. Galen grabbed the wild, snapping snake of the rope and started climbing, pulling up hand over hand, not looking down. Kishar's wings thundered above him as they thrust higher and higher. When Galen's hand finally grabbed the pommel handle, he just hung there, breathing hard, his face pressed into the crook of Tessa's knee.

She pulled her foot out of the stirrup, and he managed to find it with his left boot and swing himself up into the saddle rig behind her. He tried not to collapse against her back. They were both laughing so hard with relief Galen fumbled the straps to buckle himself in and nearly tilted the arrows out of the quiver on his back. Tessa turned and kissed him, hard.

And Kishar flew to the next nest.

Two more times and two more nests destroyed, it didn't get any easier or any smoother. Climbing back into the saddle after the third one, Galen sagged against Tessa's back, his legs trembling with the effort to balance himself riding pillion behind the saddle. ~That's enough, Kishar. I can't do any more today.~

He sucked breath into his lungs fast and hard. His legs burned, his hands were raw, his mouth tasted of nasty, greasy dust. His head swam with fuzzy pain that crawled up the back of his neck and pounded his exhausted brain with a hammer.

Kishar landed at the camp mews, and Galen's stiff body woke up. Tessa unbuckled him, and he slid out of the saddle and landed prone on the ground between Kishar's taloned feet, arms and legs spread, nose pressed into the grass, and stayed there. Until the smell of roasting meat and hunger started chewing up through his stupor.

He wobbled his way to standing. His talent reservoirs weren't close to being replenished. Cold as it was, he was going to have to lie bare-ass on the ground but in a tent and with double or triple blankets on top of him. Naked. In a tent. With Tessa. And, hey, now he was warm again. Then a blast of icy sleet pelted him. He ran for the cooks' tent.

Tessa heaved the saddle rigging to Kishar's back, and he stood. She arched her back and stretched side to side. Even her toes ached. After a tenday of searching out urbat clutches, she looked back at their first day with fond memory. It hadn't been that easy since. At least she could feel the sun begin to warm her back. It wasn't raining, and it wasn't sleeting. The too brief Ending Summer few days of warmer weather finally showed up with its respite from the persistent icy-drizzle, wet-snow weather of the past tendays of Fall.

"You should let me do that, Tessa. Galen reached around her and threaded the cinch strap through its ring and pulled it tight. "This rigging is too heavy for you.

She laughed. Oh, blessed Adalta. It even hurt to laugh. "I've been doing it by myself since Kishar found me. Do you think it all of a sudden got heavier? Or I got weaker?"

The bushy-haired wagoneer, Bren, walked around from behind Kishar. "Don' know how it happens but seems t'me love makes a woman weak and a man strong. You can tell by the puffed chests of the proud-male-pigeon-parade walk." He slipped Galen a little drawstring pouch that clinked and a rough, fist-sized block of black wood. "A busy Mi'hiru messenger whispered somethin' to me 'bout you needin' this.

Galen turned sideways from Tessa, stuffed them in his jacket pocket, and pushed aside her head-twisting curiosity with his elbow. "It's good to see you, Bren. And even better to see the supplies you brought. The food's so monotonous it even bores the cooks. And extra blankets will be much celebrated. He grasped the small man's forearm. "What news of Readen and the Itza Larrak?'

The grin permanently applied to Bren's face flipped upside down. "Captain Ethyn wants t'meet in the cooks' tent when you're done gettin' Kishar ready so that I can tell all three of you, he replied. "You c'n have somethin' hot to drink afore you take to th' air again.

They finished fastening the rigging's myriad straps and buckles. Kishar raised his head and looked over his shoulder. ~Your father comes.~

Tessa felt her heart drop so far she was afraid to move, afraid she'd step on it. Galen grabbed her hand, and she looked up at him. "Should we tell him?"

"We have to tell him sometime. Is it better now or later?"

~He will look at you together, and he will know.~

Tessa heard a definite note of amusement in Kishar's voice. "I'm glad we found something to amuse you, Kishar. I have been worried that you were finding nothing to be happy about lately."

Galen's laugh was a worry-sharp bark. "Do you know why he's here, Kishar?"

~He is bringing fifty of his men to guard this camp.~

Tessa's heart rolled a little further along the ground. "Is he staying?"

Kishar hesitated and cocked his head, apparently listening to Me'Cowyn's Karda, Arib. ~No. He'll return to join Daryl with the rest of his troops.~

Tessa held Galen's hand between them with both of hers, pressed close, and looked up into his face. "Yes. We tell him." And they turned to watch Connor Me'Cowyn land.

"No." That was the first word out of his mouth when he landed. Galen stepped up to help unsaddle the Karda.

"That's all you have to say, Father?" To her surprise, Tessa's voice was steady—it-doesn't-matter-what-you-say-or-what-you-do steady.

"This man..." There wasn't a hint of subtlety in the look of disgust on his face as he grabbed the saddle from Galen and carried it to the tack lean-to.

He turned back to face Tessa, Galen now standing next to her. "This man is a nothing. Daryl has told me about him. He is unethical. He has no family. We know nothing about him or about the kind of people he comes from. You have no guarantee his talent will breed true."

"Breed, Father? Breed? Is that all I am to you? A broodmare you can buy a stud for?" *How many times will I have to argue this?*

Connor looked away and let out an exasperated breath. "Of course not, Tessa. You are my daughter, and I love you. But to hold our family's place, to remain Me'Cowyn, you must have talented children. It isn't just important to me, it's important for you and your children, to our hold. There is a growing resistance to the rule by strong talent, and I don't want to see us dragged down. I don't want us to lose Me'Cowyn Hold. It would be a victory to the resistance, and it could precipitate a struggle that would take years to end. It might not end well for us. For you, Tessa. For your family."

"It doesn't matter, Father. All that doesn't matter. We are bonded."

"I see no bonding opal around your neck."

Tessa put her hands on her hips, leaned forward, and said, her jaw so tight the words struggled to come out, "We have been busy, Father. We are the only ones who can go inside the circles. We are the only ones who can fight the monsters on their own ground."

Connor's face went white. "I thought that was a rumor. I thought it was a false rumor. He held his hand out as if to reach for her.

She wondered how hard it was for him to ignore all the facts he didn't want to hear.

"Tessa, your talents aren't gone. They are only blocked. What if going inside the circles damages you somehow. Damages..."

"Damages my worth as a broodmare, Father?" She moved closer to Galen who stood, firm and silent next to her, not flinching at Connor's words. He was letting her stand for herself. But she could feel his anger build.

Galen looked down at her. She nodded and he hooked his arm with hers. "We are finished with this conversation." He inclined his head slightly at Connor. "Sir." The muscles in Galen's jaw bunched, and his arm was so taut it trembled with anger as fierce as hers. They walked away to their meeting with Captain Ethyn in the cook's tent. Connor followed half a step behind. His angry heat burned at Tessa's back.

Captain Ethyn, arranging maps on the table, was not much taller than Tessa, his shoulders and chest broad. Short, thick, blond hair progressed down the sides of his face to a short, thick, blond beard. Tall, dark-haired Lieutenant Jayme, his sleeves too short for still-growing arms, set down four mugs of hot cider clustered in his over-large hands, managed not to spill anything, and took his seat at the end of the table. Connor, his face a mask of hot ice, sat next to him.

Kishar spoke first. ~The news we have gotten through the Karda relays is not good, Bren. I hope you have a better story for us.~

"Does anyone ever get used to hearing a Karda in their head?" asked Bren.

Bren sounded so much like Captain Almryk.

Tessa looked at Galen.

His eyes dropped, and he swallowed as though there was a knot twisted in his throat. He picked up the mug of hot cider, and its steamy fog obscured his face. "It's a new miracle every day, Bren."

Tessa laid her hand on his leg, and he smiled at her, a quick, side-ways I'm-fine smile. The wonder of it—that she could know what he felt, and that he could know she did, was still so new she shivered and turned her head to look at the map the captain spread on the table. She pinned the corner closest to her with her mug.

Ethyn laughed, but his eyes were somber. "I hope you have news of a miracle for us, Bren."

"No. Not good news. The urbat attacked three more villages. The Itza Larrak is with them inside some sorta shield bubble. They move closer to you every day. The last attack was three days ago. Daryl managed to get there with a wing of Karda Patrol and several Mi'hiru before the village was lost, but them urbat did a lot of damage. And

SHERRILL NILSON

the Itza Larrak came close to destroying the town. It pushed a veil of terror before it that left grown men crawling on the ground until Daryl landed three riders with Air talent. They made a circle and did something to stop it. But it was close. And awful."

Connor cleared his throat. "Anyone who fell under the psychic field the monster threw was killed by urbat." He looked away from the table. Lines of worry marked his face, and darkness shadowed his eyes. "It's happened in two other villages that were nearly destroyed. One of them was in Me'Cowyn Hold. The Karda warned me and I got a troop there as soon as I could. If I hadn't happened to have three other strong Air talents with me to counteract it, it would have destroyed all of us. "

Tessa hid her shock. Connor Me'Cowyn was one of the strongest Air talents on Adalta. That he'd needed help terrified her.

Connor went on. "They like to attack just at dusk. Darkness doesn't bother the urbat. They use it to hide in. Walls don't do much to deter them either. They don't fly so much as make great, bounding leaps, but those leaps are up to seven meters high."

Bren scrubbed a hand hard around his face. Tessa could see the weariness in his tight shoulders. He'd driven the wagoneers and the patrol that guarded them in a fast, grueling trek to bring in the supplies they needed. "Two Karda, a patrol, and a Mi'hiru have been lost.

Tessa closed her eyes. She knew something like that had happened. Three days ago, all the Karda in the camp and nearby had flown their mourning dance. Their too-familiar song of grief tolled like great, deep, slow-ringing bells and hung heavy in the air for a full afternoon. The whirling double helix had reached far into the high clouds and spread out for a kilometer. Just remembering made her bones reverberate.

"Renewal," she said, her voice soft and sad, for the Karda, the Mi'hiru, and the villagers lost.

"Renewal."

"Renewal."

"Renewal."

Galen asked, "What of Readen? Where is he?"

"No one's seen him," Connor said, looking at the captain rather than Galen. "We assume he's still at his hold, and there are a lot of mercenaries gathering there. Rumor says he is trying to hire a couple of companies out of Akhara."

There was silence while everyone tried not to speak the words Tessa could all but see as if printed in large letters over each head. Connor was the one who said it, his voice hard and angry. "Daryl should have stripped Readen of his lands and mines for his treason."

The captain shifted and leaned his chair back. His eyes closed then opened as if he had seen something behind them he didn't want to acknowledge. Tessa watched him chew on his mustache.

Akhara Quadrant was too often in a more or less permanent state of revolt. Mi'hiru hated to be posted there. Keeping independent of what she'd heard them call a nasty nest of vicious vipers was a constant struggle. Readen's mercenaries would be hardened fighters.

But how hard will they fight for Readen if they discover they are fighting alongside monsters from the circles? Are they that hardened?

Kishar spoke, ~Tell us the news you are reluctant to share, Holder.~

Connor looked across the table at the black Karda just outside the tent with the golden Ket beside him. Finally, he said, "They'll be here well within the tenday. The Itza Larrak and the urbat have turned this way. They've bypassed several villages, and they marched all night, every night for the past two days. Like I said, darkness..."

There was a volley of piercing screams from above, and Kishar's voice shouted inside Tessa's head. ~Urbat come from the circle. Tessa, with me, now. Galen, you must fight on the ground.~

Tessa leaped up, twisted around the end of the table, and jumped for Kishar's knee and up into the saddle, fingers flying on her straps and buckles. They were in the air before she finished. They circled up twice, and she had her bow out and strung before she looked back down at the camp. Bren's wagons pulled to form a rough circle around the tents and the horse paddock. Galen walked the circumference, a thick tangle of thorny bushes and vines coiled out of the ground behind him, exploding with wicked thorns. Still only half buckled in his saddle, her father watched, looking back and forth between her and Galen. He looked up at her, and she could see something in his face she never expected to see. Dawning respect. Even awe.

She looked toward the circle north of the camp. *Oh, where did that many urbat come from? There must be three, no, maybe even five hundred of them.* For a tenday she and Galen had hunted and killed urbat, destroying eggs and killing live urbat wherever they found them. They'd flown for miles over the southern quarter of the circle, scouring it for nests and packs. And they'd found them, small clutches and groups of ten to twenty at a time. Destroyed them. Yet here they came, so many more. A deep, wedge-shaped rank of deadly black monsters flowed over the dark ground toward her.

Her heart fell flat and heavy on top of her stomach, leaving an aching void in her chest. All their efforts over the past days had seemed so much and been so small.

Then the urbat stopped a kilometer from the camp, well inside the circle. Holding close rank, they dropped to their haunches and went still—eerily immobile. The preternatural triangle of armored black statues gleamed against the dark dead surface.

Tessa looked back toward the camp. A tall column of Karda, so many she couldn't count them, circled above it, some with riders, her father among them, some alone. They moved with the coordination of a flock of swallows, in a whirling, ever-changing, ever-circling formation, kilometers high, kilometers wide, waiting for battle.

Chapter Thirty-Four

Galen stepped out of the way as the last wagon from the third camp moved into place. His thorny hedge expanded and filled in the final gap. They'd worked through the returning cold weather for a full day and night to consolidate the three planters' camps inside a double circle of wagons, and it took Galen that long to extend his hedge. He fell back onto the ground, cold and exhausted, and looked up into the leaden sky. "That looks like Krager's Tarath."

Captain Ethyn stood above him. "Kishar and Tessa are right behind him. I'm guessing the urbat and the Itza Larrak are closing in. We succeeded in diverting them from Readen, but oh, how soon success can turn to terror." The young captain tried a smile, and his words were even, but Galen heard his nervousness.

It matched his own.

He rolled to his feet. "Ah, but it will put an end to all the boring waiting."

Ethyn snorted. "I could use a little more boredom and a lot less urbat." He waved two troopers over to unsaddle the incoming Karda and bring food and water. The cooks were keeping big kettles of hot mash ready for the Karda and kettles of soup for riders and troopers all the time now. Intermittent drizzle and sleet took a toll on everyone. The few warm days were long gone. Cold was back. Wet cold.

Kishar back-winged and landed beside them, kicking up a miniature storm of leaves and dead grass. Tarath landed on the shortened landing field, his giant wings cupped to brake, and he loped toward them. Krager unbuckled and slid off, steadying himself with a hand against the tall sorrel. Lines of fatigue scored his face. He took a deep breath and stretched his head to one side then the other.

Galen linked his fingers with Tessa's and said to Krager, "Let's get to the cooks' tent and find something hot to drink. How close are they? Tessa and I counted just under five hundred waiting inside the circle. How many more are coming with the Itza Larrak?" He dodged and pulled Tessa out of the path of a planter carrying a bundle of long poles tipped with heavy spear tips of urbat metal.

Krager slapped the captain on the shoulder and left his hand there till they reached the tent. "It's good to see you, Ethyn. It looks like you and Galen have been busy. Your fortifications look good. The urbat might be able to fly over them, but they're a lot easier to kill when you shoot from underneath. Their armor doesn't protect underbellies."

"That's what Tessa and Galen said. The planters aren't trained troopers, but they're not defenseless. They know they're prime targets. They know that's why they're here, to draw the urbat to this one place, and why they've been working so hard. We're protecting them and the other civilians as much as we can, but we know they'll have to fight. I'd rather be out there, but…"

"I know, Ethyn. But I'm afraid the fight is coming to you. You're close to the circle, and we don't know how many more urbat are out there. Tessa and Galen gave us their best estimate, but they aren't certain. We can't even get more than an idea of how many we've been chasing. They're hard to count."

Krager's voice hardened. "The urbat target the Karda's wings. Too many are dead, and severe injuries have grounded too many more. Tarath lost a couple of flight feathers when we got careless. That won't happen again."

A cooks' assistant brought four steaming mugs to the table. Krager picked up a mug and turned it around and around in his hands. "Right now, we're fighting a running battle and doing some damage, but they'll be here within the day. And then the advantage shifts to them. The urbat and the Itza Larrak can retreat into the circle, regroup, and return. Our forces don't have that option. Only you,"—he tilted his head to Galen— "and Tessa can follow them there."

"The Itza Larrak," said Tessa. "What about it? How much threat is it?

"It can push a psychic field out that leaves men crawling on the ground and horses screaming in terror. Daryl has a circle of Air talents constantly working to combat it, but they are tiring.

He looked at Tessa. "Your father helps when he can. His lightning bolts seem to have an effect on the creature's shields. Daryl's circle of Air talents help keep its powers contained, but they can't ever let up. Too often they are outrun. But the running is coming to a stop. Here."

He rubbed his tired eyes with the heels of his hands. "Everything you and Galen told us about how the urbat attack has changed. You said they attacked in a disorganized swarm. Their only tactic was to overwhelm. But now, the Itza Larrak controls them, organizes them into vicious and efficient fighting units ranging from as small in number as six and as large as eighteen. Ranked and orderly and directed. That's bad enough, but the Larrak is big, and it's powerful, and we don't know what more it can do."

There was silence for a brief moment. Then Tessa asked, "And Readen? Where is Readen?"

"And the guns, the akenguns. Where are they?" Galen felt Tessa's hand on his leg.

"No sign of either, thank Adalta."

Tessa and Kishar circled above the battleground, above the screams, the smells, the blood, the clash of sword, the twang of bows. On the ground below them, Galen pushed a wall of rock and dirt, smothering urbat in a snarl of earth and vegetation, vines reaching to tangle, to strangle, to kill.

He stumbled. Tessa's heart skipped, and she grabbed at Kishar's mane. Galen was either tiring or losing power or both. He'd need to replenish soon. He disappeared beneath her as she flew on toward the supply wagons inside the thorn wall. She needed more arrows.

Planters stationed every three meters inside the circle of wagons and hedge held long, sharpened poles with urbat metal spearheads now dripping with ichor. Others dragged dead urbat into piles. An ugly yellow miasma swirled around them, and Tessa gagged at the stench.

Kishar landed a few feet from a supply wagon, and she dismounted, her body stiff, tired, and cold, ever colder. Two troopers came running with large buckets of water and hot food for Kishar and meat wrapped in bread for her. One of them handed her a cup and she filled it three times before she was satisfied.

Tessa looked toward the sun. Dim through the low clouds, it was still too far above the horizon to the west, much too far above. The hours of this day were forever hours, and the urbat numbers didn't seem to be decreasing fast enough. This day was going to stretch through the night and into another.

She reached into the back of the fletcher's wagon, stuffed both quivers as full as she could with the urbat-metal-tipped arrows from his rapidly depleting stores and went back to Kishar.

She leaned against his shoulder and ate her food too fast. His withers were damp with sweat in spite of the cold drizzle. ~It is well to have a moment of rest. You are tiring,~ Kishar pathed to her.

~You're tired too, probably more than I am. You're the one carrying me, not the other way around. I'm fine. Just discouraged.~

~Abala tells me Daryl wants to see us before we go back up.~

~Let's go then.~ Tessa didn't know much about battle strategies and tactics, but she was sure having Karda and Marta overhead able to relay telepathic messages and running reports of the battlefield through Abala was invaluable to Daryl and the other commanders.

There was a thunder of wings behind her at the shortened landing field outside the thorn fence. Her father and his Karda, Arib, came through the guarded gap barely big enough to admit them. Both Karda and foot soldiers fought hard to keep the landing field open.

Connor waved a hand at her, asking her to wait. Arib loped up.

Connor finished unbuckling and slid off. He nodded at her full quivers. "I've run out, too."

His hand lifted toward her then dropped. "Tessa. He looked away then back. "Tessa. I watched you up there." He pulled two empty quivers from his rigging and started filling them from the diminishing supply. "I'm good with a bow." His head was down, concentrating on his quivers, not looking at her. He filled one quiver and turned away to buckle it to a ring below the saddle pommel.

"I know you are, Father." Tessa hated the twisted feeling in her throat, the little girl voice that came out of her mouth. She turned to head for Kishar.

"You're better."

She turned back.

"You're better than anyone I have ever seen. No one should be able to shoot like you do. So fast. So accurate it's uncanny." His head came up, and he looked at her.

Her throat tightened, and pressure built behind her eyes. "Thank you, Father." *Why are those words so hard for me to get out?*

He lowered his head and reached for her hands, holding them for a minute. His voice low, almost a whisper catching in his throat, he said, "I'm so very proud of you."

They stood that way for several minutes, his hands firm on hers, so much between them that wanted speaking, that needed speaking and yet couldn't be spoken.

Then he stepped back, and his voice returned to its usual dictatorial tone. "I still don't like him. That Galen. I can never accept him. But I am proud of you." He finished filling the second quiver, jumped from his Karda's bent knee to the saddle, and they loped away while he was still buckling in.

Tessa turned back to Kishar and fastened her quivers to either side of the saddle. She breathed in till her lungs could hold no more air and let it out. *All right, then. I don't know what to think about that. But I don't have to right now. Back to the air and more killing.* Kishar took off, and she didn't bother buckling herself in for this short hop to see what Daryl wanted

She worried at her lip with her teeth, her eyes on Daryl. *He has to be more tired than I am.* They circled once, giving those on the ground time to make a space for them to land. And to grab their hats and cover their eyes when Kishar touched down and dust flew.

"Don't dismount, Tessa," Daryl called. He strode toward them, Merenya behind him. Tessa could see the lines of strain in Daryl's face, but his voice was strong and confident. He put a hand on Kishar's shoulder then looked down and reached to adjust a buckle. "The straps of his rigging have stretched. I'll readjust them for you."

Tessa looked at the two guardians. "Why do you think the Itza Larrak doesn't come out from its shields and fight? It's a powerful force. It's as if it's hiding."

Merenya laughed. "Daryl and I were just having that discussion. It can't, Tessa. For one thing, it has to keep the urbat organized and controlled. For another, it is the Itza Larrak. The last Larrak. It won't risk itself so long as it has urbat to do its fighting."

Her face lost its temporary look of merriment. "Those lines the nanobots are creating are for communication. There is no other Larrak for it to communicate with on this planet, so it must find a way to reach others of its kind. It is trapped here on Adalta alone. That makes it vulnerable, too vulnerable to risk coming out and actually fighting."

She smiled. "I'm going back up there. Between us, Connor and I ought to be able to break that shield. And Ballard is doing a good job leading my troops." Ballard was her son and heir. She left, wrapping her long sheepskin vest and rain gear tight around her. The sleet was getting heavier.

Daryl moved around the Karda, talking as he tightened buckles. "I'd like you and Kishar to do reconnaissance inside the circle. I need to know what's going on. Abala is giving me his Karda's eye view on what's happening and relaying reports from Marta and the other Karda. He thinks there's more activity near the circle. The urbat broke through the forces we had trying to block them from the circle, and they're thick there. We don't know what they're doing. None of the Karda can get close enough to see what's happening. They're endangering themselves to get as close as they have been. So, I need a report from you."

"Yes, sir. We'll do that and let you know." She paused. "Daryl, why is my father in the air and not on the ground commanding his troops?" Ordinarily solemn and severe, Daryl's eyes flashed what Tessa thought might even be called a twinkle. "He's put his troops under my aegis. He said he'd be better up there killing urbat and pounding the Itza Larrak. He's a formidable archer, Tessa. Almost up to your standards. And his Air talent is part of what is keeping the Itza Larrak from pushing his force field of terror over the Karda. They are not immune." He fastened the last buckle on Kishar's rig. "His lightning strikes are deadly. He's the only person I've heard of who can literally strike with lightning."

Daryl slapped the Karda's shoulder, and she and Kishar took off again, headed for the circle. *My father? He's talking about my father. How did I not know that?* It was hard to think of her father in this new way. As a strong fellow warrior and not just the father obsessed with her talent-breeding problem.

She could see Altan's Toldar Guard fighting up the hill from the northwest. Prime Guardian Hugh Me'Rahl's Rashiba Guard on the hill's other flank. The Itza Larrak was at its apex surrounded by dead trees and snarling urbat. Behind it, too close, was the edge of the circle.

Both Hugh and Altan shot arc after arc of searing flame, scorching through the ranks of urbat. There was a trail of smoldering dead urbat behind them, along with the bodies of too many of their troops. She knew they weren't happy about having to fight uphill. Their progress was slow. The urbat just kept coming, and they were so hard to kill.

Karda without riders darted in and out, seizing urbat whenever they could. They carried them high above the field of battle and let them fall deep in the forest.

Karda Patrol and Mi'hiru fliers threw nets, lifted the trapped urbat high and dropped them to their deaths. It gave Tessa a special thrill to see those shining circles of death flying through the air and spread over the field of battle like silver half-bubbles. *I must remember this picture to tell Kobe. His nets are making a difference.*

A crew of planters, scarves tied across their faces against the stench, untangled the nets from the dead urbat to be used again. Other planters stood guard around them armed with urbat metal spears, even hoes, and scythes. Six Karda flew tight circles above them, darting in whenever an urbat came close.

An urbat jumped/flew high, and its talons pierced the wing of a Mi'hiru's bronze Karda. Tessa sucked in a breath at its scream. Wings were so vulnerable. The Karda managed to shake it off and get high enough to glide to the runway. It loped through the gap in the thorn wall to where the healers were set up—for both Karda and human fighters and for the horses of the various Mounted Guards, though they were limited to the edges of the fight. They were impossible to control near the urbat.

But there were too many Karda, horses, and soldiers on the ground that hadn't been able to get away fast enough. The sleek and sinuous black-armored bodies of the urbat swarmed over great mounds of feather, flesh, and bone.

On the hill near the circle, at the center of a tight guard of urbat, the massive figure of the Itza Larrak stood inside a visible, iridescent force field. Opposite, beyond the fighting, at the edge of the tall trees of the forest, a circle of men and women, arms linked, and heads bowed, moved forward with every bit of ground their forces gained. Their hair blew wild, and their cloaks flapped in the twisting wind that whirled round and round them.

Tessa watched, her head moving back and forth between the linked men and women and the Itza Larrak. Every time it pushed its thick, viscous shield forward to force its terror into the battlefield, a fierce wind whipped around the group, and the shield shrank. Every time the fighting got too intense ahead of their tight circle, forcing them back, the Itza Larrak's shield grew, pushing terror and the urbat ahead of it. Its hands never stopped moving—sharp, choppy movements throwing spells.

The Larrak made a sudden broad gesture with its taloned hands. Tessa watched the troops fighting toward it falter, their organization splintering. Troopers fell to the ground, hands covering their heads, mouths open wide with screams lost in all the noise. Horses screamed and bucked in terror, wheeling, running in every direction. Urbat tore into them. Other urbat rushed toward them.

Then her father shot an arrow into the bubble. An arrow clad in a bolt of bright white lightning. And again. And again. The arrows didn't pierce it. They hung in it, and the shield flickered until their fire died. That's what he was doing in the air. No one else on Adalta could handle lightning like her father. Pride melted an edge off the anger at him she'd carried for so long.

The Larrak reeled back and glared up at Connor. Its hands moved faster, and it flung its arms above him, taloned fingers spread as if it threw something.

Connor's Karda faltered, but her father and Arib had strong shields, and they recovered fast.

Tessa looked to the south, toward the tight circle of men and women behind the lines. A whirl of dust and leaves and gravel roared up around them, and the wave of terror passed. Men stood again and fell on the urbat with increased frenzy.

She and Kishar circled high for several more minutes, watching the arcane battle. She couldn't determine if one side was winning. She thought the ranks of urbat might be thinning. And they seemed slower, their movements stiffer. But then so were the human fighters. And the Karda. The air turned colder and colder by the hour, and icy rain mixed with sleet fell harder.

Then the two of them veered away into the circle and headed north, beyond the clamor of the struggle. Tessa's ears rang in the silence of the air above the Circle of Disorder. It was even warmer here. No rain. No sleet. They flew for an hour, making wide, overlapping circuits before they headed back toward the battle. The only live urbat they saw were wounded and crippled, making their way back into the safety of the circle.

But there was no safety for them there. Tessa shot, over and over, killing every monster they saw until once again she ran out of arrows. ~Kishar, do you think there are no more coming? Do you think...~

~Let's fly higher, Tessa, to be certain.~

She pulled her goggles down. Kishar leveled off at about eight hundred meters. Even with the extra distance lens, it was hard to make out detail on the ground, but Kishar could. ~What do you see, Kishar? ~ She was too tired to meld her vision with his, and she didn't need to.

It was several minutes before he spoke. ~Scattered clutches, half-buried. More than I want to see. But no moving urbat except near the battle.~

Tessa's whole body shuddered with relief. Her arms and shoulders ached, and her fingers were so sore she didn't know how she could draw her bow again. ~Let's get back. You relay that message to Daryl. Take me to the healer's area. Maybe they can do something about my bleeding fingers. We can't stop. There are still too many left to kill.~

Chapter Thirty-Five

Galen checked his sword belt one more time and went over Ket's rigging. Testing straps. Tightening buckles. ~We won't be up there long, Ket. I need an overview. I've watched you fight. You are very good, but don't you think you are taking too many chances?~

~I certainly hope I am able to do what every Karda up there is doing right now. That question is insulting.~ He snorted, his tone regal, his nares flared.

~I didn't mean to insult you. I am sorry. I'm not used to worrying about anyone. I have more people to worry about now than...than... well, I don't know.~

~Kishar comes.~

Dust and dry grass flew, and Kishar touched down beside them. Galen went to help Tessa unbuckle. She slid down, and he held her tight, his cheek pressed against the top of her head. Her goggles dug into his face. He didn't care. ~I hate this. I hate that you are in danger all the time, and I can do nothing about it. I can't protect you.~

Her arms around him, her hands clenched together and pressed hard into his back. ~I don't need protection. I just need you. And I can't protect you either. I can't even tell you to stop and refill when I can see you badly need it.~

He pulled back, his hands cradled her face, and he brushed his lips across hers with a feather's touch. ~I have something for you.~ He stepped back and pulled a black bag from his pocket.

~Now? We're in the middle of a desperate fight, and you think it's time to give me a gift?~

He put the bag in her hand. ~Open it.~

Tessa looked down at the small bag and back up at Galen. Her fingers closed around it, feeling for the shape. ~This looks like what Bren brought you days and days ago that you wouldn't let me see.~

~Sort of. It took me a while to finish them. To get them perfect.~ He held his breath.

She took her time loosening the strings and tipped out two dark ironwood carvings on silver chains. Matching pendants of brilliant iridescent opals held by crossed arrows intertwined with vines and leaves.

~I made it for you. I mean them for us.~

Large tears formed in the eyes of this brave, courageous, indomitable woman he loved. He dropped one in her hand and held out the other. Her mouth quivered. She touched it with a shaking hand and whispered, "Will you put it on me?"

Galen reached around her, slipped the chain over her raggedy hair and rested his forehead on hers. ~Now it's your turn.~ He ducked his head, and Tessa reached to drop the other chain around his neck.

He blinked at the incandescent flash between the opals that sealed their bond. His breath stopped, and radiant joy flared.

The dark figure of the Itza Larrak spread its enormous wings and lifted into the air out of the middle of the urbat ranks, something large and bulky clutched to its chest, its shimmering shield around it. Galen and Ket watched as it arrowed higher and faster. Galen could only admire its ability to maneuver between and around, shooting through the flying Karda until it was high above. Merenya's firebolts flared, and Connor Me'Cowyn fired from below the Larrak. One lightning arrow stuck in its iridescent shield for an instant. When it fell, it left a large, round, black mark.

Before Connor could shoot again, the shimmering bubble around the Larrak disappeared for an instant, and something large fell away from it. A fire bolt from Merenya singed the tip of the Larrak's wing. The bubble snapped back. An urbat fell, its stubby wings a blur, straight onto Connor Me'Cowyn's back. Its teeth and talons sliced at him and the straps of his rigging.

Connor knocked it away with his bow arm, and it fell, beating stubby wings to slow its fall. Half a dozen arrows pierced it, and it tumbled away to the ground.

Horrified, Galen saw the Larrak drop a second urbat and knock Connor from his seat on Arib.

The great Karda screamed, flipped to vertical in a wing-over turn, tucked its wings tight, and arrowed in a fast stoop to try to get under the falling body.

A sorrel without a rider swooped in and caught Connor on her back, but his sudden weight threw her off balance, and he slipped over her side. He grabbed her mane with one hand. He swung his legs and stretched for a hold with his other hand. One foot was almost over her back, and Galen let out his breath. Tessa's father was safe.

But then he slipped. Galen watched in horror as centimeter by centimeter, Connor slid down, his foot slipped off. His weight ripped out the handful of mane he grasped. There were no straps and no rigging to catch hold of.

"Go, Ket," Galen screamed, and the big gold arrowed down.

Connor fell again, twisting and wheeling through the air, arms flailing, reaching for something to grab. His chestnut slid under the sorrel and tried to catch him, but he missed, and Ket swooped in below them.

Galen stood in his stirrups, leaning against the straps of his rigging as far as he could. He caught Connor by one arm. There was a sickening pop as Connor's shoulder dislocated, and he screamed. For an instant, Galen thought his own arm would pull loose, but Ket flipped hard in an acrobatic maneuver, and Connor landed across the saddle pommel in front of Galen.

Connor grabbed one of Galen's leg straps and lay there. His head and shoulders hung off one side. His legs hung off the other. He gasped for air, sucking his breath through his teeth from the pain. Gashes on his head and shoulders dripped blood down Galen's leg.

Galen pressed back as hard into the cantle as he could and grabbed Connor's jacket with both hands. Ket settled into a long glide toward the landing meadow and the healers

"Don't even try to talk, Galen said. "And especially don't try to move."

Finally, Connor said, his words forced between gasps, "Thank...you."

"Yeah, I've always been good at catching bodies falling from the sky. I haven't missed yet. It's a talent I was born with."

Connor's body shook. Galen thought it was fear and relief. Then he realized Tessa's father was laughing.

Tessa tried to swallow, cleared her dry throat, and rolled her aching shoulders. She looked beyond Kishar's head, squinting, trying to see through the growing dark. She had to wipe frozen tears from her lashes. They flew a wide wheel back and forth, in and out of the circle, searching the ranks of urbat. Trying to determine if they were shrinking. Marta and Sidhari soared up beside them as they crossed back above the battle, and she sensed Marta and the two Karda pathing.

Kishar said, ~Sidhari and Marta say the Itza Larrak is moving, maybe retreating. Galen is headed straight for it. He's getting close.~

Relief and anxiety fought a war in Tessa's stomach and chest. She took a deep breath. She was so tired, so scared, so terribly tired. Her arms ached from drawing back on her bow again and again. The ends of her fingers had blistered—again. Overused muscles in her legs cramped, little spasms shooting through them from hours, from days of shifting her balance over and over as Kishar twisted his way back and forth across the battlefield. For three days and nights, the urbat never stopped attacking.

Every time one of their units lost too many, they dashed back toward the circle, and a reorganized, reinforced unit came out fighting.

Few evaded Tessa's arrows, but she couldn't get them all. Three days and nights of blood and death. It had to end today. And today was almost over. The air was so still and cold Tessa's lungs ached.

Flying big, easy arcs high above the battle allowed the messages from her tired body to get through, telling her how little strength she had left, how cold she was. She alternately clenched and stretched her hands. Her quivers were almost empty again. She'd broken three bowstrings.

Kishar tilted to vertical, and Tessa's insides gave the familiar lurch as his sharp turn pressed her back in the saddle. They headed back for more arrows and a fast session with the healers for her blistered fingers. She and Kishar were the only ones who could cut off the urbat's refuge inside the circle. She couldn't quit now. They were back in the air in minutes.

In the dead abelee trees below them, too close to the circle for Tessa's comfort, blending into the growing darkness, was a tight knot of urbat, and in the center of the knot stood the Itza Larrak, its wings half spread, its blue-black body huge.

A menacing, eerily beautiful blend of humanoid, insect, and metal. The oily, iridescent bubble arched above it. Large, opaque patches marred it where fire bolts and lightning arrows made their marks. Around it was a circle of urbat, six deep, sitting on their haunches, facing outward, waiting, guarding.

She was so very tired. She blinked, not trusting her eyes. The Itza Larrak's bubble flickered. An arrow stuck, halfway through it. It flickered again, and the urbat surrounding it stood, restless, their ranks less orderly. The monster's arms made three sharp gestures. The outside rank of urbat stiffened, and several fell.

~It's losing control, Kishar. I think it's losing control. Look.~

Galen was less than a hundred meters away. Earth erupted, plants sprouted and grew to catch urbat and bury them in the dirt. Ballard led a train of Merenya's Anuma troops to guard his rear and pick off survivors. His, Me'Rahl's, Daryl's, and Altan's forces spread in a half-circle around Galen. They fought to force the ranks of urbat closer and closer together and into Galen's path. But Tessa could see they were taking heavy losses.

But the urbat weren't reacting as fast. Their movements were sluggish, jerky. Four silver nets arced down and trapped four urbat. Troopers with mallets raced toward them and pounded stakes through the nets, trapping the monsters. Their struggles were weak, futile. The troopers surrounded them, guarding their prisoners.

Altan and Daryl aimed bolt after bolt of fire through the ranked urbat, reaching for the Larrak's shield. Their troops hacked away at the enemy with swords and long spears. When the urbat fell back to run along inside the circle to try to flank them, if they weren't killed by Tessa, they were picked off when they came out by Karda and troopers with urbat-metal-tipped arrows, spears, and flying nets.

Marta and Sidhari flashed past Tessa. Sidhari's wings folded like the fletching on an arrow. She stooped and streaked across the field, snatched the urbat that popped up to attack from behind Altan. Her wings flared to beat her way back up, and she snapped its head off with a twist of her clawed foot like beheading a chicken.

Tessa swallowed hard. That was close. Too close. She and Kishar landed, and a healer came running to work on Tessa's fingers. A trooper filled her quivers for her, most of the arrows recovered from the battlefield dripped with ichor. They took off again. She searched the bloody battlefield and found Galen. He was safe. Tired but safe.

Her father was nowhere she could see. She hoped he'd landed to replenish his supply of arrows or maybe even rest for a few minutes. His arm had been healed, but he'd had little chance to rest, and drawing his bow must hurt—a lot.

Merenya on Pagra circled above the Itza Larrak's bubble, just above the reach of the urbat, firing firebolt after bolt, each bolt eating further and further into the shield. Its shimmer was blotched and dull where her bolts landed. She looked up at Tessa, waved a tired wave, and looked back down.

The Itza Larrak's wings snapped open, and it powered up with an ear-piercing, shrieking scream. Pagra's wings faltered, and she shook her head. Tessa saw Merenya's mouth move, but she couldn't hear her words. Merenya reached forward to grab Pagra's mane, one arm around the Karda's neck. The Larrak's shield dropped for an instant and its metal wing slashed up through Pagra's, cutting half her left wing away. A wide crimson arc of blood spurted through the air.

Pagra's scream slammed against Tessa, and Kishar swooped toward them. Merenya looked up at her, arms tight around Pagra's neck, tears streaming into her hair, and the injured Karda spiraled down, a river of blood trailing. The older woman smiled a sad, sweet smile.

"We can catch her, Kishar. We can catch her. Merenya," Tessa yelled, standing as high in her stirrups as her straps would let her as Kishar followed Pagra down. "Get out of your straps. Reach up. Kishar can grab you and carry you down."

Merenya turned her head away to bury her face in Pagra's mane. Then it was too late. Rider and Karda hit the ground in the middle of a swarm of urbat and disappeared.

Tessa curled over the saddle pommel. Deep, racking sobs tore from her. A Karda screamed above her, and she jerked her head up.

~Tessa.~ Kishar's voice was sharp. ~Hang on. ~ He folded his wings and dropped straight at the Itza Larrak, talons on all four legs extended, and tore into the top of the Larrak's shield, leaving long, black scars deep in its surface. Kishar swooped his way back up through a crowd of screaming Karda who were flying circles around it, riders pelting it with arrows, and twisting bursts of wind and fire.

The monster landed in the middle of its circle of urbat guards. It looked up and screamed another piercing cry. Four Karda close to it faltered in their flights, but Kishar hovered in the air above it, unaffected, and screamed back.

Hours later, as day moved toward night, Tessa's strength was nearing its end. It was so cold her fingers cramped. Her feet felt frozen to the stirrups. When she looked down into the battle, the urbat were retreating, moving slow, their movements jerky and uncoordinated. The Itza Larrak fought to extend its bubble to cover the ones who came near enough.

Galen was nearing the end of his strength, too, she feared. He was no longer pushing dirt. He could still raise vicious brambles with thorns. He couldn't kill the urbat, but he could hold them fast so the troopers coming behind could. The urbat 's movements slowed—their metal joints stiffened in the frigid cold. And Galen could move through them faster.

The troops behind Daryl, Ballard, Hugh Me'Rahl, and Altan converged in a semi-circle, forcing the monsters toward the Itza Larrak. Bolt after bolt of fire sliced toward the Larrak's shield. Connor's lightning arrows were leaving dark blotches.

The circle of Air talents moved forward and surrounded the captured urbat. Tessa thought they were setting up a psychic shield around them, blocking the Itza Larrak's control. It was no longer trying to throw the force field of terror at the troops. Its hands flew, forming arcane symbols, sparks flying from its talons.

~Now, Tessa,~ said Kishar. ~Now we hit him.~ He stooped, arrowing toward the Itza Larrak's damaged shield. His talons ripped through it, tearing a great hole in it's surface.

Tessa grabbed the pommel, and he wheeled in an impossibly tight turn. ~Shoot. Shoot now. Aim for its wing, Tessa. Shoot.~

She clamped her legs, ignored the pain in her blistered fingers and took sight. Three time she shot, hitting the juncture of its wing and body.

It screamed. Urbat rushed to it. Swarming around and under it. Its talons sparked symbols in the air and the hole it its bubble closed. Six Urbat outside it fell dead, but the shield was whole.

Dragging its wing, it climbed on top of four urbat and the bubble began moving back, faster and faster into the dark, into the circle.

~We follow and watch.~ Kishar flew higher.

It kept moving. Urbat falling like dots in a macabre line behind it.

~What is happening to them, Kishar? Is it the cold? Is the cold killing them?~

Kishar was silent for a long time. Then he spoke. ~It steals their strength, their essence, their life force to keep itself alive. To keep its shield strong against us.~

~Can we kill it?~

Just ahead was the eerie orange and green glow from the fissure that split the surface of the circle.

The Larrak moved faster and faster, more urbat falling behind. Its shield grew opaque and strong.

~Not now, Tessa. It's too close to its locus of power. But we will.~

They watched as the monster slipped into the midst of the vivid orange haze with the black symbols swarming around it. Is shield dropped away and slowly it descended into the chasm.

Tessa held her breath until it burst from her lungs. It didn't reappear. Kishar flew circles around the haze that boiled out of the split in the dark ground for almost an hour. The Itza Larrak didn't reappear.

Tessa leaned over the pommel and pressed her face into Kishar's mane. She sobbed. She sobbed her relief. She sobbed her grief for Merenya. She sobbed until she exhausted herself, and Kishar finally turned for the long flight back.

Torches flared along the edges of the landing field, and Karda after Karda glided to land. A few remained in the air, watching. She saw Sidhari land and lope from the end of the field. Marta jumped off, and her legs collapsed under her. She just sat there, leaning back on her hands, her face to the sky. Sidhari stood, head down, beside her. Altan fell next to her, wrapping her tight in his arms.

Tessa spotted troopers half carrying Galen, stripping off his clothes, into a lop-sided tent. One came running with a pile of blankets. Kishar touched down as close as he could without collapsing the tent, and Tessa flew out of the buckles on her rigging and into the tent. She lay as close to him as she dared. He turned his head and smiled at her, then Adalta reached for him. Tessa didn't move away.

She could hear Kishar talking to Daryl and Hugh Me'Rahl, telling them what he and Tessa had seen when they followed the Itza Larrak to its lair. ~The urbat will begin to recover inside the circle. The Itza Larrak will rebuild its wing. But it will take time, and it will be spring before they become a real threat again. Except for the Lines of Devastation. It will put more effort than ever into them, now.~

Hugh spoke aloud. "We'll have to put more effort into controlling them, then." He put his hand on Daryl's shoulder. "You are not fighting this alone, Daryl. Stephan Me'Gerron sent word before I left Rashiba that they are beginning to grow in Toldar's circles. I've asked Guardian Turin of Akhara to join us in Toldar Prime—he' s expected there for the bonding ceremony for Altan and Marta and Tessa and Galen. Ballard says he will fly there with me. He's leaving half his troops here and sending the rest back to Anuma to watch the circles there. Merenya already had people working on the lines there."

He sighed, and Tessa could almost see him scratching his beard and rubbing at the deep worry lines in his forehead. "And we have another complication. I've had an emissary from the ship. We have some decisions to make about that."

There was a long silence, then Daryl said, his voice so tired Tessa wondered how he was still standing—how any of them were still standing, "We can't solve anything now. Now we need to help the healers with tents for the wounded, do what we can to help them get rid of this horrid stink of disease. Then I'll see what the cooks can do in the way of a celebration. We haven't won the war, but we won this battle."

Kishar's pathed voice said, ~And we learned much.~

Their voices moved away, but Tessa didn't notice. She was already asleep.

Epilogue

Four tendays later Tessa and Galen landed outside the mews in Toldar Prime, tired, cold, and hungry. They'd hopped from village to village and from winter storm to winter storm in a zigzag line all the way from Restal, carrying the warning of the horrors that were coming. Connor Me'Cowyn met them inside and helped Tessa with Kishar's heavy rigging.

"I was beginning to wonder if you were going to make it." He heaved the saddle up to a stand and laid the saddle blanket over it to dry.

"Wondering or hoping, Holder Me'Cowyn?" There wasn't a note of teasing in Galen's voice.

Tessa kicked him in the ankle. ~Don't push him. I think he's trying to accept this. He's not shouting.~

Kishar and Ket both shook their heads and blew hard—a Karda laugh.

Connor reached out his arm. With a slight hesitation, Galen clasped his forearm.

"I would like a moment of your time, Galen if Tessa could finish grooming your two Karda," said Connor, with a polite nod to Kishar and Ket.

"Father—" Tessa began.

"Don't be concerned, Tessa. I know I can't stop you. And I don't think I want to. I only want to talk to him. The keep is crowded with people coming for the strategy meeting and the bonding celebration, and the mews is quiet at the moment. This is a good time."

Galen stood for a moment, looked at Tessa, and said, "We can talk in the feed room. You groom, Tessa, and I'll put mash on the stove to heat for them. It's been a long, cold flight. Several long, cold flights." He tossed Tessa Ket's brush and headed down the mews aisle.

Galen pulled two big metal buckets down from a shelf, added water from the spigot at the big sink, and set them on the wide magma stone stove next to it. "Who's here for the meeting?"

"That's not what I want to talk to you about." Connor scooped grain from a bin and added it to the heating water. "When I get my temper under control, I can sometimes think straight."

Galen looked at him. Connor's mouth quirked in a wry grin.

"I've talked to a lot of people about you since I arrived. Daryl, Krager, Marta—even Altan had some good things to say about you. Only some, and reluctant, but good. I know what your father has done, what you did that got you so badly burned. I've seen what you've done since, and I see how Tessa feels about you."

"They like you—not because you're the Kern. You probably don't have to be a good person to do what you do as the Kern. Maybe even more important, I see how Kishar feels about you. He's not an impressionable young girl."

Galen picked up the long wood paddle and gave the thickening mash a stir.

"Tessa is my only child, my heir. My wife, Aldra, is past the age for bearing children, so I won't have another. Me'Cowyn Hold is the oldest hold in Restal. One of the first holds established outside Rashiba when the colonists began to spread out. My ancestors settled here because it was so far from Rashiba. Their laws and customs were very different from the other colonists, and there was friction—to use a polite word. The laws of my hold concerning women and property came to us from an ancient and frankly, restrictive religion. The religion didn't survive, but those restrictive laws did. Tessa becoming the

Austringer is forcing us—me—to look closer at those laws. To look closer at the possibilities for change. But they are old and well-established."

"You're afraid Tessa will not be strong enough to be holder after you." Galen leaned against the wall, one leg cocked, eyes half-closed. He was tired, there was a long strategy session ahead of them before they could rest, and he didn't see the point of the conversation. "I can assure you that she is."

"You're right. I know better now. It took me a while to appreciate what and who she is. I had to get past a lot of my own...issues. But I know she can do it. I also know she doesn't have to do it alone, and she won't ever choose someone else. She's chosen you. Marta has told me about you and your father. So, I hope you will think favorably about what I am asking you." He took a long breath. "I would like you to take the name Me'Cowyn when you and Tessa bond."

Galen dropped the paddle, and hot mash splashed on his hand. He shook it and turned to run cold water over it, his back to Me'Cowyn. He put both hands on the edge of the sink and leaned into them, head down—Connor's words buzzing in his head. He felt Connor's hand land softly on his shoulder then drop away.

Connor's next words were just as soft. "Talk it over with Tessa. I would be proud to have you become Galen Me'Cowyn. For who you are, Galen, not just for your bond with Tessa."

Not be Galen Morel? Not be the everlasting disappointment? Not be Kayne Morel's son? Galen felt so light he wondered if his feet had left the ground.

Still in their worn, wet, travel-worn clothes, Galen walked with Tessa into Guardian Stephan's large conference room. Magma stones glowed in the massive stone stove on the hearth at the end of the long, narrow room. Sun shone from tall mullioned windows at the other. It was hot, stuffy with the smell of wet wool and travel weary bodies.

All four quadrant guardians were present—Galen assumed the enormous man with the cruel face was Turin of Akhara. Young Ballard sat next to him, his face hard with anger and grief. Tall, silver-haired Stephan stood at the windows, Marta and Altan beside him. Prime Guardian Hugh and Daryl had their heads together over the brittle pages of an ancient book.

Hugh looked up at Tessa and Galen. "I'm glad you are finally—and safely—here. Find seats, and we'll begin with the report of your winding journey here."

For two days they discussed, argued, and discussed the strategy and tactics for eliminating the threat of the Itza Larrak and its urbat. Some learned from the ancient books like the one Daryl and Hugh studied.

Guardian Turin agreed to set up his troops on the lower Tarana river close to the border with Anuma and Toldar, and not far from Rashiba. Galen suspected he hadn't intended to travel back to Akhara in the vicious cold of winter—he didn't fly—and wanted to be stationed as far away from the northern mountains where the mercenaries Readen hired from Akhara were likely to pass through. Turin was probably glad to have them out of his quadrant.

The focus was on the battle with the alien Itza Larrak, the Lines of Devastation, and the urbat. Readen was Daryl's problem.

The akenguns weren't just Daryl's problem, though they knew Readen had them. All four guardians and Hugh knew the guns wouldn't be used only in Restal. Readen's defenses were discussed, and Altan, Daryl, with Galen's help when he could, were assigned the problem of getting them back and destroying them.

The troops from Anuma, Toldar, and Rashiba that were still in Restal would remain there, and reinforcements would make their way as the weather permitted. Finder Mirela was called and promised a list of strong Earth and Air talents to attack the lines, beginning with the longest. They were growing everywhere. The cold wasn't affecting them, Galen and Tessa reported. Guardian Turin had to be convinced that he couldn't attack them on his own, that it took several strong talents and several days. However strong he might be, he wouldn't be enough.

Tessa reported again about the journey of the Itza Larrak to the chasm, and how it might be possible to weaken it by trapping, separating, or killing its urbat and how they could work that into the strategy.

Marta would continue to work with unpartnered Karda to keep watch on Readen's hold, the circles, and the lines in a more methodical manner. If she could

Mirela promised the strongest Air talents she could find to send to Restal to examine the captured urbat to discover how they might be controlled, how control of them might be ripped away from the Larrak. She'd go herself if Marta could find a Karda to carry her. And troops to go with her. And plenty of blankets.

Finally, Daryl said, "It's late and we're not going to finish this tonight. Let's take tomorrow and celebrate. Celebrate what we've done. Celebrate the bonding of the four warriors of legend."

Galen laughed and the tension in the room dissolved. The meeting ended.

No one left completely happy. No one went away convinced they could win the war. Except Ballard whose grief wouldn't let him think anything other than victory.

It was the morning of the third day. The day devoted to the bonding celebration for the four fighters of legend. At the far end of Toldar's landing field Tessa, on her father's arm, at the opening of a circle of more Karda than she'd ever seen. She glanced at him. She knew she looked beautiful, and for the first time since he realized she'd reached the age to mate, she didn't dread the attention she drew.

Her spiky silver hair had been tortured into soft curls bound by a silver circlet set with five deep-blue aquamarines. A single long, black flight feather hung from it behind her left ear. Her dress was a shimmering, silken column of silver that left her right arm and shoulder bare. On her left wrist over a slim, long sleeve, she wore a silver archer's arm guard, studded with a dozen small aquamarines.

Her bonding opal, mounted between carved, black ironwood arrows linked with vines, hung on its silver chain just above the hollow of her breasts. A small, decorative quiver of black-fletched arrows hung on one side from a belt that hugged her just above her hips, her sword in a matching scabbard on the other.

They stepped into the circle filled with fragrant flowers from the greenhouses, and on a raised hill across the circle from her, there, beneath a young, rare native darisa tree, Galen, tall and beautiful, one hand on its slender trunk, watched her walk toward him. Tessa's breath caught.

His eyes turned brilliant green with emotion. The scar on his cheek was gone, and in its place was the trefoil abelee leaf tattoo. Eight polished oval buttons of dark green malachite, striped like the growth rings of a tree, decorated his high-necked, black tunic. A gleaming gold feather hung from a malachite hair clasp behind his right ear. His sword was in a tooled, black leather scabbard. Embedded in its hilt was another, larger malachite cabochon.

Marta and Altan stood on the other side of the tree. Overlapping bands of tiny bronze feathers trimmed the deep V-neck of Marta's Mi'hiru-green tunic, wrapped the ends of the long, loose sleeves and the hem. She also wore her sword—in a gilded gold scabbard—by her side. A narrow gold circlet shone in her long mahogany hair. A bright bronze feather hung down her back. One hand rested on the arm of a nervous and uncomfortable Bren.

On her other side stood Altan in a tunic of deep brown velvet with thin gold piping in a double row around the stand-up collar and sleeve cuffs. His bonding opal, set, like Marta's, between two Karda, gleamed on the dark fabric. The sword hanging at his waist was in a well-worn, scarred leather scabbard. Tied to the hilt were three bright copper feathers as long as his sword.

Tessa and her father reached the others, and she took Galen's outstretched hand. Connor and Bren stepped away.

Marta spoke first, her voice just above a whisper. "Altan, you feather my nest. You teach me what I need to be taught. You hear me when I speak my truth. I am honored to face the world by your side. My hand and my heart are yours. I promise to guard your back, to uphold you when you are right and argue with you when you are wrong. I promise to trust you, and I promise always to be worthy of your trust. She reached her hand to touch his bonding opal. " I, Marta Me'Rowan, give you this, my promise.

Altan bent his head to rest on her forehead and curled his fingers around her bonding pendant. "You crossed galaxies and fell from the stars so I could find you, to bless my life with your courage, with your will, with your love. I am honored and inspired that you agree to be by my side, steadfast and strong, that you agree to stand with me, and sometimes in front of me. I promise to stand by your side; I promise to hold you with love, to protect you with love, to argue with you with love. I will build a nest for our fledglings and help you push them out when it is time, knowing that together we can teach them what they need to fly. I, Altan Me'Gerron, give you this, my promise." They stood, heads together, hands clasped, each on the other's opal.

Then Galen spoke, his voice at first low and thick with emotion, then growing in strength and clarity. "Tessa." He cradled her bonding opal in his fingers. "My love for you grew and entangled me like a vine with a flower that bloomed into a strong, powerful woman with spiky silver hair, with thorns that pierced me like your arrows and broke through the cold that froze my heart. A vine that grew with the tenacity that freed me to grow, freed me to be worthy of you. You bring me hope. You bring me courage. You bring me faith in myself. Now, we are family. I, Galen Me'Cowyn, give you this, my promise."

Tessa's eyes flicked to her father. He watched Galen, smiling, then he looked at Tessa and his smile deepened. She swallowed her shock and took a deep breath. She placed one hand over Galen's fist, and her other grasped the bonding pendant on his chest. "I love you, Galen." She steadied her shaky voice. "Galen Me'Cowyn, you are my ground. You are the soil in which I plant myself. You give me what I need to grow, to bloom. You are the strength in my heart that blossoms with hope for our future. I promise to be your friend, your companion, your sanctuary, your lover. Together we will cultivate the garden for our children, so they grow in health and safety. I, Tessa Me'Cowyn, give you this, my promise." And, silently, with joy that threatened to burst out, ~I love you. You give me the courage to let my hair grow back. And I should kick you in the shins for this surprise.~

The four of them turned to face the circle. Their hands fell away from the bonding opals, and brilliant rainbows of light flashed around and around.

Galen reached with his hand to grasp the slender trunk of the darisa tree, revered for its beauty and its ability to survive, to bend, to spring back from the harshest winds. He bowed his head and above them the tree burst into hundreds of five-petaled blossoms. Tessa looked up, and a lacy white cloud of them drifted across her face. Galen reached his hand and brushed her cheek.

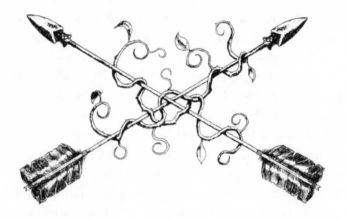

Acknowledgments

I could not have written this book without my sister, Alice V. Brock, author of the prize winning mid-grade historical novel, *A River of Cattle*. I've had support and encouragement from all my talented family, including Phil Vincent (who's writing a thriller titled *Varuna*), Jeri, Abbie (who gave me the German word for seed—Kern), Rachel B., Heather, Myrna, Daniel (for the fight scenes), and my friends Monica and Lorrie—all of whose careful reading made the book so much better. Thanks to Kurt Nilson, whose cover makes Tessa and Galen come alive and whose illustrations add so much.

Special thanks to story editor Nathan Riding, to Reina-Shay Broussard, proof reader and more, and to Eve Church for her final read-through. Thank you to Jody Thomas at the West Texas Writing Academy, to Margie Lawson of the Lawson Writer's Academy. It takes a village to write a book.

Visit my website at www.sherrillnilson.com. I sometimes post working-version scenes from the next novel in the series, occasionally working versions of the next book cover, etc., and I will appreciate your comments. Join me on my Facebook page: Facebook.-com/SLNilson, at Twitter @sherrillnilson and sherrill.nilson on Instagram. You can email me at SherrillNilson@gmail.com.

Please read on for an excerpt from *Falling: Adalta Vol III.*

FALLING ADALTA VOL III

CHAPTER ONE

Fifteen riders on magnificent hawk-headed flying horses circled the landing field just outside the small town of Flat Rock. Hugh monstrous dog-like creatures, half metal-half flesh, with scales of armor, swarmed over the walls into the village. Their stubby metallic wings beat with a ringing Daryl Me'Vere, astride his Karda, could hear from high in the air. A sound he hated. He forced down the pressure building from his chest into his throat—hatred, anger, fear for his riders and for his people below.

At his signal, Karda and riders swooped across the field, snatching unwary monsters, the urbat, in their wicked talons, carrying them high above and dropping them to their deaths in the middle of the throng attacking the gates. Other riders aimed arrows at the urbat tearing through the streets after townspeople, most of whom fought with swords, spears, axes—whatever was to hand and sharp.

Daryl and Abala dropped down to about twelve meters, twice as high as the urbat could reach with their stubby wings and massive bodies. They crossed the walls, circling the village. Screams and cries and urbat snarls and howls rose, and he heard the clang of swords and hoes and scythes against the urbat armor. The savage brutes swarmed through the small town, and Daryl shoved down his anger. He needed to fight urbat, not his emotions.

Below him, a terrified unarmed villager stumbled to his knees, an urbat half flying, half falling directly at him. A second villager ran to shove his short-bladed spear overhead at its belly and impaled the creature. The impact knocked him down, but he scrambled to his feet, put his foot against the urbat, pulled his weapon free and slashed it across the throat. Thick, yellow ichor ran in runnels between the cobblestones.

Daryl flew on, drew on his talent, and fire bolts, long, narrow bursts of flame from his spread fingers, incinerated every urbat he caught in the open, careful of the villagers and the buildings. He fired and fired until Abala peeled away to beat his way up into the air and beyond the walls.

~What are you doing, Abala? They're still fighting.~ He spoke telepathically.

~And you have depleted your talent. You are so tired I can feel you sway in the saddle. We have other work to do. Another kind of monster to find.~

Daryl scrubbed his hands through his hair, wishing Abala didn't know him so well. When frustration tried to clamp down on his chest again, he shoved it away to take long, deep breaths, pulling strength from the air, the clouds, the sky. Restoring his power through elemental Air was difficult--impossible for most--but Daryl was a formidable talent and there wasn't time to land to draw power from deep in Adalta.

They flew a sortie over the fields and trees around the village, searching for the Itza Larrak, the alien being who controlled the urbat in its fight to control the planet and call back others of its kind. He strengthened his shields against the alien's powerful psychic force field and flew low over the forest and fields below.

Off to his right, a small group of men trapped in a red stone quarry fought off ten urbat with picks and long, heavy pry bars—only two of them armed with swords, another with a short spear. They were going to lose.

The telepathic Abala spoke in Daryl's head. ~You are too depleted of talent to use fire bolts.~

Daryl stopped him before he could go on. ~Just get us a little closer.~ And Abala dove.

Daryl extended his arm, spread his fingers, and a bolt of fire flew toward an urbat, burning it to stinking cinders. Abala flew, wings near vertical, in a tight circle around the fight, and Daryl struck another, and another—every urbat separated far enough from the fighting men, who finally drove the rest of the monsters off and ran for the village gates.

Abala straightened and beat his wings hard to gain altitude. They wheeled around to circle the village again, widening their circle over brown fields near the river and the forest to the east wearing a haze of new green leaves, but never out of sight of the village. Daryl split his concentration between drawing in power from the air and searching for the Itza Larrak. The monster driving the urbat, controlling them—its minions—its creations.

~There. In that small grove of pines at the far edge of the runway,~ Daryl pathed. ~I can feel the Larrak.~ He knew better than to waste his power on attacking it. Its shield was too strong for just one fighter. He'd had ten powerful talents fighting it last fall. It killed one, almost killed another, and escaped. Not unhurt, but still it escaped into the Circle of Disorder where he couldn't follow. He looked as closely as he could through the monster's pearlescent shield. The wing Tessa, the Austringer, and Kishar, her Karda—the only ones who could follow it into the circle—had nearly severed, was repaired.

They would fight it a different way this time.

The big roan Karda peeled off toward the village, landed and loped to a stop. On his heels landed Nuala, a delicate, light brown Karda with sharply contrasting black wing stripes and Mi'hiru Steffa on her back.

Steffa dropped a handful of quarrels into her quiver, pulled her small crossbow from its holder, slid out of the saddle to the ground, adjusted her sword belt, and started after Daryl.

He stopped and turned to speak to her.

She spoke first. Her small frame tense and determined. "Don't tell me to go back up there and just watch that monster."

Her face was a tight as the white-knuckled grip on her crossbow. Daryl just nodded and headed for the gates.

Just outside the wall a circle of six people formed, securely guarded by armed villagers and four patrollers. One of the gates opened enough to let two more women slip through and run to join them. One of them called to Daryl, between pants for air, "Where is it? Are we close enough? I can almost feel it."

"The stand of pines to the southeast of the landing field. I felt its force field shoving at Abala and me. Form up here against the wall close to the gates. I'll help you locate it and monitor you until you find it." Not a hint of the worry about how well prepared they were showed on his face. He'd swallowed it. It tasted like bitter medicine.

The woman stopped when she reached the circle, bent over, hands on her knees, breathing hard. A woman already seated cross-legged on the ground looked up with anguished questions in her eyes. The first spoke between panting breaths. "Brey is alright. Your son is fighting with the patrol, but he's alright. And Maddy is on the roof of your cottage with three quivers of arrows and a spear, firing as fast as she can."

The eight people, all strong Air talents formed a tight circle on the ground, knees touching, and stilled. Daryl watched, walked to one man, touched him gently on the shoulder. "Ground, first." The man straightened, then relaxed into the cross-legged posture Daryl knew these people might need to hold for hours.

The Itza Larrak controlled the urbat. And it could throw a psychic wall of terror that froze anything without strong shields—human, animal, or Karda. It stepped out of the pine grove onto the edge of the landing field. Tall, broad, covered with light-absorbing black armor that seemed part of him. Part metal and part flesh, the Larrak was an eerily beautiful blend of insect and humanoid with enormous pierced metal wings that never entirely stopped moving.

Daryl drew on Adalta and strengthened his shields just as the wave of terror reached the circle. The eight people swayed, straightened, and held firm, whispering the spell words they'd worked on for the past four tendays.

After a few minutes, the circle swayed again, then righted itself, pushing a psychic field that rocked the Itza Larrak. They settled in for the long battle for control.

Daryl breathed deep, the band of anger and fear for these people that seemed permanently clamped to his chest eased, and he filled his lungs fully perhaps for the first time since he'd gotten the call that Flat Rock was under attack. He dropped to his knees, placed his hands flat on the earth and began to draw power from Adalta, filling the power vacuum inside him, feeling it move up through him from deep in the heart of the planet. He knelt there for several long minutes.

Then he stood, drew his sword, flexed the fingers of his left hand, and headed through the gates at a fast trot. Abala was back in the air searching for unwary urbat. Daryl took a last look at the circle of eight Air talents. It swayed and recovered, swayed and recovered, but it held fast against the Itza Larrak. And he could feel the power from Adalta gathering above them.

Daryl, Finder Mirela and her teams of Air talents worked all winter, studying the urbat captured during the last battle before winter fell and the extreme cold of winter on Adalta stopped the urbat attacks. He hoped the spell they'd developed worked. Then he dismissed them to the back of his already crowded mind and fanned the tiny ember of hope they left room for. It would work or it wouldn't. There was nothing more he could do.

Daryl ran through the gates, Steffa on his heels, and grabbed the arm of the first patroller he saw. "Krager? Where's Armsmaster Krager?"

"Sir. The fiercest fighting is between the grain storehouse and the tavern. You'll find him there. I was waiting for you. To watch your back."

"Let's go then, Wingman Arden. Tell me what you know on the way."

The two men and the Mi'hiru jogged toward the center of the small town, checking each intersection for signs of fighting. Suddenly Arden grabbed Daryl's arm. "Down there, sir. Look." His voice rang, not with danger, or with the thrill of the fight, but as if he saw something impossible to believe.

There, in the middle of the next intersection, were four urbat, milling aimlessly, weaving around each other, sometimes a head would droop, the urbat shaking it furiously. One pawed at its face, leaving deep, weeping red scratches down its muzzle.

"What's wrong with them?"

Steffa fired her crossbow, crippling one. Daryl waited till the others were as close together as he thought they would get, shook out his left hand and shot three fire bolts, incinerating them just as their heads seemed to clear and focus on the two men.

His lungs filled again. All the research he and Mirela and her team did over the winter on the six urbat captured at the end of the battle at the Circle of Devastation last fall paid off. The Itza Larrak had lost control over these urbat, at least for a moment. A significant moment.

He didn't stop to explain or celebrate but headed around the corner to the town square where the fighting was most intense. Krager was in the midst of it, watching, shouting orders, and fighting, never missing a smooth stroke of his two swords aimed at the urbat's few vulnerable spots. He roared when he spotted Daryl. "Come join the party, Guardian, Mi'hiru. Sorry we couldn't wait for you." And he beheaded an urbat on a backstroke.

Daryl smiled inside at the astonished look on Arden's face at the ordinarily phlegmatic armsmaster. Then he was too busy fighting and taking advantage of the sporadic disorientation of the urbat, to smile at anything. Steffa moved along the edge of the square, crossbow loosing bolt after bolt. Tipped with razor heads of urbat metal, they could pierce the creatures' armor, sometimes killing, sometimes wounding them for others to finish off.

Finally the last of the monsters started running for the gate, some stumbling, a few confused and wandering—soon dead at the swords of the following patrollers and fighting villagers.

Krager walked up beside him. "What, in the name of Adalta, happened here?"

"The circle of Air talents worked, thank blessed Adalta. They held off the Itza Larrak's psychic field and interfered with its control of the urbat." He scrubbed his hands through his hair and rubbed at the back of his neck, feeling the adrenaline sustaining him leaching away. His head ached, and he forced himself not to tremble by gripping his sword hilt so tight his hand hurt. "Send small teams through the village. Check every house, every building, under every rock. Gather the wounded here in the main room of the inn." He waved at the building behind Krager. "I need to check on the Air team; then I'll be with the wounded." He strode off back toward the gates, fearing what he would find. Krager, already shouting for his teams, headed in the other direction.

When he cleared the gates, Daryl broke into a run, the clamp of fear closed in on his chest again. All eight of the Air talents sprawled on the ground, eyes closed, bodies not moving. He skidded to a stop when one of the men rolled over, pushed himself up on one arm, and raised the other, hand fisted in a victory sign.

His voice hoarse and weary, he grated out, "We did it. We forced it away. We forced the Itza Larrak to back away and sent the urbat home with their damn tails between their legs." Then he fell back, exhausted.

***

Several hours later, after he was certain the village was clear of the vicious creatures, Daryl moved along the makeshift aisle between pallets crowded into the main room of the village tavern. He knelt beside a young guardsman, his arm torn, one side of his face shredded. He was half-healed and half-conscious. "I'm going to finish healing your wounds now, Boren."

There was comprehension and not a little fear in the boy's eyes, but what he said first was. "How many did we lose, sir?"

Daryl made a mental note to talk to this boy's lieutenant. He might make a good squad leader. "Not as bad, this time. And you're not one of them."

"Will it hurt?" Boren's voice was faint as if he was afraid he didn't have enough breath in him to speak.

"You'll feel some heat, but it's okay if you decide to sleep through it. You've done your duty. Now it's time to let someone take care of you."

The urbat left horrible ragged wounds. The hastily slapped on bandages told Daryl he'd gotten enough triage healing to stop the bleeding, but the sick, stinking miasma the urbat left over every battle lingered. It was always strongest where there were wounded, and if it weren't removed, the wounds festered and turned putrid.

He cupped his hands a few inches from the boy's face. His eyes never left Daryl's.

Daryl concentrated, ignoring the weariness that threatened to prostrate him. He reached down through the bedrock beneath the village, searching for rivulets of underground water. A surge of power reached for him, and he drew on it, siphoning away the heavy, sick urbat stink, letting it pass through him, pushing it deep into the ground. Earth and Water power moved through him, and he focused it on the shredded cheek, checking for infection, closing the long gashes with delicate care.

He sat back on his heels, shoving away his frustration that he could do no more, as usual, not letting a hint of emotion make it to his face. "You'll have scars, Boren. It's been too long since the battle with the monsters for the healing to ensure smooth skin. But they'll be superficial."

The boy tested the muscles in his cheek and discovered he could smile, even if it were a small smile. "There was others hurt worse`n me. I told the healers to let me wait."

Daryl turned his attention to the injured arm and drew more talent force from the planet, and concentrated on the healing. He lost himself as he knitted blood vessels, muscles, and tendons, repaired a deep score in the bone, and finally closed the final layer of skin.

"You'll have scars here, too, but you'll have full use of your arm."

The young man made a fist and grimaced.

"I know. It still hurts. It takes a while for your body to finish the healing. Your arm will be sore, and you won't be able to use it to the fullest for a couple of tendays." Daryl patted his good arm. "At least the urbat stink is gone—from you if not from the room."

But Boren was asleep

Daryl levered himself back to his feet and looked around. The wounded lay on pallets with a few cots for the more severe cases. The less severely injured leaned against the walls waiting their turn. With so many, the healers had to ration their battlefield healing, only doing what they must to stabilize the worst and get all of them inside the tavern.

He let his eyes and his talent senses roam over the room. He noticed fever spiking in three of the guard lying there. He caught a healer's eye and motioned to the three men. She nodded.

He raised his head and sniffed. At last, the healers with strong Earth talent had removed the foul, stinking miasma hovering over the wounded. One more reason they were tired and their talent stretched thin. One more reason why the less severely injured, like Boren, had to wait so long for healing. Many would have scars.

Then he felt something else. A tiny nudge at his senses. He wound his way through to a young woman lying on a cot near the doorway and knelt beside her. Her name was Ana, one of his regular Karda Patrol wing, and fiercely loyal to him, he knew. She had taken a slash low to her side. It wasn't the wound he felt. That was closed and shallow enough the intestines hadn't been compromised. He sucked in a breath. She was pregnant, and the shock threatened the small life inside her.

He took her hand, and she opened her eyes. She trembled with fear. "I thought I would be all right when the Healer finished with me, but there's something else wrong. I have just enough talent to know it, but not enough to fix it. I don't know..."

He could feel her hysteria rise. "May I?" he asked, with his hand just above her belly. She nodded, and he rested his hand on the blanket. He let his consciousness sink into her, find the little spark that was new life, ground it, strengthen it's shaken connections to the larger life that was the planet Adalta and to the mother-to-be. He felt the muscles of her abdomen relax.

"What is it?" she asked. "Did the healers miss something? A leaky blood vessel?"

A rare grin cracked Daryl's face for the first time in forever, and he sat back on his heels. "You have something to tell Jack, Ana. I'll send him to you as soon as I see him."

Her eyes widened, and both hands flew to her belly. "I'm pregnant?" Her eyes went frantic. "Is it all right? Have I killed it?"

"No. It's decided to stay." He put a large, sword-callused hand over hers, his smile as light as his heart. "A new life. I'm glad I'm the one who discovered it. I needed that sign of hope and regeneration. Thank you, Ana."

Something in him relaxed for the first time in months since he first learned of his brother Readen's perfidy, since he'd been shot with a poisoned arrow--at Readen's order, since he'd come too close to being garrotted--at Readen's order.

Too pragmatic to believe in signs and portents, nevertheless, and irrational as it seemed, Daryl felt a tiny smile inside. He walked on through the wounded, speaking to each of the injured as he passed. Thanking the troopers and assuring the villagers that they would have the help they needed to rebuild and repair the damage from the urbat attack.

Three village councilors waited for him on the wide covered porch of the tavern, two women and a man—faces drawn with pain, anger, and fear.

"Will they be back?" Headwoman Surana's right arm was in a sling, her left arm supporting it. She shifted on her feet, and pain flashed across her face. "Perhaps we could meet in my home. It's not far."

Daryl nodded and followed the trio to a small, brick one-story home. A young girl sloshed buckets of water across the steps. It ran red with blood and strings of thick yellow ichor. Her skirt was tied up out of the way, and Daryl saw thick bandages wrapping both legs.

She noticed his look. "I been to the healers. I be all right." She moved aside, and they entered, doing their best not to step in the bloody water.

Inside, a small boy slumped, half asleep, in a chair at the stone table that took up much of the kitchen-living area. Both his arms wrapped in colorful bandages torn from one of the curtains on the window beyond him.

Surana shook her head at Daryl's questioning look. "My family is not as bad off as some of the others. My bonded is unhurt. He's the blacksmith and made sure to keep one of the weapons made of the monster's metal bones close by him. Unlike some, who thought since we'd heard of no attacks all winter, they were over, that our walls were high enough, strong enough, and we'd be safe inside them."

She sat, almost fell, into a chair. "They were wrong. Please seat yourself. I can stand no longer. Mina will finish washing the blood and the ichor from the porch and come to make us some tea. And we could all use a sandwich, I think. You are welcome in our home, Guardian. May our table provide you sustenance, may our land provide you work to suit your heart and hands, and may you find safety within our walls for your rest." She paused. "And may the work our land provide you be less bloody than this day's."

The boy lifted his head, and his mother said, "Go to your bed, son. You've helped as much as you can. Now you need rest."

He looked at Daryl, at the sword on his hip, and his lips went tight and flat. He forced words between them, "Where were you? Where were your soldiers? Why were you so late?"

"To bed, now, Arlen," his mother said.

The boy backed away into another room, his eyes never leaving Daryl's. The accusation blazing in them burned deep in Daryl's chest. It would do no good to tell the boy he and his patrol had been fighting at a village forty kilometers away—an attack even more devastating than this one. That one of his patrol wing members and a Karda were dead. That he'd been fighting urbat since winter season had changed to early spring in village after village. That every trooper, every patroller he had was tired to the bone or injured or both.

"He lost his best friend. He's an apprentice healer, and he couldn't save his best friend, guardian. Please forgive his anger," said Surana, her words low, weary, unapologetic.

The male counselor, Davris, said, "You are always too easy on that boy, Surana. he needs discipline." His words were harsh, angry. "We hold no blame for you, Guardian. We are grateful that you arrived when you did. Your Karda Patrol saved us." His fawning, conciliatory tone grated on Daryl.

The other woman, Bettis, spoke. "And we wouldn't have needed so much help, Davris if you had agreed to spend enough to raise our walls this winter, like we were told. Or agreed to pay our blacksmith to forge more weapons like we were told. Or agreed to train our young people to fight like we were told. I think it might be time to change our town charter. If all three of us have to agree on an action, too often no action is taken, and today we've had a harsh lesson."

She pulled her blue cloak, banded with the distinctive dark red embroidery of a healer, tighter around her. "I'm exhausted, and I still have patients to see to. Let's figure out what we do next and get this meeting over with." Bettis looked at Daryl. "We won't let those monsters defeat us."

Surana ignored Davris. "Three young men were cutting wood in the forest and spotted the urbat. They warned us. Thank the lady Adalta for that. We were able to prepare. But one of the monsters they saw was not an urbat. It was taller than a man and walked on two feet, dark as night with yellow eyes and enormous wings. It had to be the Itza Larrak. Thank Adalta, Bettis realized in time that it was throwing a psychic field of fear, and she organized our Air talents. They, at least, paid attention to your warnings and orders."

"When the Austringer and the Kern were here, they warned us about what it could do," said Bettis. "We've worked hard on our defense against his terror attack. Without the information you and Mirela sent…" Her words trailed off, and her eyes looked at an empty distance.

Davris snapped his words out. "We had prepared, whatever these women tell you. We had. And we killed a lot of urbat. We drove them off."

Daryl sat straighter in his chair. The last thing he needed was to get in the middle of a village squabble. The girl Mina handed him a mug of hot, strong tea. The warmth in his hands was welcome. Early spring might be warmer than the cruel winters on Adalta, but sometimes it was hard to believe the season was changing. "You are fortunate you had strong enough Air talents to block it." He didn't tell them that had they not been able to block the Itza Larrak, most all of them would be dead. He'd found too many villages, too late, that hadn't been so fortunate. Even one was too many. There'd been more than one.

A loud cry sounded from the sky, and Daryl heard Abala's words in his head. ~Tessa, Kishar, and Galen approach.~ There was a pause then Abala added, humor in his voice, ~Yes, Ket, too, of course.~

Daryl caught himself before he slumped in relief. "Surana, The Austringer and the Kern are approaching your landing field. With the help of your best Earth and Water talents, Galen can clear the diseased stink from the urbat, and salvage the armor and metal bones from the ones you killed. We'll leave them with your blacksmith. Tessa will talk to your village defenders about strategy. I could see your walls had almost reached high enough. You'll be able to repair today's damage and finish them, with luck, in possibly a tenday and a half. Galen will also bury the urbat for you if you collect them in one spot."

He tilted his head toward Davris. "Do not worry about the costs. Restal's treasury is hard hit, but I will see about resources for you. Planting season is still tendays away, so every worker you have can be put to building up your walls. If you need more Air and Earth talents to help you fire the mud bricks and haul rocks, I'll see what I can do about that."

He stood. I'll find them somewhere, somehow. "I'm heading for Me'Mattik Hold to make sure he sends troops and funds to help you."

There was a long and uncomfortable silence. The three village leaders stared down at the table.

"What is it? Do you think he won't help? He's your holder. It's his responsibility."

Surana finally looked up. "He's gone. He and his troops are gone. Meryl went to see him to ask for help on our walls last Deciday. His hold is abandoned, only servants and a few guards remain."

Daryl looked at her, a terrible sickness of dread opened a deep hole in his chest. "Gone?"

Bettis said, "Gone. North. To your brother Readen's hold with all his troops to join Readen's revolt against you, some of them our sons and daughters, willing or no. We are at your mercy, Guardian."

Daryl looked back and forth between the three of them, unable to form words.

"Many who weren't willing to go were able to hide in the forest—if the urbat hasn't killed them. They wait to see if you will accept their service. They don't want to be known as traitors because they refused to follow Me'Mattik," said Surana. "The ones close enough when the urbat attacked fought with us. We can use their help."

Bettis's face twisted with disgust. "Me'Mattik is not a strong talent for a holder. Probably doesn't have much more than I, a simple village healer, do. He believes your brother is fighting you on behalf of those with weaker talent—against the custom of rule by strong talent. That's Me'Mattik's reasoning."

Surana snorted. "His excuse, you mean. He is a traitor to Restal."

"I hope you will not hold his treason against us, Guardian," said Davris. His eyes shifted back and forth between the other two councilors. "We are completely loyal to you. You are the true leader of Restal."

There was a long silence. Then, still sitting tall and straight in his chair, in a voice quiet and controlled, Daryl said, "You will have what you need. I'll see to it."

Inside him, another layer of pain formed ice around his heart.

Available on Amazon

About the Author

Sherrill Nilson used to raise horses. Now she writes about flying horses—with hawk heads and wicked talons. Author of the Adalta Series, she's been a cattle rancher, horse breeder, environmentalist, mother of three, traveler to exotic places–even a tarot card reader. She lived in Santa Fe (where she built a straw bale house) and Ruidoso, NM, San Francisco, and Austin after leaving the hills of Eastern Oklahoma and her ranch. Now she's back in Tulsa where she started.

Her studies for her PhD opened her to the world of ancient myth and story. Writing all those many papers and her dissertation suited her. So she took a leap of faith and did what she's always wanted to do—write fiction. She started writing Karda and Hunter–the first two books in the Adalta series. She's now working on Falling, the third book, and lurking in the back of her mind is another series about the trees deciding whether or not to leave Earth.

She lives, reads, and writes SciFi/fantasy (and occasionally poetry) in Tulsa, Oklahoma—back where she started as the oldest of seven kids (don't ask to drive). Three of whom are writers.

She doesn't have a dog, a cat, or even a bird, but she does have an old Volvo convertible and loves to drive around in her sunglasses with the wind blowing her hair. It's how she gets her vitamin D.

You can reach her through SherrillNilson.com or email her at sherrill.nilson@gmail.com, on Twitter @sherrillnilson, on Instagram.@sherrill.nilson. She would like to hear from you because she wants to know what you think about her books. She says it makes her a better writer—and makes her write faster.

CPSIA information can be obtained
at www.ICGtesting.com
Printed in the USA
LVHW091610220719
624869LV00002B/336/P

9 781732 272910